SEPHIROT

GORDON BONNET

LITTLE BUSTARD BOOKS

CONTENTS

To my amazing wife, Carol Bloomgarden, who refused
to let my voice be silenced.

CHAPTER I

MALKUTH

It had been a completely ordinary day for Duncan Kyle until the moment he fell through the floor of his living room at a little before two in the morning.

A slow day at Carthen, Douglas, and Prescott Financial Consultants. Dinner with his girlfriend, Libby, followed by drinks at his apartment and the happy but never certain outcome that she intended to spend the night with him. They had not fallen into a contented doze until nearly midnight, and Duncan fully expected to sleep until his alarm went off at seven o'clock. So it was something of a surprise when he opened his eyes in the pitch darkness, and turned his head toward his clock to see that it was only 1:54.

His mouth was sandpaper-dry. He swallowed, throat muscles contracting on nothing, and reached toward his nightstand for the bottle of water he kept there. His wrist contacted the bottle before his searching fingers did, sending it tumbling to the floor. It gave a light clatter as it landed on the hardwood.

Empty.

He swore under his breath, and swung his legs out of bed. Libby made a small, childlike noise in her sleep, mumbled something incomprehensible, and then was quiet. He stood, and walked out of his bedroom, naked, not even bothering to take his robe from its hook on the back of the door. He padded down the hall toward the kitchen. Moonlight shone through the living room window, turning the furniture and carpets a silvery gray. The window was open, and the curtains fluttered in the humid July breeze, looking organic, like some kind of sea creature swaying in the current. He went along his sofa, brushing his fingertips along its rough cloth surface, and passed in front of the television.

Then the floor caved in.

There was a grinding, rending crash, and the smooth surface tilted beneath his bare feet. He reached out for something to grab, and caught a projecting strip of the subfloor, but it snapped off in his hand. With a cry, he fell into darkness, with pieces of hardwood flooring, insulation, and dust raining down around him.

He landed on his side, a rough edge of the tumbled mass of debris tearing a long scratch across the skin of his back and left shoulder as he came slithering to rest. The impact knocked the wind out of him, and for a time he lay, gasping and coughing while the dust drifted down, his thoughts as shattered as the world around him.

It was only two minutes afterwards, but it felt like a great deal longer, that he braced himself on his elbows and sat up. Grit and wood slivers dug into his arms, legs, and butt as he forced himself upright.

"Earthquake...?" he croaked, and coughed again. "Libby?"

He had never been in an earthquake, and he had a vague memory from one of his high school science classes that upstate New York wasn't on a fault zone, but he couldn't think of any other ready explanation. He looked upwards, and struggled to his feet. There was a gaping hole in the ceiling, perhaps fifteen feet overhead, and he could see a bit of his living room through it. A corner of the sofa and one end of the coffee table tipped perilously near the edge, along with trailing wisps of fiberglass and loops of electrical wire.

Better move out of range. It'd suck to take a coffee table to the head if there was an aftershock.

He moved to the side, out of the likely landing area should the coffee table fall, and called again, louder, "Libby?"

There was no sound from his apartment. In fact, there was no sound at all. He looked around, and that was when he realized the oddest thing yet, something that had been knocked clean out of his mind by the shock of what had happened.

If the floor of his apartment caved in, he should have fallen into the apartment below his. If things were normal, he would have landed in the living room of Mrs. Elena Gonzales, a sixty-something widow who was a mother hen type to the entire apartment building, constantly inquiring about the tenants' health, eating habits, and love lives. And although going through the ceiling stark naked into Mrs. Gonzales's living room would have occasioned an apology, he had no doubt that she would have been more concerned with whether or not he needed to go to the emergency room than the fact that he happened not to be wearing any clothes.

But wherever he was, it was clearly not *anyone's* living room. The light was dim, coming through a row of slot-like windows high up in the wall. What he could see amongst the shadows was a dingy gray brown. The air was cool, and smelled of age and mildew. Near him, and covered with broken pieces of two-by-four and particleboard, was a jumble of wooden boxes. In one corner was a worn marble statue of an angel, angled toward a wall made of rough stone, its hands covering its face as if it were weeping. The end of one wing was missing, and piles of broken ceramic jars partially covered its feet. The wall behind the statue had a shelf cut into it, and it held untidy stacks of leather-bound books. Tumbled blocks of fallen masonry lay strewn on the stone floor where in places the facing had peeled away, leaving bare rock and earth showing underneath. Farther away, almost invisible in the darkness, was an arched doorway through which he could see nothing but blackness.

Had he fallen through Mrs. Gonzales's apartment, too? Maybe he was in the basement of the building. Was there a basement? But immediately, he doubted this guess. This didn't look like any basement he'd ever seen. It looked more like his imagined idea of catacombs, or a dungeon beneath a medieval castle.

He rubbed his face, and then dragged his fingers backwards through his hair. "Fuck," he said, his voice creaking in his dry throat. "What do I do? Sit around and wait to be rescued? Or try to get out on my own?"

There was clearly no way to reach the hole in the ceiling and climb through back into his apartment. There was nothing big enough or sturdy enough to use as a makeshift ladder. If help didn't come from overhead, there was no escape in that direction.

He shouted again, up toward the hole, "Libby! Help me!"

Silence.

He waited, watching, for some minutes. If there'd been an earthquake, or at least a cave-in, shouldn't the noise have alerted someone? Shouldn't there be voices, sirens, noises of rescue equipment being moved? Libby wasn't a heavy sleeper. No way could she have slept through all this.

He called out again, "Libby!" and was again met with complete silence.

Then, with a sudden gush of relief, he realized what the answer must be; he was dreaming. He'd wake up soon, and Libby would be right there next to him, and he'd tell her all about it, and they'd have a good laugh. But why was he dreaming this weird scenario? He reached up and touched his shoulder, wincing as his fingers brushed the oozing and aching scrape.

Then he had a second realization; he must be having a lucid dream. He'd never had a lucid dream before. May as well enjoy it, and explore a little. He walked around the room, avoiding the worst of the fallen debris, but still yelped once as his bare foot contacted something sharp and painful. Hobbling, he went up to the bookshelf, and looked at the battered and dust-covered spines, barely readable in the gloom. The books were bound in dark leather, and were ancient, to judge by the faded writing.

Liber Ivonis. Cultes des Goules. De Vermis Mysteriis. Unaussprechlichen Kulten. Necronomicon.

All were in languages he didn't speak, to judge by the titles, so he moved on.

He made a complete circuit of the room, and ended up standing before the doorway underneath the arch. A set of three stone steps led up to it, but beyond it was completely lightless. A cool breeze flowed from the door, carrying with it a faint aromatic scent, and he shivered.

If it was a lucid dream, maybe he could control it. He said out loud, "I want my robe!" feeling vaguely foolish as he did so.

Nothing happened.

"How 'bout a flashlight?"

Still nothing.

"Shit. I thought lucid dreams would be more fun than this. That I'd be able to fly and teleport and do magic. And that there'd be lots of scantily-clad women. What do I get? Rocks and broken crap and dust."

He took two steps up, peering into the darkness.

Walking stark naked into a dark hallway in a strange place seemed unwise, so he stood there, uncertain. Another shudder rippled over his bare skin, and he retreated into the room, and found a wooden box to sit down on.

It being a lucid dream didn't mean that there might not be a monster hiding in the dark. At least it seemed safe in here. Also, if this wasn't a dream, and there really had been an earthquake or something, it'd be better to stay put.

It was several hours later, Duncan couldn't be certain exactly how long, that he finally gave up on that idea. He had slept uneasily for a time, his head in his hands, but thirst kept waking him up. Why couldn't this have happened after he got his drink of water? He got up once to pee in the corner of the room, returning to his seat on the box after peering cautiously up through the hole in the ceiling. The coffee table and the sofa remained visible through the gap, but the light hadn't changed. It was still dark, with only the faint, shimmery quality of the moonlight on edges and corners.

Shouldn't it be morning by now? Or at least near dawn? It still looked like the middle of the night. And why hadn't Libby noticed anything? Heard the noise, or at least noticed that he was gone?

He shouted, "Libby!" up toward the hole, again, to no effect. Then he returned once more to the box.

He had been told before that he lacked imagination, that he was solid, reliable, and stable, but not creative. Honestly, it was true enough. Accountancy and financial consulting had been a good choice of a career. He was a steady employee, could be self-motivated when he needed to, but his best qualification was that he took direction well. He was good with details, sharp about numbers, fast, and efficient. But other than that, he was mostly interested in what he called "guy stuff" —sports, news, friends, food, beer, and sex. So he had filled his life with those things, and considered himself lucky if he had a baseball game to watch, a full fridge, and a steady girlfriend. He wasn't good at thinking outside the box, largely because he'd never had to.

Now, he was out of the box, and he didn't like it.

He stood up, stretched, yawned. "Well, if this *is* a lucid dream, it sucks."

He walked back to the archway, which appeared to be the only exit from the place, and again took two tentative steps up. There was once more that brush of cool air against his bare skin, carrying with it a trace of some unidentifiable spicy odor. He reached out his left hand, and his fingers touched the rough stone of the wall. Extending his right hand out and upward, to avoid if possible cracking his head on any low obstacles, he plunged forward into absolute darkness.

The passageway was smooth and unobstructed. There was familiar coolness of hard-packed dry earth beneath his feet. His left hand contacted nothing but rock as the tunnel slanted gradually upwards, and his right hand touched nothing at all. The air became progressively cooler, and goose bumps stood out on his arms and chest. Finally there was an angle to the right, and the incline increased, but he became aware of a change as well in the light. There was a faint grayness, not enough to make out any objects, a shift subtle enough that at first he thought was a trick of the eye. He realized, though, that he could see his hand in front of him, vague, but visible when he moved it. The light continued to increase, until he could see the contours of the stones that made up the wall, the smooth surface of the floor.

All at once, the tunnel opened out into a wide room. The light was still dim, and he couldn't see the other side of it from where he stood, but it was at least better lit than where he had come from. There was a window cut into the stone wall near where he stood, but too high to peer out of, and through this a chilly breeze flowed. He shivered, once again wishing for and not getting his robe, which probably still hung from a hook on his bedroom door.

He went up to the window. All he could see out of it was a rectangle of gray, featureless sky. He hooked his fingers over the edge of the sill and tried to find toeholds so he could lift himself up and find out more about where he was. He succeeded, after one failed attempt that left him with a scraped knee, but finally ended up with his elbows propped on a broad, flat sill almost three feet deep, the lower part of his body dangling, pressed uncomfortably against the cold stones.

He was looking out over a landscape he'd never seen before.

A skittering sense of panic rushed through him, like a rock skipping on the surface of a lake, leaving little shuddery ripples behind.

Where the fuck was he? His heart pounded in his chest, sweat standing out on his skin despite the chill. This couldn't be a dream. It was too real. But it couldn't be real. It was too dreamlike…

He looked out through the window, the breath whining in his throat, elbows aching from supporting his weight on the rough-hewn rock. There were undulating hills dotted with brown, scrubby plants and rust-colored stones. The aromatic smell was stronger. It was a dry, desiccated odor, and he was reminded of a passage in one of his college history texts that described the spices the Egyptians used when they embalmed dead bodies.

It wasn't a comforting thought.

He hung there, feet dangling, for some minutes. Nothing moved. There was not a sound, no bird song, no rustle of little animals in the leaves. It looked like an artist's depiction of a dying world, a world where everything wise enough and mobile enough had long ago departed. There was a tired, ruddy light coming from somewhere behind him and whatever strange building he was in.

He briefly considered climbing through the window, but it wasn't possible from his vantage point to tell how high up the window was in the wall, or if there might be a sheer drop on the other side. In any case, the vista in front of him looked singularly uninviting. Finally, he pushed himself out and away, and landed with a soft thump on the floor inside.

His thirst was becoming unbearable, and for the first time, the thought crossed his mind that he might be trapped. He still wasn't certain if this was a dream, but in the end, it didn't matter much. While he was there, what he felt *was* the reality. If in a dream, he spent days without water and finally perished of thirst, would that mean the agony, the terror, the despair would be any less?

He padded across the earthen floor, moving away from the window. Whatever this room was, it was considerably larger than the one he'd fallen into. The far edges were obscured in shadow.

He stopped, suddenly, and shouted, "Is there anyone here?" Even his voice sounded thin, sapped of all of its blood and vitality. He stood still, listening, not expecting any response, and getting none. A faint noise, whether caused by his call, or not related to him at all, came from the darkness. It was a dusty, dry creak, like stone on stone, quiet enough that when it ceased he half convinced himself that it had been his imagination. No human voice, nor even the rustling and squeaking of mice or other small, subterranean animals, followed.

A shudder rippled through his frame, and his eyes blurred for a moment with hot tears. His chest heaved, but he fought the sensation back, and started walking again, toward the dark side of the room.

There was more fallen masonry in the middle of the room, and he added a bruised shin to his other injuries before he cleared the rubble. He slowed as the light from the window diminished, but kept walking even after he had descended once more into total darkness.

Despairing thoughts echoed in his mind, loud in the oppressive silence. *Buried alive in the crypt. Left here, alone and naked, to die slowly. How long will I keep walking before I give up? Or will I finally drop from exhaustion, hunger, and thirst? My body will lie here and slowly mummify, and no one will ever find my bones.*

The room, whatever its function to those who had constructed it, was immense. Long after the light was gone, he kept walking, and other than small pieces of fallen stone, his tentative feet and outstretched arms encountered nothing. He walked more confidently after a time, still moving forward, although with no clear idea of why.

When he finally struck the opposite wall, it was with a glancing scrape to his left shoulder. He stopped, and swore loudly, massaging it, fighting down a combination of rage and frustration that came welling up from his belly.

And then, he heard the same sound he had heard before—a grating noise, like the grinding of a stone mill-wheel, this time from nearer at hand.

He turned his head in the dark toward the sound, and shouted, "Hello?"

The faintest of creaks answered him.

He put out his left hand, and walked along the wall toward the sound, fingertips lightly brushing the stone. He had only gone about twenty feet or so when the wall took a sharp turn to the left, and the floor sloped down-hill. Straight ahead, but still too distant to illuminate anything, he saw something that set his heart pounding against his ribcage.

Firelight.

Fire meant inhabitants. And even hostile inhabitants were better than a solitary death in an abandoned catacomb. He had been in this place for how long? Perhaps ten hours? And already, he was ready to risk anything in order simply not to be alone in the dark. The light flickered and wavered, its quality somehow more alive than the dreary ruddiness of the sky outside the window.

He walked steadily downhill toward the light, which soon revealed itself as coming from another stone archway. He looked down at his own body, now just visible. The red light glimmered garnet on the bloodstains on his legs and across one side. Without any conscious will, he ran, his bare feet thumping on the packed earth of the floor, only slowing as he came, squinting, into the full firelight shining through the opening.

He hesitated for a moment on the threshold, and then stepped through the arch.

The room was stone-walled, as all of them had been, but this one had a ceiling so high it was out of sight. There were no windows. In the center of it, and taking up most of the room, sat a huge statue of a Sphinx, its face angled away from him. The thing was enormous. The top of its head was barely visible in the gloom. Its hind legs, smooth-carved and rippling with muscle, towered over him. The massive paws alone, resting on the ground directly in front of him, reached nearly to his waist.

Walking silently, he made his way around to the front of the Sphinx. Directly between its forepaws was a huge bronze brazier, in which a fire burned steadily. But more importantly, beneath the brazier was a stone basin with a pool of dark, still water, reflecting the light from a surface like a mirror.

His thirst surged tenfold. He said, in a thick croak, "Water. Thank god."

Immediately there was the same grating noise he'd heard before. And the Sphinx's head moved, angling downward. Rock dust came down in a trickling stream from the sides of the neck. His thirst forgotten for the moment, he looked up into the statue's immense face.

And then the Sphinx's eyes opened.

The eyes were glossy, liquid, alive. The irises were green flecked with gold, the pupils an inky black, the whites as smooth and unblemished as polished alabaster. It regarded him with a gaze that was curious, intelligent. Duncan froze, body and mind, in such a balls-clenching panic that he was unable to utter a sound.

And then it spoke.

"You're naked," the Sphinx commented.

"I know," he was able to gasp out, after a moment.

"I thought you might." The Sphinx's tone was conversational, its voice deep, resonant, like a cello. "It just seemed odd."

He looked down at himself again, and then back up at the Sphinx's face. "I... I wasn't wearing any clothes when I fell through the floor of my apartment, and ended up here." He swallowed painfully. "Can I drink from the pool?"

The Sphinx's mouth curled upward a little in an ironic smile. There was the same creaking grate of stone on stone, and another thin tendril of dust spiraled downward. "What does that mean, *can you drink*? The water is right there. Have a drink if you wish to."

"You won't grab me, or hurt me, will you?" His cheeks burned at how cowardly it sounded.

"Of course not. Why would I do that?"

He moved forward and knelt down, reaching out to cup his hands into the water. He saw his own reflection. His hair was disheveled, his face pale and grime-streaked, an ugly scrape across his shoulder. Above him, he saw the reflection of the Sphinx looking down at him. Its smile widened, and he caught a flash of sharp white teeth.

"Of course," the Sphinx said, "the first thing you should learn here is that everything you see and hear is a lie."

He looked up in alarm. The thought, *What would it feel like to be bitten in half?* bounced through his skull, and he braced himself for the pounce, for the teeth to pierce his torso, tearing sinew from bone. But the Sphinx didn't move. It simply continued to watch him.

There was another frozen moment, but he recovered more quickly this time.

Fuck this. If it killed him, it killed him, but he'd be damned if he didn't have a drink of water first. He scooped up water in his hands. Even the feel of it against his skin was delicious. He took one drink, then another, and another.

It was as if he had never known what it was to quench thirst until now. He stood again, sated for the time being, rivulets of water leaving trails down his chest. He backed away from the Sphinx, who still regarded him with an amused expression.

"Better?" it asked.

"Yes."

"Good. There are many hard ways to die, but thirst is certainly one of the worst. And there you have the second lesson you must learn—fear may be a necessary companion, but it is a poor guide."

"Who are you? And where am I?"

"Those are two different questions, of course. Which would you like me to answer first?"

He ran his arm over his mouth, still wet from the pool. "Who are you?"

"Look at me. Who do you think I am?"

He leaned his head back till his neck ached. The Sphinx craned its own massive head downward, its shining eyes looking into his. There was a brief moment when his mind teetered on the edge of complete incredulity, and he wondered if he was neither dreaming, nor lost, but had simply gone insane.

No. No, that was not possible. How...?

He said, in a small voice, "Maria?"

"Ah," said the Sphinx.

"You look... you look like my sister..."

"Do I?"

"Just like. *Exactly* like." And as he watched, the resemblance became closer. The angle of the nostrils, the sardonic lift of the eyebrow, the way the carved waves of hair fell against the shoulders. Had he not seen it at first, because he was so thirsty and afraid? Or did its face change when he thought he recognized her?

"There you are, then," the Sphinx said.

"But Maria... Maria died." The old grief rose in his chest, a painful grip on his heart.

"Did she?"

"A car accident. When she was seventeen."

"A pity."

"She was my twin sister. My only sibling."

"It must have been hard for you." There was a hint of mockery in its voice.

"But you're not Maria. You look like her, but you're not her."

"No," the Sphinx admitted. "You're correct about that."

"So the fact that you look like her... that's a lie, too."

"That is one way of looking at it."

"Am I dreaming?"

The Sphinx didn't answer for a moment. It finally said, its voice thoughtful, "If I told you yes, might I not be telling the truth?"

"Of course."

"And if I said no, might you still be asleep and dreaming?"

"I suppose."

"Then what is the point of asking?"

He shook his head, rubbed his eyes with the heels of his hands. "What the hell is this place?"

"Yes, that was your other question. Where are you?"

He looked up, waiting, but the Sphinx didn't say anything more. It continued to watch him, its green-gold eyes glittering in the firelight.

"Well?" he finally said.

"It is a hard question to answer," the Sphinx said. "What is this place? I could tell you what it is called, but what would a name tell you?"

"It's a start."

"Yes," the Sphinx said, its voice deepening until it made his innards vibrate, a sound as rich as the bass pipes on an organ. "A start. That is exactly what it is."

"What is it called?"

"It is called Malkuth."

"Where is it?"

The white of teeth showed again, just for a moment. "All around you."

"But..." He took a deep breath. "Damn it all, you know what I mean."

"Do I? Are you so sure of that?"

"Fine. The Sphinx talks in riddles. I get that. I remember that from my college English class. I guess I have to be specific. Where is this place, relative to my apartment?"

"Did you not say that you fell through your apartment floor, and that is how you came to be here?"

"Yes."

"Then you know the answer, do you not? It would appear that this place is beneath your apartment."

"But I know that's not true!" he shouted. "There's no place like this underneath my apartment."

"Suit yourself," the Sphinx said.

"Look, all I want to do is get back home. Or wake up, or whatever. How do I do that?"

"I think that you humans have a saying, do you not, that the only way out is through? I believe you will find that to be the case here."

He regarded the Sphinx's face. No wonder it looked like Maria. Maria would have liked this. She always loved riddles. "You said that everything here was a lie. Are you lying now?"

"Oh, of course not," the Sphinx said. "I wouldn't lie about something *that* important."

"So how do I get through, then?"

The Sphinx looked down at him, its face in a sardonic twist. "Do you want some advice?"

"Sure."

"The best way to get the information you need is to ask the right questions."

"How do I know what the right questions are?"

The Sphinx's stone mouth opened slightly, and it gave a *basso profundo* laugh that vibrated the floor beneath his bare feet. "Well, that certainly wasn't one."

"You are a pain in the ass," he said, scowling. Then he looked down, and said to himself, "This is fucked up. I'm talking to a statue."

The Sphinx inclined its huge head. "At your service."

He took a deep breath, and looked back into the Sphinx's face. "Okay, look. Let me start with some simple questions, before we move on to the big stuff. I haven't seen any trace of anyone else since I arrived. But there's a fire burning here. Who keeps the fire going?"

"My attendants."

"Where are they now?"

"How should I know? It's not like I get out much."

"But who are they?"

The Sphinx smiled. "Who are *you*?"

"I'm Duncan Kyle!" he yelled. "And why can't you give a straight question a straight answer?"

"Because I really don't think you know what you're asking, most of the time. You humans are like that, you know. You think things are their names, and if you know the name, you know the thing itself. You throw words around as if they were meaningless, or as if they mean whatever you want them to, and could mean something completely different tomorrow. Then you blame each other when there is confusion." It paused, and blinked its enormous, glistening eyes. "If you were asking for my attendants' names, I can't tell you that, because I don't know the answer. As for *who* they are? They are silent. They come to feed the fire and replenish the water in the pool. They don't talk to each other, nor to me. How can I know who they are, who they would be if they were like you, alone and naked in the dark? How would I know what they love, what they hate, what angers them, what fills them with grief, what fills them with lust? They never tell me such things. And even if they did, I do not doubt that much of it would be a lie. Humans, I think, are as good at lying to themselves as they are at lying to each other."

"Playing with words, and shifting meanings, isn't the same as lying."

"It might as well be. It has the same effect. Deceiving yourselves and everyone around you."

"But you said you lie, too."

With a creak, the Sphinx shrugged its mighty shoulders, sending a thin cascade of sand pouring down from its sides. "Oh, touché," it said, its deep voice dripping sarcasm.

Weariness rose in him. Maria had loved intellectual sparring. He didn't. "Look, just tell me how to get out of here, and I'll leave."

"That is simple enough. There are two ways out. The way you came in, and the other exit, that is on the opposite wall. If all you want is to leave, those are your options."

"Good. Because this whole conversation is pissing me off. Thanks for the water, and all." He turned and peered around the right side of the Sphinx, and in the middle of the wall was a dark stone archway that was the twin of the one he'd entered through.

"May I offer you one other piece of advice?" the Sphinx said, and he turned as the Sphinx's head swiveled ponderously toward him, its jewel-like eyes full and alert and not necessarily friendly.

"Certainly."

"If you find your way out of these walls, it would be wise not to be caught outside at night."

"Why?"

"Because it's not safe, of course," the Sphinx said, its voice full of high good humor. "You always want to be safe, don't you?"

"Safe from what?"

"Danger."

He smacked the heel of one hand against his forehead. "Are you absolutely forbidden from giving me any actual information? Because if all you're going to do is give me vague hints, you might as well shut up."

The Sphinx flashed a smile at him. "As you wish." It turned its head slowly until it was facing forward, and there was a little shudder and a soft creak as its body stiffened, its face resumed its still impassivity, and the stone lids shut over its eyes.

Silence fell.

He looked up toward the Sphinx, which once again simply looked like a huge statue, and waited for its eyes to open again.

Nothing happened.

"No, but seriously, what danger?" he said, to no effect.

After waiting nearly a minute, he scowled, and said, "Well, *shit.*"

Okay, he was *done* with this dream. If it *was* a dream. Time to get out of Dodge. Maybe by this time, Libby would have woken up, or the rescue crew would have arrived, or whatever. In any case, he was done playing around with all this.

He strode back into the archway by which he'd entered the room, once again letting his fingertips trail along the stone wall. The light diminished and finally vanished altogether, but his footfalls were confident and regular on the smooth floor. Uphill and into the huge room with the window. The light was brighter now, enough to see and avoid the rubble in the middle of the room. Evidently outside, whatever passed for day was happening, although the view through the window still showed nothing but the same featureless rusty gray light as before.

Across the room, back into another arched doorway, and back into the dark. His heart pounded. The sudden longing for being home, in his own apartment, in his girlfriend's arms, washed over him. He broke into a run, barely realizing he had done so, and burst into the room with the boxes, books, and angel statue with his chest heaving in what were nearly sobs.

He looked up toward the ceiling, and had a rush of sheer terror.

The hole was gone. Where before there had been a view into his apartment, the corner of his sofa and coffee table visible, there now was only the rough facing of cut stone, intact and solid.

He gave an inarticulate cry, and retreated until his bare back pressed against the chill surface of the wall. His frantic glance darted around the room, and his mind reached desperately for an explanation. Had he taken the wrong path? No, there had been no other turnings, no way to get lost. And it was definitely the same place into which he had fallen. The boxes, the statue, the shelf with the books, even the piles of broken ceramic were still exactly as he remembered them.

Only the debris that had fallen from his apartment floor, and the hole in the ceiling that was his portal back home, were missing.

And now he did cry. Helpless weeping seized him, shaking him like a wolf shakes a rabbit. His knees buckled, and he slid to the ground, the stones tearing a long scrape down his backbone, and he sat on the earthen floor, one hand over his face.

After a time he looked up, his eyes bleared with tears, and drew one arm across his face, looking upward again with a desperate hope.

The ceiling was still intact. The words *trapped* and *no way home* rang inside his skull, and then his mind went blank.

Hours later, after pointless wandering that took him through a maze of rooms, each filled with ruined statuary, broken stone and pottery, and stacks of moldering books, Duncan found himself once again standing before the Sphinx. He knelt, shaking, and drank from the pool. His hunger was now extreme. He hadn't eaten in... how long was it? He couldn't even begin to figure it out.

"Tell me how to get home," he said, his voice ragged.

The Sphinx spoke, without opening its eyes. "I told you. The only way out is through. You found that going back was impossible, yes?"

"Yes. Why?"

"I cannot answer that, for the very good reason that I do not know."

"Why am I here? What happened that brought me here?"

"I think that if you do not know the answer to that already, then anything I could tell you would be meaningless."

"Try me."

The Sphinx opened its eyes a little. A crescent of shining white, green, gold, and black shone beneath its half-closed lids. "You have been condemned to wander through the ten worlds," it said, its resonant voice taking on an oratorical tone, "making your way through them one by one, learning the lessons that they can teach, and only after you have met the challenge that each one represents will you be able to return back home victorious."

He stared at the Sphinx, his mouth hanging open a little. Finally, he said, "That's bullshit."

"I know," the Sphinx replied. "It was the best I could do on short notice."

"So you don't know."

"No, sorry."

"You're a lot of fucking help."

"Hey," said the Sphinx, sounding a little aggrieved. "We all do what we can."

"I'll be leaving, then."

"Good luck," the Sphinx said, its voice gaining a sarcastic edge.

"Please don't add, 'you'll need it.'"

"I wasn't going to."

The Sphinx's eyes closed.

He muttered, "Poser," under his breath, and walked toward the other exit from the room, through the arch on the right side of the Sphinx's front paws. This opening led into another tunnel, once again smooth underfoot and with no low hanging obstacles. It sloped upward, gradually at first but then more steeply, and once again he found himself moving into vague light that colored the walls, floor, and his own body a dusty gray brown. After perhaps a hundred yards, he stepped through another arch into a narrow room that was clearly some kind of atrium. Along the wall to his right, a row of mullioned windows, their sills just over his head, let in the tired illumination from the still-overcast sky. The light had dimmed now. Noon had passed. It was closer, apparently, to the nightfall that the Sphinx had warned him about.

Set in the wall with the windows was a huge set of timber-frame doors, cross-banded with iron strips. A pair of enormous rings hung from ornately-carved brackets in the center of each, at slightly above head height. There were more piles of debris scattered about, but the floor was mostly clear and unobstructed. He padded across the room toward the doors.

He was ten feet away from them when he realized that what looked like vague, amorphous lumps in the shadows were actually something other than fallen rubble and refuse.

They were skeletons.

There was the jolt of adrenaline, and sweat stood out on his chest and forehead despite the chill air coming in through the windows. He walked forward, more slowly now, toward the nearest one, which was seated against the wall to the right of the nearer door, its head tilted in a way that suggested sleep rather than death.

The skeleton was dressed in leather and metal armor, and had a heavy cap with a flat nosepiece. He knelt down next to it, and reached out and touched the sleeve. The leather cracked and crumbled into powder under his fingertips, and an iron fastening fell off and landed on the floor with a faint *thud* that sounded loud in the silence.

There was still some skin clinging to the bones, but it had dried and stretched and split. It looked insubstantial, inorganic, like a film of gray plastic. The skull was heavy and apelike, the leg bones long and massive but straight. Duncan was a little over six feet tall, and regular gym visits kept him well-muscled, but when this individual was alive he would have been able to pick him up one-handed.

There was something odd about the skeleton, though, besides its size. Leaning in, simultaneously thinking, *Why am I doing this? In horror movies, this sort of thing never ends well*, he looped his index finger under the broad chin, and lifted the head. It had thick brow ridges, and from underneath the cap a fringe of dark hair still protruded. He turned it a little. The remnants of tendons gave a dry, brittle creak.

It was the teeth. There was something inhuman about the teeth, especially the molars, which were thick, heavy, and ridged with deep grooves. He reached out with his other hand, and put his fingertips against the face, and pulled downward on the jaw. There was a cracking noise, like breaking ice, and the mouth popped open.

The jaw had two rows of teeth, both on the top and bottom.

He recoiled, and stood, his breath whistling in his throat. It wasn't human. It was a troll. Or a giant. And a deeper fear, one from scary stories in childhood, bubbled to the surface.

When he turned, the skeleton would come to life. It would stand up, the bones rattling against each other, and come after him...

But the skeleton showed no signs of life, even after he turned away and then back. In fact, he couldn't remember ever seeing anything that looked deader. The jaw gaped forlornly, the head tipped at an awkward angle. He walked past the doors, and up to three other skeletons that lay sprawled on the floor. All were similarly huge, and in fact were even bigger than the first one. If he had come upon these first, he would have known instantly they weren't human. The cheekbones were thick, and angled up from the side of the skull like arches. One of them had lost its cap, and a heavy ridge ran from front to back along the top of the skull, beneath a tangle of wiry black hair.

Lying on the floor next to the nearest skeleton was a massive wooden cudgel, the end festooned with metal spikes. A little further away was a short, curved sword with leather wrapping on the handle. A crude skin pouch, tied with a frayed cord, was clutched in the long-nailed fingers of the nearest skeleton. Everything had been preserved, mummified by the dry air. There was no way to tell if the remains were ten, a hundred, or a thousand years old.

This was a dead world. Everything. The plants outside, the giants in here, all of it. All dead. But then he knew that this couldn't be true—something kept the Sphinx's fire burning, kept water in the pool. He shuddered, and walked toward the doors.

He reached up, and grasped the iron rings. He pushed, leaning all his weight into them. At first, they didn't move, and he wondered if they were locked, or barred from the outside, or so frozen with age that the hinges wouldn't move. But there was a deep groan, and the doors swung outward. Light came through the space between them. Finally there was a gap wide enough for him to squeeze his body through.

Outside the door the ground was bare, covered by fine earth, rusty brown in color. It might not have been watered by rain in a century. Craggy rocks protruded in some places, and there was the same desiccated vegetation that he'd seen earlier from the window, rattling in the cool breeze. The sky was a uniform gray, with only a vaguely brighter spot near the horizon that showed where the unseen sun must be, now near setting.

Nothing to eat, that was evident immediately. He put one foot in front of the other, heading downhill and away from the doors. There wa nothing edible here. He could go back to the Sphinx's room if he need to drink, but he'd still die if he didn't find anything to eat. His belly was sunken already, his muscles weak and shuddery, after perhaps twenty-four hours without eating. He couldn't imagine what it would be like to slowly starve.

Probably peaceful, though. At some point, he'd get so weak that he'd lose consciousness and never wake up. As long as he had water, it wouldn't be so bad. He resolved, at that moment, never to get too far from the building, where there was the only source of water he'd seen.

He turned around and stared at the edifice he'd just left. It looked more like a geological formation than a structure raised by hands and intent, as if the underlying bedrock had simply produced these enormous windowed walls in a volcanic upheaval eons ago. The seams between the huge stones were so narrow that a knife blade would not have fit between them. The building itself sprawled sideways and back like an oddly geometric lava flow, cresting the hill where it sat, a temple as imposing as the Pyramids or Stonehenge or the ziggurats of Ur.

He walked down the hill, through clumps of dead plants that scratched his bare legs as he went past them. They were the source of the spicy odor—as his passage bruised the dry stems, there was a scent like oregano or thyme, left behind like a ghost of former vitality, years after they last grew and thrived and were green. At the bottom of the hill was an empty river course, its rocky bed barren of life, with only a fringe of dead grass along the edges to show where living things had once grown. The wind was stronger here, and in the distance he heard a low susurration, like the distant noise of ocean waves. He walked up the hill on the other side, a higher vantage point than any in the area other than the temple itself.

He stood on the crest of the hill, the wind ruffling his hair as he slowly turned a full circle from the temple and back again. There was nothing, as far as he could see, other than the scrub-covered hills rolling off into an uncertain distance. Nearer at hand was an upswept rock formation, ending in a jagged edge. But everywhere devoid of life, desolate, empty.

"This place is a tomb." Even his voice sounded lifeless in his own ears. "I'm fucked. I'm going to die here."

Perhaps it was the weakness from hunger, or the despair of having no way out, that kept him from weeping again. That storm, once past, did not return. He turned, the dust clinging to the soles of his feet, and made his way back toward the temple as the sun set behind the hills to his left.

He felt, rather than saw, the change. The light didn't fade immediately. Nothing in this world of gray and brown could be that well-delineated. But there was a gust of wind against his back, and the temperature went down. If it hadn't been so dry, he would have been convinced that a storm was brewing. He swallowed, and his ears popped.

There was a deep, resonant clang, sounding impossibly loud in the silence, as the two huge doors at the front of the temple slammed shut.

He broke into a run, his bare feet thudding on the ground. He kept running from sheer momentum and desperation even after he saw that it was pointless, that the front of the massive doors were smooth, with no handholds, and the gap between them was far too narrow even to slip a piece of paper between, much less a hand.

He fell to his knees in front of them, bowing his head, still too exhausted and weak to cry. Wild thoughts echoed in his skull. He'd never get back up, and he'd die, just like the mummies inside. He tried to think of his body's soft, pliable flesh, that had given him pleasure and pain, that because of his youth cooperated with his desires so naturally that most times he didn't think about it at all, being dried out, clinging to his dead bones. He looked down at himself, his chest, his hands, his legs, his penis. Soon, this thing he called "me" would be gone, and what was left would feel nothing. Soon. Maybe only a day or two. And then, after that... his body would never move again. And here it would lie. Forever, as long as this world existed.

It was the idea of never feeling anything again that terrified him the most. Death itself was a single event, like snuffing out a candle. But after that, not to have sensation, even pain, was impossible to imagine.

He thought of lying down and simply waiting, but some innate determination wouldn't let him give up quite yet. He stood again. By this time it was almost totally dark, but he could still feel the wind against his naked body, twisting around him like the caress of light hands. He turned outward, away from the doors, deciding that he would stand as long as he could, meet whatever danger the Sphinx had warned him about head on if it were possible to do so.

What had the Sphinx meant, "don't get caught outside at night?" What danger could it have been referring to? It said that it never left its room, knew nothing about what happened out here. Perhaps it was just being ironic. Or lying outright. It had told him that it lied, that everything here lied. There wa nothing that he saw during the day that looked dangerous.

And it was as he was thinking these comforting thoughts that he was grabbed from both sides by rough hands, his arms pinioned behind him. He cried out, but a hand came over his mouth. He tried to kick, but his legs were held tightly, and he was lifted into the air. There was a cold breath of a voice behind his right ear, a bloodless voice, as if the air itself were speaking.

"A living one?" it said. There was no way to tell if the speaker was male or female, young or old.

A cold finger pressed against his chest. "Yes," another voice said. "Alive. It's warm. But how? Where did it come from?"

"Inside," said a third. "There must be a portal inside. Perhaps there is a way out, after all."

"There hasn't been a living one for thousands of years."

"We need its warmth," said the first voice, and there was a sharp inhalation near his neck, as if his captor was drawing in his scent. "We can take its heat, then find the portal it came through. And then we won't have to tend her fire any more."

"But if it comes from outside, what if there are more still inside that came along with it?"

"We will find them, too." The voice near his ear spoke in a silky whisper, quietly, almost lovingly. The hand moved cautiously away from his mouth. "Where do you come from? Did you come from outside? Who came with you?"

"I came from my home," he said, desperately trying to think of an evasive way to speak, to talk in circles without saying anything, as the Sphinx had. Fear and the weakness of hunger defeated him. "I don't know how I got here."

"It must know," one of the voices said, becoming harsh. "It can't get here without knowing."

"I just want to get back home," he said, and gave a feeble attempt at twisting his way free, but his captors' hands only dug into his biceps and his ankles more firmly.

"You'll leave the world when we have what we want," one of the voices said.

"What do you want?"

A voice breathed right into his face, with a gust like a fog of ice crystals. "Heat."

Hands pressed against him, against the skin on his chest, hips, legs. Cold hands. His own body's warmth was being drawn away. A haze clouded his mind as his body cooled, but he heard the voices becoming stronger, more solid.

"It has much heat."

"This much will last us for a long time."

"It has been such a very long time since we have fed."

"Perhaps we can leave it with a little. It would be a pity to drain it dry, as we did the last ones."

"They didn't suffer, they merely went to sleep."

"Leave it its breath. The bit of warmth that will be left behind isn't enough to make a difference to us. Then perhaps it will live, and if it comes back, we can feed from it again."

They're Heat Vampires. His mind whirled. He now couldn't feel his own body, and but if he'd had the strength, he'd have laughed. At least now he knew what it wa like to feel nothing.

He didn't have long to think, he knew that. His consciousness was already dropping away, like a stone falling into water, sinking out of sight. Only one chance, and after that, he'd never respond to anything, ever again. He struggled feebly, and heard his own voice say, in words that sounded sludgy and indistinct, "I'll tell you how I got in."

Hands pulled away from him, and there was hiss of indrawn breath. "Where? Where is the portal?"

"There's a room," he said, "if you go from where the Sphinx is, down the hallway, into a huge room with windows…"

"The Great Room," one of the voices said.

"There is another hallway that leads from there, down to a… it looks like a storage room. The portal is in the ceiling. There are many of us where I came from. Lots more… heat."

There was an excited rush of whispers.

"We might be able to get through."

"All of us?"

"Yes, all. And then there would never be want of heat. It said so."

"Perhaps it is lying."

"But perhaps it is not."

"What if she finds out?"

An angry hiss. "We've served her long enough. She can't stop us."

"But we promised!"

"She made us promise. If she forced us, it wasn't a real promise."

"I told you we shouldn't have entered the temple and killed her guards."

"Shut up."

A hand pressed over his heart. "Let us finish with this one, first. Perhaps we can get through, and perhaps not. But we have this one here, now. And it has more warmth that we can take." A murmur of assent. Hands came back one at a time, against his neck, against his thigh, cupping his genitals. Once again there was that horrible feeling of being drained, and his thoughts drifted away. It didn't hurt. It was like going to sleep after an exhausting day.

"Stop," said one of the voices. Duncan barely heard it. The word seemed to have no meaning.

"What?"

"She said if we kill again, she would end our lives, too."

"She lies. You know she lies."

"What if it wasn't a lie? We've taken enough from this one. We can feel again, for a while. Let us get rid of what is left of it, and perhaps she won't know. Then we'll find the portal, and get into its world, and we'll all be able to feed as much as we wish to."

"Yes," said another. "That is wise."

"What if it was lying, though? I asked it earlier, and no one had an answer. She lies, perhaps it lies, too. What if the portal isn't where it said?"

"What warmth it has left is nothing. Better to give what is left of it to the sea, and then we will find the portal if it is there."

"Perhaps," said one of the voices, in a sly tone, "we can quench her fire, and end this world first."

"Not until we know we can escape in time."

"No. Not until. But that would serve her right, for enslaving us. Kill the flame, then leave her alone in the dark, with the world dying around her."

Another hissing of assent. "Let us give this one to the sea. Let the sea kill it, not us."

His body was lifted, and there was the jostling sensation of being carried along, but there was no clutch of fear, nothing but a desire to sleep. The wind ran its fingers through his hair, fluttered across his skin. He didn't feel cold, although what was left of his conscious brain knew that he was, deathly cold, perhaps beyond recall.

There was a change in angle as those carrying him ascended a steep hill, and he remembered the cliff edge he'd seen from his vantage point on the hilltop earlier. They were going to throw him into the sea, he knew that, but even so he was unable to summon up any fear. Perhaps the impact would kill him. He had read years before that people who jumped from the Golden Gate Bridge often didn't drown, but were killed when they hit the water. If he somehow survived the impact, of course, then he'd drown. There was no way he could swim, not in his present condition.

He opened his eyes. His eyelids were leaden. He could see, far beneath him, a dark ocean, laced with phosphorescence, surging and receding, and smelled salt. The hands gripping him tightened, pulled backward, and there was a forward surge and he was thrown outward into the empty sky.

Air rushed past him, but there was none in his lungs with which to scream. He plummeted downward as silently as a shot bird.

CHAPTER 2

YESOD

The first sensation to come back was vomiting, over and over, puking up what felt like gallons of water. It wasn't salty. Duncan's mind, still in a whirling mist, asked the question, *Didn't I fall into the ocean?* but the thought slipped away unanswered. The water had a mineral taste, a leafy taste, like the smell of river water from fishing trips with his dad as a child. It came up until he'd been purged of everything, was hollow and lifeless, like an empty clay jar.

He opened his eyes. His head was hanging downward, and he was looking at the still surface of a lake. It was not completely dark, like the place he'd left, but a deep, indigo twilight. He couldn't feel his own body, nor tell what he was resting on, nor answer the question of why he hadn't drowned.

A female voice, full of care and compassion and as opposite to the hissing breaths of the Sphinx's Caretakers as anything he could imagine, said, "You swallowed enough water to drown an ox. You'll feel better now that it's out of you."

He tried to respond, but he heard his mouth utter only a wordless groan. A streamer of drool fell from his lips, slipped into the water beneath him, and disappeared. He gagged again, but nothing more came up.

The voice laughed. "You're making noise, you'll be all right." He was lifted, turned over, and a soft cloth wiped his face and his upper chest. He was looking up into a beautiful face that smiled down at him, a smile that held none of the sardonic wryness of the Sphinx. She was a young woman, he could tell that despite the dim light. Moonlight caught the edge of a flawless jawline, a straight nose, the elegant curve of her neck. She was clad in some thin, light-colored wrap, like a tunic, and as she turned her head there was a quick glint from a headband with a single jewel, holding back a cascade of dark hair.

He opened his mouth again, moved his tongue and lips, swallowed with difficulty. "Where..." he was able to get out, and in his own ears his voice sounded muffled and cottony. "Where am I?"

"You don't know? This place is called Yesod." She gestured upward with a bare arm. "You fell out of the sky. I saw you fall, straight down, like a bolt of lightning cleaving the air. It is fortunate I know how to swim, or you'd be dead. As it was, I thought you might drown before I could get you ashore."

He tried to smile a little. The way she said *You fell out of the sky* so prosaically made it sound like such things happened to her every day.

She placed one hand on his shoulder. He could see it but not feel it. His whole body was sunk in a blank numbness like anesthesia.

"You're very cold," she said. "We're far enough from my home that I can't take you there, not as you are. You could not make the journey. But I have a blanket with me, and I'll wrap you in it. It's a warm enough night, and no rain on the way, thank the gods. I'll be warm enough without, but naked and chilled as you are, I fear that you'll take your death if I don't warm you quickly. I'll get the blanket, and then kindle a fire. Don't be afraid, I'll only be moments."

The face vanished. He looked up at a deep blue sky with what looked like a million stars, each glittering with a fierce energy. The thought occurred to him that if he lived, what would come back first would be pain, but at the moment, there was only exhaustion. He closed his eyes, and his consciousness drifted away.

Duncan was awakened by shivering. Convulsive, agonizing, helpless shudders racked his body. He was terribly cold and desperately hot at the same time, and he thought, *I'm feverish*, but again the idea simply drifted across his mind like a stray balloon. Every muscle and joint ached. She was next to him again, and he heard the crackling of a fire nearby, but she had him covered from the waist down with a soft blanket, and was rubbing a warm, dry cloth across his belly and chest and arms. It felt good, but the pain was so much worse that his consciousness could only fix on the sensation of her caress for a moment before it was once again swallowed by the pain. He moaned, and even that was caught and torn by the chattering of his teeth.

"You're warming up," she said. "It'll hurt for a while. I think you were near death from the cold, before even you came to fall into the lake. The heavens must be a frosty place." She smiled, and her hands stroked the side of his neck. "Try to relax. I have dried jasmine and other herbs wrapped in a cloth, good medicine for warming the skin and bringing life back."

She brought it near his face, and there was a sweet, floral odor. The shivering abated a little, but he was still aching and weak and his limbs would not obey his will when he struggled to make them move.

"Don't," she said, as if she'd read his thoughts. "Don't try to rise. There is no reason. I will care for you until you are well and strong again. I have no reason for haste, and you are unable to travel. We can stay here in this place as long as you need. You may be at ease." The cloth caressed his skin again, leaving a trail of tingling warmth behind it. "Sleep. It is the best cure for all ills. I will not leave you."

And again his mind slid downward into unconsciousness for a time.

When Duncan awoke, it was morning. The fire had burned low, and the woman was curled up near him, asleep herself, head resting on the crook of a shapely arm. The sun was barely over the horizon, but he could already feel its warming rays against his face. He turned his head, activating a hundred small pains in his neck and upper back, but the desperate agony of the previous night was gone.

He lay in a grove of huge, gnarled trees whose crooked branches swept almost to the ground. They were festooned with silvery-gray leaves and small green fruit. The grass he lay upon was soft, and a gentle breeze set the bell-shaped blooms of some tiny wildflowers nearby nodding and dancing. He sat up, and the blanket, which had been pulled up to his neck, slipped down to his waist.

The woman heard his motion, and her eyes opened. She sat up herself, yawned and stretched like a cat, and then looked him up and down.

"You appear to be feeling better."

He frowned at her, and his belly clenched in a moment of incomprehension. He looked at her face, golden-brown flawless skin like satin in the sun, deep brown eyes, shining black curls.

"Antonia?" he said, his voice quiet, disbelieving.

"No," the woman said, shaking her head with a smile. "Diana. You mistake me for someone?"

"You look like my... my ex-girlfriend," he said. "Antonia Syriakis."

"Ex?" She stood, walked over to a satchel that sat on the ground nearby, and knelt to open it, her back to him. "Foolish woman, if she chose to leave you."

"I chose to leave her. She was a nutcase."

Diana pulled a small leather bag from the satchel. "Then doubly foolish for troubling you so. But I am not her."

"The Sphinx looked like my sister."

"I do not know the Sphinx." She shrugged, as if the question did not interest her much. Then she returned to where he was sitting, and dropped into a cross-legged position next to him. "But perhaps it is wise not to trust appearances. What is your name?"

"Duncan Kyle."

She took a piece of spiced dried meat from the bag, and a handful of fruit that looked like apricots. "Then here, Duncan Kyle. Eat this slowly. Your strength will come back the better if you do not try too much too soon. I have water in a skin, and some good wine. Once we see if your belly will tolerate a little food, I will bring you something to drink."

He took a bite of the dried meat, and munched it slowly. It was strong, a little peppery, and tasted of cinnamon and allspice. His stomach accepted it gratefully, and he was finished with all of what she had given him in short order. After that, she brought him some water, and then a drink of dark red wine from a wineskin on a leather cord.

Afterwards, she helped him to lie back down, and pulled the blanket completely off him so that the sun, now fully up, could warm his skin directly. If she was bothered by the fact that he was naked, she didn't show it. She took the jasmine-scented cloth and once again rubbed him, starting from his face and working her way down his body. As she was stroking his sides, there was a surge of warmth in his groin, and he felt himself getting hard.

"There is another good sign," she said with a laugh. "But perhaps you should not expend energy in that way too soon." She worked her way down his legs, to the soles of his feet, and then wrapped him in the blanket again. "Sleep again, now that it is day. Let the sun heal you. Perhaps by the evening, you will be stronger still." She let her fingers brush his face. "And then we will talk further."

He closed his eyes…

… and when he opened them, it was once again the warm, azure twilight into which he'd fallen the evening before. He had slept the day away, so soundly that he was unaware of the passage of time.

Diana knew immediately as soon as he awakened. She was sitting with her back to one of the huge trees, but when she saw his eyes open she stood and walked over to him, and knelt next to him. Whether she had watched him the whole time as he slept, or had gone away on her own business and then returned, he had no way of knowing.

He was fully himself again. Better, perhaps. He could not remember ever feeling so completely alive. Whatever her treatment, it had worked. Could the food she had given him been drugged? He could sense his heart pumping in his chest, the rush of blood flowing through arteries. He needed to stretch his muscles, or run, or lift weights, as if energy flowed through him, clear and lambent as sunlight, restless like the flame of a fire. He was still hungry, but even that was pleasant, a deep heat in his belly. He had a raging hard-on.

She leaned over him, smiling. "You seem well." Knowledge and laughter danced in her eyes.

'I feel well."

She pulled the blanket back a little, and rested one hand on his chest, letting a finger trail across one nipple. He groaned.

"Perhaps we should not talk, first," she said. "You won't think clearly, I don't believe, in your current state." She unknotted the belt at her waist, and opened up her tunic, let it slide off her shoulders and to the grass behind her. Underneath it, she wore nothing at all. The moonlight touched her breasts with the softness of silk.

"So let us finish your cure," she said, and pulled the blanket all the way from him.

I can't do this... My girlfriend... Libby. It's cheating. But I need it... I need it so bad... Then she straddled his lap, and all thinking was done. He gave himself up to pleasure.

She never relinquished control. Brought him close, backed off, brought him closer, and again slowed, smiling down at him. When she finally gave him release it *was* a gift, and none of his doing. His orgasm arced through his body like lightning. She came moments later, hands on his chest, fingertips digging into his pectorals, her backbone flexed like a bow, head thrown back, shouting her ecstasy to the sky. Afterwards they stayed linked for a time, both drinking in deep draughts of cool evening air as hearts slowed, tensed muscles relaxed.

He finally said, "Whatever ailed me, I think that cured it."

Diana laughed, and leaned over him. The moonlight gleamed from the jewel on her headband. "I would have you well and whole. It appears that you are."

"Very well, thanks. But you didn't have to do that, you know."

"I know." She raised one eyebrow in a quizzical fashion. "You regret it?"

"No. But just because I was turned on, didn't mean..."

She touched his face, and her dark eyes looked into his. "I take what I want. There was no coercion." One corner of her mouth turned upward a little. "I don't know that you *could* coerce me. I wanted you, so I had you. You enjoyed it, yes?"

"Very much."

"I did as well. Then there is no need to talk about this."

"I guess not."

She pulled away from him, and then lay down next to him, draping one arm across his belly, and pressing a cheek against his shoulder. "How did you come to fall out of the sky, half-frozen?"

"I was thrown over a cliff. It was in another world. I know it sounds ridiculous."

"How do you know that?"

"What? That it was another world?"

"No, that it would sound ridiculous to me."

"It sounds ridiculous to *me*."

"Ah." She did not speak for some minutes. "Do not make the mistake of thinking that anyone else sees what you see, thinks what you think."

"I suppose not."

"What world was it that you were in?"

"All I know is that it was called Malkuth. Everything there was dead."

"If everything was dead, who threw you from the cliff?"

"I'm not sure who they were. They were the Caretakers for the Sphinx, but I don't know anything more about them. Maybe they were alive, but it didn't seem that way. I think perhaps they were ghosts. It was night. I could not see them. They stole my heat, using their hands. A little more and I would have died."

"You nearly died as it was. My half-brother is a healer, and I have learned some of his art. I believe that it saved your life. But a short while longer and you would have been beyond recall."

"Yes. Thank you."

"You're welcome," she said, her voice formal, mimicking his, and then she laughed. "Do not take so much on yourself. Perhaps I have saved you for my own reasons."

"What reasons would those be?"

"One of them you just saw." She stroked his abdomen lightly. "But there could be others. You needn't know those. You will find out when you need to."

"What is this place?" he said. "And why do you look exactly like Antonia? The Sphinx—she was in Malkuth, in the world I just left—her face was like my sister's. You could be Antonia's twin. You even... you even make love like her."

"Do I?"

"Yes." He paused, swallowed. "I'm sorry if I've offended you."

"You haven't."

"It's just that none of this makes any sense. I landed in Malkuth when the floor of my apartment collapsed, and I thought I was going to die there, of thirst or starvation. Then the Caretakers found me, and nearly froze me to death, and threw me over a cliff into the sea, but I ended up here. I still don't have any idea what is going on."

"Why do you need to understand? It might be that some things are only to be experienced, not explained."

"But there has to be an explanation!"

"Not necessarily. Perhaps there are no explanations, at least not in the way that you mean. Things simply happen because they happen, and in all the world, there is only one true reason for doing anything."

"What is that?"

"Because you desire it."

She slid her hand downward, and gently raked her fingertips through the curls of his pubic hair, still damp from their earlier encounter. He made a sound a little like a purr.

"You understand, then," she said, and smiled against the bare skin on his upper arm.

After a moment, he said, "Do you want to fuck again?"

Her hand slid lower still. "You need to ask?"

So they did.

Afterwards, he slept, as the stars and the moon wheeled overhead. It was a warm evening, and even the blanket was unnecessary, so he lay curled on his side on the grass, only stirring once or twice the whole night. He woke as the eastern sky was filling with rosy light, yawned, and sat up. Diana was nowhere in sight, but her satchel was still sitting on the ground near the remains of the previous evening's campfire. He stood and stretched, his backbone cracking pleasantly, and after taking care of his bodily needs he walked around the area for a while.

He examined the green fruits hanging from the low branches, and decided that he was in an olive grove. He wandered aimlessly, looked in Diana's satchel for food but found none, and finally went for a swim in the lake that lay, still and clear and warm, only a few yards from their campsite.

He dove from a rock, his body piercing the water like an arrow. As he swam in the same lake he'd plunged into when he'd fallen out of the sky two days ago, he considered his good fortune. He'd landed in a nice place, even if he'd almost drowned on arrival. It was better than Malkuth, anyhow, even if there was something weird about it, something that he couldn't quite put his finger on. He wondered idly where Diana had gone. Maybe she'd bring back food. The one thing that was certain is that he was ravenously hungry.

He finished his swim, then dozed on a rock near the lake's edge, letting the sun dry his wet skin and hair. After a little while, he heard a noise, and turned his head. Diana was emerging from the grove. She was still wearing the light tunic, and desire stirred again in him on watching her walk toward him. At her shoulder was a bow and a quiver full of arrows, and hanging from a cord at her waist was a pair of rabbits.

"While you were idling, I've been hunting," she said. "Are you hungry?"

"Famished."

"Kindle a fire, and I'll see to the rest," she said. "There's flint and tinder in the satchel." She pulled a small knife from a sheath at her belt, and with an expert hand skinned and cleaned the rabbits.

He had never started a fire with a flint, but there was something in his pride that was stung by her comment about *idling*, and he couldn't admit that to her. He pulled some stalks of grass, and found more dry shreds along with a small knife and a piece of flint in a wooden box in the satchel. After a few fumbling tries—*Get fire from a rock? How do you get fire from a rock?*—he was able to strike a couple of sparks, and create a little smoldering pile of grass, twigs, and leaves. He added a few sticks, and some chips of wood and charcoal that were the remnants of the earlier fire, and a few minutes of blowing and poking resulted in merrily crackling flames.

The olive grove had dead wood in plentiful supply, and before long he had a nice blaze going. Diana cut up the rabbit meat and skewered the pieces on slender branches along with some chunks of apricots like the ones he had eaten the day before, then tossed the skins and other remains into the long grass near the lake's edge and washed her hands and knife in the shallows.

"Toast these in the fire," she said, handing him one of the skewers. "Not too long. They're young and tender, no need to toughen them by overcooking."

The smell soon had his empty belly growling and his mouth watering, but as she said, it wasn't long before they were ready to eat. She removed her skewer from the fire, and delicately removed the pieces one at a time with her fingers, and he followed suit.

By this point he would have eaten almost anything remotely edible, but even taking his hunger into account, he thought that this meal was the most delicious thing he had ever tasted in his life.

After eating and washing up, they sat on the ground as the flames died down.

After a time he said, "What happens now?"

"What do you mean?"

He frowned. "I don't know, exactly," he said, fumbling a little. "I mean, here I am. I still don't have any clothes, not that you seem to mind much, and not that I really do either, actually. But I have to get home, somehow."

"Why?" She drank from the wineskin, and handed it to him.

His frown deepened, and he took a pull of rich red wine from the skin. "Don't I?"

"No reason I can see." She leaned across to him, and kissed him. He tasted the wine on her tongue, and that ended any questions he might have had for the time being.

One day passed, and then another. A week, then two, then time fogged out, lost its meaning except for night following day. Diana took Duncan hunting, and after a few fumbling attempts, he took down a young stag with his arrow. The skinning and gutting left him feeling a little sick, but it didn't stop him from enjoying the venison that evening.

His jaw at first darkened with stubble, and then one day he felt the unfamiliar sensation of drawing his hand across a prickly beard. The soles of his feet, tender from wearing shoes day in and day out, toughened until he could run beside her through the woods and not feel every twig on the path. The sun burnished him bronze from head to toe, and he found that for the first time in his life, he was able to forget about whether he was clothed or not. Back home, he often went shirtless when the weather was warm, but it was always with a measure of self-consciousness. After a few days had passed here, he found himself wearing nothing and not thinking about it at all.

His desire for her, though, didn't wane. It was rekindled morning and evening, and was morning and evening satisfied. Still, there was an uncomfortable knowledge that she had him in tow. They were sharing the hunt, and he was no longer weak and in need of care, but there was never any doubt who was in control.

One evening, after the meal and lovemaking were both done, and the air cooled around them into a twilit calm, his mind once again fluttered with unease. He still knew next to nothing about her. Who she was, why she was here, why she had rescued him, why she took him on as a companion and a lover. And every time his questions approached the topic, she deflected them, or enticed him into activities that he was honestly all too easy to distract into.

"How long can we stay here?" he said, as he lay stretched at length on the grass, his head in her lap.

She gestured around her. "Do you see any here demanding that we leave?"

"No. But I think I should be trying to get back home."

"I don't see why. If you like it here, stay."

"I do like it here."

She shrugged. "Well, then."

"It's not my home, though."

"No. But I cannot see how that matters." She ran her fingers through his hair. "Is it so important to return home?"

"I don't know how to get home in any case. I want to, but I don't know how."

"That is a problem."

"So you don't know, either."

"No." She shrugged. "I know the world around us, but how to get back to your own world, I could not say."

"So you really don't know about Malkuth? The place where I was, the world that had the Sphinx and the temple and the Caretakers?"

"I know only what you have told me about it. And from what you have told me, I do not understand why you would want to go back there."

"I don't. But if I understood how I jumped from there to here, I might know how to jump from here back to my home."

"Only if the paths are the same. There is no certainty that is true."

"No. So, like I said, what now? We can stay here in this grove, which is pleasant enough, but I feel restless. I feel like I should be doing something more than swimming and hunting and sleeping and having sex."

"Why?" One dark eyebrow rose slightly, and her eyes gleamed with a curious intelligence.

He rubbed his hand across his face. "I don't know. If you'd asked me two weeks ago what I wanted out of life, I'd have said that the things I just mentioned are all I need. I know you said explanations aren't important, but I think I have to figure out why I've been dumped into what looks very much like a dream, but apparently is not. I can't simply accept this."

She smiled, and slipped out from beneath him.

He raised himself on his elbows, and she stood up, straightening her tunic and brushing off a stray piece of grass.

"Suit yourself," she said.

"Wait a moment," he said, and she paused, and looked down at him with a questioning expression. "Aren't *you* a little curious about how I got here, and why? I fall out of the sky into the lake, and you rescue me, and are willing to feed me and take care of me and make love to me, and that's all? No questions?"

"Questions lead to answers," she said, and for the first time her voice sounded a little perturbed. "And answers aren't always what they appear to be. Nor what you might want. What if you got answers, but they weren't the ones you hoped for?"

He pinched the bridge of his nose between thumb and forefinger. "I don't know. Like I said... what more could a guy want, you know? A beautiful woman bringing me food and jumping me every time I get the urge. But..."

"But what?" she said, and her voice had a hard edge.

"There's something wrong, here." He stood up suddenly. "You've talked about others, but the only one I've seen is you. You say that I am free to stay here forever, but I get the feeling that the last thing I really am is free. After you healed me, I wanted you, and I wanted what this place was. I was taken in at first. But now I want answers. I want the truth, even if it's harsh. Even if I'm dreaming, or have gone insane, and this is somehow all a delusion."

Diana stepped near him, and she gave him an alluring smile. He looked at her, stared deep into her dark eyes.

He hadn't noticed before, but her smile didn't ever reach her eyes.

She put one hand on his shoulder, and let it run down his bare back. "The truth isn't important," she said in a soft voice. "Your mind is only going to mislead you. Follow what your body wants, instead." Her gaze moved downwards, and she chuckled. "See? Your body knows what it wants. Better than your mind does."

He pushed her away, and at the same time pushed away his own physical need.

The realization was like a sudden chill in his heart. She was taking from him, just like the Caretakers had, only a different way.

"No," he said. "I want answers. I see what the attraction is for me. What man wouldn't? But what are *you* getting out of this?"

Her lips pulled back in a sudden, and unexpected, snarl. "Think carefully, Duncan Kyle. Put your feet on this path, and you won't be able to turn back. I could protect you, if you stop now."

"From what? What do I need protection from?"

The snarl turned into a triumphant grin. "From us. This world isn't a delusion. But when you find out what it really is, you'll wish it was."

Despite the warmth of the evening around him, a chill twanged its way up his backbone.

"What? What is it?"

She didn't answer for a moment. Her eyes were on his, evaluating, considering. Finally, she said, "Putting it in terms you'll understand, it's a hunting preserve."

"Hunting for what?"

Her gaze was cold, pitiless. "Whoever finds their way in."

"So others..." He tried to ignore the sick feeling in his belly, the way he had ignored his lust earlier. Desire was now light-years away, nothing but ashes left of the pleasure he had had of her.

"Have found their way here? Certainly. Not from Malkuth, at least not recently. There are other paths in."

"So you knew..."

"... about Malkuth? In other words, did I lie? Of course I did. I know all of the worlds, and the paths between them. I told you what you needed to know, and what you wanted to hear."

"But if you are a hunter, why did you keep me?" His eyes widened a little. "No. I see. You kept me as a pet. For a time, right? Eventually, you'd have tired of me, too, so even your talk about my turning you against me by asking questions was a lie. Sooner or later, you'd have gotten bored with me, and then, what? You'd have killed me outright?"

"No, we never do that. Hardly sporting. You always have a chance to escape." She let one finger trail down his chest, and her mouth turned downward in a mockery of sympathy. "Of course, none ever has. The outcome is never *really* in question. We always win."

"We?"

"I told you. My siblings live near here, and our parents. And there are others, farther off. You and I are far from alone. On the day you fell here, while you slept, I went to them and told them to keep their distance. That I had found a pet, as you put it. That I wanted some privacy to play."

"So your family is all like you? Using people and then killing them?"

"You put it so brutally." She sighed. "But surely you've heard about us. Some hints about us have gotten through, even to your world. They get most of the details wrong, but the essence is there. You've heard of Actaeon, yes?"

He shook his head.

"I never found out how he got here. It was from your world, I'm certain, so he must have stumbled on a portal, poor thing. He came upon me while I was swimming. He watched me for a while. I knew he was there. I'm hard to sneak up on, you know? A hunter becomes sensitive after a time. So I let him watch. And then, I could see that he was pleasuring himself. Who can blame him? It's natural enough, I guess. But at the time, it angered me."

"Because you weren't in control."

Her eyes narrowed a little. "Yes. You understand me well."

"What did you do?"

"They say I turned him into a stag. But that part is a lie. I was kind enough to let him finish. Then I went to him. I picked up my bow on the way, and notched an arrow to the string. I didn't bother to dress. He was frozen to the spot, frozen with mortification because of being caught that way. I looked down at him, his garments still askew, his hand around his pathetic little manhood, and I laughed. At that point he still thought I'd spare him, I think. But I leaned in close to him, and I whispered, 'I think you'd better run.'"

"What happened?"

"He ran. For a short while, at least."

"That's horrible."

Her white smile flashed out at him. "Not everyone thinks so. I've been deified in your world, did you know? The goddess Diana."

Realization struck him with a jolt like an electric shock. "Diana? Like the Roman goddess?"

She gave a little gesture with one long-fingered hand. "So it would seem."

"But I thought..." He swallowed. "I thought the goddess Diana was some kind of, you know... fixated on being a virgin."

"A virgin?" She shrugged. "I am what I choose to be. I am a virgin in the sense that I never give myself to anyone. I only take what I want, for my own satisfaction. But perhaps *virgin* is the wrong word, after all. I prefer to think of it as *selective*." She gave him an appreciative look up and down, and he suddenly wished, for the first time since his arrival, that he was clothed. "Once you were well enough, I was going to let you run, too, as I had with Actaeon. But as you recovered, I realized that your body pleased me, and that I wanted you. So I took you. I didn't hear you complaining. And at least you had a nice last fling, right? If you had to choose a way to spend your last weeks alive... think of it. Making love twice a day, hunting next to a beautiful woman in the sunshine, good wine to drink, sleeping under the stars. It's what you'd have chosen, right?"

"Not knowing what you actually are."

"You really believe that? You credit yourself with far more forbearance than I think you are actually capable of."

"And you credit yourself with far more allure than you actually have."

He expected her to become angry, but she laughed. "Come, now. I've been honest with you. I admitted to you that I wanted you, you should admit the same about me. And you should be honored. I haven't kept a pet in some time. Most of them end up like Actaeon. An arrow" —she reached out one finger and pressed it to his chest, right above his left nipple—"here. And that is the end. A quicker death, and less painful, than many you could hope for. But still, I can't expect you'll see it that way."

"No. I don't."

She shrugged again. "It doesn't matter, though. If it means anything to you, in what will be your last few minutes, I did enjoy you. You gave me a great deal of pleasure." She put one cool hand on his cheek, and kissed him on the mouth. "And now," she said quietly, "run, little rabbit. Run for your life."

He stared at her, didn't move.

"I'm serious," she warned. "You'd better run. After enjoying your body so, I would hate to end it without any sport. But if you don't run, I will be forced to shoot you where you stand."

"Why?" His voice was hoarse. "Why are you doing this?"

"I told you. The only reason to do anything. Because I desire it." She walked slowly toward a gnarled olive tree, beneath which sat her satchel, bow, and quiver. "I soon will tire of encouraging you to run," she said, her back to him. "I expected you to show more spirit than to give up before you've even started. It is, of course, your choice."

And he turned and ran.

He darted between huge old olive trees, then down a hill, and along a path he and Diana had used while hunting. He leapt across a little tumbling creek in one bound, leg muscles taut as steel bands. The path wound away uphill, but he turned aside into an open woodland, zigzagging his way amongst tree trunks and past craggy outcrops of gray rock, crusted with lichen and moss. He'd hunted with her many times; he knew she'd track him with no difficulty. Desperation surged through him, tingling with adrenaline. A good huntress knows her prey. She'd done this many, many times before, and no one had ever escaped.

He expected at any moment to feel the jolt of an arrow between his shoulder blades. What would it feel like, to be pierced to the heart? It would be a different death than the one he had expected at the hands of the Caretakers. Better, though, than being drained of his heat and left to mummify in the dead world of Malkuth. Here, at least, he was given one last chase, and even if it would end with his bleeding his life away into the grass, there was something exhilarating about it. Malkuth had been desiccated and barren. Yesod was brutal, fierce, and pitiless, but vitally, desperately alive.

The path he took climbed slowly, steadily uphill, and his strength flagged. His breath came in ragged gasps, and sweat was running down his chest. He slowed, ducking behind a trio of broad trunks that looked like good cover, and leaned over, hands on his knees, coughed, and spat into the bushes. Had he lost her?

At that moment, an arrow whickered overhead, embedding itself inches deep into a nearby tree.

Sprinting again. Heart thudding against his ribcage. The staccato beat of bare feet striking the ground. Another arrow whirred by, the wind of its passage brushing his cheek, and he thought, She was playing with him. He'd seen her fell a deer from fifty yards away. If she wanted to, she could put a shaft right through him. She wanted the sport, the thrill of the chase. And just as she said—when she tired of it, she'd end him.

He struck another broad path, one he'd never seen before on his hunting treks. It was well-maintained, but open. The lack of cover was one problem, but the other was that he recalled that Diana had referred to "us." This path wasn't kept clear by one person, nor was it for one person's use. There were others like her, hunters the same as her. Would they kill him on sight? Or know that he was her prey, and hers alone, and leave him to her to finish off?

He crossed the path, and dipped into the deeper woods on the other side. He still saw no one. Not even Diana, of whom he had not caught a glimpse since his run began. But there was a merry peal of laughter from somewhere very close.

A thought, near hysteria, bounced around in his brain. *She's found me. I'm about to die.*

Then, a different thought cut through the fear.

He'd thought he was going to die when the Caretakers caught him, and against all odds he'd survived. He was not done yet. He was not done till there was an arrow through his heart. If she finished him, he was damn sure going to make her work for it. He button-hooked to the left, through a stand of dark-trunked trees with heavy, glossy leaves, and started a short, steep climb, leaping from rock to rock.

The pursuit, certainly right on his heels, made no sound.

Suddenly he came out into bright sunshine, and in front of him was a cleared space with a small, open-sided temple. It was not a sprawling monstrosity like the one on Malkuth, but a neat, columned building of light-colored marble. Behind the row of columns was an altar, on which lay a wooden staff, a knife, and a basin.

For sacrifices? If he was not killed outright, was that what she had planned? But sacrificed to whom? To herself?

The idea struck him as preposterous, and he laughed, but he grabbed the knife as he ran across the flagstone court, intending to circle behind the temple and then downhill and away. The temple itself filled him with a chill foreboding. It had an air not of desolation and emptiness, like the huge complex in Malkuth, but active evil. If he tarried there, he would die.

He almost made it.

He was about to leap from the edge of the wall down into the grassy verge, a drop of only a few feet, when an arrow grazed his naked thigh. It cut a deep gash across his skin, and then skittered on the stones and into a shadowed corner of the temple.

He gave a cry of pain, and grabbed his leg. He looked down. Scarlet oozed from between his fingers. He turned to see Diana walking slowly up the hill, an arrow notched to her bowstring. She wore a broad smile.

"Well run," she said. "Not many have lasted this long against me." She looked down at the ceremonial knife in his right hand. "You've hunted with me enough to know that an arrow is far swifter than a knife."

He backed up, passing between two of the stone columns and into the cool shade of the temple. "You don't have to do this."

"Have to?" She gave a peal of laughter. "I have never *had* to do anything."

"Why would you kill me if I gave you nothing but pleasure?"

"Because killing you also gives me pleasure. Because the chase is pleasure. Because seeing you standing there, naked and trembling, knowing you are minutes from death, gives me pleasure." She pulled the bowstring, flexing the wooden bow. The point of the arrow was aimed at his breastbone. "But if you wish to plead for your life, I will listen. That will also be pleasant to me."

His halting retreat ended when his back touched the cool folds of woven fabric. He reached behind him with one hand, and his hand brushed some sort of cloth, perhaps a tapestry or a curtain. There seemed to be a space behind it, but he dared not turn to look.

"Pleading wouldn't change the outcome," he said. "So why embarrass myself by doing it?"

"Well said," she said, whether sincerely or in jest was impossible to tell. "You show courage. I will make your end quick. Such a gift a goddess can bestow." She pulled the bow taut. "But wait," she said, as if it were an afterthought, but he knew everything she did was planned, considered, deliberate. She released a little of the tension on the string. "Perhaps I will spare your life, if you will tell me one thing."

"What is that?"

"How do you get from one world to another?"

"I thought you already knew that. You said other people have come here, and you have hunted them. And you know about the worlds and the paths from one to another."

"Oh, yes. We do. We know what the worlds are. But we do not know how to create the portals between them. I think you do."

"I don't."

"So a portal appeared, from nothing, as you needed it, when you were on the verge of death? I find that difficult to believe. The others who came here, they have always looked lost, as if they stumbled in by accident. Your arrival was... convenient. For you, at least."

"I was almost frozen to death, and then I nearly drowned. I would have died if you hadn't rescued me."

"*Almost* and *nearly*," she said. "And yet here you stand. I think you *do* know how to travel from one world to the next. Tell me that, and I will let you live. I may even let you accompany me as my brothers and sisters and I go hunting in new lands." Her beautiful brows drew together in a mockery of sympathy. "Of course, you may not really know, or you may choose not to tell me. Either way, it would be unfortunate for you."

He wasn't sure why he reacted as he did. His rush toward her was so sudden, and so unexpected, that she hesitated for a moment, then flinched as she released the arrow, and it flew wild.

He heard the *twang* of the string, and a metallic *ping* as the arrowhead struck stone somewhere above and behind him. He leaped forward and swung the knife at her, but fear and inexperience defeated his first attack. The knife blade merely grazed her shoulder, slitting open the sleeve of her tunic.

She gave a howl of anger, cut off as his momentum drove him into her, his shoulder hitting her hard and low. His greater weight bowled her over, and knocked the breath from her lungs in a great whoosh as they tumbled together to the floor. She recovered her composure instantly. She had undoubtedly tracked many prey in her long, long life, and this was surely not the first one that decided to fight back. She tore at his bare chest, growling like an animal.

They clutched, striving against each other in a death battle as they had striven against each other in love only a day before. She grabbed his wrist, and with surprising strength slammed it against the stone floor.

He gave a cry of pain and let go of the knife, and it clattered out of reach.

Now they were bare hands to bare hands. She had dropped her bow as well, not that it would have been useful in such combat. And to his surprise, he found that they were equally matched. He had never been a fighter. A few tussles in middle school were all he had to his credit. He had thought that this tireless huntress would be more than a match for him, that his death was only a matter of time.

Could he kill her? He was amazed the thought even came to mind. He had to try. It was her or him. He reached for her throat, but her free hand came up and raked nails across his cheek, drawing blood. A lithe, powerful leg twisted beneath him, her knee planted solidly in his abdomen. He was flung away from her, and slid toward the curtained wall, one shoulder scraping painfully on the flagstones.

He rolled to the side, trying to come to his feet, but she was on top of him before he could regain his balance. Now both knees were against him, and she shoved him backwards. Head and shoulders landed against the curtain, and the fabric tore and cascaded around them.

There was a moment, almost comical, as they struggled to free themselves from the heavy weight of the cloth. He grabbed at the curtain, pulled it down around her head, trying to entangle her further to buy himself time. She gave a snarl of anger, but he was able to free himself, get at least to his knees.

He looked behind him, hoping that the space there was an exit from the temple, at least a thread of a hope for escape. It was a mere alcove, barely four feet deep.

The back wall was blank, dark brown stone, different from the light marble from which the rest of the temple was constructed. But there was no escape that way. He was trapped.

Diana pulled herself free of the curtain, and stood. She took a step back, and grabbed the heavy wooden staff from the altar, the only weapon still within reach. Her black hair was in disarray, her eyes smoldering with rage. She advanced, pointing the end of the staff toward him.

She was going to spear him with that thing. That would hurt way more than an arrow through the heart.

Once again, he backed up, as she prodded him forward with the blunt end of the staff, her face twisted with anger.

His back and his butt touched the wall. He expected the cool roughness of stone against his skin, an unrelenting solidity that would be an incongruous coda to the dreamlike worlds into which he had fallen. Instead, behind him was a springy, smooth surface, unlike anything he'd ever felt. It was a little like plastic, a little like water, and a little like the surface of a trampoline he and his friends had played on as kids. He pressed himself into it, and it gave, stretching like elastic.

"A portal?" she said, and her upper lip curled in a snarl. "I knew you were lying."

He reached back into it, and it flexed against the palms of his hands. "A portal to where?"

"You can't get out that way!" she screamed at him. "My prey never escapes!"

She lunged forward, aiming the staff at his heart. He grabbed it, held it, his muscles straining, and looked into her eyes. And for a moment they were perfectly balanced, immobile.

"This one does," he said, and launched himself backwards. The membrane tore, like a balloon bursting, and he was blown from one world to another by a shriek of futile anger. He almost pulled her through with him, but at the last moment let go of the staff, and she teetered on the edge, and then recoiled back into the sunlit groves and hillsides of Yesod. The air around him exploded into fragments, abrading his skin like shrapnel, and he landed on his back on some hard, dry surface, with the wind shrieking in his ears.

And the curtain from the temple, sucked through the portal behind him, twisted down through the air and settled over his prone body like a shroud.

CHAPTER 3

HOD

Duncan had once read a story in which the wind had a human voice. It was the first thing that went through his head upon regaining his senses, lying on his back on hot sand. *The wind is screaming with a human voice.* But if it was, this voice needed no pause to breathe. It brayed its violence in one continuous note, a wide-mouthed shriek of unchallenged power. It was dark, but the heavy curtain from the temple still lay over his face. The air under it was dry, with the sharp odor of dust and ozone.

He pulled his covering back and peeked out, then immediately ducked under again. The air was whirling, and in the moment of a glance that communicated nothing about his surroundings it scoured his skin, stung his face. From the calm summer woodlands of Yesod, he had fallen into the midst of a desert sandstorm.

There was obviously nothing to be done. No one could stand up in such a maelstrom of air and grit and dust and survive, even if he'd pulled the curtain around his body. Breathing would have been not difficult, but impossible. Better to lie prone, hanging onto his protection with a desperate grip, and hope that it would end quickly.

Would it have been better, an easier death, if he'd let her kill him?

With an effort he banished the self-pitying voice from his head.

No. Even she didn't know how the portals appeared. And twice, they showed up when he'd needed it, when he was about to die. She would have killed him, one way or the other, if he'd stayed in Yesod. If he was here, he had a chance. Maybe more than a chance.

He pulled the curtain around him, held on tight, and tried to breathe slowly and steadily, without coughing.

It seemed hours later that he realized that the sound of the wind had quieted. It still blew, and the edge of the curtain had pulled up off his right foot, exposing his toes to the abrasion of the flying sand. His foot was painful, and likely bleeding, but he dared not move to look at it, or reach down to pull the fabric back over it. A few minutes later, the screaming air calmed to a rippling flutter, and he once again peeked out from underneath his shroud.

The sky was brown and blue—brown as the streamers of dust pulled away, and blue where they passed. To one side, the sun hung low in the sky. He wriggled out from under the curtain, and found that his left leg was buried in warm sand up to his thigh. He was lying half on his side. It had been impossible, while the sandstorm raged, even to tell which direction was up. He had caught a piece of the blanket underneath his hip as he fell, and the wind had flopped the rest over him. Fortunately. If the curtain had blown away, he would have been flayed alive.

He coughed, sneezed, and pulled himself free. The air was hot, but there was no moisture in it. There was nothing but sand as far as he could see. He stood up, pulling the curtain over his shoulders like a cape, and the end of it snapped out behind him.

It looked like the Sahara. Back to the possibility of dying of thirst.

He took a step, and a searing jolt of pain sizzled across his upper right leg where Diana's arrow had grazed him. He looked down at the injury. It was caked with sand, the dried blood blackened and stuck to his skin and leg hair, but it wasn't actively bleeding any more.

He needed to find a place to clean this up soon. It looked likely to get infected if he didn't.

He took a tentative couple of steps, his bare feet sinking ankle-deep into the loose sand at every pace. With an exhausting effort considering the short distance, he staggered to the top of the nearest dune. A sea of beige sand spread out in every direction he turned. Perhaps a quarter of a mile away, though, when he faced away from the sun, a lighter-colored object poked up above the ridge of the dune, something that had angles and peaks instead of the smooth, undulant surface of sand. Having no better plan, he set out toward it.

He fell to his knees more times than he could count as the grains slithered out from underneath him. Sand coated him, stuck in the hair on his head and legs and chest and groin, until his skin was abraded raw. At first, his intended goal looked no nearer, and he spent some time convincing himself that it was not a mirage. After being lost for a moment behind the crest of a dune, however, he saw it clearly enough to be certain that it was no illusion. The object was no longer a wavering vagueness in the distance, but was recognizable as a tent.

Closer, and the tent had flags of red and green and orange. Closer still, and it stood near a rock outcropping and a pair of palm trees, to which the corners of the tent were securely anchored. Nearby was a small but deep pool of water.

He pulled the curtain around his waist, and called out, in a voice that was barely a croak, "Help? Is anyone there?"

A head, itself covered almost completely with cloth colored a rich canary yellow, poked out through a flap of the tent, and a hand motioned him toward it.

"Come on," the shrouded figure said. "I wondered if I would have to come get you. The haboob is not done with us for the night. The waves always come in threes, and that was but the first."

He looked up at the sky, which was violet-tinged with the approach of sunset, but in the east, building like the surf, was a brown cloud with rolling, boiling edges, mounting up even as he watched. There was a sizzling crackle in the distance as lightning flashed, and a few seconds later the deep voice of thunder.

Lightning in a dust storm? The idea sent a chill through him.

"You'd better come in," the cloth-covered figure urged. "You won't survive another. The first was barely a skirmish."

The wind was picking up already, and sand stung his face. The flags on top of the tent, tied to flexible poles, snapped like whips.

He brushed what sand he could from his skin, then ducked through the opening and into the warm dimness of the interior.

The figure turned, and with a practiced motion, secured the tent flap with what looked like about a hundred buttons. His eyes adjusted as he stood there, the wind beating on the tent's sides, making it flex like the breathing ribcage of some great beast. The flames of two large brass oil lamps fluttered in the moving air, their yellow light casting deep shadows across the interior. He hitched up the curtain around his waist, and dropped into a kneeling position on the thick rug that covered the floor.

"Where am I now?" he said.

"Now? Now, and always, this place is called Hod." A face turned toward him, but not one he could see. It was still covered with some kind of soft mesh, no doubt to screen out sand and the harsh sunlight. But a strong, work-hardened hand came up, and undid the mesh, twisted it to one side and across a shoulder, exposing the gray eyes, long, beaky nose, and good-humored mouth of a middle-aged woman.

Maybe he should have expected this by now. Was everyone he met going to turn out to be someone he knew, in another guise?

She looked at him quizzically. "Is that look because you expected to find someone else? Or because you're repelled by my rather unfortunate face? Or because of something else entirely?"

"It's happened in both of the other places I've been. The people I've met... they look like someone I know. You look like a woman I work with. Her name is Tania Reade. But I'm betting that's not what you're called here."

"No," the woman said. "My name is Fatima."

"I'm Duncan."

The howl was building to the horrific levels that he'd heard when he first arrived here, a hellish, unearthly scream. The tent shuddered under the force of the wind and sand.

"How does this tent not blow away?"

"When you live here, you learn how to deal with the haboob. It comes during this season. The tent is tied, and weighted, but it also bends with the force of the wind, and does not try to stand stiff against it. That is the secret to survival, you know. Flex, flow, and spring back. Sometimes if you fight, you get..." She made a puff of breath across one hand, and shrugged and smiled.

He sagged a little, and did not respond.

"You look exhausted and hungry. I'm certain you have questions, but they can wait until you are fed and clothed, and have had a chance to sleep."

"You have clothes? Other than your own, I mean."

She smiled, and unlike Diana's smile, this one went all the way to the eyes, making the corners crinkle into maze of fine lines. "Yes, I am a widow, and I still have my husband's clothes, packed in a chest. Were he still alive, he would have given you clothing without hesitation, so I feel no shame in doing likewise."

"You have no idea how nice that sounds. I've been naked for weeks."

She stood, and went to a wooden chest that sat in one corner. She lifted the lid. It was made of some old, dark wood, with intricate carvings he couldn't quite make out in the dim light. She lifted a neatly-folded stack of clothing from the chest and closed the lid, setting the bundle on the top with some reverence.

"There," she said. "This should provide you. You are nearly the same height and build as my husband was. I think they will fit well enough."

He stood and went to the chest, still clutching the ends of the curtain around his waist. Tidily folded on top was a robe, white but with fine blue stitching down the seams, and a thin belt made of dark leather. He looked over at Fatima. She had discreetly turned her back to him. He dropped the temple curtain to the floor, picked up the robe, and slipped it on. It was made of cotton or some other lightweight cloth, and was loose and airy, with wide sleeves tapering to the wrists. He folded first the right, then the left of the robe across his body, and pulled the belt around his waist, cinching it snug with a simple brass buckle. It was an unfamiliar garment, but surprisingly comfortable in the dry heat.

It was amazing what clothing did. And what being naked meant. Clothed, you're an equal. It gave you the choice of whether to be seen, be known, right down to the skin. He'd been a fool not to realize what it signified that Diana was clothed and he was nude.

He returned to where he had sat, and dropped to a sitting position. "Thank you. That's much better."

Fatima turned, smiling again. "I have tea. You should drink. The desert air parches you much faster than you realize."

"No, I know I'm thirsty. Thanks."

A tall metal samovar sat on the floor, on a little wooden platform. It had a long metal pipe through the center, and a thin wisp of smoke twined up from the pipe. She turned a spigot near the bottom, pouring out steaming tea into two small cups, and brought one to him. He took a sip. It was strong and sweet, and tasted a little of cardamom and cinnamon. She set a brass plate with bread and cheese on the rug in front of him, and sat down cross-legged opposite. He took a piece of each, his stomach rumbling. The bread was coarse and chewy, the cheese strong-flavored and sharp.

"This is delicious," he said, his voice a little muffled as he chewed.

She smiled.

After a short while in which both of them simply sat, drank their tea, ate, and listened to the storm, he said,

"You told me you knew I was here. That you wondered if you'd have to come and find me. How did you know?"

"We always know. We who live here. When someone comes, we always know it. I do not know how."

"So Diana, the woman in Yesod, who rescued me, she was lying when she said she just happened to be in the right place to drag me out of the lake and save my life?"

A wry quality came into Fatima's smile. "Diana? So that's what she's calling herself now?"

"Yes."

"Hmm."

"It isn't her real name?"

She shrugged. "It's as real as any other name that she'd give. But in answer to your question, yes. She was lying. She certainly knew that you had gone through a portal into her world. It was fortunate, of course, that she was nearby—had she been miles distant, she would have known but might not have arrived in time to save you." She looked at him curiously, and a thin eyebrow went up a little. "She rescued you? She and her people are not often so kind to new arrivals."

"That came later," he said. "She saved me, and took care of me until I was healthy again, but then..." He stopped. He shouldn't trust this woman simply because she looked like Tania. He'd trusted Diana, and look where that got him.

"She made you the prey in their hunt."

"Yes." He pulled up the hem of his robe a little, showed her the long gash on his leg. "It's how I got this."

Her brow drew together in concern. "I did not know you were injured. All I thought was to get you inside before the next blow from the haboob struck. You must let me clean that wound. Otherwise, it may fester. I have a salve for such injuries. It has great benefit. With luck, it will leave barely a scar when it heals."

She took a small vessel with water that had been sitting to the side of the samovar, and moved it onto the top, next to the little smoking chimney. After a few minutes, she tested the water with a finger, and evidently it met with her approval. A cloth bag hung near the door to the tent,, and she went and rummaged through it and finally drew out a strip of clean linen cloth.

"Lie back and I will clean this," she said.

He was too tired to argue, and did as he was told. She dipped the cloth in the warm water, and gently cleaned away the dried blood, sand, and dirt caked around the wound. The pain made him wince more than once, but it was bearable, and he knew it was necessary. Finally the gash was clean, but bled a little. She went to the chest where she'd found him clothing, and came back in a moment with a small wooden box made of some strongly aromatic wood. She opened it, and showed him a greenish cream.

"My husband had some skill in the healing arts. He bought this from a trader we met in Tannar some years ago. It stings a little going on, but will stop the bleeding, and make it heal cleanly." She rubbed a little of the cream onto the arrow graze. He jumped at its peppery bite. Afterwards, she gave him a wide band of linen cloth. "Here. I will let you wrap this yourself, as I have done all that I can do in seemliness. Do not be afraid to tie it firmly. The cream will keep the bandage from clinging to the wound as it dries."

Again she turned away from him. He sat up, hitched his robe higher, and wrapped the linen bandage twice around his upper leg, ending by tying a clumsy knot in the ends. He tugged on them to test their tightness, then readjusted his robes to cover himself.

"There," he said. "I'm done. Thanks for this, too. Thanks for everything."

She turned back with a smile, and did not answer, but put everything she had used back in its place. The soiled and bloodied piece of linen she'd used to clean the injury she disposed of by opening one button on the tent flap, and thrusting it out into the storm, which by now was abating.

"Now," she said, "sleep. There will be time for talk tomorrow. Sleep, and let the haboob blow itself out. Tomorrow the weather will be clear and kind."

He took one of a stack of pillows that sat against the tent wall, put it behind his head, and then lay back.

"Can I ask one question?" he said, as she prepared her own place to sleep, on the other side of the tent.

"Certainly."

"What is happening to me? Why am I being bounced from place to place like this? Nothing I've ever done in my life was anything like this."

She blew out one of the oil lamps, and the light in the tent dropped by half. "I do not know the answer for certain, but you are correct that there must be a reason. Perhaps you are able to jump between the worlds for some purpose you have yet to determine, but which will become clear later." She picked up the other oil lamp, and held it in front of her. The flame light flickered over her features, at once familiar and unfamiliar, and she smiled a little. "One thing, however, I can tell you. The worlds you are moving through... their inhabitants have one thing in common. They all want to be able to do what you appear to be capable of, by nature—to jump from one place to another. So you must be careful. Because there are ones who will trick you, convince you that you have gone mad, even hurt or kill you to find that out."

A sudden chill struck him, and his eyes narrowed as he looked at her, smiling down at him. "Even you?"

"Me?" She laughed. "No. Not me. Perhaps, years ago, when my husband was alive, we would have been tempted by such knowledge. But now, I am content where I am."

"How can I believe you? Everyone else I've met has lied to me."

A strong gust of wind shook the tent, making one wall bellow inward. Fatima gave a little shrug. "At the moment, you should believe me simply because it is better than the alternative, which is to go back out there and meet the haboob again. But tomorrow, we will speak more, and perhaps I can give you other reasons." She blew the flame out, and the room was plunged in darkness.

Duncan woke the next morning to light streaming in through the open tent flap. He blinked, yawned, and stretched, and squinted out into a vista that was composed of only two colors, a stripe of bright blue, and a stripe of beige. He sat up, winced as the motion pulled on his injury, and spent the next few moments unwrapping the bandage to check on the wound. The linen strip had a little blood on it, but was mostly stained green with the salve Fatima had applied the previous evening. The gash looked clean, with no inflammation, and he re-wrapped it tightly, adjusted his robe, and walked barefoot outside.

The sand was already hot underfoot, but the sky was a sparkling sapphire blue, with not a single cloud, and no trace of the ominous brown streaks that heralded the approaching sandstorm. Fatima was down by the little lake, filling round-bottomed clay water jugs, and he walked down toward her. Near the bottom of the swale the sand gave way to sandstone, and the footing was easier.

She turned as he approached and smiled at him. Her head was covered, but the mesh she had worn over her face was still pulled back across her shoulder like a veil.

"Good morning." The dipper she used to fill one of the jugs never slowed. "The haboob has turned the water murky, but it will settle out. This water is very pure, and very deep. We are lucky to have such a spring."

He dropped into a sitting position with his back against one of the palm trees. "Tell me more about this place."

"What do you wish to know?"

"Anything you'd like to tell me."

She considered for a moment, the dipper hanging loosely from one hand. "It is beautiful. As you can see. Beautiful and harsh, like the sun that governs it. You must come to term with its rules. It will not conform to yours."

"How do you survive?"

"I and the others in my tribe have learned to deal with what the desert does. We rely on each other heavily. My family has lived here by this spring for generations, and these palm trees produce many baskets full of dates every year. I trade water and dates for meat, bread, and cheese. We care for each other, and see that no one goes without if ill fortune strikes."

"My father used to say, 'We have to hang together or we'll all hang separately.'"

"Precisely. Your father was a wise man."

"I don't think he made that saying up."

She shrugged. "Wisdom can also be found in recognizing the wisdom of someone else." She picked up two of the jugs using a rope handle that she slung across her shoulder. He stood and picked up the other two in the same fashion. They were surprisingly heavy, but she wasn't bothered by their weight.

At least that was one thing that hunting with Diana had accomplished. He was in way better shape now than he had been before all of this started. He'd have looked like a fool, struggling with these, while Fatima carried them without breaking a sweat. He followed her back uphill toward the tent, and they stood them next to one of the tent walls in the shade, their round bases partly buried in the sand.

"You said that there were other questions you had for me," she said. "Have you eaten yet?"

"No."

"Then come inside out of the sun, and we will eat and talk." She went into the tent, and unbuttoned a flap on the wall across from the doorway. There was an immediate cross-breeze which, if not cool, at least took away some of the oppressive and pervasive heat.

"I do what is necessary in the early hours," she said, tearing up the remainder of last night's bread, and placing it on the brass plate they'd used the previous evening, adding a handful of dried dates from a mesh bag hanging from a hook on the tent wall. "Before noon, the heat will make it impossible to work, except in dire need, and I usually take a rest. You would be wise to do the same."

He picked up a date and put it in his mouth. Compared to the dates he'd had, purchased in plastic from the grocery store, this one was soft and sweet, with an indescribable perfumed taste like nothing he'd ever eaten.

After they'd eaten in silence for a few minutes, he said, "Most of the questions I have, I don't think you'll know how to answer."

"There is no harm in asking, even so."

"I suppose not." He looked down, and frowned. "I mostly want to know how to get back home. Diana told me she knew about the worlds, and the paths between them, but she obviously didn't know how to get from one to the other herself, or she'd have done so."

"That is correct."

"And neither do you."

"No." She gave him a thoughtful look. "What is it in your world that you wish to return to?"

He didn't answer for a moment. He had been about to say, *Everything*, but realized before he spoke that it would not be the truth. He missed his girlfriend, he missed the familiarity of his life, but honestly, there was little else about his existence that he had any real attachment to.

Finally, he said, "I'm not sure. It's home. I don't know how else to say it."

"That is a reasonable answer. Were someone to come to me, and offer me a life in a different place, with verdant woods teeming with fruits and nuts and wild game, all within easy reach, and no sandstorms and killing heat and drying wind, I would choose, all in all, to stay here. The pull of home is very real."

"I might feel different if I knew why I was here. So far, it's all random, as if I'm being thrown from place to place as part of some arbitrary game."

"Are you unhappy?"

The affirmative died on his tongue. "Actually," he said, with a lopsided smile, "I feel more alive than I ever have. Even when I was running from Diana, there was part of me that felt like if I'd died then, if she'd shot me with her arrows, I still would have been given an opportunity to live that was far beyond what most people get." He shook his head. "She said that to me, you know? When she thought she'd won, that she was seconds from putting an arrow through my chest, she said that it is how I'd have chosen to live the last couple of weeks of my life, if I'd had the choice. I told her she was wrong, but I'm not certain she was."

"It is perhaps easier to say this when you are not facing a drawn bow."

"That's true." He lay back, hands cupped behind his head. "Both of the places I've been have looked okay at first. Well, Malkuth was pretty bleak, but it didn't seem dangerous, and Yesod was very close to paradise. Then in both cases, something changed, and nearly killed me. Is that going to happen here? I mean, you've been friendly so far, but so was Diana. Diana was *very* friendly," he added, a sudden blush heating his face, and one of Fatima's eyebrows arched a little. "You're not suddenly going to try to murder me, are you? Because if so, I'd prefer it if you'd tell me now, and skip all of the preliminary nonsense."

She laughed. "I have no intention to kill you."

"And that won't change? You won't suddenly remember that you're an undead vampire, or something, and try to rip my throat out?"

"No. You are a guest, both to our world and my humble household, and I owe you the honor and respect and kindness that all guests receive. But even did I not owe you a guest's care, I would still have treated you as I did, and as I will continue to do. Truth be told, I am happy for the company." Her smile faded. "It is hard sometimes, being alone."

"How did your husband die?"

She looked down, and was quiet for some time.

"I'm sorry to bring back bad memories."

She looked up. Her quick, easy smile flashed across her face, but then was gone again, replaced by an old, familiar pain. "Bad? No, they are not bad memories. It is not so long ago that I do not still grieve him, but he was a kind man and a loving one, and I have no bad memories of him, nothing that does not bring me joy to recall, with the lone exception that our time together was too short." She cleared her throat, and her expression became resolute. "Izem was thrown from a horse, and landed badly. I knew he was injured beyond my ability to treat, and that he would either mend or end without regard to what I did. I cared for him as well as I knew how. He lingered for two days, but never spoke again. He breathed his last while cradled in my arms."

"That's sad."

"It is. But all living things die, and to be held tenderly by the one who loves you the most dearly as you make the transition is the best that anyone could hope for."

"My friend Tania," he said. "The one who looks like you. She also lost her husband, but it was in a freak car accident."

"Car?"

"Like a wagon, I guess. But it goes by itself, and fast. It is something we have a lot of in our world."

She nodded.

"His car flipped. He broke his back, and also lived for two days afterwards. It was a little over a year ago when it happened."

Again, there was a curious lift of an eyebrow. "That is also when my husband died. Strange."

"So you really don't know why I keep seeing people who look like folks I know?"

She shook her head. "Perhaps that, too, is something you will need to figure out on your own. The reason may be something that only you would understand in any case."

He ate another date. "So, what now?"

She smiled. "Now, we clean up after our meal."

"I meant, what do I do now? What do I do about my situation? I appreciate your hospitality, sincerely I do, but I am still stuck in a world that isn't my own, and I don't know what to do next."

"I do not see what you could do. Perhaps the only real answer, for now, is to fall in with my routine, and wait to see what happens. Therefore, we should clean up after our meal. Then, afterwards, I will find you shoes to wear. Already the sand will be too hot to walk barefoot, as you are. As you may have noticed, however, my people do not wear shoes indoors. There is a pouch on the inside of the tent door to place them when you come inside."

"Okay."

"Then, if you are willing, you can help me with the four other water jugs. There are the dates I harvested yesterday morning still to set out to dry. I could not leave them out in the storm, and they still have another two days in the sun and open air before they will store without spoiling. Then we take a rest until late afternoon. If they were not delayed by the haboob, my cousins will be arriving by evening, and will bring meat and bread and cheese. My Uncle Anir will be with them, I hope. He is wise and may be able to answer more of your questions than I can."

"That'd be nice."

"I'm certain," she said. "To be left in ignorance and doubt is the most uncomfortable of states."

The morning and afternoon passed with the completion of chores and a long doze in the tent, as the dry breeze made the sides of the tent ripple and flutter. Duncan woke before Fatima did, and went over to the wooden chest where she had found clothes for him. He opened the lid. It swung upward without a squeak on finely-wrought brass hinges.

Inside, folded with reverent care, were more clothes, including an embroidered shirt and pants that could only be wedding finery. There was a fancy braided leather belt, coiled and tied with a cord. Two books with covers made of some sort of cream-colored skin lay in one corner, but both were in a curling, sinuous script that he didn't recognize.

At the very bottom was a short, straight sword with no scabbard, wrapped in a piece of oiled silk. It was obviously of outstanding workmanship. The grip was wrapped with thin strips of leather, the cross guard carved with a design like fish scales. A single orange jewel, perhaps a topaz, was set into the pommel. The blade's surface had a swirling marbled pattern, and shimmered like satin.

"I have not looked at that sword for a year," Fatima said quietly from behind him.

He startled, and looked around. "I'm sorry. I shouldn't be snooping. I was curious about your husband."

"It's not a problem." Her expression was watchful, interested, inscrutable.

He looked up at her. "Was your husband a soldier?"

She shook her head. "Only when it was necessary did he wear that sword. But it was given to him by his grandfather, who used it in earnest in the old days when there was war in these lands. The southern tribes once made raids on us here in the north. But we have had peace with them for many years now."

He wrapped the blade in its silk covering, and set it down in the chest with care.

"I do not think you will find answers in the past, Duncan." Her voice was gentle, but so much like that of his friend and coworker, Tania Reade, that a shudder went up his spine. "Neither my past nor yours. Any answers that matter will only be found in the future. I do not believe you will find the purpose for which you have come here at the bottom of a wooden chest."

"What if there isn't a purpose?" Even in his own ears, the words sounded bleak.

"There is always a purpose. Even if we never find out what it is, the universe is so laid out as to make a pattern. It may be a subtle one, or so grand that our sight cannot encompass it all. But that does not mean it does not exist."

"There's no difference between a pattern you can't see and a pattern that doesn't exist."

"No? Your world is really so small, that it all fits inside your little skull?" She gave him a playful smile.

He frowned. "All I know is what I've experienced. I don't know any other way to make sense of things." He gestured with one hand, quick, frustrated motions. "And none of this makes sense."

"You have survived a journey through two worlds, and are still alive and sane and healthy except for a scratch on your leg. I wonder how many have come so far?"

"Diana said that no one had ever escaped from Yesod."

"I think that was a lie. But I have no doubt that few have."

He looked down. "I wish I had never gotten up for a drink of water that night. I'd still be safely in my apartment."

"You don't know that."

"I suppose not," he said miserably.

"My father once told me that all questions are worth asking except for one—'What would have happened had I done things differently?' In all the universe, it is the one unknowable thing."

"I just want to go home." He was on the verge of tears, and lowered his head in shame, hoping she wouldn't look at him, wouldn't meet his eyes, knowing that if he did he would not be able to stop himself from weeping. "I don't understand any of this, and I want to go home."

She put one hand on his shoulder. "Speak with my Uncle Anir," she said, in a gentle voice. "He has traveled far, and read deeply. Perhaps he can put your heart and mind at ease."

Anir arrived shortly before sunset, as the air cooled and the shadow of the tent elongated like a spear pointed toward the eastern horizon. Anir was a tall, imposing figure of a man, dressed in a white robe a little like Duncan's, but his belt was twisted with a silver band that had an inlay of dark blue polished stones. He was darker than Fatima, with a neatly-clipped beard and mustache, and a long, saturnine face. He was accompanied by about a dozen men and women of varying ages, an equal number of children, and horses for riding and hauling full packs of goods.

Fatima gave Anir a kiss on each cheek, and he gave her a smile that was there and gone in an instant. Her greetings from her other family members, especially an older woman whom he guessed was Anir's wife, were more effusive.

After the courtesies were over, Anir looked over at him as if noticing him for the first time. He got the impression, however, that there was little that escaped his awareness. Anir's eyes were dark, and glittered with a subtle intelligence.

"So," Anir said, in a deep, resonant voice. "This is the visitor."

"Yes, Uncle," Fatima said. "He came last night and I gave him lodging and food, as you instructed me."

The words jolted him. *They knew I would come?* But then he remembered Fatima saying that they always knew when someone jumped into their world. Perhaps all she meant was that her uncle had given her instructions in that eventuality.

"That is good," Anir said, and then to Duncan, "What is your name?"

"Duncan Kyle."

"What is your native world?"

He frowned. He hadn't thought of his home and his apartment and his life as simply being part of another place, on equal footing to the three odd worlds he'd visited.

"We call it Earth," he said.

Anir nodded. "Earth. And from which world did you most recently come?"

"Yesod."

Anir's dark eyebrows rose, eyes opening wide in surprise. "And you arrived here alive?"

"His only injury was an arrow graze on his leg, which I have treated," Fatima said.

"That you survived at all is a testimony to your skill and courage," Anir said. Clearly, he had impressed the older man. "We see few arriving here who have taken that path. I do not doubt that there are others who find their way there, but who never leave Yesod. Those unfortunates, I suspect, are now nothing more than piles of moldering bones."

Duncan shuddered.

"For my part, I give you welcome, and I wish you a calm and pleasant stay here, until you find your way to whatever path opens before your feet. I am certain there are questions in your mind, and perhaps I can answer some of them, if the answers lie within my knowledge and understanding. And from you, I wish to hear more about the places you have visited, and about your own home. But first, there are goods to be unloaded, and our evening meal. Afterwards, Duncan Kyle, we will speak more of this."

Two young men helped Anir unload the baggage from the pack horses. They didn't speak to Duncan, but allowed him to assist while talking quietly amongst themselves, casting curious glances in his direction but averting their gaze when he met their eyes. Others unpacked bags and boxes, and Fatima was given cloth sacks with dried meat, loaves of coarse bread, and cheese, each round head with a waxy rind and tied across with string.

After unloading, all pitched in together to prepare a meal, simmering some of the dried meat with fruit and spices. Anir had also brought along clay jugs of what turned out to be strong dark ale, and by the time the meal was completed there was laughter and chatter from everyone assembled. Even Duncan had gained some measure of tacit acceptance. He was passed the beer jug for the third time by one of the quiet young men he'd helped with the baggage earlier, and it was accompanied by a flashing smile and a thwack on the back.

After the meal was completed, and the remains cleaned up, Anir leaned back, and gave Duncan a thoughtful look. The sun had set an hour previous, and the sky was indigo, with the pinprick silver of stars piercing the night one by one. A low moon, just past full, glowed a deep, rich orange in the eastern sky.

"Now, Duncan Kyle," Anir said. "We have come to the time for questions and discussion. My niece has told me a little of your journey thus far, but I would rather hear it from your own mouth. There is no tale that benefits by a longer chain of retellers."

Duncan, relaxed among this pleasant company, with a full belly and his tongue loosened by the ale, related a detailed retelling of his travels, beginning with the collapse of his living room floor. It felt as if it were years ago, and already almost as if it had happened to another man, somewhere else, someone he had only heard of, never met. He led them through the dead catacombs of Malkuth, told them of his conversation with the Sphinx and his near death at the hands of the Heat Vampires.

Then it was onward, to his fall out of the sky and into the lake, and his time in the woods and glades of Yesod. He didn't give too many intimate specifics about his time with Diana, but it was clear that his listeners could read through his words. He had mentioned that when he'd first fallen through the floor of his apartment, he'd been naked, and they knew that he had still been naked when he arrived in Hod in the midst of a sandstorm.

The upshot was obvious. The two young men who had helped with the unloading of the goods gave each other a grin and a nudge in the ribs, and one of them gave Duncan a light punch on the arm and laughed good-naturedly.

Anir's long, melancholy face looked less approving, but he didn't say any word of criticism. "You are fortunate to have avoided Yesod's snares. Not many are so lucky. Diana and her kin are not known for their merciful hearts."

"I found that out."

"It is curious that twice you have found a portal when you were on the verge of death. It is unusual, that."

"Is it?"

Anir didn't quite smile, but a corner of his mouth turned upwards just a hair. "Were it not, I think there would be a great deal more people going to and fro through the ten worlds. And there would be far fewer deaths from misadventure, if escaping it were so easy."

"It isn't anything I'm doing. At least, I don't think it is."

"Which makes it even more curious. The paths between the worlds are known mostly to adepts, and the ones who jump them are highly skilled magicians. Even so, much of what these men and women do seems to me accidental, haphazard. They go from one to the other without certain knowledge of how or where they are going, and usually perish in the attempt." He stroked his pointed beard thoughtfully. "You, on the other hand, have escaped certain death twice over, three times if you count falling into the violence of the haboob upon your arrival here. And truthfully, you appear to have no knowledge at all."

He bristled a little, but didn't say anything.

Anir was immediately aware of having breached the laws of courtesy. He bowed, and said, "Your pardon. I spoke thoughtlessly."

He shook his head. "No, it's all right. You're correct, after all. I'm blundering around. I don't have any idea what I'm doing."

"It is modestly said. But I have been demanding information from you, rather than letting you speak your mind. Perhaps there are questions you would like to consider."

"I have two. One is from simple curiosity—I've noticed that in each place I go, there is one person who looks like someone I know back home. In Malkuth, the Sphinx looked like my sister. In Yesod, Diana looked like a former girlfriend. Here, your niece Fatima looks like a friend of mine. I don't see what that could be about."

"Nor I," Anir said. "I shall consider it. But like you, I am hard pressed to see what that could mean."

"My other question, though, is how do I get home? This place is nice enough, although I have to say I don't know how you ever get used to sandstorms, and the heat. But you have all been wonderful, and Fatima honestly saved my life. So I'm not meaning this as a criticism, but I want to go home."

"Yes. I am certain that you do. But I do not know how to manage the portals. I have read what is written about the ten worlds. Far to the north, there is a sprawling city that I have visited twice in my life, and they have a library there, the largest one in the world, filled with the writings of our world's greatest scholars and philosophers. I have seen the books that tell of the Sephirot, the ten worlds that make up the universe. And they also tell of the paths between them. It is dangerous knowledge. I only read enough to convince me that to seek out more would be to seek out a level of risk beyond anything I would wish to face, for gain that would be elusive at best. But men do seek out that knowledge." Anir gave him a long, considering stare. "Some will kill for it."

"Diana offered to spare my life if I could tell her how to jump from one world to another."

"I am certain that you know she would have killed you even if you had told her."

"Yes. But I couldn't tell her in any case, because I didn't know."

"Hmm." Anir looked up at the star-strewn blackness over his head. "It is an excellent question. There is clearly something about you, Duncan Kyle, that allows the portals to appear, and you to pass through them with no more difficulty than a man walking through a door. It is odd that others have striven and died for that ability, which you can do with no effort at all."

"I don't feel like I'm controlling it."

"Something in you is doing so," Anir said firmly. "No one could do what you have done accidentally. It may be that you are not yourself certain how you accomplish these things, but still, there is something in you that has that knowledge. Perhaps it is like the knowledge we have in our bodies, how to walk, how to run, how to move our mouths when we speak, how to do every common task we undertake. We do it all without our minds giving the command, and if we think too hard while we are doing these things, we cannot do them. Only when we let our bodies command themselves, without interference, do we become fluid, graceful." Anir considered for a while. "Seek that fluid self, seek to understand it, and maybe you will be able to discern the path home, and get there as easily as I put one foot ahead of the other. I cannot tell you anything further than that, but perhaps it will be enough. My heart tells me that by the time your travels are done, you will know far more about these matters than I do, and my words will appear to you as those of a child."

"Perhaps." But the bleak thought arose in him that if no one knew more than Anir did, he might never see home again.

It was in the middle of the night when Duncan was awakened from a sound sleep by a noise of metal on metal. Then he heard confused shouts of alarm, harsh laughter, and a woman's scream. He sat up suddenly in the total darkness, his head spinning.

Nearby Fatima stirred, and she said, "What is happening?" in a sleepy voice.

He went to the door of the tent, which had only been tacked down by a few of the many buttons in the pleasant night, and put his head outside. There was a flurry of motion nearby, hard to discern even with the brightness of the moon, now high in the night sky.

Then he heard Anir's commanding voice rose in the darkness. "How dare you attack our place, southern swine?"

Another harsh laugh came in answer, and then a mocking voice called, "We dare what we wish, old man."

Fatima gasped. "It is the southern raiders. They have not been seen in this place in generations. Why have they returned?"

But he knew immediately. It was no coincidence that they came only a day after his arrival. And he suspected that Fatima, whose mind was agile, was in no real doubt, either.

"What is it you want?" Anir called back to the leader, scorn in his voice. "Our goods are but things of no great worth. We have no gold, nor jewels, nor anything thieves such as yourselves might desire. And you will pay dearly to take any of our people, if you are slavers, like your forefathers."

If the words were meant to sting, they had little effect. The leader laughed again. "We want no gold. And your women and children would be burdens to us. I believe you know what it is we come for."

"I would have you say it out loud, so that the heavens can hear you," Anir thundered.

From the shadowed figure, standing perfectly still downhill from the tent, near where the spring lay, the voice came back. "Give us your visitor, and we will leave."

The hairs on the back of Duncan's neck prickled. There was a murmur of outraged voices from Anir's family, who were camped on the other side of the rock outcropping.

"You would ask us to deliver him into your hands, to face torture and death?" Anir said, and his voice was filled with outrage. "You know my people better than that."

"Then keep him," the leader said. "We will kill any who stand in our way, and take him all the same."

"I have to go to them," Duncan said in a fierce whisper.

"Have you lost your senses?" Fatima whispered back. "They want what you know. When they find that you don't know how to create a portal, that you know as little as they do, they will slit your throat and leave your body for the jackals."

"I can't put you all at risk."

"You barely know us. You have known me for a day, my uncle and his family for only a few hours. You would risk your life for strangers?"

"No. I would risk my life to help people who, with no thought of gain, showed me nothing but kindness."

She was silent, but he heard her moving in the darkness behind him. A moment later, she put something cold and hard into his right hand. "Here. At least you will not face those animals unarmed."

It was her husband Izem's sword. He swallowed. It had only been a little over a day ago that he had defended himself against Diana's onslaught with a sacrificial knife, and been saved by what now appeared to be mere luck.

But his fingers curled around the grip of the sword, and he said, "Thank you. I will try to use it well."

He reached out with his left hand, and undid the remaining buttons of the tent flap. He climbed out. The sand was dry and warm under his bare feet. Moving as silently as he could, he launched himself downhill toward the figure of the man he had still only seen as a black silhouette.

The change of distance and angle made moonlight catch on his adversary's face, and what he saw almost stopped him in his tracks. It didn't look human. Powerful legs, waist kilted with a short leather skirt, a muscular bare torso, thickly knotted arms folded across the chest. But the head was a grinning jackal face, long ears erect, eyes glowing orange. It took only a breathless moment for him to realize that the man was wearing a mask, but in that moment, he felt that he was attacking a god, a monster, a specter of Anubis come to life from the walls of an Egyptian sarcophagus.

The man heard him coming, saw him running down the dune, and he parried Duncan's sword thrust with the casual motion of a man swatting away a fly. The sword was flung back and knocked from his grasp. It flipped through the night air, and was lost. The masked leader reached out and took hold of his arm, swung him around effortlessly, so that his back was pressed against the man's chest. Behind him, Fatima screamed, and there was the sound of running footsteps.

A knife blade was laid across his throat, cool and deadly.

"No farther," the leader said. "Stop. No one moves, or I cut this man's throat."

In the night, there was not a sound but Duncan's panting breaths, and the light hiss of the wind on the sand.

"What do you want with me?" he said, not daring to move.

"Do not play the fool with me," the leader said, his voice full of good humor. "I do not have the time, and sadly, I fear that you do not, either. I want to know how you came here. You have control of the pathways. We need that knowledge."

"Why?"

"Let us say that Hod has been slim pickings, of late. We are looking for richer grounds."

"I'll tell you," he said, "as soon as we leave the camp, and Anir and his family are left in peace."

The jackal-man laughed. "You do not appear to be in a position to negotiate. What power to compel me do you have?"

"That depends on how badly you want to know."

There was a moment's silence, and the jackal-man guffawed. "He plays his hand boldly! Very well, then, I will game with you, at least until I tire of it." He paused. "You bargain with your life, that is not enough for you?"

He cleared his throat, tried to move away from the dagger's edge, but the man's grip was like steel bands. "No. I want more."

"What more do you want?"

Duncan's mind reached blindly for ideas. He had to try to think like one of them. What would he do, if the situation was reversed?

"I will tell you how to jump, in exchange for these people's lives, and my own, and a cut of whatever you get from your first raid in another world."

"What if we come away with nothing?"

"Then you owe me nothing but my freedom."

"And what if my people are killed on this other world? What then?"

"That's the risk you take. If you're not willing to take a risk, then stay home."

Again, a roar of laughter, both from the leader, and from several of his men. Was he making headway? But the knife was still against his neck.

"Let us be clear, here," the jackal-man said. "You wish something in payment for your knowledge, which is reasonable. Like a bold ruffian, you ask for more than only your life. But I am no child who can be tricked into bargaining away what I have, and get nothing in return. Before we go further, you will tell me how to create the portals and navigate the paths. Or, better still, create a gateway, here, now."

Was it that the jackal-man didn't trust him—or did he know Duncan was lying, and was calling his bluff?

"I don't want to do that with these people watching," he said. "Do you want them all to have this knowledge as well?"

The leader snorted with scorn. "They are nothing. I know their kind. If they had the knowledge, they would be afraid to use it. Now,"— his arm tightened around Duncan's chest— "do it. Either tell me how to create the gate, or show that you can do so. I have enjoyed this conversation, but we have far to go tonight, in this world or in another."

He didn't respond, didn't move.

"Did you not hear me? You spoke readily enough before. Tell me how the gateways are created. I tire of this."

He said, in a thin voice, "What if I told you I don't know how?"

The jovial tone in the leader's voice was gone in an instant. "That would be unfortunate for you. And if we then had to take our frustrations out on your friends, you understand that we could hardly be expected to do otherwise, given the circumstances."

"He doesn't know," came Fatima's voice, from somewhere nearby.

"Oh?" the leader said, and the knife pressed a little harder against his throat, right over his carotid artery. "Then tell me, woman, how did he arrive here, if he did not know the way himself?"

"He came," Fatima said, "because I summoned him. I have studied the deep magic, and I called him here."

The man's grip relaxed, as doubt struck him. "You summoned..." the leader began, but in that instant, Duncan twisted around like a snake and drove his knee up into the man's crotch.

The breath went out of him in a great whoosh, and he doubled over, the knife in his hand forgotten for a moment. But it would only be a moment. Even hurt, this man was a killer, and would not lose his prey if he could.

Duncan was still too close to land a punch, but he grabbed the man's mask, and shoved as hard as he could. The leader took a step back, stumbled, and lost his footing. He went over backwards into the spring with a tremendous splash.

The jackal-man's followers roared with anger, and there was the sound of fighting. But Duncan leaped on top of the fallen leader, trying to hold his head under water, as the man struggled and sputtered. He was far more powerfully built than Duncan, and rage and pain gave him even greater strength. He turned, grabbed Duncan by the shoulders, and in seconds Duncan found the tables turned. He was forced under water, his back scraping on wet sandstone, his hands beating ineffectually at his captor's arms.

There was a tremendous impact, and the jackal-man's grip slackened. Duncan came up, coughing, taking in huge gulps of air. He saw, in the faint moonlight, the huge man's shape in front of him. Light glinted on the point of a razor-sharp sword blade protruding outward from between the man's ribs.

The jackal-man looked downward at the sword point piercing his chest, with a surprised, disbelieving expression. He looked up at Duncan. Beneath the snout of the mask his mouth opened, as if he were going to say something, but all that came out was a gush of black. Then he collapsed to the side, his blood fouling the clear water of the spring.

There was a whisper of noise. Duncan knew what it was immediately from his hunts with Diana. Arrows, more than one, followed by the thud of impact. Fatima lurched once, twice, three times. Then she fell into his arms, and they, too, collapsed into the shallows of the spring.

The sounds of fighting surged around him, but he barely heard it. He struggled forward until they were both on dry land, and cradled her familiar face in his hands. He put his mouth near her ear, and said, his voice pleading, "No. You can't die."

She said, "All things die, Duncan Kyle. I can die. It is the easiest thing in the world." She attempted a smile. "I wonder which world I will go to now, and by what path?" She grimaced. "Stay here. Stay and help my people."

And her eyes went blank, under the yellow moonlight, as the fighting raged around them.

He laid her on her side, but turned her head so her sightless eyes faced the stars. Then he leaned over, his face covered by his hands. He had thought that the despair he'd experienced in the catacombs of Malkuth, his terror in being the prey of an amoral huntress in Yesod, was powerful. But here, despair like he'd never known welled up through him, a terrible need to put right things that would not be put right until the worlds ended and were rebuilt anew. He let his head drop until his hair was almost touching the ground, put his hands palm downward against the still-warm sand, and crouched, motionless, next to her still body.

"I can't bear this," he said, in a half sob. "I can't. I can't."

Grains of sand slithered out from underneath his fingers, as if they were being blown by the wind. But there was no wind, nothing but screams and shouts and the clashing of weapons nearby. He pressed harder, willing himself to be covered up, swallowed in the earth.

And the earth responded. He was sliding, slipping downwards, falling headfirst into an ever-deepening hole in the desert. He heard a voice—it may have been Anir's—calling, "Duncan Kyle! You must help us! They are slaughtering us!" But sand poured inwards with him, and he tumbled in, the larger rocks scoring long scrapes on his arms and legs. Then the sand was gone, and there was nothing but empty air, but he still did not open his eyes as he fell, his body flailing and limp.

The impact, when it came, took his breath. He lay there for nearly a minute, gasping like a beached fish, unable to sit up, unable even to open his eyes and see what was around him. But when he did, he had the disorienting feeling that one has at waking from a dream, the momentary wondering, *Was that real? Where am I?*

He lay on his back in a patch of sunlit lawn, closely mown. A rose garden in full bloom, with a neat edging of red brick, was about three feet away. There were large trees swaying in a warm and gentle breeze, and farther away, a clipped hedge of what looked like holly.

He tried to move. He had sand all over his face, sand in his hair, sand inside his robe. He tried to sit up, and failed.

Then he heard a voice, full of concern and distress, calling, "Mr. Duncan! You poor boy! How did you get all the way out here? And in such a state, too. Your parents will be ever so furious at Doctor for letting you escape!"

CHAPTER 4

NETZACH

D uncan squinted up into the face of a rather ugly middle-aged woman wearing a neat, dark servant's dress and apron. A white bonnet held back her iron-gray curls. She clasped work-hardened hands together, and said, "Oh, dear. Dear me. We need to get you back inside. I do hope Doctor won't blame me, but it wasn't *my* fault, after all."

She reached out a hand, and he took it. She helped him to his feet, and then fussed over him, brushing the sand off his shoulders. "*Look* at you, Mr. Duncan! Whatever can you have been doing? It looks as if you rolled in the dirt. And in your nice white robe, too! I don't know if Mrs. Nevins will ever be able to get those stains out."

He looked down. Instead of the cream-colored cotton garment with blue stitching that Fatima had given him, he was now dressed in an old-fashioned white terry-cloth bathrobe. His leather belt with the silver buckle was gone, replaced by a simple tie made from the same material as the robe.

He looked back up at her, and cleared his throat, wincing a little at the dryness. "Who are you? Where is this?"

The woman's face crinkled up into a hundred sympathetic creases. "Oh, Mr. Duncan, you poor thing. We'd thought you'd taken a turn for the better this morning, but you're still feverish." Her voice took on a condescending tone, as if she were talking to a very small child. "I'm Mrs. Banks. I do your room every day, as I've done since you were that little. I've helped to care for you since you fell ill, three weeks ago."

"Ill?"

"Scarlet fever, dear." She applied gentle pressure to his upper arm. "Now, we must get you back indoors. I'd send you right to bed, which is where Doctor would want you, but you'll need a bath first. I'll call Mr. Garrett once you're comfortable. He'll see you to your bath."

"Mr. Garrett?" The world spun around him. The aromatic odor of roses surrounded him, powerful enough to overwhelm the senses. It didn't look real. The greens and pinks and reds of the garden were almost too bright to look at.

Her brows drew together in sympathy. "Your gentleman," she said, still in the same patronizing voice. "Don't you fret yourself, now, Mr. Duncan. Your mind will clear soon enough, now the fever's broke."

She conducted him uphill and around the corner of the holly hedge, and ahead was an enormous house built of stone and heavy timbers. A two-story glass-walled conservatory was nearest to them. In the windows were huge potted palm trees, orange trees, and lemon trees, with smaller flowering plants tumbling beside them like a colorful waterfall. They crossed a flagstone patio to the left of the conservatory, on which sat tables and chairs and a large parasol in a wrought-iron stand, then went up three steps and through a sliding glass door into the house.

He had never been in a manor house. His family was solid lower-middle class. Still, he recognized opulence and wealth when he saw it. If the outside of the house and Mrs. Banks's mention of servants weren't enough, one glance inside was sufficient to communicate to him that these people had money the likes of which most don't see in a lifetime. His bare feet made no noise on the cold, polished surface of marble flooring. A huge sunroom, with wicker chairs, a piano, and a long, glass-topped table in the center, opened to the left. Down a hallway the marble gave way to hardwood, burnished to a satin finish and the color of rich copper. Oil paintings of people in ornate, uncomfortable clothing, their expressions remote and grim, lined the walls. He almost stopped to look at one of them. The face had a familiar look, despite the odd setting and odd garments.

Mrs. Banks said, "Come, now, Mr. Duncan, we must get you to your bath," and gave a little nudge that kept him moving.

The hall ended in a wide foyer, three stories high, with windows all the way up to the ceiling. The sunlight was blinding, reflecting from immaculate white walls. She guided him to turn, and they ascended a curving staircase, the steps covered in a runner made from lush green brocade. More paintings lined the wall, figures dressed in red and blue and royal purple, colors so intensely saturated that Duncan had the incongruous thought, *I need sunglasses to look at these,* something that had never occurred to him even in the harsh sunlight of Hod.

Mrs. Banks helped him to the second floor landing, then down another hallway, much more dimly lit, and into the open door of a sumptuous bedroom. It had a thick wool carpet, dyed a pale green, polished cherry-wood furnishings including a writing desk, a dresser, two large cabinets, an overstuffed chair upholstered in the same green brocade that had covered the stairs, and a four-poster bed. Here were the first signs of disarray he'd come across in this world—the bedclothes were a twisted mess, half on the floor. One of the pillows lay in the middle of the bed, its pillowcase partly pulled off.

"Now don't you worry, Mr. Duncan," Mrs. Banks said. "I'll fix that right up for you. You just sit here"—she directed him to the overstuffed chair— "and don't you move. I'll go get Mr. Garrett to draw your bath and help you to it, and I'll see if Doctor can be found. I must let him know you were playing the truant on us but are none the worse for wear, as far as I can tell, and God be praised for that, for we'd never hear the end of it if you'd relapsed because of it."

He sat in the chair, and Mrs. Banks scuttled off to find the other servant and the doctor. He watched her go, a perplexed expression on his face.

Be on guard. This wasn't what it appears to be. It was another of the worlds that Anir had told him about... what had he called it, the Sephirot? And the people in these worlds all wanted the same thing—to be able to do what he did. They tried sex, they tried violence, and now they'd try something else. When this world turned on him—as he knew it would—his survival could depend on paying close attention to everything around him.

He stood, cautiously, still feeling the vertigo he'd had earlier. The room didn't spin too badly as he rose, holding onto the arm of the chair. A little sand crumbled from his robe onto the carpet.

Sand from the deserts of Hod. But where was he now? Mrs. Banks never did answer that question.

He did a slow circuit of the room. There were more paintings, but instead of portraits these were landscapes, vistas of rolling hills and mist-covered mountains and glistening azure lakes. One wall had an inset bookshelf lined with leather-bound volumes with names like *Divine Songs* and *The Gigantick History of the Two Famous Giants* and *Original Stories from Real Life* and *A Description of a Set of Prints from Scripture History*. He opened one of them. *Hymns for the Youth.* It turned out to be a child's sacred songbook set in an archaic-looking font. The children in the illustrations were uniformly cherubic, with rosy cheeks, blond curls, and small, pink, bow-like mouths. The girls were clad in green dresses with pinafores, their heads encircled with lace bonnets, the boys in what looked like sailor suits, topped with round straw hats.

There was a noise behind him, and Mrs. Banks came bustling back in. She gave him an indulgent laugh. "Oh, Mr. Duncan, you *did* love that book when you were a boy. Brings back memories, don't it, looking at the sweet pictures? I bet you still know every one of the songs by heart, just as you did when you were in school."

He didn't answer, but closed the book and returned it to the shelf. Mrs. Banks turned her attention to the bed, straightening the pillowcases, and then stripping the rest of the sheets, replacing them with a practiced hand with fresh ones retrieved from a cabinet nearby.

Another person entered the room. He turned to see a tall, balding man, dressed in somber attire, carrying a large brass kettle.

"My, that was fast, Mr. Garrett!" Mrs. Banks said. "Shall you go to your bath, Mr. Duncan? You'll feel ever so much better."

"The water was already on to boil, Mrs. Banks," Mr. Garrett said, in an uninflected voice. "I've let Doctor know what happened. He'll be here to see the young master once he's out of the bath." Mr. Garrett gave a little nod toward Duncan. "Sir?" He turned toward a door near the bed that was a little ajar.

He followed Mr. Garrett through, and found himself in a tile-floored bathroom containing a porcelain sink with brass fittings, a gilt-framed mirror, and a small, octagonal window. A large claw-footed tub stood to one side, and a toilet with a chain instead of a handle in the corner. Mr. Garrett went to the tub and gave a brass spigot, with only a single tap, a sharp twist. Water flowed in. He added the hot water from the kettle and after a moment tested it with his finger.

"It is still a shade cool," he said. "If you find it chilly, I shall fetch more hot water from the kitchen. I had Cook put another kettle on."

"No, I'm sure it's fine."

They stared at each other in silence for a moment.

Mr. Garrett cleared his throat, and said, "May I help you with your robe, sir?" in a voice that held traces of indulgence and embarrassment in equal measure.

"Oh. I guess so." He untied the belt, and pulled it back. Mr. Garrett slipped it from his shoulders, and he went to the tub, and stepped in.

The water was cooler than his usual preference for a bath, but not uncomfortable. He settled in with a sigh, the sand of Hod slipping from his chafed skin. The scrapes and scratches he'd received over the past day stung a little as the water covered them, but it was wonderful, as refreshing as the skinny-dip he'd had in the lake in Yesod.

"There is a towel for you, sir, on the little table, as usual," Mr. Garrett said. His tone was cautious, as if he wasn't sure how much to say. Again, Duncan had the sense that the man was speaking to a child. "I shall fetch a clean robe for you. Perhaps later you will feel like dressing? But until Doctor has seen you, it would not be advisable. I shall, however, prepare your shaving needs, if you wish."

He rubbed his scruffy jaw, now covered with several weeks' growth of beard. "Sure. That would be wonderful."

Mr. Garrett nodded, and took scissors, a straight razor, and a small bar of white soap out of a little cabinet, and laid them out neatly on the vanity. He also took out a green glass bottle stoppered with a cork.

"Your pardon, sir," he said. "I will take your old robe to be washed, and retrieve more hot water for you to shave with. If you need anything, I will return momentarily."

"No problem."

He was left alone in the bathroom, and after a cursory washing of his face, hair, and upper body, he lay back in the water to consider his situation.

He'd fallen into a nineteenth century English manor house. What the hell? And what should he do now? These people weren't going to talk straight to me, the way Fatima did, nor even lie to him outright and then jump me, like Diana. He could see that already. There was something else going on here. The trick would be finding out what it was.

Garrett returned as the bath was cooling to uncomfortable levels. Duncan gave himself one more quick wash to make sure that all the sand was gone. He looked down. Beige grains coated the enameled bottom of the tub. He stood, dripping but refreshed, and Garrett handed him the towel without being asked. He dried himself and wrapped the towel around his waist, then went to the sink to shave. It was already plugged and filled with hot water.

"Sir?" Garrett said. "If you would?" Garrett already held the razor and the bar of soap.

"What?"

"I will shave you, if you wish."

He gave the man an incredulous look. "No, that's okay. I'll do it myself."

One of Garrett's eyebrows rose a fraction of an inch, but he gave a little bow, and said, "As you wish, sir."

He had never shaved with a straight razor before, much less starting from weeks' worth of beard, and shortly into the endeavor he regretted not letting Garrett do it for him. He used the scissors to trim his facial hair. The result was a ragged, moth-eaten mess that made him smile involuntarily at his own reflection as he looked in the mirror. He got the bar of soap to lather, applied some to his face, and proceeded to scrape the razor down his cheek. He ended clean shaven, with only a couple of little nicks that bled scarlet for a moment. Garrett, hovering behind him, applied some of the liquid from the green glass bottle to a bit of cotton, and dabbed them on the nicks. It had a strong smell, and stung, but the bleeding stopped immediately.

He rubbed his jaw. "Much better."

Garrett bowed again, and after helping him into a clean robe he took the wet towel and cleaned up the sink.

Duncan padded barefoot back into the bedroom. Mrs. Banks had finished making the bed and was setting a silver platter on the table next to it. She lifted the cover from the platter, revealing china plates with what looked and smelled like scrambled eggs and thick rashers of bacon. A cup of what was unmistakably coffee sat next to it. The pungent combined aroma made his stomach rumble.

"I hope you can eat at least some of it, Mr. Duncan, sir," she said. "It's been ever so long since you've had solid food, I thought a little something to eat might do you a good turn. Doctor hasn't said you're ready for it, so if you'd like to wait until you've seen him..."

"No. I'm starving."

"Oh, that's delightful," she said with feeling. "Your parents will be beside themselves with joy, they will. Now, you sit back. Only eat what you can, sir, and take it slowly."

He sat down on the bed, leaning back on the pillow. Mrs. Banks retrieved a small wooden table, shaped like a picnic bench, from underneath the bed, and laid it across his lap. She placed the platter in front of him and handed him a cloth napkin, which he draped across his lap, then stood, her hands clasped in front of her, watching him.

He took a bite. The eggs were piping hot and delicious, the bacon rich and crisp. The coffee was strong and a bit on the sweet side.

"It's wonderful," he said, his mouth full. "You don't have to worry, I'll eat it all."

"Oh!" Mrs. Banks's voice rose to a squeak. "What a blessing, sir! The whole household has been *that* worried about you!"

Breakfast was finished post haste, and Mrs. Banks cleared away the empty platter with a cheerful efficiency borne of relief and long practice.

Mr. Garrett emerged from the bathroom shortly after-wards, said, "If you need anything, sir, I will return after Doctor has visited you," and he also exited into the dim hallway, shutting the door soundlessly behind him.

He was left alone, wrapped in a soft robe, propped up with pillows on the plush cushion of the bed, in the greatest comfort he'd experienced since falling through the floor of his apartment.

This looked like Earth. But it couldn't be. It was more like his world than any he'd been in, but there was still something wrong. He couldn't let the coziness and the good food and the servants waiting on him hand and foot lull him into a false sense of security. It was like the other places he'd been. They threw you off balance, made you think things are okay, then the other shoe dropped hard. No reason to expect different here, just because everything was luxury. Luxury after physical hardship, he realized, was just as enticing as sex. But here, that was all it was; an enticement. What would happen when he refused to play the game—that he'd have to see.

Ten minutes later he had fallen into a light doze, and the bedroom door opened to admit a little, grizzled man, dressed in a tight-fitting dark suit. He had bushy gray eyebrows, and a thick, unkempt mustache. He wore a cloth hat, a little like a British driving cap, and carried a large leather bag.

"So, Master Duncan, the fever's broken, I see," he said, placing the back of his hand on Duncan's forehead. "Your skin is cool. First time in three weeks. You nearly died, young man."

"I did?"

"You did. Scarlet fever. Worst case I've ever seen. Raving, you were. All manner of things. Terrified the servants, but they knew you weren't in your right senses."

"What did I say?"

The doctor gave him a speculative frown. "Now, then. No need to go into all of that, seeing as how it's over. You're still weak, I'll warrant, and in need of healing. Put your strength after that instead of wondering about what happened in your delirium. It's all over."

"No, I want to know, Doctor. What did I say?"

A pause, and another curious look. "Very well, if it'll settle your mind about it, it'll likely do no harm, as long as you don't dwell on it." He sat in a chair next to the bed and leaned back, considering. "Dreaming, you must have been. Nightmares, some of them. You were chilled, shivering as if you'd been in a blizzard, yet sweating rivers, and you said that the servants were stealing your heat when they touched you. Screamed at them, you did, said you'd tell them what they wanted to know if they'd only let you live."

"I said that?" A chill of a different sort settled into his belly.

"You did. More than once. At other times you were being hunted by a woman who was trying to kill you with arrows. We found you at the end of the hallway, it'd be about a week ago. You were raving about it, while looking up at a painting of your Aunt Clara. She was a great beauty, your Aunt Clara was, pity what became of her. You claimed that she was after you. We got you back to bed, and I have medicines that induce sleep. Those helped, for a little.

"But then just yesterday, you nearly tore your bed-clothes to shreds, saying you were fighting a man with a dog's head, and he was trying to drown you. Your fever was high, higher than any I've seen in my career. I thought we were going to lose you, then. But it broke during the night. Your man Garrett told me he was with you when it broke, and the sweats came back, and you relaxed into a deep, dreamless sleep.

"He thought at first you were dying, but I came in, and your heart was still beating strong and sound, and we realized that against all hopes and fears, you'd triumphed. But you gave Mrs. Banks a turn this morning, getting up and going out into the garden by yourself. Sunshine and fresh air can't have done you any harm, though, I'd say. If you're up to it this afternoon, you can go and sit on the patio and take a bit more, but ask for help and don't scare the life out of the servants by going alone and telling no one where you are."

The doctor then proceeded to examine him, touching the sides of his throat, pressing his abdomen, looking into his eyes and ears and mouth.

"The swelling in your throat has gone down," he said, after a time. "Is it still painful to swallow?"

"A little."

"That will go away, God willing, if the disease is truly gone. And I have not known scarlet fever to relapse once it's broken, so I think you're safe enough as long as you don't do anything foolish."

"That's good."

"I've no doubt that your memory will return, but it may take a while to come back to normal. Mrs. Banks said you didn't recognize her this morning. Do you know me?"

"No," he said. "Other than the fact that you're the doctor."

He chuckled, making his copious mustache flutter. "I'm Doctor Carruthers. I've known you since you were a babe in arms. But don't fret. Your mind will be back to itself sooner or later. You've been through enough to kill a weaker man, God be praised for your constitution. It's no great wonder that you're still shaken by it. Be patient, and you'll recall what you need to when you need to."

There was a noise from the hallway, and he and Doctor Carruthers both turned their heads. A pair of figures stood in the shadow of the doorway, unrecognizable in the dim light. Carruthers said, "Oh, Mr. and Mrs. Kyle, come in, I'm just finishing. Your son is going to be all right."

Through the door walked a tall man with a handsome, angular face and chestnut-brown hair streaked with gray, dressed in an elegant but antiquated suit that looked as if it were made from heavy silk. He gave Duncan a stern and unsmiling, but approving, look. The woman next to him was clad in a floor-length green satin dress with a lace bodice, flowing sleeves, and a tatted hair net studded with what looked like small emeralds covering a knot of nearly black tresses.

"Oh, Duncan," the woman said, clasping her hands to her breast. "We thought we were going to lose you!"

And Duncan said, in a thin voice, "Mom and Dad?"

"Excellent," Doctor Carruthers said, quietly. "At least you know your own parents. That is a positive sign."

"But..." he started, and then closed his mouth.

Careful. Don't reveal too much. You don't know who is on whose side yet.

The two people standing in front of him *were* his parents. Their faces were exactly like them, down to the last detail. The clothing and hairstyles were different, old-fashioned, but even so, there was no doubt.

"You're Dennis... and Thalia... Kyle." His voice was tentative, as if he were straining to remember. It was easy enough to feign, even if the strain came from a different source.

Relief flooded Mrs. Kyle's face. "They said you didn't know anyone. Mrs. Banks... she was dreadfully upset, even though we told her that high fever can do that, and that your memory would surely come back."

"No doubt of that at all, I'd say," Doctor Carruthers said. "It may take days or weeks, however."

"We've no problem exerting our patience now," Mr. Kyle said. "Now that he's out of danger. We thought we were losing you, Duncan. We had the whole household praying."

"I couldn't bear the thought," Mrs. Kyle said. "After losing Maria, you're all we have left." A pair of tears coursed down her cheeks. "But you'll be fine, God be praised. Take your ease, and let Mrs. Banks and Mr.

Garrett care for you, as they have for years. Don't exert yourself, and listen to what Doctor Carruthers tells you. He'll know how best to see you through convalescence. You're so impatient sometimes, let yourself relax..."

Mr. Kyle put one hand on his wife's arm. "Thalia, don't worry the boy with your prattle, now. He'll be well again, and you shouldn't fret him. He's still weak."

Mrs. Kyle gave a quick nod and a sniffle, and said, "When you feel ready to dress for dinner, let Mrs. Banks know, and we'll have Cook prepare you something really special."

"But not until he's strong enough," Doctor Carruthers warned.

"Of course," Mrs. Kyle added.

So Maria was dead in this world, too. And his parents... they were acting like his parents, despite the weird clothing. Could it be...

He pulled himself up short. No. This had to be a lie. Everything so far that had seemed real at first had turned out not to be. They were using his knowledge and his past against him somehow. Now was not the time to drop his guard.

"Rest," Mr. Kyle said. "Come, Thalia, let us leave him in peace." He looked at the doctor. "Are you done, Carruthers?"

"Yes." The doctor picked up his bag. "Nothing more for me to do here. Nature and time and fresh air and the Good Lord will take care of him now."

They left the room, closing the door quietly behind them, and their voices receded down the hallway.

He got up, and pressed his ear to the door. All he heard, before the three moved out of earshot, was the doctor saying, "Keeping him quiet for now is the most important thing."

The day passed in calm, and Duncan saw no one until Mrs. Banks brought him lunch. She set the tray on the table next to his bed, then encouraged him to nap.

"I think I'd rather go outside," he said. "I feel fine, honestly."

Mrs. Banks gave him a dubious look. "You shouldn't stress yourself, Mr. Duncan," she said. "You don't want to relapse. It's what Doctor Carruthers was worried about."

"Doctor Carruthers told me that scarlet fever almost never relapses," he said firmly. "And sunshine and fresh air would make me feel better. I know it would."

"Well, all right, then," she said, still not sounding as if she were very sure of it. "I'll see you down into the garden. It'll be sunny still, I'd think, although your father said there's likely to be rain by nightfall."

He allowed himself to be conducted down onto the patio and seated in one of the chairs near the parasol. Mrs. Banks brought along with her a folded blanket, and insisted on tucking it around his legs even though the sun was shining and it was comfortably warm, with a light breeze.

"Now, if you need anything, Mr. Duncan," she said, "I or Mr. Garrett will be out to check on you every so often. Don't you be wandering off, now, but sit there and take some sun and fresh air. You'll not hasten your convalescence by doing too much too soon."

His sore throat and vertigo were both completely gone by now. Even so, he didn't argue.

Whatever game these people were playing, for now he had to let them play it. And he'd go along with it, at least for the time being. What he needed most at this point was information.

But as he watched Mrs. Banks's back receding, as she trotted up the stairs and into the house, he gave his situation some thought.

What if they were telling the truth? What if he did imagine it all, the Heat Vampires, and Diana, and the jackal-man in Hod? What if it actually was all the product of delirium in a high fever?

But that would mean that everything before it was also part of his imaginings. Libby, his apartment, his job, and living in Colville, New York. How could that be?

He looked around him, at the holly hedge and the lawn furniture and the conservatory, and farther off, the rose gardens from which the powerful floral scent still wafted on the breeze.

Maybe this was his real life, and everything that he remembered came from the illness and fever. How could he tell the difference?

Something in him rebelled at even asking this question. His initial impression was right. There was something wrong here. Anir, in the deserts of Hod, had told him that in other worlds the inhabitants wouldn't try to kill him, they would try to make him think he'd gone mad.

He couldn't let them get to him. What he remembered of his life, and the worlds he'd been in, couldn't be delusion. If there was a delusion, it was here.

Wherever here was.

Garrett and Mrs. Banks each came out once to check on Duncan, and both times he said, in as cheerful a fashion as he could manage, that he felt fine and needed nothing. Eventually, they left him alone on the patio, and he didn't see anyone else from the household for a little over an hour. Bored, he got up, folded the blanket neatly and left it on one of the wrought-iron tables, then went back into the house.

The marble floor of the entryway was chilly underneath his bare feet, so he turned left and went into the sunroom. It was wide, with huge windows and skylights. There was a tall potted palm in the corner, standing behind the grand piano, whose polished wood surface shone like a mirror. He looked at the brass plate in the center of the key cover. It said, "John Broadwood & Sons, London, 1877."

Well, that narrowed down what time period they were trying to mimic. He narrowed his eyes. Not that he believed any of it was real. But he had to admire their attention to detail.

He wandered out of the sunroom and down the hallway. He looked up at the portrait that Mrs. Banks had hurried him past that morning. It was his mother. He knew that now, and some part of him had realized it then, even if his conscious mind couldn't quite grasp it. She was clad in a dress made of heavy, emerald-green satin, and wore a white hat trimmed with folds of lace. A fan was in one hand. She had a distant expression, unsmiling, like someone deeply preoccupied with something many miles away from her surroundings.

Whoever these people were, they were not his parents, any more than the Sphinx had been Maria, or Diana had been Antonia, or Fatima had been Tania Reade. It was all part of the illusion.

But they had even gotten their personalities right, he thought, as he considered his interaction with them earlier. Thalia Kyle was a perennial worrier, always anxious about what Duncan did, and when he was younger she fretted every time he had the sniffles. It had worsened after Maria died, and when he'd gone away for college, he had lied more than once about his health. When his mother called, he had made a practice of always saying that he was "doing fine."

Dennis Kyle, on the other hand, was a stern, distant man, not exactly unfriendly but not someone to whom he had any sort of bond other than the automatic one that comes from the parent-child relationship. Dennis worked hard as an electrician, and had been running his own business since before he and his sister were born. He provided for the family, was steady and reliable, but otherwise inaccessible. Even at Maria's funeral, Dennis Kyle had not shed a tear for his daughter, but had remained stone-faced throughout, as the rest of the family wept and hugged each other. He presumably felt something, but no one, possibly including his wife, knew what that might be.

Duncan continued down the hallway toward the front of the house. But instead of circling to the base of the staircase to the second floor, he went around the rear side of it, toward the glass-fronted door into the conservatory. It looked like an interesting space, and he hadn't seen what, if anything, was beyond it. But as he turned, he saw a shut door on the wall that angled along the underside of the stairway. Without knowing why, he reached out and turned the knob. It opened silently, revealing stairs that led downward, presumably into a basement. There were no windows, as far as he could see. The room, whatever it was, lay underground. There was a glow from the flicker of gaslights, the first of them halfway down the staircase. The wall alongside the stairs was bare and unadorned, and looked dingy.

Curious, he took one step downward, but that was as far as he got.

"Mr. Duncan!" said an alarmed voice.

He startled, and turned, and there was Mrs. Banks, staring at him with eyes wide with alarm. "Whatever can you be doing, going down there?"

Wow, she came out of nowhere.

Feeling a little like a child caught with his hand in the candy bowl, he said, "I saw the door, and I wanted to explore a little."

She took his arm and pulled with surprising strength. He stepped back up through the door. "There's nothing down there that concerns you," she said, reaching around him and shutting the door firmly. "Just the washing and cooking and cleaning, and you leave *that* to the servants. Stay up here in the fresh air and light where you belong. Doctor would *not* want you down there."

"Why not?"

She gave a fluttery motion with one hand. "Close air and damp, and, it's just not a place that you should be going, of course." She laughed, a tight, nervous titter. "It's much nicer upstairs, you know. Ever so much nicer."

"I was only curious."

"Much better things to be curious about than nasty below-stairs," she said firmly. She gave him an ingratiating smile. "If you're feeling that well, Mr. Duncan, maybe you'll be ready to dress for dinner this evening? I know it would do your dear mother good, but only if you're up to it. Perhaps for now, you should take a nap, and harvest your strength so that you're well enough."

He allowed himself to be propelled by the elbow back down the hall, past the portraits, and up the stairs.

How much exertion could eating dinner be? He suppressed a laugh. But he knew one thing—there was some reason she didn't want him down in the basement other than the close air and damp. He'd find out what it was sooner or later. If he could elude Diana the Huntress, he could get the better of Mrs. Banks.

As he was going up the stairs, passing the row of portraits on the wall, he deliberately slowed his steps so he could examine them more closely. He tried to twist his face into a passable impression of fatigue, and dragged his feet a little. Mrs. Banks didn't push him, but her brow wrinkled with worry. He looked at one portrait of a handsome man of about thirty with his hand on the shoulder of a seated woman with a quirky smile. The woman, he saw, was clearly Tania Reade.

Or should he call her Fatima? Who was she here?

"Who are these people?" he asked.

"Them?" Mrs. Banks said, stopping in the middle of the staircase and gesturing at the painting. "They're your cousins, Leona MacGregor and her husband, Harris. Harris died, was it a year ago? Maybe more. He was in a horse-drawn carriage, and for some reason the horse startled and the wagon overturned. He lingered two days, poor man."

"And her? Is his wife still alive?"

Mrs. Banks shifted her weight from one foot to the other. "No. Sad to say, she died only last week. Robbed and murdered right on the streets of London one evening. Nowhere is safe, and London is worse than most."

She gave him a little tug to keep him moving. They passed several portraits of people he didn't recognize, then at the top of the staircase there was another familiar face. A man in riding clothes, standing next to a handsome chestnut stallion, smiling as he looked off into the distance.

He pointed. "Is that Uncle Liam?"

Mrs. Banks's face brightened. "Why, yes, Mr. Duncan! You recognize him, then?"

"Yes." The man was definitely his father's younger brother, recognizable despite the odd setting and garments. "He's still alive, isn't he?"

"Oh, yes! He's alive and well, and lives not so very far away. A great man for the horses, is your Uncle Liam. Horses and dogs, and your uncle is a happy man."

Odd how some people had their right names, and others didn't. There had to be a pattern here, but for now, he wasn't seeing it.

As they turned down the hall toward his bedroom, he looked up, and in the dim light he saw a portrait of Diana—or Antonia—high on the wall. She had an intense gleam in her eye, her head tipped a little to one side. She wore a low-cut dress of deep, pine-green satin that had been painted so that it looked luminous. A silver circlet held back her dark curls.

Remembering what Doctor Carruthers had said about his dreams, he made a quick guess. "Aunt Clara?" he hazarded, looking over at Mrs. Banks.

"Why, yes! Your memory is returning, as Doctor said it would. But you do have a way with picking out portraits with sad stories. Your Aunt Clara was a wild one, she was. May still be, God willing, but the family would be none the wiser either way."

"The doctor said that I was looking at her portrait during one of my nightmares."

"Yes. Terrifying dreams, you must have been having, poor thing. But understandable, considering what happened to her."

"What did?"

"You don't remember that part, then?" Mrs. Banks said. "It was about fifteen years ago. You were only a boy. Your Aunt Clara took it in mind to marry a young man below her station. Her father would have none of it, and told her as much, thinking that would be enough. And it would have been, for most young women. But she ran away from home, and the young man too. He was an apprentice to the accountant down in the village. They were living wild, out in the forest south of here, for some time, carrying on in ever such an inappropriate fashion, I heard." A blush spread over her plain face. "Eventually he was caught and brought home and returned to his apprenticeship, because his contract with Mr. Cavanaugh at the accountancy still had two years' service left. But your aunt was never found. Hasn't been seen since."

"Strange," he said, but the response was more to his thoughts than to what Mrs. Banks had said.

There were pieces of reality here, pieces of truth. Mixed in with falsehood. Some names changed, some the same. What was the pattern?

"It *was* strange," Mrs. Banks said, pursing her lips in a disapproving fashion. "To think that a young lady, raised right as she was, would turn wild like that. It boggles the mind, it does."

He turned away from the portrait, and continued down the hall toward his bedroom, running into no further familiar faces. Mrs. Banks's face relaxed a little when it appeared that he wasn't asking any more questions, and showed every evidence of docility.

"Now, you take a nice nap, Mr. Duncan," she said. "The bed's all made up and tidy for you, and there's nothing for you to fret about. You take a nice sleep, and Mr. Garrett will come up when it's time for dinner to see if you're feeling up to dressing and coming down."

He lay down on the bed, and cupped his hands behind his head. "I'm sure I will, Mrs. Banks."

Wouldn't miss it for the world, in fact.

Garrett came up to Duncan's bedroom when the reddish rays of sunset were slanting across the lawn. Without being asked, he lit the gaslight near the door, and Duncan, who had been in a light doze, blinked at the greenish-white flame in a groggy fashion.

Garrett said, "Are you feeling well enough to dress for dinner, sir?"

"Sure." He sat up, and Garrett immediately went to a tall cabinet on the other side of the room. He selected a shirt, jacket, and trousers, and pulled underwear and socks from a drawer underneath. A pair of dark leather shoes was retrieved from a different cabinet.

"May I assist you, sir?"

He had anticipated this, but it was still awkward at best. He hadn't been helped into and out of clothes since he was a toddler, and the idea of one grown man helping another completely healthy and able grown man to dress struck him as bizarre.

Best to go along with it. If he was going to be up to shenanigans later, the less suspicions he roused now, the better.

He was glad for the help, however, when it came to tying the tie, which was not the simple four-in-hand knotted straight tie he wore to work. What did they call this thing? An ascot? He wasn't sure. But Garrett silently tied, straightened, and pinned the thing into place. He caught a glance of himself in the mirror inside the open cabinet door. He smiled. He looked like an actor in a play by Charles Dickens. Probably the character of the spoiled young rich guy who took advantage of widows and orphans, and then got his just deserts in the end.

Garrett looked him over with a frown, dusted an invisible speck from his jacket lapel, and then gave a little nod. He turned and escorted Duncan back down the hall of portraits and the curved staircase, but at the bottom he turned right, and conducted him into a part of the house he hadn't yet seen.

Garrett opened a door with a cut crystal doorknob, and held it for him. He walked into an opulent dining room, with a gaslit chandelier, marble floors, and a table set with bone china plates and sterling silver tableware. Red wine already sparkled in glasses. Through a long window at the back, he could see the tops of the trees in the conservatory in the fading light.

Mr. and Mrs. Kyle were already seated, but when he entered, his father stood and gave a little bow at the waist.

"Mr. Garrett informed us that you would be joining us. I am pleased that you have recovered so much in a single day."

"I feel fine, thank you," he said, and added, after a pause, "Father."

His mother looked over at him. "You shouldn't over-do." She picked up her cloth napkin and twisted it in her hands. "You'll bring on your fever again if you eat too much. But your father thought some ordinary dinner would be nice. And a little wine might be calming."

"I'll only eat what I feel like I can."

A door at the back of the room opened, and a pair of servants he hadn't yet seen brought in a platter of perfectly sliced roast beef, garnished with parsley and pearl onions, and two porcelain dishes, one contain-ing cooked carrots with butter and dill, and the other asparagus spears. The smell was mouthwatering. The servant with the beef platter set it in front of Mr. Kyle, and gave him a cautious, questioning look. Mr. Kyle gave the servant a quick nod without meeting his eyes. The servants then deftly arranged beef, carrots, and aspara-gus on each of the plates, covered the serving dishes, placed them on a sideboard along the wall, and then retreated silently whence they had come.

He kept his eyes on his parents, wondering if they'd say grace, or if there was some sort of protocol to be followed. Certainly there hadn't been in his household while he was growing up. Everyone just dug in. He waited until his father had taken his first bite to cut a piece for himself, and the meal proceeded in silence.

The beef was a little on the tough side but flavorful, the vegetables done perfectly. It was the most homelike meal he'd had since his precipitous arrival in the catacombs of Malkuth. But the quiet was unnerving. His mother looked fretful. Between bites she looked from her husband to her son, and her hand kept pulling her napkin through her fingers.

It was obvious she was expecting something to happen, or someone to say something. But what?

And nothing happened. The tension in the room waxed. Mr. Kyle ate his dinner, drank his wine, and ignored it all, which, Duncan reflected, was exactly how his father had acted when there'd been difficult times at home. Mrs. Kyle, on the other hand, finally stopped even pretending to eat. Duncan, remembering how unpredictable the other worlds were, forced himself to eat everything on his plate, and considered asking if he could have seconds, or even getting up and serving himself some without asking, before deciding against it. Were seconds frowned upon in this place?

"Mother," he said in a quiet voice, trying not to startle, but Mrs. Kyle jumped as if stung anyway.

"Yes, dear?" she said, her voice quavering a little. She cleared her throat, and said, in a steadier fashion, "What is it?"

"What is this place called?" He popped a carrot in his mouth, and said, "I've been trying to remember, but I can't bring the name to mind."

Mr. Kyle looked over the table at his wife, and one eyebrow went up slightly. But he said nothing.

"It's..." she started, and then stopped, swallowed. "It's your *home*, Duncan."

"I know that. But the whole place, you know, everything here. What is it called?"

She tried to smile, failed, and then said, "Well, I don't know if it *has* a name. Perhaps you should ask Doctor Carruthers tomorrow."

"Why would Doctor Carruthers know?" he said. "How about you, Father? Can you tell me what the name of this place is?"

"You look flushed, son," Mr. Kyle said. "The fever might be back. Evening is always the time that's the worst for a relapse."

"I feel fine." He leaned back in his chair. "But I do want to know why you won't answer my question."

The three of them sat there for nearly a minute, silent, Mr. Kyle scowling, Mrs. Kyle fearful, Duncan defiant. How long they would have stayed that way, locked in a frozen triangle, he didn't know, but the door at the back of the dining room opened, and the two servants who had served the table came in and commenced clearing the plates, and it broke the icy silence.

Mr. Kyle stood, tossed his napkin on the table, and said to the servants, "Let Jenkins know that I'll take my brandy in the library," and walked out of the room.

Duncan looked over at Mrs. Kyle, who also rose, and said, "Well, I think you've upset your father very much," in as stern a tone as she could manage.

He said, "Why? What was so upsetting about that question?"

But she didn't answer, only gave him a tight-lipped glare. She exited the room the same way as her husband, and he heard her heels clicking as she ascended the staircase.

He looked over at the servants, who were taking the dishes toward the door. He met the eyes of one of them—a young man, perhaps only five years his senior, with dark hair and jaded, deep brown eyes.

"Guess I better learn to keep my mouth shut, right?"

The young man gave him a slight shrug, and said nothing.

"You bringing all of that downstairs?" he asked. "Would you like some help?"

The man's expression changed to an alarmed frown. "No, sir," he said, in a hoarse voice that didn't sound as if it got used often. "That won't be necessary. Me and Akers here can manage it right enough."

"What's down there, anyway? Down below-stairs?"

But he had gotten as much out of the man as he was going to. The two servants gave him a suspicious glare, and then carrying their load of plates and dishes, they maneuvered their way through the door and disappeared.

Not knowing what else to do, he sat at the table a while longer. The servants had taken away the platters, so seconds were out of the question, but he poured himself another glass of wine from a decanter that had been left behind, and drank it as the evening deepened around him. Then he stood, wiped his mouth with his napkin, and made his way back upstairs to his bedroom. The gaslights along the hallway were low, casting long shadows on the carpeted floor. He opened the door quietly, stepped inside, and closed it again. Moonlight illuminated the lawn in stark grays and whites, but as he looked out, he saw scudding clouds building to the west, heralding the rain that Mrs. Banks had mentioned earlier. For now, though, the sky overhead was still clear, and studded with stars.

Duncan peered up at the sky. This window faced north. He should be able to see the Big Dipper. He remembered that much from his Earth Science class when he was in high school; you could see the Big Dipper in the northern sky all year long. But he didn't recognize any of the constellations he saw. So he wasn't on Earth, however much these people wanted him to think he was.

There was a quiet knock on the door. He jumped a little, swallowed, and said, "Yes?"

"It's Garrett, sir, with a little something to help you sleep."

"Come in."

The door opened, and Garrett entered, dapper as always, carrying a brass tray on which sat a small glass with a clear red liquid.

"A bit of valerian, sir," he said, setting the tray down on the night stand. "Doctor suggested it, saying it would help you to sleep soundly."

"Thanks, but I'm not ready to go to bed yet. I've done hardly anything all day long."

"Doctor told me that I should make sure you drank it before I left."

"Then you'll have to stick around for an hour or two, because I'm not going to drink it until I'm ready to go to sleep."

Garrett's eyes narrowed slightly, and he seemed to be trying to think of a reason to argue. Finally he said, "Very good, sir. Shall I help you change into your night clothes before I leave?"

He thought of saying, *I haven't worn pajamas since I was thirteen years old. I can get naked without your help, dude*, and had to stifle a bray of laughter.

"No," he said. "I'm fine."

"Very good, sir," Garrett said again, and turned to leave.

"Say, Garrett?" he said, and the man half turned back toward him.

"Yes, sir?"

"Why would my parents have gotten so angry that I asked them what the name of this place was? And refused to answer?"

"I couldn't say, sir."

"Couldn't? Or won't?"

He cleared his throat. "I should say, sir, that if they would not answer the question, it is not my place to."

He took a step toward the servant. "So this isn't actually England, then."

"Good night, sir," Garrett said, the ghost of a smile playing around his lips. "Be sure to drink the valerian. Doctor Carruthers and your father agree that sleeping the night through would be the healthiest thing for you."

He stepped outside, and closed the door.

Well, that was ominous. He glanced at the glass full of scarlet liquid. Healthiest? That sounded like a threat. But either way, he'd be damned if he drank the valerian, or whatever that actually was.

He took it to the sink and poured the contents down the drain, then returned the empty glass to the tray.

He knew he couldn't do anything for a while. They'd be sure to be watching. So he may as well chill and give them a chance to tire of guarding the door.

He amused himself for a time reading *Original Stories from Real Life*, which turned out to be moralistic and preachy enough to be mildly funny. All of the stories were about children who disobeyed their parents and either fell afoul of the law and came to bad ends, or else repented of their willfulness and begged for forgiveness. Some of these came to bad ends, too. The illustrations were archaic, with stern, righteous-looking parents, angelic good children, and scowling, villainous bad ones. Worst of all were the evil men and women who tempted the bad children into sin. Their simian visages hardly looked human.

After reading for perhaps an hour, he stripped off the uncomfortable clothes he'd dined in—he'd taken off the jacket and tie soon after coming back to his bedroom—and tossed them over a chair. He looked down at the healing arrow graze on his upper thigh.

How the doctor would explain that? Most likely that he'd cut myself while he was thrashing around, delirious with fever.

He donned the robe he'd worn earlier, which Garrett had left, neatly folded, on the foot of the bed. He was debating whether enough time had elapsed to make a safe exit from the room when he heard the creak of a footstep near the door.

He ran lightly to the bed and lay down just as the door opened a crack, then a little wider. Duncan tried to relax his face into a passable imitation of deep sleep. The footsteps came into the room, walking quietly, heel-to-toe, first to look at the tray, then up to Duncan's bedside. He forced his lungs into deep, regular breaths. There was a clink as the tray was picked up, and the footsteps receded toward the door. A faint grating noise sounded as a hand turned down the gaslight to a flicker.

He opened his eyes a slit, to see the tall, stooped silhouette of Garrett in the light from the doorway. Then the door closed.

Duncan had to give him time to get to the servants' quarters, or wherever he slept. Then it was time to be off to explore this place.

He counted to a hundred, slowly, did it again, and then judged that he had as good a chance then as ever to get out of the room unnoticed. He stood up, tightened the belt of his robe, and padded barefoot to the door.

He opened it enough to stick his head out. He saw no one but the faces of the line of portraits, looking down at him with stern, humorless expressions. He walked down the hall, wincing at each creaking floorboard, and then down the long staircase to the first floor.

Beams of moonlight interrupted by streamers of cloud came in through the huge window in the front foyer. The dining room was empty, as was the sunroom at the back of the house. He turned toward the conservatory, and the door to the basement. He looked around, half expecting either Garrett or Mrs. Banks to grab him by the shoulder, but he was alone.

He turned the handle, pulled the door open, and de-scended the stairs.

Mrs. Banks had been right about one thing. The air was dank, musty, smelling of dishwater and mildew overlain with the odors of cooked food and garbage. He reached the bottom of the staircase, and his foot stepped onto the coolness of rough flagstones.

He looked both ways. One side opened onto a narrow room with metal tubs, washboards, and scrub brushes, the other into a broad kitchen. A huge old cast-iron pot-bellied stove stood in one corner, the chimney passing upwards through the wall. Pots and pans were laid out haphazardly along a wooden table, along with knives, spoons, and ladles. Hanging from the wall were tied bunches of onions, garlic, and herbs, and baskets of potatoes, carrots, turnips, and squash sat on the floor.

Why *had* he wanted to come down here? Mrs. Banks had told the truth. It was the kitchen and laundry. No secrets down here, and no way out of this place.

That was when a hand clamped down on his shoulder. He gasped and whirled around, almost losing his balance on the damp stone floor. It wasn't Garrett or Mrs. Banks, though. The hand belonged to a slatternly woman, with long, dirty, unkempt hair and a smudge of soot on one cheek. She wore a shapeless gray dress. The woman grinned, a smile that was missing both front teeth, and her small, cunning eyes glittered up at him.

"You're the Other-Worlder, then?" she said, in a creaking voice. "The one Nevins told me came here this morning."

He gaped at her, and then nodded.

"Thought so. You haven't the look of one of them."

"One of them?"

"People from this world. They all have that weaselly look." She put her face close to his. "What did they tell you?"

He recoiled from her, but she kept her grip on his shoulder. "That I have been here all my life, and that I don't remember any of it because I was sick with scarlet fever."

She laughed, and the laugh ended with a cough. "That's a good one, that is. Creative, you know? Oh, lord, yes."

"Who are you?"

"I'm Jennet. I'm the scullery maid." She gave a mocking little curtsey. "And who might you be, sir?"

"Duncan Kyle."

"Ah," she said. "That explains why them upstairs is 'Mr. and Mrs. Kyle' this go-round."

A shudder vibrated its way up his spine. "What is the name of this place? They wouldn't tell me."

"It's called Netzach. They're superstitious about it. You find the name of something, you own it, and they don't want to give you that power. Breaks the spell."

"So why are you telling me the truth?"

She didn't answer for a moment, but her grip tightened on his shoulder. She finally said, "I got no reason to lie."

"Why not? Aren't you one of them?"

"Me? No." She coughed again. "Stumbled into here when I was a girl, and they've kept me since. I come from some other world. Not Netzach."

"Where?"

She frowned, and looked down. "I'm not sure, just now. Maybe your world, I don't know. I was only a little thing when it happened." Her glance darted back up to his face. "But that's what they do, you know. They drive you mad, then keep you. Keep you forever." She shook her head, and her fingers dug painfully into his shoulder muscle. Her creaking voice dropped to a whisper. "You stay here long enough, and you'll start believing their lies. And when you do, that'll be that. You'll never leave. Just like me."

"Why? Why do they want to keep me? Why did they keep you?"

Jennet shrugged. "It gives them, what's the word... It makes them solid. Without us, they're ghosts."

"Substance," he said, his voice quiet. "That's the word you want."

"Yeah. Substance. That's the word, right enough. We give them substance. They'll use you up, though, like they did me. Unless..." She stopped and frowned, mouth hanging open slightly. "You know how to get out of here? How'd you get here, I wonder?"

"From Hod."

Careful. He couldn't trust her just because she was talking against the others. It could be a trap. She could be as dangerous as they were.

"Hod," she repeated. "Don't know where that is. But they will. Did you come here deliberately?"

"Why would I do that?"

She gave another cackling laugh. "That's a good question. But you know how to make the doors, do you? They'd keep you here to find that out."

"I don't know," he said, but Jennet caught the evasiveness in his voice.

"Fine. Keep your own counsel, then. But if you do know how, don't let on to them upstairs. They'll never let up if they find that out. As long as they think you found your way here by accident, they'll eventually forget about you, once you get swallowed up by the lies they tell themselves." She leaned forward and said, in a conspiratorial whisper, "They're nothing, really, you know? Lies that have learned how to take human shape."

He pulled away from her. There was still no noise from upstairs. He had no doubt that if his absence was noticed, this would be the first place they'd look, given the interest he'd shown earlier.

"I should go," he said. "Are there any other people here, people who aren't from Netzach?"

"I know of two. There may be more. Yancey, he works with the groundskeeper. He came here when he was little, like me. He won't be any help. He's been here so long he's forgotten everything but what he thinks he knows about this place." She gave him a thoughtful frown. "If you can get leave to go down into the town, you might talk to Jack Holland. 'Tis but a twenty minute walk, if that. He's the blacksmith. He came a few years ago. Wouldn't say from where, but settled in like he owned the place. Takes no guff from anyone, and hasn't the slippery look the rest of 'em have. I think he's an Other-Worlder, like you and me and poor Yancey. Couldn't hurt to give him a visit. But be careful. They know you talked to me, they'll be watching you every minute."

He gave a quick look up the stairs. "Thanks. I really appreciate the help." Moved by sudden compassion for this bedraggled figure, he said, "If I can find a way out of here, do you want me to take you with me?"

She looked at him narrowly for a moment, as if she thought he was joking. But she released her grip on his shoulder, and patted his arm roughly.

"Naw. I know how to deal with them upstairs. I jumped worlds once, by accident, and look at me. I'll not do it again." She gave him a crooked smile. "But it was kindly thought of, sir, and I'll not forget that." Her head twitched suddenly, like a dog scenting a rabbit. "Now go. You'll do no one any good if you get caught down here."

He turned, and padded his way back up the stairs. He opened the door as silently as he could manage, and peered out. The darkened hallway was empty. He turned toward the staircase, but there was a quiet creak directly ahead of him. A footstep. He flattened himself against the wall, and then edged his way back past the door to the basement. He went across the hall at a run, into the empty dining room. The moon was covered by clouds, and as he stood, wondering where he could go from there to avoid the unseen person he'd heard on the stairs, the first drops of rain pattered against the skylights.

There was the noise of footsteps, and a voice said, "Mr. Duncan!"

He turned to find Mrs. Banks, clad in a nightdress, standing in the doorway to the dining room. "Whatever can you be doing up at this time of night?"

This time of night? It was only a little past eleven o'clock. He looked toward the window in time to see a flicker of lightning glancing across the darkness, and thunder rolled in the distance.

"I woke up hungry," he lied. "I thought that the servants might have left some food on the sideboard, so I came down to check."

"Well," she said, a little dubiously, "they'd never do that. It'd spoil, of course, and attract mice. But you shouldn't eat this late in any case. It'd settle heavy on your stomach, and that's not good if you've been ill. I'll have your breakfast nice and early, don't you worry. For now you need to go back to bed and get your rest, and try to sleep despite the storm. Shall I see you up?"

"No, that's okay. I know my way."

"Best you don't leave your room till morning."

"I know."

She gave him a suspicious, and not particularly friendly, look, but said, "That's all right, then. I'm only considering your well-being, you know. Good night, Mr. Duncan."

"Good night, Mrs. Banks."

He went up the stairs toward his bedroom. "And I don't trust a single thing you've said," he whispered into the darkness. "All in all, I'll take Jennet over you, even if she is a little on the creepy side."

He was so keyed up that it took him two hours to sleep, so he lay on his back, hands cupped behind his head, and listened to the thunderstorm roll past. He finally fell asleep at perhaps a little after one o'clock, and then slept so soundly that he was still deep in slumber when Mrs. Banks knocked on his door the next morning. He opened his eyes, blinked, and squinted at the window, which showed a rectangle of unblemished, rain-washed blue.

"Come in," he said in a voice still groggy and slurred, and she opened the door with a smile that was utterly unlike the stern demeanor she'd had the previous evening.

"Gorgeous morning, Mr. Duncan," she chirped, and set down a silver platter on the nightstand. "Cook has made you a lovely breakfast. I know you'll enjoy it ever so much."

"I'm sure I will," he said, as Mrs. Banks retrieved the lap table from underneath the bed and arranged the food and drink on it.

"You're looking well and rested this morning," she said, giving him a mischievous smile, "despite your being up and wandering last night. Whatever can you have been about?"

"I told you," he said, munching on a piece of toast with marmalade. "I was after food. I was hungry."

"Yes, well, here the food is, even if you had to wait," she said with a coquettish laugh.

"It's great." He took another bite. "I think I'd like to go for a walk down into the village today."

Immediately the concern was back. "Oh, Mr. Duncan, do you think that's wise? After how sick you've been?"

"I'm not sick *now*," he said. "And I'm tired of inactivity. I think a walk would make me feel better."

"Well, perhaps I'll speak to Mr. Garrett, and see if he could accompany you—"

"No," he said firmly. "I don't want Garrett. I'm perfectly capable of going alone. It's only a twenty-minute walk, and I feel perfectly healthy."

Only a momentary narrowing of Mrs. Banks's eyes betrayed her thoughts. He had the impression that she almost asked, "How do you know how far it is?" but to ask that would be to admit that they were all lying, that he really *hadn't* lived there his whole life.

She finally said, "Well, if you think that's wise."

"I think it's fine. I can't stay an invalid, being fed in bed like a little child, forever."

"Two days is hardly forever," she said, but even this objection was feeble. "But you're a grown man, Mr. Duncan. Go ahead on your walk whenever you want to."

"I'll leave after breakfast, and after I have a chance to wash up and dress." He gave her a little smile that made her frown deepen, and her head tilt. "And tell Garrett I don't need him to come dress me and shave me, either. I know what I'm doing."

"Very well, Mr. Duncan," she said, in a flat voice. "You'll let me know if you need anything."

"You'll be the first to know."

After finishing breakfast, Duncan rooted around in the cabinets for the most comfortable clothes he could find. He settled on a white linen shirt with an absurdly high collar he left unbuttoned, a pair of tan trousers, a beige cloth cap a little like the one the doctor had worn the previous day, and brown leather shoes. The sun was still shining, so he decided against a jacket.

"I wonder if this is one of those places men never went out without a jacket?" He studied himself in the mirror inside the cabinet, and then added, "Never mind. This isn't really England in the eighteen-seventies anyway. I don't give a damn."

He walked out of his bedroom and down the hall, then trotted down the staircase, only to have a near collision with his mother.

"Duncan, dear," she said, her voice full of worry. "Mrs. Banks told me of your foolish idea to go down to the village. Whyever would you want to do that?"

"I need the exercise. Why shouldn't I?"

"Well"—she gave a vague gesture with one hand— "it's more that you'll be wearing yourself out for no reason. What can you want in the village?"

"Nothing, Mother." He had to stifle a wince at using the word. She wasn't really his mother, but for now it was best to go along with this little let's-pretend. "I just want to get out in the fresh air."

"And look at you!" She fastened the top button of his collar. "In your shirt sleeves! What will people think?"

He grimaced, and tugged on the collar. "Probably, 'he looks more comfortable than I am.'"

"You *are* in a mood today," she said, clicking her tongue disapprovingly. "If I can't talk you out of it, perhaps Mr. Garrett..."

"No. I won't have Garrett dogging my footsteps. I'm leaving now." He turned away from her, and had his hand on the front doorknob when she spoke again.

"Be careful who you talk to," she said, in an odd, un-inflected voice.

"Oh, I will." He opened the broad front door of the house and stepped out, then shut the door firmly behind him.

The first thing he did was to unbutton his collar.

It was only after he walked a little way down the drive that led up to the doorstep that he realized that he had no idea which way the village was, but he saw a middle-aged man wearing suspenders and a shapeless gray cap kneeling in a long, narrow rose bed that bordered the walk.

"Hey," he said. "How do I get to the village from here?"

The man squinted up at him with a perplexed expression. "You don't know, Mr. Duncan?"

"I've been ill. I don't remember."

"Ah, yes. So I'd heard. Well, glad to see you up and about. Go down the drive until you reach the lane. Take a right, downhill. It's nary twenty minutes, fifteen if you're in a hurry."

"You're Yancey, aren't you?"

"Why, yes, sir, I am." The man gave him a shy smile.

"Maybe my memory is returning." He returned the smile. Jennet had been right; the Other-Worlders did look different. They were more... real. "I'll be on my way, then."

"Have a nice day, sir."

"You do, as well."

He continued walking, across a bridge spanning a tumbling little creek, and then uphill through a grove of oak trees whose branches curved over the drive like cathedral arches. Small blue and white flowers dotted the ground, and a light, gentle breeze caressed his face and ruffled his hair.

Wow. They were really going all out making this place look nice. Was this all for his benefit? And was any of it real?

He came out from under the trees as the drive reached the lane, turned right, and descended a long, low hill. Wide fields of grain, blue-green under the sunshine, swept away to the left. To the right were more trees. He had walked ten minutes when he saw the first sign of other inhabitants, a small, neat house with a tidy garden, and a woman in a green-checked dress hanging laundry on a clothesline. She turned and gave him a cheerful wave as he passed, and he returned it with a little nod. Other houses appeared as he continued his walk, then a tavern, already noisy and crowded despite the early hour. J. A. Abercrombie, Book-Seller. Harkness & Davies, Barristers At Law. Thomas D. Cavanaugh, Accountant.

He got many curious looks from passersby. People turned and followed him with their gazes as he passed. Still, he thought, it was nothing that couldn't be explained by the news having reached the village of his lengthy illness. If he hadn't talked to Jennet, he could easily have dismissed it as nothing but idle curiosity. He refrained from engaging anyone beyond returning smiles, and wandered through the center of the village without speaking to anyone.

He walked for nearly a half-hour before stumbling upon the blacksmith's shop. He came on it suddenly, on a little side lane that branched out from the main road to the right and ran steeply downhill toward the creek. A roughly-hewn sign nailed above the door said *J. C. Holland, Blacksmith*, but he would have known in any case from the assortment of metal tools, wrought-iron chairs, plough blades, and axes in the front yard. He hadn't wanted to ask anyone for directions. Better that no one know where he was going, if Jennet had been right about the smith being one of the only Other-Worlders in the village.

He went in through the front door, which stood a little ajar. Inside was more ironmongery, a long counter with various tools of the trade, and a broad, leather-bound ledger, standing open and covered top to bottom with rows and columns of orders for goods.

"Hello?" he called.

There was a noise from farther in, and after a moment, a tall bear of a man stepped through a curtain at the back of the room. He topped Duncan by at least four inches, and Duncan was himself a little over six feet tall. He had a ragged mop of wiry black hair, a bushy beard of the same color, and thickly-muscled hairy arms. He regarded Duncan with an expression that hovered somewhere between reserve and outright suspicion.

"Good morning to you, young sir," he said, in a voice that was courteous enough.

"Are you Jack Holland?"

"I am."

"Do you know me?"

"Should I?"

Time to take a chance on Jennet's advice. Push on the world a little, and see how it responded.

"I live in the manor house up the road. I'm Duncan Kyle."

The man looked him up and down. "If you say so."

He took a step forward. "They tell me there that I've lived in that house all of my life. That I've been ill with scarlet fever and that's why I don't remember any of this. What do you say about that?"

"I'm not going to say anything. Do you believe it?"

"No."

"Well, then."

They regarded each other in silence for a moment. "I talked to Jennet. The scullery maid."

One bushy eyebrow went up a little. "And what did Jennet the scullery maid tell you?"

"That she, and you, and I, and Yancey the gardener, are all different from the rest of the people here."

"She told you that? Jennet the scullery maid should learn to keep her big mouth shut."

"So you're saying she's lying?"

"Listen," Holland said, and his voice lowered, "I got no reason to talk to you about this. I came to terms with where I am, and who I am, and who all these others are, years ago. If you don't like it, leave."

"You know I'm an Other-Worlder, like you are. Let's stop dancing around. What is it that they want from me? The people in the manor house up on the hill?"

Holland stared at Duncan for some time in silence. Finally, he said, "I think you know the answer to that."

"They use us to make themselves real."

"Did Jennet tell you that, or did you figure it out yourself?"

"A combination of both."

"Then why are you talking to me about it?"

"Just call it checking my sources."

Again, there was a long pause. Jack Holland, apparently, was not to be rushed or pushed. "I don't know what you want me to say," he said. "You already got your answer. They'll take from you if you let them. I stopped them, so I stayed sane. The others? I don't think Jennet is all there, and Yancey's mind is gone. But you know there's another reason. They can't get out of here. Whenever a new one arrives, they cluster around him like fleas to a dog, trying to find out how he did it, where he came from, to see if they can get through the door themselves. If they think you can lead them somewhere else, they'll do everything in their power to stop you from leaving yourself."

"Why? Why don't they want to be here? The place is idyllic."

Holland gave a gruff laugh. "You think so? You're more'n half lost already, then." He moved forward suddenly, smoothly for such a big man, and reached out toward Duncan. Duncan recoiled a little, but Holland had no ill intent. He merely grabbed Duncan by the shoulders and spun him around, suddenly, toward the still-open door to the shop.

And for a fraction of a second, he saw something different than the wooded, peaceful glade next to the little dirt road he'd come down. For a flash, what was outside was gray, foggy, amorphous, nothing but vague shapes with no real borders. Only for a moment—then the trees and the edge of the road were back. As if to convince him of its solidity, and that what he'd seen wasn't real, a sparrow landed on the top of a rake handle leaning on the front steps, gave a fluid, melodious little song, and then flew away.

"You see?" Holland said. "Catch 'em off guard, and they can't keep up. They're fast, but not if you surprise 'em. I know what they are, now, and I can see 'em either way, if I want. Trained my eyes, like. Doesn't bother me. But they're exerting all their power to keep you fooled. You'll have to be cunning."

He licked his lips, still looking out through the door. "So that... that gray fog... that's what Netzach really is?"

He nodded. "What you're seeing is all what they take from you. If you were different, this place and the people in it would look different. But yeah. Take away the appearances, and that's all that's left."

He turned back toward the smith. "Why do you stay here?"

Holland's dark eyes turned distant for a moment. "Got nowhere else to go. Came here when I was a young man, twenty years old. I'd killed a man in a pub brawl. Wasn't fond of the idea of hanging for it, so I ran. I stumbled on a doorway. I don't know how to create 'em myself, or I'd have found a better place, I suppose. Got here, and once them as live here figured out I didn't know anything of interest, and wasn't going to swallow their nonsense, they left me alone. You don't have a reason to stay here, I'd guess?"

"No."

"You haven't the look of a killer about you," Holland said, with a grim laugh. "Then I'd get out as soon as possible. They'll keep at you until you tell them what they want to know, and after they'll keep you out of spite and a desire to hang on to what they have."

"I don't know how I make the portals. I just seem to do it."

"All the more reason to get the hell out of here, then."

"I'll do what I can."

The smith nodded, and Duncan turned back toward the door. As he walked out of the shop, he saw an elderly man, leaning on a cane, standing next to the stairs that led up to the front porch.

"Morning, Mr. Kyle," the man said cheerfully. "Nice to see you up and about."

How long was had that old man been listening to them?

"Nice to feel better."

"Hope you continue to be well and whole," the man said.

"Me too."

Duncan passed him, the man watching as he returned to the road back toward the village. It was only as he was almost out of sight under the overhanging trees that he turned suddenly, and saw the elderly man still standing there, but featureless, like a ghost in a spectral, misty landscape. Once again the colors and details flooded back instantly, and the man, still watching him, raised a hand in farewell.

He returned the salute and kept on walking.

He did that, over and over, on the way back to the manor house. It was mostly to keep reminding himself that Jennet and Holland were right, none of what he was seeing was real. He got his biggest shock when the house itself came into view. Yancey was still on his knees in the rose garden, a bit further up the drive, and Duncan first turned away, then spun around on his heel toward the manor with his eyes wide open.

What he saw was terrifying. A jagged ruin of a house, with sharp angles and spikes and spires, great holes in the roof, and empty eyes for windows, standing on a hill with the mist curling around its foundations. Everything was white, gray, and black, except for Yancey, a little figure of unmistakable bright color and solidity in the vague, shadowy foreground. Then, as before, it was all back in its previous opulence. As if to reinforce its reality, the breeze brushed his face with the scent of roses.

"All right," he said. "I'm about done with this charade. I'm not playing any more."

He strode up the drive, giving Yancey a curt nod as he passed, and then up the front stairs and into the house. He hadn't gone three steps when his father came out of the sunroom, his face stern and disapproving.

"Son," he said, "your mother told me how rude you were to her this morning. You owe her an apology, and me an explanation."

"I don't owe you anything." He gave his father a hard stare. "Who are you?"

The man in front of him drew himself up, his lips tightening with anger. "I'm your father, as you well know. Are you feverish again? Because that's the only explanation that would excuse your behavior."

"Oh, knock it off. I'm not feverish again. I wasn't feverish the first time. Stop lying to me. I know what you people are doing, and why. I talked to the blacksmith."

For the first time, a quick flash of alarm spread across Mr. Kyle's face, but it was gone in an instant, as quickly as the vision of the gray, foggy reality of Netzach had vanished.

"Jack Holland is a rogue and a liar."

"I think you're wrong. He's telling the truth. Everything else here is a lie."

There was a noise behind him, and he turned to see Garrett and Mrs. Banks standing there, both wearing grim expressions. When he turned back toward Mr. Kyle, he saw that Mrs. Kyle and one of the servants who had served the food had appeared a little way off down the hall, and were standing, watching him.

"You can't stop me from leaving here."

Now would be a good time to find a portal, he thought. *Don't make me a liar, too.*

"I think we can," Mrs. Banks said from behind him, and two pairs of hands grabbed his arms.

"You can't resist forever," said his mother's voice.

It sounded so real, felt so real... He closed his eyes. No. None of it was. It was all images they've taken from him, somehow, to shape themselves into reality. Without him, they were nothing.

Then he opened his eyes, and saw what he'd seen from the bottom of the drive—an empty, shell-like ruin of a house, broken, splintered timbers, jagged shards of glass in bent window frames. Five wraiths, faceless and formless, swirled around him, reaching for him with wispy hands that appeared to be made of fog.

And behind the ghost that was all that was left of Dennis Kyle was a gossamer door, pale gold in the gray mist. In any other setting, it would have been invisible, like strands of spider web in the morning breeze—here, it shone like a beacon. He effortlessly shook off the grasping hands, whose only hold on him had been his belief in them, and stepped through the door.

He heard their voices calling, "No!" but they were of as little substance as their bodies. The spectral house, and its ghostly inhabitants, winked out like a candle flame.

CHAPTER 5

TIFERET

D uncan was immersed in blackness. It was too complete even to be night. This was nothingness, nonexistence, an absence so complete that it wasn't even emptiness. *Empty* implies a boundary, a container, outside of which there are the ordinary things of life. Here, there was nothing to contain, nothing inside or outside, just a disembodied awareness floating in infinite space.

He recalled as a small child attending church with his grandparents, and hearing the minister reading from Genesis—*The world was without form, and void*. He hadn't understood the verse then.

Now he did.

There was no sense of the position of his body, and he could not feel his own limbs. It was as if he, too, had become nothing, along with the rest of the world, when he stepped through the door in the phantom world of Netzach.

He could think, though, and hear his own thoughts.

What happened to me? Am I asleep? In a coma? Dead?

The latter wasn't likely, although he couldn't rule it out.

But then he heard another voice, a different voice, saying, "Increase stimulation of the reticular ascending pathway by five percent," and another answer, "Increasing."

Other sensations came to him. He was, quite suddenly, aware of his body again, but still could not move. There was a feeling of gentle pressure behind his head, back, buttocks, heels. A gentle brush of air moved against his left cheek, as if someone had passed near him.

"Any response?" came the first voice.

"Yes," said the second. "Spontaneous activity beginning in the prefrontal cortex and sensory pathways."

"Excellent. Increase by another three percent, then hold there. We may be getting him back at last."

And the sense of breathing, of air going into and out of his lungs, came upon him in a rush. He could feel blood flowing through his veins. His hands and feet tingled. He realized that he was lying on his back, on some soft surface, naked but covered up to mid-chest with a sheet, and had a momentary panicked thought that he might be back on Yesod, at Diana's mercy.

His eyes flickered open.

"Got him," said the first voice, full of relief.

His field of view was limited to what was right above him—a white ceiling, dimly lit, and a vague blur of machines and wires in his peripheral view, along with some moving figures he couldn't at first make out.

A tall, rotund man with wire-rim glasses and a shock of snow-white hair moved over him, looking down at him with a paternal smile.

"Well, Mr. Kyle," he said. "Welcome back. You've been gone for a long time."

He licked his lips, grimaced, and said, "Where am I?"

"Saint Stephen's Neurological Hospital, Colville, New York."

He cleared his throat. "Colville doesn't have a hospital called Saint Stephen's."

The man nodded. "No. In your time, it didn't."

"In my time?"

The man frowned a little. "You shouldn't be stressing yourself by asking questions."

"That's what they told me in Netzach. It was bullshit there, it's bullshit here." He coughed, and a jolt of pain arrowed through his head. He winced. "I'm more stressed by being evaded and lied to."

"No one is going to lie to you, Mr. Kyle," the man said. "Let's start with the fact that I'm Doctor Caleb Marshall, and I've been supervising your case for some time now. What's the last thing you remember?"

"Jumping through a door in Netzach, and everything went black."

The man shook his head. "No. From your life before. From when you were here in Colville."

Duncan frowned. "I got up in the middle of the night, and my apartment floor caved in. I fell into another world."

"So you do remember right up to the moment of your stroke." Doctor Marshall patted his arm. "That's good. It means that you haven't lost as much of your higher cognitive function as we'd thought at first."

"Stroke?"

"You suffered a cerebral hemorrhage. Your girlfriend found you, unconscious, on the floor. It is fortunate she did, and called an ambulance, or you'd have died. But with the medical care at the time, there was little they could do. They stabilized you, put you on life support. But they couldn't repair the damage that had been done."

"How am I alive, then?"

"About eight months after your stroke and subsequent coma, a technique was developed to place critically ill or terminal patients into cryostasis. This slows down metabolism, aging, and the progress of the disease if it's progressive in nature. Put simply, it buys us time. Patients can be brought out of cryostasis when medical researchers learn how to treat their conditions. In your case, it only recently has become possible."

"How long was I asleep?"

Doctor Marshall hesitated. "Mr. Kyle, I really don't think—"

"No." His voice became stronger. "Tell me."

"One hundred fifty-six years."

He struggled to sit up, despite the pain, but Doctor Marshall put a hand in the center of his chest and gently pushed him back down.

"I know how upsetting all of this must be. But you mustn't become agitated. Your condition was, until very recently, extremely fragile, and the repairs that were done to your neural network are still healing. You will do yourself no good at all by struggling to get up, and could undo everything we have tried so hard to accomplish."

"That sounds way too similar to what the people in Netzach said. They took that tack. 'You've been sick. Don't overtire yourself. Here, let us care for you.' It was all lies. It didn't fool me then, it won't fool me now."

Doctor Marshall smiled and shrugged. "We're not trying to fool you. I can assure you that I can convince you, should you desire proof, but that will have to wait until you are further along in your healing. Your body has been through a lot, and so has your brain. Give yourself time to recover." The doctor squeezed his arm. "At this point, you have all the time in the world."

At some point Duncan slept. He opened his eyes more than once to dim light and figures moving around in the shadows. Clips were attached to his fingers, then removed. Others were affixed to his temples and upper chest and remained in place longer. He supposed, in his fogged, dreamlike state, that they were monitoring his vital signs somehow. He slept again, and woke up with a beam of sunlight across his room, falling in a golden rectangle on the white wall. He needed to pee, and was hungry, but otherwise felt reasonably well.

He looked around for something like a nurse's call button, and saw nothing. Finally, he said, "Hey." When that elicited no response, he said it louder.

A tall nurse, with curly hair and freckles, came into the room. "Awake, Mr. Kyle? How are you feeling?"

"I need the bathroom."

"We can take care of that." She went up to his bedside, and slipped a hand beneath his shoulders, and helped him to a sitting position. "Sit there for a moment, and make sure that you don't feel dizzy. If you think you can stand up, I can get you a robe."

"I think I'm okay."

She retrieved a white terry cloth robe from the closet and draped it over his shoulders, then helped him to maneuver his arms into the sleeves.

It's just like the one I had in Netzach. I won't trust these people either. I won't. I won't.

But he allowed her to help him to his feet, and he tied the robe closed, then shuffled carefully to the bathroom.

Afterwards, he let her conduct him back to bed, resettle him under a sheet and blanket. A screen with regular blips that could only be his heartbeat on a screen was inset in the wall behind his bed, along with various other green glowing squiggles that he could not interpret. He no longer had sensors on his skin, so he assumed that somehow, they were monitoring his vital signs remotely.

One hundred fifty-six years. A century and a half. But it had to be a lie. They'd lied to him everywhere else. Each place, it had always been about getting him to cooperate, to give in and tell them how to get from one world to another. And each time, the ante had increased. In Malkuth, it was a simple physical threat. In Yesod, Diana tried to tempt him with sex. In Hod, it was the pull of friendship and loyalty and honor. If he hadn't been halfway through the portal already, he would have stayed to fight beside Anir and his family, and he would either be dead or in the hands of the jackal-man's followers. Then in Netzach, they'd tried to convince him that illness was preventing him from remembering reality, and that he should trust them instead of his own intuition.

What would it be here? The approach was similar—convincing him he'd been sick. But that was only the trappings. This was more serious, he was certain of it. Whatever they had going on here, they were not going to be as easy to see through as the phantoms of Netzach.

The next time she came into his room, he asked the freckled nurse where he was.

"Saint Stephen's," she said.

"Not the hospital. The whole place."

"Colville, New York. You never left Colville."

"Bigger than that," he said. "What's the world called?"

She raised her eyebrows, and smiled. "The world?" She shrugged. "It's just called the world."

Knew it wasn't going to be that simple.

"I'm trying to see what I remember."

"Your memory should be intact," she said. "The neurologists said that most of the damage was in the part of the brain involved in conscious awareness. Your memory and sensory centers weren't affected, except that you weren't registering much of anything while you were comatose."

"Did I dream?"

"Do you remember dreaming?"

"I think so."

She nodded. "Doctor Marshall and the others on your team actually stimulated you to dream, because when dreaming and REM sleep is suppressed, the individual suffers a serious cognitive decline. It was discovered about fifty years ago that stimulating various dreams in coma patients has excellent success in minimizing lingering deficits once the organic cause of the coma is reversed."

"So what I remember after falling in my apartment..."

"... is almost certainly dream content," she finished. "I think if you consider what you remember from those episodes, you will easily convince yourself that it cannot be reality, however intense those memories may appear to you now."

Another attempt to convince him that the other worlds he'd visited didn't exist.

"It was pretty surreal," he said, managing a smile.

"Dreams are like that. I wouldn't worry about it."

"I'm not worried."

But, he thought, *I'm also not going to let you convince me that it never happened.*

In the mid-afternoon, Doctor Marshall came back with two other physicians. One was a small African American woman with a round face, high cheekbones, long wavy gray hair tied back into a ponytail, and small, square plastic-framed glasses. The other was a gangly scarecrow of a man with a shock of bright red hair and a neatly-trimmed beard. They were introduced as Doctors Felice and McAlpin.

"How's our miracle man?" Doctor Felice said in a quiet voice, while looking at the readout on one of the monitors.

"Not sure what to think about all of this," Duncan said.

"You are in second-place for recovery after the world's longest cryostatic coma," Doctor McAlpin said, his voice considerably more animated than his colleague's. "First place beat you by five days."

"Cool." His voice reflected his lack of enthusiasm.

"I'm sure it's been an adjustment," Doctor Felice said. "And will continue to be. We'd encourage you to exercise as much as your physical state will allow. Our research has shown that the faster you get back to gentle, regular activity, the faster you will recover in all ways. We did muscle stimulation while you were unconscious to keep your muscles from atrophying, but it is no replacement for actual exercise."

"I'm still pretty weak."

"That should dissipate," Doctor McAlpin said. "Even with a century and a half of medical advances over what you remember, it's still hard on the body to be bedridden. But now that the neurological problem is repaired, the physical issues should follow suit after a short recovery period."

"You must be patient with regards to your readjustment," Doctor Felice said. "This has been a tremendous emotional shock, and you must not underestimate the strain that places on you."

"I'm *not* patient," he said. "I never have been. When can I get out of here?"

The three doctors made momentary eye contact, and then Doctor Marshall smiled in a paternal fashion. "It's a little early to think of leaving. If your recovery continues on its present course, we expect that you would be able to leave the hospital temporarily, and under supervision, for short periods. You've been through a lot, Mr. Kyle. It's far better not to rush things."

"Supervision? By whom?"

"By a hospital staff member, of course. Someone who would be qualified to deal with any problems should they arise."

His eyes narrowed. This was all bullshit. He hadn't had a stroke, and therefore everything they were telling him was false.

"I wonder if I could see images of my brain scan that show the damage from the stroke?"

Doctor Felice shrugged, and pushed her glasses up her nose. "If you're curious, we can have images sent up from radiology. You have a computer link here in your room, so you can access them from there. We'll have one of the nurses bring you a facet. She'll show you how to gain access, and then you'll be able to see all of your medical records, as well as use the internet." She smiled at him, showing a row of perfectly even white teeth. "I think you'll be pleasantly astonished at how much information technology has improved in a hundred fifty years. You picked the right time to be reborn."

He smiled back at her, still holding tight to his determination not to believe a single thing any of them said. "Choice had nothing to do with it."

She met his gaze levelly. "I was speaking figuratively, of course. But I think you know that."

"Yes," he said, his voice quiet. "I think I know exactly what you mean."

After his evening meal, the freckled nurse brought him a rigid, lightweight piece of translucent plastic, about twice the size of a sheet of paper.

Duncan, sitting in a chair in his room with his feet on the edge of the bed, said, "What's this?"

"Naturally, you aren't up to date on our technology," she said, smiling. "Put one finger on the surface, and sweep left to right."

He did as he was told. The sheet of plastic lit up, and there was a meteor shower of glowing lights across its surface that coalesced into a three-dimensional image of a bespectacled man with dark skin, short cropped brown hair, and intense brown eyes sitting behind a library desk. Duncan held the sheet up in front of his face, turned it this way and that. The image of the man rotated, just as if it were an actual miniaturized human floating in space, a few inches in front of the screen.

"This device is called a facet. It's similar to the laptop computers you had back in the twenty-first century." She gestured at the man's image. "Talk to him," she urged.

"What should I ask?" he whispered.

And the man answered, in a friendly voice, "Whatever you want to know."

"Wow," he said, impressed despite his determination to meet everything he saw here with hard-edged skepticism.

"I'll leave you with this," the nurse said. "You have complete access to whatever is on the worldwide archive systems. This would include factual information, such as history and science, as well as hundreds of thousands of works of fiction, including books, movies, and serialized film. Your own medical records are accessible, too. I believe you told Doctor Marshall you would like to see your brain scans? All you have to do is ask. The world is at your fingertips, as long as you know what questions to ask."

The nurse left the room.

He held the sheet of plastic gingerly, as if he were afraid to hurt the image of the Librarian. After a moment, he poked at the image, and his finger went right through it.

"You're not real?" he said.

"Not solid matter, no," the Librarian said. "But whether I am real or not depends on your definition of *real.*"

"A computer simulation."

"A hologram, to be precise." The Librarian gave a courteous nod. "Would you like more information on how I was created?"

"Maybe later." The Librarian nodded again. "There's some stuff I want to know before that. First, what is the name of this place?"

"You will need to be more specific with your question," the Librarian said. "Demonstrative pronouns such as *this* and *that* only make sense if the person to whom you are speaking knows the referent to which they point."

"The whole world. What is the name of the whole world?"

The Librarian did not answer for a moment. He finally said, "It is called Tiferet."

"What does that word mean?"

"It means Place of Balance and Healing."

"Who gave it that name?"

Another pause. "I do not have access to that information."

"When I was last in Colville, New York, the whole world was called the Earth. Or the Universe, depending on how far you want to go. Am I somewhere different than that?"

"I do not have access to that information."

"I thought you know everything?"

The Librarian gave him an indulgent smile. "That is incorrect. I only have access to information that is in the worldwide archives. There is much, therefore, that I do not know."

"What is Sephirot?"

The answer came immediately. "Sephirot is a mystical schema that encompasses the journey of the soul toward enlightenment."

"Says who?" Duncan's voice was scoffing, not that the Librarian would be likely to notice that.

"This view would be held by individuals who espouse that particular mystical tradition."

"In other words, the people who believe in it believe in it because they believe in it. Very helpful." He leaned back, holding the screen propped up in his lap. "Is Tifer-et one of the worlds of the Sephirot?"

"To those who espouse this tradition, everything is part of the Sephirot. I am unable to answer whether this tradition is reflective of reality, however, as the evaluation of the veracity of various mystical traditions is outside the scope of my function."

"Who should I ask, then?"

"You might ask a priest. They are generally considered qualified to answer spiritual questions, although some consider them biased in that regard."

"Thanks. I'll get right on that. Oh, by the way. What year is it?"

"In the most common calendar, it is the year twenty-one seventy in the Common Era."

That seemed about right, if they'd told the truth.

"Have I really been in a coma that whole time?"

"I do not have access..." the Librarian began, but Duncan cut him off.

"I know, I know. But look. Doctor McAlpin told me I was in close second place to the world's longest reemergence from a cryostatic sleep. That must have made the news, right? Check for my name. Duncan Lukas Kyle."

A pause. "There is a press release from only twelve hours ago. It was released into the archives from a spokesperson for Saint Stephen's Neurological Hospital, Colville, New York. Would you like me to read it to you?"

"Sure."

> Doctor Caleb Marshall, senior neurologist at Saint Stephen's Hospital in Colville, New York, has just announced that one of his patients of longest standing has been successfully reawakened from cryostasis. Duncan L. Kyle, who was put into stasis after a stroke in twenty-fourteen, has spent the last one hundred and fifty-six years in suspended animation. Marshall and his colleagues, Doctor Annabel Felice and Doctor Douglas McAlpin, recently perfected a technique for repairing the kind of damage that Mr. Kyle had suffered, and after surgically reconstructing the part of the brain that was damaged, they resuscitated him from his coma.

> "Mr. Kyle will have a bit of a rude awakening," Doctor Marshall told reporters. "Given that the last thing he will remember

occurred a century and a half ago. Our staff psychologists and social workers are already preparing for the task of transitioning Mr. Kyle to life in the twenty-second century. We, and he, have a monumental task ahead, but one that I am confident will have a successful outcome."

Doctor Marshall added that only one other patient, Kerry Ann Landis, was in stasis for a longer period, and that only by a few days. Miss Landis is still working with mental health specialists to facilitate her return to the world.

The Librarian's voice ceased, and once more, the little figure looked out at Duncan with a placid expression.

"And you know what happened to me that put me in a coma. You have brain scans and everything."

"You suffered a stroke of the right ascending pathway of the reticular activating system. Would you like to see images of the affected area?"

"No," he said. "It wouldn't mean anything to me, anyway."

The Librarian fell silent.

"Well, this is all very convincing."

The Librarian gave a little bow.

"So I suppose everyone I knew in twenty-fourteen is dead by now."

"Although am unable to answer a generalization like that with any certainty, the likelihood is high that this is a true statement."

"So there has been no particular enhancement of human life span in a hundred fifty-six years?"

"The current average human life span is ninety-two years for men, ninety-eight years for women."

"So people still don't get to the two-century mark."

"The oldest verified age at death was Célimène Marie Jouglard, of Saint Jean-Saint Nicolas, Hautes-Alpes département, France. She died at the age of one hundred forty-nine years, six months, and two days."

"So no chance, then."

The Librarian didn't answer.

"That's cheerful." He scratched his head. "Oh, well, it's better than ghosts or crazy huntresses or jackal-men with swords. I wonder what's going to be the hitch here? Because nowhere I've been yet has turned out to be what it appeared to be at first, and I have no reason to believe that this place will, either." He gave the Librarian a wry smile. "But thanks for the information."

"I am always here if you need me," the Librarian said, and the screen turned back to a translucent gray.

The evening passed, with Duncan watching all of the hospital staff closely, looking for a means of ingress.

In Netzach, he had lucked out by running into Jennet the scullery maid. How long would it have taken him to figure out what was going on had she not trusted him?

Even so, in Netzach he'd known something was amiss. The pieces of the world that didn't make sense were obviously drawn from his past, his imaginings, his memories. Here? It was all seamless. There was no chink in the armor.

At least that he'd found yet. The only thing to do was to watch and wait. And not to trust anyone too quickly. This puzzle wouldn't be an easy one.

He slept. And dreamed perfectly ordinary dreams. A nurse came in in the middle of the night to check his vitals, which she did by touching the screen behind his bed and copying down a few numbers that flashed past. The twenty-second century apparently had dispensed with thermometers and blood pressure cuffs. Afterwards, he slept again, and didn't wake until an aide brought him breakfast the next morning.

"I'd like to shave and shower," he said, munching on a piece of bacon that was pretty good, considering the hospital food he'd had.

"You'll need to clear that level of activity with the doctor," said the aide, a tall man with a melancholy, horsey face and short salt-and-pepper hair.

"That's considered 'activity?'"

"Certainly. You could become dizzy while in the shower, or slip. One of the doctors from your team will have to sign off on this. However, it should not take long once the request is submitted."

"Fine," he said. "Although I do wonder what you'd do if I decided to lock myself in the bathroom and showered without permission."

The aide gave him a mournful look. "Please don't. You don't recover faster by ignoring the doctor's orders."

"Yeah, yeah." He waved a hand at him. "I'll follow protocol. No unauthorized showering, I promise."

By midday, Duncan was getting the impression that he was being constantly monitored.

He was served an excellent lunch by a dour elderly female aide who came and went without saying a word. After a trip to the bathroom, he opened the door to find two orderlies in his room, sweeping the floor and casting surreptitious glances in his direction. After the orderlies left, he waited about five minutes and then got up and headed for the door, and had gotten a few feet down the hall when the melancholy aide who had brought him breakfast came up behind him and said that it was time for his medication and for checking his vitals.

He acquiesced, but as the afternoon crept on, he felt restless and bored. After an unsuccessful attempt to garner more information about his situation from the Librarian, he decided to investigate the history of the world since his presumptive stroke in 2014. He found a complete account of events in the intervening century and a half, including a list of world leaders, wars and skirmishes, and events (apparently a meteorite had turned a good part of the city of Lagos, Nigeria into a large smoking crater early in 2132). Science had made commensurate progress, at least if the Librarian was to be believed, and he lost himself for a time in reading about medical and technological advances.

But after a time he grew restive, and set the facet down on the bed. He tried to make another attempt at a walk down the hall, only to be intercepted at the door of his room by the tall, freckled nurse who had looked after him the previous day.

"Up and about, Mr. Kyle?" she said with a smile.

"I'm feeling fine," he said in a querulous tone. "Except for the fact that I'm going to go stir-crazy if I don't get some exercise."

"We have some exercise equipment on the second floor, but you won't be able to use it..."

"... yes, I know. Until it's cleared by the doctor. Why haven't the doctors been back, by the way? If my condition is all that fragile, you'd think they'd be around."

"They have other patients to attend to, Mr. Kyle," the nurse said, her friendly smile dimming somewhat. "They run a very busy schedule, and now that you're improving, you don't need the constant monitoring that you did before you awoke."

"I don't think I need monitoring at *all*. In fact, I'd very much like it if I could have some clothes and a ticket out of here."

"Well, you can't be discharged yet," she said firmly. "You will still be under observation for some time, I'm afraid."

He turned, and plopped down into the chair next to his bed. "So in this century, you have the authority to hold people against their will, indefinitely, for some imaginary condition? I never thought Colville, New York would turn into a police state."

A flush spread across the nurse's face. "I hardly think that's fair. After all, the doctors here saved your life, and all the staff here has cared for you and nurtured you back to health. Looking after your best interests hardly makes Saint Stephen's a police state."

"Oh?" He put his feet up on the bed. "Suppose I was to stand up, and walk past you and out of the door, and then down the elevator and out of the hospital. What would you do?"

"If I couldn't talk some sense into you, I would have to call the doctors."

"And what would they do?"

"Well, I... I don't know. Really, Mr. Kyle, I don't think there's anything to be gained by being so combative."

"Would you like to get out of here, nurse?" he said, smiling at her, and cupping his hands behind his head. "What's your name, again?"

"Sue Scavron," she said, frowning. "And what do you mean? Out of the hospital? I'm not—"

"No, I mean out. Right out. Out of the world. Into somewhere else."

She frowned. "I don't have any idea what you're talking about."

"Oh, I think you do. I think you *all* do. It's the same thing again, isn't it? It's just like Netzach." He held one hand up as she opened her mouth to speak. "I know, I know, you have no idea what Netzach is. Let's pretend that I believe that for the moment." He shook his head. "You folks are kind of running out of ideas, aren't you? The people in Netzach tried to convince me that everything I remembered was a lie, a fever dream, and that I should buy into their beautiful collective delusion instead. Here"—he gestured around him— "I can't say this place is all that beautiful. What's the lure going to be this time? Knowledge?"

Sue Scavron looked at him, tight-lipped, and didn't respond.

"Yeah, I bet that's it. The Librarian, right? Twenty-second century technology. Free access to anything I want to know, as long as I don't ask too many prying questions. The world at my fingertips. What else is there? I bet there are other attractions too, right?"

She backed away, still frowning at him. "You're getting agitated, Mr. Kyle. I don't think..." She turned and walked out of the room. He heard her shoes clipping down the hall, then fading into silence.

"Well," he said. "I bet that'll get their attention."

It did. A half-hour later, Doctor Caleb Marshall, his usually bland expression replaced by one of stern disapproval, came into Duncan's room. He was still sitting in his chair, the computer facet propped in his lap, watching a documentary on faster-than-light travel.

"Guess you folks went all *Star Trek*, too," he said. "Manned missions to other star systems, and everything."

"You upset Nurse Scavron very much," Doctor Marshall said.

"I bet I did. Good thing she's not real."

"What are you talking about?"

"Just like Nurse Scavron, whoever or whatever she actually is, I think you know perfectly well what I'm talking about. You are a little better at hiding what you're after than the folks in the other worlds, that's all. But I'll play along. Tell me about this place, Doctor Marshall. Doctor Felice said I'd picked a good time to be reborn. Why?"

Doctor Marshall's eyes narrowed, but he said, "Well, we've put an end to war and poverty. About seventy years ago there were technological breakthroughs that revolutionized food production, and significantly limited the wanton ecological destruction that your era was engaged in. We live in a society that to you will seem very much like a paradise."

"Nice. What's in it for me?"

"How do you mean?"

"If I'm going to stay here, I want to know what I'll get out of it."

"You'll want to pursue some retraining and education, but unlike in your time, all education is free and open-access. You can follow any intellectual pursuit you wish, and contribute to society in whatever way you choose. You'll find that here, you will be truly free."

"What about the fact that everyone I knew is dead, though? That kind of sucks."

Doctor Marshall nodded. "Unfortunate. But the reality is that death is still with us. We stay healthy far longer, however, and can cure many diseases that were fatal or debilitating in your time. A man of your current state of health can look forward to another ninety years of vitality at the very least. And, I should add, the opportunities for pleasurable pursuits are very much more open than they were in your time. We have holographic simulators for any diversion you choose, from sports, to adventure, to interactive games, to encounters of a sexual nature. Something to suit all desires, and without the incessant and puritanical moralization of pleasure that your time reveled in. You will find our society open and welcoming. Conformity is a thing of the past."

"As is asking questions, I presume?"

Doctor Marshall didn't answer.

"Look, doctor, this is not about me being obnoxious. I've been through this whole rigamarole several times before, and I know what you people are after. I can somehow jump from one world of the Sephirot to another, even though I'm not exactly sure how or why I do it. And I know that after some preliminary messing about, it'll turn out that you want to get me to let that information slip, or you'll cajole me out of it, or whatever. So can we skip the foreplay, and get right down to business, here? Because frankly, I don't believe one single fucking thing you're saying, and I'm tired of pretending that I do."

"Now, Mr. Kyle," Doctor Marshall said, "you are incorrect that we want anything from you other than a continued improvement in your health. But I will say that your belligerent attitude is not going to help you along your road to fitting in to our society. You'll find us amenable to all manner of opinions. In fact, we are a far more open society than the one you remember from before the stroke, accepting of many different and fluid standards for behavior. That said, you are accomplishing nothing by being deliberately obtuse."

"So I'll get anything I want as long as I play along. Knowledge, happiness, sex, anything. But I can't ask too many questions."

Doctor Marshall bristled a little. "I understand your disorientation at the situation you find yourself in. But you must look at this thing rationally. There is a world here that is yours for the taking, and is far more beautiful and pleasurable than the one you left behind. Surely even the short time you spent working with the computer facet confirms that idea."

"I have a different idea," he said. "Why don't you take that facet, and stick it up your ass? Sideways?"

Doctor Marshall didn't answer. He simply stared. Duncan stared back.

And Doctor Marshall turned on his heel, and walked out of the room.

"Wonder who he'll get to come see me next, the CEO of the hospital? Or maybe a psychologist."

But no one else visited Duncan that afternoon or evening, not even to bring him dinner or check the monitors in the room. The hospital staff were leaving him well alone. He saw nurses and aides walking past his room, and even caught one of them glancing in at him, but no one spoke to him or came into his room.

Okay. The light was fading from the sky, and the first few stars were appearing. He was not going to sit around the hospital room and wait. First opportunity he got, he was getting right the hell out. And unless they wanted to fight him, they'd have to get out of his way. A surge of confidence rushed through him. He found himself almost wishing for a confrontation. He could take Doctor Marshall, and that skinny ginger guy, Doctor McWhatever. Let them try to stop him.

The fact remained, though, that he was still clad only in a robe. Once more, clothing was going to be an issue. Then he decided he didn't really care. He chuckled to himself. He'd walk out of there bare-ass naked if he had to. What were they going to do? Arrest him?

His bellicose mood increased with his hunger. He was sitting up in bed, trying to find out from the computer facet whether the "mystical schema" that the Librarian had told him about earlier included any information on how to make doorways appear when you needed them. The Librarian was once again patiently stonewalling him at every turn, and Duncan had just decided to give up and find someone from whom to demand food when there was a soft noise of footsteps, and a man stepped through his door.

He frowned and looked up. The man had turned back and was shutting the door, quietly. He was dressed like an orderly, but had a furtive manner. A plastic bag, stuffed full of something, hung from his left hand.

The man turned back toward Duncan, and put his finger to his lips.

It was his uncle, Liam Kyle.

Duncan opened his mouth to speak, but Liam shushed him again, and said in a whisper, "I'm not supposed to be here, and you don't have much time. It looks like they're not watching you, but they are. There are monitors all over the place. I took care of a few of them for you, but there are a lot more. I'm surprised I got this far, but it won't take long for them to get here." Liam threw the bag to him. "Clothes. Get dressed and follow me."

Duncan tossed aside the computer facet, and upended the bag. A pair of faded jeans, a sweatshirt, boxers, socks, and two beat-up sneakers fell out onto the bed.

Without saying anything, he stood up, shucked his robe, and quickly donned the clothes.

"Forget the shoes," whispered Liam. "Just bring them along. Come with me."

"Liam..." he started, but his uncle shook his head.

"Later. And I'm not Liam. I'll explain once we get out of here. If we can."

He went to the door, opened it silently, and peered out. He beckoned with one hand.

Duncan padded after him, feet silent on the cold tile floors. The nurse's station looked empty at first, but as he passed it, he saw someone in aide's scrubs lying face down on the floor, partly behind the desk. He looked at Liam in surprise, but he was already past the desk and heading down the hall. Duncan gave a glance back toward his room, and over the door there was a little red light, flashing on and off.

No question what that meant. It was a remote sensor, which he'd just set off. It meant he'd escaped.

Liam, or whoever he was, got to the end of the hallway, poked his head around cautiously, and then turned right and went off at a trot. He followed. About twenty feet further, there was a door on the left that opened into a staircase, and they went inside, but to his surprise, Liam went up the stairs, not down it.

"But..." he started, and again Liam anticipated his question.

Liam shook his head. "No. Up. You've been underground the whole time."

"There was a window," he said, jogging up the stairs.

"You thought there was."

They went up four staircases, each time turning at a landing, passing a door and two more bodies slumped on the tiles. Whether unconscious or dead, he didn't ask. Both wore suits made of some sort of metallic-looking cloth, had helmets on, and were of indeterminate gender. He stepped gingerly past them, and they ascended another set of stairs. By this time, he was winded. But they were approaching the fifth landing when from behind them came the unmistakable sound of pursuit.

"Uh-oh," Liam said. "I think the Huns are about to sack Rome." He was smiling, and looked totally relaxed.

The easy good cheer in his face was so much like his father's younger brother that he couldn't stop himself from saying, "You look *so* much like my uncle..."

"You'd have thought," Liam said, using a slide card to unlock a door on the fifth landing, and holding it open, "that you'd have learned not to trust appearances three or four jumps ago."

A blue-white beam zinged past, blowing a neat hole in the wall right where he had been standing moments before. The heat and the sizzling electricity of its passing stung his face.

Liam let out of a war whoop. "Whoa, mama," he shouted. "Set those phasers on stun, you sonofabitch! You could kill someone!" He slammed the door shut, and grabbed a nearby bench and slid it in front of the door. He added a couple of chairs and an empty gurney on wheels, although what good that would do wasn't clear.

He noticed that the door he'd exited through had a sign that said, *Secure Ward #15-A. Unauthorized Entry Prohibited. Use of Lethal Force Allowed.*

"Slow 'em down," Liam said. "Best we can hope for at this point."

Behind them, the pursuit had encountered the blocked door. There were sounds of banging, swearing, and a couple more blasts on whatever weapon had created the bolt of energy earlier.

"You're enjoying this, aren't you?" said Duncan, following Liam as he took off at a run.

"All in a day's work," he shouted back.

Well, if he wasn't Duncan's Uncle Liam, he sure acted like him. They ducked around a corner as he heard the gurney crash over behind him. Duncan remembered his dad being scandalized when he was discussing football at Thanksgiving dinner, and Liam said, in all apparent seriousness, that the only sport he liked was co-ed naked bungee jumping.

There was a glass-fronted double door ahead of them, and Liam barely slowed down as he stiff-armed both doors open. They swung back and slammed into the walls, almost rebounding hard enough to knock Duncan down as he flew through them seconds later. Then down some steps, and into what appeared to be...

... a formal garden?

A tall clipped hedge lay directly in front of him, bordered by a row of enormous sunflowers. Two lion statues stood on either side of an arbor through the hedge. Although night had been falling, to judge by the view through the window of his room, here it was full daylight, with the sun shining down from a flawless blue sky. He stared, trying to figure out how to make sense of this place, but Liam grabbed him by the arm and shoved him forward.

"Go inside!" he shouted. "Quickly."

"What kind of hospital is this?"

"It's not a hospital," Liam said. "I thought you knew that."

"What is it?"

Another shove, and Duncan stumbled through the arbor.

"It's a prison," Liam shouted, and sprinted off down the lane between the hedgerows and out of sight, leaving him alone.

"A prison?" he said to himself, but at that point, his pursuers, whom he still had not seen, burst through the front door of the building he'd just left. In the moment's glance he had, he saw more of the silvery uniforms, helmets with dark, glossy shields over the faces, and guns. Lots of guns.

He turned and sprinted after Liam. Great. Another world where he was being chased by people with weapons. He ignored a stitch in his side, trying to listen for Liam's footfalls ahead of him. Was it too much to ask for a world where everything wasn't trying to kill him?

The lane between the tall hedges ran straight for a time, and then took a sharp turn to the left. Standing in the corner was a cluster of bright sunflowers in full bloom, but he barely registered them as he ran past. His bare feet made little noise in the soft grass underfoot, and the sounds of pursuit diminished and finally disappeared. His path was straight, with no branches or turns, for about a hundred yards, and when he reached the first gap in the hedge, he slowed to a walk and turned to look behind him.

He saw no one. Whether the silver-suited guards had followed him in, there was no way to tell. Perhaps they'd gone the other way? If they'd come this direction, surely they would be visible by now.

The path ran on straight for some way, but he turned left through the gap to find himself in another, parallel lane, with the same tall hedges, trimmed meticulously to a flat surface that was almost artificial in its perfection. He turned right, for no particular reason, and almost immediately reached another corner, marked by another clump of sunflowers.

It was a maze. A labyrinth. The hospital, or prison, or whatever it was, they didn't have to worry much about escapees, because if someone got out, they ended up caught in the maze. That's why the guys with the silver suits didn't follow him in. There was no need to.

He walked a little farther, and then it occurred to him that he had no idea where Liam went. His rescuer had vanished into the labyrinth as well, but there was no way to know whether he'd taken the same path. The mown lawn beneath his feet preserved no marks, and there hadn't been time for a message to be left, or even a broken branch as a clue. As far as he could tell, Liam might be in an entirely different part of the labyrinth.

Still, being lost in a maze was preferable to being chased and shot at, and even preferable to being cooped up in the hospital under the care of people whose intentions were doubtful at best. He kept walking, stepped through another gap to the left, and this time turned left, following a lane for about fifty yards before it, too, turned a corner marked by the bright, eyeless faces of sunflowers looking down at him from a height of about ten feet.

He wandered on, not even trying to keep track of his path. It was pointless in any case. There were no landmarks, no way to keep track of where he was, and he didn't have any ultimate goal except for avoiding capture for as long as possible. Also, finding Liam and asking him some pointed questions. Clearly some of what Doctor Marshall and the others in the hospital had told him were lies, but was it *all* false? He had doubted from the beginning that he'd actually had a stroke, that a brain aneurysm and subsequent coma accounted for all of his experiences maneuvering his way through the Sephirot. But there was no way to tell how much else was truth.

And, to be honest, the lure of knowledge had been tempting. The Librarian had given him a glimpse of an access to information the likes of which he'd never experienced. It made the internet he knew seem as antiquated as the *Encyclopedia Britannica*. If it was real, if everything Doctor Marshall had told him about this world hadn't been a lie, then this was the first place he'd been in where he could actually have considered staying.

He came to a four-way crossing, and went toward the right. No, he wouldn't stay here even if he found out that what they were offering him was real. There was too much that was awry, too much that Marshall and Felice and the rest were being evasive about. Even the Librarian—he balked every time Duncan had pushed him to answer questions about the Sephirot and what this place actually was. Given his past experience, he was pretty sure everything he was seeing around him was just appearances, designed to suck him in.

But designed by whom?

He didn't have an answer to that.

The path went straight for some time, and then came to another crossroads. This one had a larger central space, with a neat diamond of gravel in the center. In the midst was a granite pedestal on which stood a nude bronze of the god Apollo, holding aloft a sundial. He frowned. The overall effect wasn't of menace. It was more like a hedge maze in a formal English garden than it was a construct to trap prison escapees. He stopped by the statue, listening, and heard nothing but the soft breeze rustling the branches of the hedge, making the sunflowers that stood at the corners sway, nodding.

"Liam!" he shouted.

No answer.

"Liam, if you can hear me, try to find the crossroads with the sundial. There's a—" he looked up at the bronze image, whose stern face was pointing in his direction—"statue of a naked dude holding a sundial here. I'm going the direction that the arrow of the sundial is pointing. If I see any more landmarks, I'll yell."

There still was no sound. He sat down, back against the base of the statue, and put on the shoes Liam had given him, and which had been unnoticed in his hand ever since. Then he struck off down the path pointed out by the sundial arrow.

He'd wandered a little farther when a chilling thought occurred to him. What if the labyrinth had no exit? The more he thought about it, the more likely it seemed. If it really was to keep hospital escapees from getting away, an endless maze of paths with no exit would be the way to do it. Anyone trapped inside would be unlikely to find their way back to the entrance, and would eventually starve or die of thirst.

If they really did want to get information from him, they wouldn't have let him go that easily. There was something else going on here. Was there another reason they didn't follow him in?

Maybe they were afraid to.

A chill twanged its way up his backbone.

But thus far, the labyrinth was nothing more than an endless network of linked grassy pathways, lined by neat, but impenetrable, walls of some close-branched hedge. He tried to wedge himself between the branches, to see if the walls could be breached, should he find himself at some point with only one hedge between himself and freedom, but the tight network of leafy twigs foiled him. The branches were too wiry and tough to break easily, and too flexible to climb.

The only way out of the maze was to find an exit. If there was one.

He wandered aimlessly for another half-hour or so, without encountering anyone or anything. Retracing his steps was out of the question. At this point he wasn't even sure he could make his way back to the intersection with the statue and the sundial.

He remembered hearing once that if you kept one hand on the wall, and turned whatever way you had to to keep the hand in contact with the wall, you'd eventually find your way out of a maze. He didn't know if that was true, and if the maze spread over a hundred acres, it could take days or weeks. He'd drop of hunger long before he'd find his way out.

And it still would do him no good if there was only one way out, the way he came in.

He heard a noise. It was a quiet, grinding sort of sound, like branches scraping against each other. It came in fits and starts. There was a series of four or five dry, scraping noises, then silence. Then three more. Silence. Then almost a dozen in rapid succession.

He frowned, and turned his head in the direction of the sound. It lay directly through one of the hedge walls, but how many lanes stood between him and the source of the noise was uncertain. Equally unclear was whether he should seek it out, or avoid it. Whatever the source of the noise was, it didn't sound overtly hostile.

How on earth did I know that for sure? All bets were off in the Sephirot. Nothing was ever what it seemed.

Curiosity spurred him, however, to see if he could get closer to whatever was making the grating sounds, and he found a gap in the hedge a little further on that took him in the right direction. Now that he had a goal, he paid closer attention to his path, and tried to keep the turns and angles of the maze in his mind as he slowly maneuvered his way closer to the source of the noise. Soon he realized the sound was louder than he'd thought at first. He had been, when he first heard it, at least three or four lanes removed from its origin.

Now, the crunching and scraping sound was much more distinct, and was interspersed with tapping, a sound like wood on stone. Another couple of crunches, and the tapping increased in force and volume, becoming a series of loud knocking noises, followed by a sharp crack.

Then the scraping started again.

A chill ran up his spine. The noises were still unidentifiable, but there was something sinister about them. His feet carried him forward, along a short path and around a corner. Then he turned once more through a gap in the hedge wall, to find himself looking into the largest clearing he'd yet seen.

It was a huge, octagonal grassy lawn, each face of which had an opening. All roads, apparently, led to this place. The first thing he noticed about it was the bones scattered about, drying and whitening on the brilliant green of the grass. In the middle, hunched over and with its back to him, was another statue, of some uncertain material. It appeared to be a monster of some kind. What he could see of it showed rippling muscles in a back that had a strip of long, coarse golden hair, a little like a horse's mane. But its face was turned away from him.

"Holy shit," he said, under his breath.

And the statue turned its head and looked at him with glittering yellow slit-pupiled eyes.

It wasn't a statue, of course. He had assumed it was, fooled by its immobility and its impossibly grotesque silhouette. But the thing swiveled toward him, dropped a cracked bone on which it had been gnawing, and pressed huge fingers onto the grass to lever itself into a standing position. Now that it was facing him, he saw what it was, and was frozen for a moment. The two of them, man and monster, simply stared, for one hanging second.

It was a naked, hulking thing, perhaps twelve feet tall, whose body was more or less human-shaped—legs taut as steel bands, a broadly muscled chest, and prodigiously male. The fingers and toes ended in curved talons. He looked up at the head of the creature, and there all resemblance to humanity ended. Its face was most like a lion of any terrestrial creature, but even that wasn't entirely accurate. A sloping forehead was topped with a back-swept mane of wiry hair, and the glossy golden eyes were unequivocally predatory in expression. The muzzle protruded forward, one lip curled upwards to reveal yellowed canine teeth as long as Duncan's hand. Scattered at its feet were not only piles of human bones, but shreds of clothing, including more than one of the silver suits the prison guards wore.

All of this was registered in an instant. He turned and fled, his breath whistling in his throat, and there was a snarling roar as the monster leaped toward him, the dead bone on which its teeth had been grating forgotten in favor of a tenderer cut of meat.

He turned and twisted his way through one gap in the hedge after another, every moment waiting to feel the thing's claws or teeth sink into his body. He could hear its crashing pursuit, but dared not turn around to see how close it was. After some time, the noises behind him diminished, and he allowed himself a quick look over his shoulder, which revealed nothing but the endless lanes of the maze. The creature, whatever it was, was nowhere to be seen.

He now understood why the guards hadn't followed him into the labyrinth. There was no need to. Either he'd eventually find his way out the way he'd entered, or else he'd meet the Guardian of the Labyrinth and be destroyed. He vaguely remembered some myth or other in which a maze had been guarded by a creature that ate people, but he thought that it was half-human and half-bull, a combination that had struck him as ridiculous at the time.

There was nothing ridiculous about this thing. This monster was death embodied.

Why hadn't it pursued him further? He slowed to a walk, clutching his sides. Did it lose him in the maze? That wasn't likely. Maybe it knew that all the paths ultimately led back to its lair, so all it had to do was bide its time and he'd find his way back and get caught.

He wandered on for perhaps another fifteen minutes, and still heard no further signs of pursuit. By this time, he was famished and thirsty, and light-headed from the exertion. When had he last eaten? It was lunch, but how many hours before? He flopped down on the grass, and looked up at the rectangle of blue that was framed by the ruler-straight top edges of the hedge.

There was no sense in wandering around the maze. His mind slipped downward toward despair. Either he'd end up getting eaten by the Guardian, or he'd get caught by the prison guards. He was safe here, for the time being at least, so he was damned if he'd move. If something was going to happen, it'd have to come find him.

The grass was soft beneath him, and he dozed for a time. The sun arced its way over the top of the hedge and shone full on his face. He only woke when the coolness of a shadow crossed over him.

He sat up, heart hammering, certain the Guardian had found him, and that he was about to be torn to pieces. He shouted, "Please don't kill me!" in a hoarse scream, simultaneously knowing that it would do no good, that he would have done as well arguing with a grizzly bear or tiger or rattlesnake.

A hand clutched his shoulder, and he heard a soft laugh.

"Steady, buddy," said a voice. "You're fine."

His vision came into focus, and he found himself looking up into the smiling face of Liam.

"Where have you been?" he said, trying to control the panic in his voice.

"Wandering," Liam said with a smile. "Like you have been, I guess. This place is huge. It was a hundred to one against my ever finding you."

"Did you see that monster?" he said, and sat up. "The thing in the center of the labyrinth?"

"I've seen it more than once. It's only a problem if you panic. It doesn't follow you far as long as you keep your head and do a little dodge-and-weave."

"That's what I found out."

"It knows there's no way out, so eventually its prey will come to it." Liam grinned. "So it waits. It has to be a great deal hungrier than it is to start wandering around looking for food. They keep it well fed. If there are no prisoners to be disposed of, they pick out a few of the guards who've been slacking in their duties, or maybe ones who pissed someone off, and drive them in. There's a balcony in the prison complex, up on the fifth or sixth floor, that overlooks the labyrinth. They go up there and watch the fun."

"You think they're watching now?" He looked around, but couldn't see over the top of the walls.

Liam shrugged. "Could be. I don't give a flying fuck if they do. I've been in and out of this labyrinth before. We'll wait here until they get tired of watching the entrance, and then go back out the way we came in. There's a way out of the prison complex other than through the labyrinth. This was just a place to hide out until they put away those damn guns."

"What makes you think the guards will be gone when we come back out?"

"We'll find out one way or the other."

He looked at Liam and frowned. "Wait a minute. What's in all of this for you?"

"When I found out they were holding you, I knew you had to be important to them. It was critical to spring you before your resolve weakened, and you gave them what they wanted."

He stood and looked Liam full in the face. "You didn't answer my question."

Liam shook his head, still smiling. "C'mon. You'd still be in there, in an underground cell, thinking you were recovering in a hospital some time in your world's future, if I hadn't saved you."

"That sounds nice. But it *still* doesn't answer my question. You're running all of these risks why? Out of the goodness of your heart? Because you love adrenaline rushes? Because you've got such an advanced set of morals that you can't bear to see a total stranger held captive?"

Liam smiled, and put his hand on his arm, but he shook it off.

"No. I want to know why you're doing this. But you're not going to tell me, are you? You want what they all want. To jump from world to world. But what I don't know yet is why. And before I move from this spot, I want you to tell me why it's so important to all of you people to be able to do what I can do."

There was a low growl from just ahead of them, and the Guardian stepped through a gap in the hedge. Its leonine face wrinkled in a snarl, and its golden eyes looked at him with a hungry expression, but it stopped about ten feet away, its muscles tensed, flexing its taloned fingers. One lip lifted to show a dagger-like tooth.

"That thing doesn't frighten me," he said. "I don't think it's real. I don't think any of this is real."

"That's where you're wrong," Liam said. "Oh, it might not be real from the perspective of your world, but when you're *here*, it's real as hell. You've already felt what these worlds can do, haven't you?"

He frowned, opened his mouth and closed it again, and Liam laughed.

"Of course you have. I bet you've felt plenty from wandering through the Sephirot. It can be sweet. We've heard from other people who've made it this far. If you've been here as long as Marshall and Felice and the others say you have, you've been eating and drinking, and sleeping and laughing and running and fucking. Everything that a man like you needs. You know it can be good." Liam leaned toward him, a broad smile on his lean face. "But it can be bad, my friend. You've felt that, too, I think. And you have no idea how much worse it can get."

There was another noise behind him, the noise of running feet, and he turned to see a half-dozen of the silver-suited guards running toward him, guns drawn. But they halted, as the Guardian had, and now the three formed a triangle, the top point of which was Duncan, facing Liam with his back to an impenetrable hedge. If he dodged around Liam, made a run for it, he would have to run directly into either the Guardian or the prison guards.

"So you have a choice to make," Liam said. "You can fight it, in which case you'll very likely die. If you don't think those guns, or the Guardian's teeth, can kill you, you're wrong." Liam grasped his upper arm again, and this time Duncan didn't resist him. "Or you can show us how to jump, and you can taste the sweet for as long as you want to. Knowledge, you know? That's what we have here. The knowledge of *everything*. All of your questions answered. We can give you that. You can have that forever."

He swallowed, glanced from the guards to the monster, and then looked down.

I have to get out of here. They'll kill me if I refuse.

And suddenly energy poured through him, coming from his belly and up through his chest, and surging from his eyes like twin laser beams. Where he looked, his line of sight left a glowing spot on the green of the lawn.

"Stop," Liam said, his voice rising in alarm. "You can't escape that way."

He drew a glittering line with his eyes, between Liam's feet and his own. "Why not?"

"Because you don't know the danger you're in."

He laughed. Another line, at right angles to the first, like a fiery gash in the grass.

Liam's grip tightened. "The next place after this... you haven't experienced danger yet. No one gets through the next one alive."

A third line appeared. "And my alternative is to stay here and get eaten by the Guardian, or roasted alive by ray guns? That's not good enough? I die here, I die there, same difference."

"You stay here, you don't have to die." Liam's voice rose in alarm. "You can have anything you want. You don't understand what you're giving up. And for what?

For pain and death in a world that is far worse than anything you've yet experienced."

He glanced behind him, and with a flick of his eyes, completed the square around his feet. "I don't trust you. And as far as the next world, I'll take my chances."

The square of grass gave way beneath him like a trapdoor, and he fell through feet-first. The Guardian gave a roar of rage, and there was an outcry of defeated anger from the guards. But Liam, still holding his upper arm, was pulled over and down, and came head first through the portal. Linked, one head upward and one head downward, a positive image and its negative reflection, the two of them fell together from the gold and green of Tiferet into a smoky red twilight that was like a descent into the pits of hell.

CHAPTER 6

GEVURAH

Duncan landed with a breathtaking thud, face down, on some uneven, unyielding surface. Liam's hand still gripped his arm, and it ached, the older man's fingers digging painfully into his biceps. He opened his eyes to take in a scene made mostly from scarlet and gray—an overcast sky with a crimson sun near the horizon, the rough stone façades of buildings, streets made of dirty cobbles, a fire burning in some kind of town square. A hot wind was blowing down, moaning in the tilted eaves of houses and through leafless branches of trees. He rolled over, took a deep, painful breath, and reached up to pry Liam's hand from his arm. Only then did he glance over at the man, who still had not moved.

The next moment, he was on his feet, heart hammering against his ribs, stumbling his way backwards, blindly.

It wasn't Liam Kyle any more, or, perhaps, it never had been. What lay sprawled on the cobblestone streets was a leonine monster, the twin of the one who had been gnawing bones in the middle of labyrinth, except it still had hanging on its bulging arms, legs, and torso the tattered remnants of the orderly's scrubs that Liam had been wearing.

As he stared, panting with terror, the thing opened its eyes halfway, gave a snarling cough, and a pink tongue came out and licked its lips, twisted around one long canine. It fixed him with its slit-pupiled golden eyes, and said, in a deep growl of a voice, "You should have listened to me."

"Liam?" His own voice sounded thin and whistly in his ears.

"You need to get out of this place as soon as you can. I wasn't lying about that." It coughed again. "It's killing me as I lie here. It'll do the same to you."

"What's killing you?"

"You can't feel it? It's poison. It's in the air. I knew I should have let you go when you fell, but I wanted your knowledge too badly. And I'll die of that want."

"There's nothing in the air but smoke."

The hairy lip curled in what may have been a smile. "If you can breathe it and not die, maybe you have a chance here." Another cough, this one painful and rasping and prolonged. "Maybe there's a reason why you can jump and few others can. You can survive, and we can't. We want something we can't have."

"Why are you a monster? You weren't before. You looked like my uncle."

Another baring of the teeth. "I already asked you once. You've come this far and you still believe in appearances?" There was a hitching, gravelly intake of breath, followed by a paroxysm of coughing. "I even told you I wasn't Liam Kyle. You're still not seeing past the surface. I'm surprised this journey hasn't killed you yet. Maybe what you mostly are is damn lucky." The creature beckoned weakly with its taloned index finger. "Come here."

He hesitated, staring at the thing's massive body, its long, yellowed teeth still showing.

"If I'd wanted to kill you, I'd have already done it. You never were in any real danger, not really. Not unless we thought you wouldn't cooperate any other way. We wanted what's in your brain, not what's in your guts."

He went toward the thing, slowly, and knelt down next to it. His heart was beating so hard he thought it would shatter.

"Find a way out of here. Hide. You don't know what you're in for."

"What? Can't you be more specific?"

"Don't you see the pattern yet? Each place in the Sephirot offers you one lesson and one lure, one thing to learn and one reason to give up and go no farther. If you take the lure, that's as far as you get. Here? It's not so much a lure as it is a weapon."

He looked around him at the hellish landscape, now darkening into night. "What's the weapon? Don't cooperate, and we'll kill you?"

The creature nodded its enormous head, and winced a little. "Something like that. If you're fortunate they'll just kill you. Most aren't that lucky." The creature's voice was weakening, hoarse, becoming hard to understand. "Get free of this place as soon as you can. Jump. Anywhere is better than here. What this place has to teach you is nothing worth knowing. Endurance, strength maybe, but you can learn that another way."

"I can't control how to jump."

Another dry laugh that ended with a shuddering grimace. "You're not trying hard enough. You'll have better incentive soon." There was another great, rasping breath, and the thing's eyes went unfocused. Its muscled, furred chest settled, down, down, the air hissing from its broad feline nose.

The chest didn't rise again.

He heard a gasp and a shout, and looked up to see an old woman, clad in a filthy dress, a ragged bonnet around her head, staring at him.

"A demon!" she shouted, pointing at the dead creature lying in the street. Her voice was wild, thin, like the keening of a bird.

"No," he said. "He's not a demon—"

"Demon!" she shouted again, and her bloodshot eyes turned toward him. "Evil! You consort with evil! You brought it here!"

He sprang to his feet. "I didn't bring it deliberately... he followed me..."

Why am I wasting time arguing? Do what Liam said. Get the fuck out of here.

He turned and ran.

By this time, others were coming out of houses and alleys, like the woman dressed in dirty rags, soot smudging faces, eyes dark with suspicion. They looked at Duncan as he sprinted past, then at the fallen monster, and then back at him again, uncertain whether to chase him or to let him go.

He turned down a narrow alley, past rickety structures composed of no straight lines or right angles. He heard noises of pursuit, and ducked as soon as he could down another, narrower lane that curved away and uphill. A thorny bush snagged his clothing and popped free, but not before he had a moment's panicked thought that he'd been grabbed by another taloned claw.

Finally the noises dissipated into silence, broken only by the sound of the wind. The houses here were more widely separated, interspersed by narrow fields with sparse, scraggly crops, and hillsides tangled with brambles. There was a dry, cindery taste to the air that caught at the throat, and he coughed and spat to the side of the road, clutching at his aching sides. He turned into the recessed doorway of a ramshackle building that appeared to be abandoned, and sat down on a cracked front stoop to take a better look at his surroundings.

It was fully night now, and overcast, but there was a reddish glow from the town behind him that lit the underside of the clouds and gave a ruddy cast to the shadows.

What was he in for here? Even Liam was afraid of this place. Maybe if he could find a portal quickly, and jump again before he got caught, he'd be all right.

He recalled his creation of the portals in Netzach and Tiferet.

Perhaps didn't need to find one. Perhaps he could make one.

But try as he might, he couldn't bring back the clarity of vision he'd had in Netzach, and the laser-sharp ability to cut holes in reality he'd somehow conjured up in Tiferet. Whatever those had been, they no more came when summoned than the portals did themselves.

There was no sound of pursuit. Evidently the people in the town had lost his trail, or maybe they had been more interested in the body of the monster than they were in the completely ordinary man who'd been standing next to it. After a time, he dozed, his head on his knees. It was warm enough here, although the wind was incessant, and even in his uncomfortable position he was able to sleep a little.

He dreamed dreams of falling, dreams of being trapped, dreams of being chased as his legs became heavier, heavier, and finally he fell in the middle of the road, and lay, unable to rise. At some point a creaking noise intruded into his dream, and at first it was no more than an annoyance, an irritating *non sequitur* that had nothing to do with anything happening in his sleeping visions.

But it got louder, and more insistent, and finally he said, "What *is* that?" as a hand clenched his shoulder and he jerked awake, breathing hard.

He leaped to his feet, and found himself facing a scrawny old man whose features were barely visible in the ruddy gloom. He got a glimpse of sunken cheeks, a long, beaky nose, and wide eyes.

"What're you doing on my front step?" the old man said in a hoarse whisper. "Who are you?"

"I thought..." He took a deep breath, willing his heart to slow down. "I thought it was an abandoned house."

"It ain't. I live here."

"I see that now. I'm sorry."

"Where'd you come from?" the man said, and his voice dropped even lower. He still had one hand on Duncan's shoulder, and his bony fingers dug into the muscle. He pulled his face close to Duncan's. "You ain't from here."

"I came from the town."

"No, you didn't. You ain't from here. I'm old and poor, but I ain't stupid. I can see you ain't from here. You came in from outside, didn't you? I know you did."

Faced with such certainty, it was pointless to lie. "Okay. Yeah, I came in from outside."

"You'd best hide, then," the old man said. "Them in the town will be after you. And like as not they find you here, they'll take me as well."

"Hide? Hide where?"

The old man swallowed, and a furtive look came into his eye. "You could keep going down the road, but you'll more'n likely get caught before the night's over no matter what. They got spies all around here. You get off the road, it's hard going. Thick with brambles and brush, and wouldn't do you no good anyways, because they'd use dogs to track you and the dogs can go faster in that sort of land than you can." He paused, licked his lips. "I'll shelter you for the rest of the night. I don't mind. Ain't no business of mine, what they want outsiders for, and you look like a nice boy. I got but one bed, but you can sleep in the chair and be comfortable enough, I expect. Then morning comes, we'll talk more about what you might do."

The old man pushed him toward the door of the shack, which was still open, and Duncan walked from the dim light of outside into the full darkness of the shack's malodorous interior. The old man lit a candle, and then shut the door. The candlelight sent flickering shadows across the ceiling, illuminating dark, soot-stained walls, a bare plank floor, a disheveled, narrow bed, a table with one rickety chair. He gestured Duncan toward the only other piece of furniture in the house, a broad chair with a ragged blanket tossed over the back.

"Take your rest there. I'd give you the bed, but I got old bones and an old man's aches, and I wouldn't sleep a wink. I don't know what the sunrise will bring, but it's bound to be better than stumbling in the dark."

"What is your name?"

"I'm called Gade. How about you, stranger from outside?"

"I'm Duncan Kyle."

"Duncan Kyle," Gade repeated.

Duncan pointed toward the only adornment in the place, a tarnished brass star, with the image of a haloed man in the center. It looked old. The paint was scratched, and the loop of wire that it hung from was black with age. The man's face regarded them all with the flat, unreachable tranquility of a Byzantine Jesus, his expression inscrutable. One hand was raised, with two fingers extended, in a salute or benediction.

"That's an icon of Saint Judician," Gade said. "It came from my grandfather. It's all I got of his." Gade looked over at him with a melancholy expression on his thin face. "Don't matter, I guess. But maybe Saint Judician will watch over us. I'll take his help, or anyone's."

"I suppose it couldn't hurt."

Gade's eyes narrowed. He seemed to be trying to figure out if Duncan was mocking him. But he said, "Sleep well, Duncan. And tomorrow we'll see." He blew out the candle, and there was the soft creaking noise of his footsteps on the floorboards, and then a sigh and a groan as he lay down on the bed. After that, silence.

He settled himself as comfortably as he could in the chair and pulled the blanket around his shoulders. He felt sure, as he wriggled his body to move away from something hard digging into his back, that he wouldn't be able to sleep, but sleep overcame him anyway. He fell into a deep slumber, all awareness gone, until he was brought to groggy wakefulness by the combination of the red light of morning coming in through a window and a rough noise, of uncertain origin, somewhere nearby.

He opened his eyes, blinking and trying to focus. The first thing he noticed was that Gade's bed was empty. He thought the old man might have gotten up before him, and be outside doing chores, but before he had a chance to ponder what else might be the cause of Gade's absence, the front door burst open.

Three men, heavily armored and holding daggers that glittered in the ruddy light, came into the little shack.

Gade was behind them, an obsequious expression on his face, but he wouldn't meet Duncan's eyes.

"Are you Duncan Kyle?" one of the soldiers said.

"I am."

"You're under arrest."

He jumped to his feet. "Under arrest? Why?"

The other two men flanked him immediately, and his arms were pinioned behind him. He struggled, but there was no escaping their grip.

The man who had spoken came up to him, until their faces were close. He had a fat face, with a snub nose, and his jaw was fringed with a scraggly growth of beard. "You talk nice, see? Easier all around."

"I want to know why I'm being arrested." His breath whistled in his throat.

"Oh, we got plenty on you. Consorting with a demon, bringing said demon into the town, disturbing the peace." The soldier grinned. "You're gonna have a rough time of it, I think."

"What do you mean?"

The grin widened. "Last fellow who came in from outside and was found guilty of such things, they beheaded him in the middle of the town square. About five hundred people came to watch." He drew a line across Duncan's throat with one stubby forefinger. "Poor fellow. Struggled the whole way to the block. Said his name was Benjamin Bathurst, and that he didn't come here a-purpose, he was some kind of ambassador or dignitary or whatnot and had got here by accident, and would leave soon as he could. He left, all right."

Duncan just stared.

"Kind of glad you happened along. Been a while since we had a nice beheading. Good for business, you know? People set up booths with food and trinkets and such like. Hangings just don't have the same draw, although they are a good bit easier to clean up after."

"This is fucking ridiculous," he began, but was cut off when the fat soldier slapped him hard across the face.

"I told you, you talk nice," he said, and his grin was undiminished. He wagged a finger underneath his nose. "Talking foul like that ain't gonna get you anywhere. Maybe to the block faster."

"Someone's got to listen to me." He tasted blood at the corner of his mouth.

"Oh, they'll listen, all right," the soldier said with a chuckle. "Won't change the outcome. But they'll listen to whatever you got to say." He gave a jerk of his head to the two who held Duncan. "Let's get him where he's going. Sooner we do that, sooner we'll be at breakfast."

Gade, who had been standing behind them, said, in a tremulous voice, "What about my payment? You promised me."

"Oh, right!" the fat soldier said. "How much did I promise?"

"Thirty silver pennies," Gade said.

"That's right." The soldier reached into his pocket, and pulled out a handful of coins. "Here's ten copper. We'll call it even, won't we?"

"You said thirty silver..." Gade started, and then stopped as he looked into the soldier's small, piggy eyes.

"Maybe I did. You want to bring it up to the judge, ain't no skin off my back. Why dontcha wait until Judge Bevans has done with this young fellow? I'm sure he'll be in a good mood after that. Complain away."

Gade swallowed. He still wouldn't meet Duncan's eyes. "No," he said in a defeated tone. "Ten copper is all right."

"Thought you'd see reason. Most men do, given enough information." He let the coins drop, jingling, into the old man's hand, then gave another jerk of his head. "Off we go, boys." To Duncan he said, "Don't try to escape. Don't even think about it. Be a pity if one of my men had to cut your throat before we even got to town."

They hustled him out of Gade's shack, leaving the old man looking after them, his face twisted in a mix of shame and impotent anger. But soon it was lost to view as they turned down the road back toward the town, past stony fields overgrown with gorse and blackberry, a few more houses even more tumbledown than Gade's, and finally, some stone façades of sturdier buildings. A crooked wooden sign marked the entrance of a pub called the Shield & Spear, but it was empty, with shuttered windows and a closed front door. They turned and went uphill, past the clanging din of a blacksmith's shop, an enclosure that held several pigs, and a house where a slovenly-looking woman was putting out laundry to dry. His nostrils were assaulted by the rank combination of smoke, sewage, cooking food, and rot.

Another turn and they walked past a pair of heavy upright timbers with a long crossbeam. Hanging from them were two bodies, a man and a woman, hooded, ropes tight around their skew necks. Their hands were tied behind them, but their feet dangled free, toes pointing toward the ground.

His gorge rose, and a shudder vibrated its way up his spine.

"What did they do?" he said, wondering if even asking the question would earn him another slap, but the fat soldier responded cheerfully.

"Them?" He stuck a thumb in the direction of the two bodies. "Petty thieves. Also caught fornicating without being married first. You know. Can't allow such immorality. Either one alone, they probably wouldn't'a got hanged for it. But both together was too much." He looked up at them. "Least, they both went out of the world together. Wouldn't be fair, leaving one of 'em to grieve. Romantic, ain't it?"

Duncan fought off the urge to vomit, but the rest of the walk into the town was spent in a lightheaded daze, a feeling of surreal horror.

I've got to find a portal. Or make one. I've got to. These people are going to kill me.

But no portal appeared.

"Here we go," the fat soldier said, approaching a heavy stone wall, pierced by only a single, heavily-barred gate. He unhooked a set of keys from his belt and unlocked the gate, then they all passed through and into a broad, flagstone courtyard lined with more, but smaller, barred doors.

"Let's put him in number three," the fat soldier said to Duncan's captors. "That's the most elegant cell we got, don't you think?"

One of the other soldiers cackled, and then he was pushed forward. The fat soldier unlocked the door, and they thrust him into a tiny dirt-floored room with a wooden cot and a stone basin as furnishings. The door clanged shut behind him, and there was a click as the key turned in the lock.

"Relax, Mr. Kyle," the fat one said, his smiling face peering into the barred window of the door. "You might want to spend some time thinking up some good last words. Always gives an air of majesty to the proceedings, that does. I know the spectators would be much obliged if you could do the occasion justice."

He spent the next few hours intermittently sitting on the cot, lying down and trying to sleep, and pacing back and forth in the cell, a distance of only about six feet. He was famished and thirsty, and pounding on the bars and demanding to be fed elicited only a cracked wooden platter shoved through a slot at the base of the door. The platter held a cup of tepid water, a piece of several-days-old bread, and a piece of meat of such uncertain provenance that he decided not to eat it until he was a great deal more desperate than he currently was.

He was lying on his back on the cot, in a light doze, as the minimal light coming in through the window in the door was fading into evening, when there was the sound of the key turning in the lock. He came awake instantly, but any thoughts of a sudden rush and escape were dashed when he saw a pair of guards with drawn daggers, either of whom alone could have successfully blocked the door.

"You're wanted," one of them said, gesturing with the dagger. He had an unpleasant smile on his face. "Judge Bevans wanted to see you right away. Guess you'll be getting it over with sooner than most."

He regarded him with wide eyes, and didn't respond.

The soldier laughed. "Come along, then. Ain't dignified if we have to drag you."

He stood, knees wobbly with fear.

Every time he'd been in serious danger, a portal had appeared. He had to count on that happening again. If they tried to hurt him or kill him, he'd just disappear.

Hopefully.

He went to the guards, who tied his hands behind his back with a leather cord and propelled him along through the courtyard and then up a set of stairs on the other side. There was a broad flagstone patio, and beyond that a much more sumptuous pair of doors, made of some dark wood, carved and embellished with figures and symbols, including a blindfolded Justice, holding a pair of scales, and a woman kneeling and holding shut a lion's mouth. In another corner, a sickle moon presided over the image of a howling wolf. Most disturbingly, along the door frame was the figure of a man hanging by one foot from a scaffold. His other leg was folded behind him, and his eyes were closed, but whether in death or sleep or trance was impossible to tell.

One of the guards opened the door with a key, and they entered a long, stone-floored corridor lit by red torchlight. Chains hung from the walls. The whole thing looked more like a torture chamber than a court of law.

Which was very likely what it was. To listen to those guards the previous night, it could well be a five-minute mock trial and then Duncan's head on the block.

Still, the thought that he'd escaped from dangers at least this dire was a comfort. Diana, and the Jackal Man in Hod, had certainly intended to kill him, and both had failed. It was with that optimistic thought that he was shoved through a door and into a wide chamber, where other guards stood along the walls in the shadows. Vaulted ceilings rose out of sight in the gloom, and on the near wall, the only one he could see, were rings and chains and what looked like cuffs for wrists or ankles. The place smelled of mildew and old blood.

There was only one thing in the room that was clearly lit, and it was a man. The light from a trio of torches fell full on the face of a scarlet-robed figure standing on a dais in the front of the room, watching Duncan with the effortless, malignant patience of a spider.

He was middle-aged, jowly and running to fat, with short, salt-and-pepper hair peeping out from underneath a square red cap that apparently was a mark of his office. His face was deeply creased, set in a disapproving frown. He had his hands laced on the lectern in front of him, and regarded Duncan with an expression somewhere between distaste and outright loathing.

It shouldn't have been a surprise by now, but it always was.

And he said, in a thin voice, "Gabe?"

"Silence!" the man thundered. "You will speak when you are asked a direct question, and not until."

"You are speaking to Darick Bevans, High Judge of Gevurah, you scum," said one of the guards who had brought him in. "Speak civil. He holds your life in his hands."

He stared up at the man's humorless face.

It was Gabriel Carthen. Duncan's boss. Who judged the whole world. Who kind of hated everyone.

And Duncan thought, *I'm screwed*.

Of course it wasn't actually his employer, but he'd had enough experience with the people he'd met in the Sephirot that any hope he had for his safety and freedom died.

Maria, Duncan's sister, had been enigmatic, sarcastic, and clever; so was the Sphinx.

Antonia Syriakis was gorgeous, sexy, and batshit insane. So was Diana, the huntress of Yesod.

Each time, there had been someone who had come through into the new world, some person from his old life—which was increasingly seeming like a distant dream— who had kept the essential part of their personality here.

If that was true, it was no cause for optimism. He recalled a financial consultant who had been one of his coworkers and who had been summarily fired when

Gabriel Carthen found out the man had been sleeping with Gabriel's daughter Emily.

And she'd even interceded on his behalf. Told her father that she'd been a willing participant. No good. The man's desk was cleaned out the following morning, like he'd never existed.

He was pushed forward, and stumbled a little, but kept his feet. He looked up at the familiar face scowling down at him.

"Your name is Duncan Kyle," Judge Bevans said.

"Yes."

"You came in from outside."

There was no possibility of denying it. "Yes."

"Why?"

"I was trying to escape being killed."

There was a rumble of laughter from the people who watched.

"And you brought a demon with you?"

"He wasn't a demon."

Judge Bevans's scowl deepened. "And what kind of infernal creature was it, then?"

"I... I don't know."

"You speak as one as clean of sin as a newborn baby, and yet you were seen talking to the beast. Kneeling next to it, asking it questions, listening to its counsel. If you know nothing about it, why were you holding conversation with it?"

He shook his head. "He didn't look like that in the world we'd come from. And he did nothing evil there. In fact, he saved my life..."

"You owe your life to such a creature, and yet you expect me to believe you have no knowledge of its doings? One need only look at it to know that it is a creature of darkness. What good and honest man looks like that?"

"He *was* a man before we jumped." His voice was becoming desperate.

The Judge nodded. "You used his evil power to come here, not knowing that we were protected against such intrusions."

"I didn't use his evil power—"

"Silence. If you were not in league with evil, then why did you run? An innocent man does not run from other innocent men. He stands, confident in his righteousness."

"The people in the town saw the beast, and were already accusing me of bringing in demons. I was afraid—"

"Because you knew it was true!"

"No! I—"

"You are in league with the infernal powers. Your very words give it away."

"I don't know what you're talking about."

"You have visited many worlds. Bringing death and destruction to every one. The same as you intend here."

"I don't have any such—"

"Silence." Judge Bevans looked around him. He gripped the lectern with both hands. "Do you deny that you have visited other worlds before this one?"

"I have not harmed any—"

"Do you deny it?"

He looked at the Judge.

No matter what he said, it was going to be turned around to incriminate him. It was like the Salem Witch Trials.

"No," he said.

"As I thought. And you brought evil into those worlds, too. You dare not gainsay me."

"I have never set out to hurt anyone—"

The Judge nodded. "So say all who consort with evil. They never intended it. They only had the good will toward all, never wished to harm a soul."

Again, there was a murmur of laughter from the guards and the others watching.

This was theater. Everyone here knew what's going to happen. They were enjoying watching him squirm.

"We will allow you to confess," the Judge said, opening his hands toward Duncan in a conciliatory gesture. "If you confess now, you will receive as much mercy as the law allows."

He swallowed.

Confess? Confess what? Confess to a lie?

He shook his head, a convulsive, terrified gesture. "No," he said. "I did nothing wrong."

"And that is your sworn word on the subject?"

"Yes."

Judge Bevans was unsurprised. "Very well. By lying under oath, you bring your punishment on yourself." He gave a gesture with one hand to the shadowy figures standing watch, and Duncan was seized with rough hands and forced toward the wall to one side of where the Judge was standing. The cord tying his hands was undone, but his hands were forced upward and bound with leather straps to a pair of rings in the stone. His feet were kicked apart, and then his ankles were secured in the same fashion, leaving him spread-eagled, facing the rough stone.

He turned his head and saw a huge man, stripped to the waist, approaching with a drawn dagger. The man wore a hood over the top half of his head, and dark eyes glittered through eyeholes cut in the front.

"What?" he said, aware that he was babbling pitifully, but unable to stop himself. "Are you going to stab me? But I didn't do anything…"

But the man used the knife to cut a slit in the back of his shirt. Then he tore it in half, pulling the pieces outward over his shoulders, exposing his bare back.

The man looked over at Judge Bevans. "How many?" he said, in a heavy, rough voice.

"Start with two dozen. Perhaps he'll sing a different tune after that. You may administer the punishment."

Duncan watched, heart hammering against his ribs, sweat running in rivulets down his chest, as the hooded man unhooked a many-thonged whip from a peg on the wall. He ran the leather cords through his hand, tentatively, and then gave it a low swing or two.

Now. He needed a portal now. Now. A portal. To any-where.

The muscles in his back rippled, tensing, trying to pre-pare. He clenched his teeth and closed his eyes. Then his thoughts were cut off by pain as the first lash landed.

He'd thought that the gash from Diana's arrow had been painful, but that was a mere scratch compared to this. The man with the whip knew what he was doing, waiting a full, slow count of ten between each stroke. By the eighth lash he screamed every time the whip fell. By the eighteenth he was crying.

But finally it was over. The hooded man stepped back, as if to admire his handiwork, shaking droplets of blood from the whip thongs.

Duncan hung limply from the straps binding his wrists to the rings, still shuddering with sobs.

"You may consider your confession until the morning," Bevans said. "That much mercy we will show, even to an acknowledged practitioner of hellish arts. If you are not convinced by the tale your back will tell you tonight, we have other, and worse, ways to persuade. Think carefully."

The man who had flogged him rehung the whip on the wall, and then unstrapped his arms and legs. He nearly collapsed. He was close to fainting from the combination of adrenaline, pain, and blood loss, but managed to keep his feet. When he lowered his aching hands, the torn remnants of his shirt slid from him and crumpled to the floor, and he slowly turned to face the judge, who watched him with an impassive expression.

"Till tomorrow morning, then," Judge Bevans said.

"And I die regardless." He cleared his throat to try to steady it. "Either way, you're going to have me executed."

"As a practitioner of infernal arts who brought a demon into our world with foul intent, there is no other course. However, you can go to the block and be released from your suffering easily, or only find the peace of death after further... attention from my attendants. Trust me, a flogging will seem like nothing at all if you choose that way."

He raised one hand to wipe away the tears and snot on his face. Even that motion caused his lacerated back to scream at him. He opened his mouth to answer, thought better of it, and just shook his head.

"Take him away, then." The judge gave a motion of his hand to the soldiers who had brought him in. "Bring him back in at sunrise, and we will hear what the night's counsel has told him."

He was once again grasped, none too gently, and pushed back out of the room, down the hall, and out of the building, retracing his steps back to his tiny prison cell. The guards locked him in without saying a word, and he staggered to the cot and fell face first onto it.

At first all he could think about was the agony of his raw, welt-covered back, but as he lay there, trying to slow his breathing down, the pain became manageable. But then he was taken in a different direction by fear. His mind raced through all of the horrible things they could do to his body, worse than flogging, things involving knives and red-hot brands and steel pincers. A paralyzing terror and nausea rose up in him.

He could face death. He could deal with that. But he couldn't face torture. Was it worth giving his body to them so he could have the very short-lived satisfaction of not having lied?

He turned his head and stretched, wincing at the ache as movement pulled against the crisscrossing whip cuts on his skin.

He couldn't do it. He couldn't take more. Even if he told himself now that he'd stand up for what he knew to be true, the first time they showed him the torture equipment, He'd be pissing himself and begging them for mercy.

He had not confronted the imminence of his death since his near-freezing at the hands of the Heat Vampires in Malkuth. It felt like years ago. And even then, the cold there had come with a sort of peace, not with this crimson-tinted heat and blood and agony.

He knew in that moment he would stand there and confess. His cheeks burned with shame and misery at the realization. He would tell that asshole judge whatever he wanted to hear. He'd confess to anything at this point, just to be put out of his misery in as quick and easy a way as possible.

He slipped into a light, uncomfortable doze, waking up at some uncertain time later to a tapping on the cell door. At first he thought it was some natural noise, a small animal, perhaps, or a branch rattling against the roof. But it was insistent and regular, and he came back to wakefulness and alertness, lifting his head and frowning a little.

"Hey," came a quiet, hoarse male voice.

"Yes?" he said, hesitantly, not entirely sure he wasn't dreaming.

"They did quite a job with your back, young fellow."

"Yeah. He did."

"You're a mess. Can't tell where one whip stroke ends and another begins." There was a chuckle. "I've seen worse, though. Guy last year got flogged in the town square for breaking into people's houses and stealing. Been going on for some time, but they finally caught him. Sentenced to a hundred. By the time they was done, you could see the white of his backbone. Flayed him, I'd say."

He grimaced and swallowed. "How could you survive something like that?"

"Oh, he didn't. I think he was dead at about fifty or so. But they gave him the whole hundred anyhow. A sentence is a sentence."

"Why are you here?" His voice rose in anger. "Are you trying to scare me?"

"Naw. I'd guess you're scared plenty already."

"You could say that."

"They're already setting up in the town square. I saw 'em just now. Getting the scaffold ready, sharpening the axe, all that sort of thing. Gonna be a big event."

"Why are you telling me this?" he shouted, and struggled up off the cot. He went to the little window in the cell door, but could see nothing through it but darkness and the reddish underside of the omnipresent clouds.

"Only making sure you know you ain't got much time. One way or other, tomorrow morning's it. And you got to find a way out of this before then."

"Is there a way out?"

"That's for you to figure out."

"So you're not going to let me out, or anything."

Another chuckle. "Naw. I don't got the key in any case. Ain't you seen yet that you don't get out of *anywhere* till you unlock the door your own self? Each place, it's been the same. You just ain't understood the pattern yet. But in this one, there's a clock running, and it's not gonna slow down because you beg it to. You got to figure out how to stop what they're planning on doing to you."

"Otherwise I die."

"Otherwise you die."

"So there is a way out?"

"Only if you make one. I can't tell you where it is, mostly because I don't know. And it may cost you. It may cost you blood or pain or both."

"It already has."

"I suppose that's right," the voice said. "But it ain't over. And I know one thing—you give up, it's going to be out of reach, and you'll end up with your head on the block tomorrow morning, and a couple of seconds later, falling into a basket. This place don't play fair."

Duncan said, quietly, "Maybe none of them do."

"That's right. But this one's especial harsh. You weaken for a moment, you'll be taken out like yesterday's garbage, and then you'll be forgotten."

He didn't answer for a moment.

He finally said, "I think I understand. I still don't know what I'm going to do, though."

"I expect it'll be clear when it's time. Or not. I dunno. I'm not a scholar. But what I do know is you will only survive if you grab this world and twist it yourself, instead of letting it twist you. Look at what they already done to you. You'll be carrying the scars of that whipping for the rest of your life."

"I know."

"So tomorrow, we'll see," the voice said, echoing the words Judge Bevans had uttered earlier. "I'll be really sorry if I see you on the scaffold, but by then, there'll be nothing more anyone can do for you."

The voice didn't speak again. Eventually Duncan went back to the cot, and once again lay face downward.

He spent the rest of the night alternately dozing and letting his mind run over what he could possibly do. It crossed his mind to wonder if the man who spoke to him might have been lying, but he immediately discounted that possibility.

He'd started relying more on his intuition. And so far, it hadn't let him down. And his intuition said that the guy was telling the truth. He had no logical reason to believe that, but it felt right. And that meant he did have a chance, if only he recognized it when it appeared.

He had to be ready to pounce. In Yesod, he'd had to think like a deer. Here, he needed to think like a leopard.

And those were the thoughts going through his head when the first scarlet light of morning stained the undersides of the clouds, and a key fumbled in the lock on his cell door.

"Good morning," said a familiar voice, and he squinted up to see the fat soldier who had arrested him in Gade's shack. He was once again accompanied by two helpers, who stood behind him, leering at Duncan eagerly.

"Oh, look at you," the fat soldier said, gesturing at his welt-covered back. "They did you good, poor thing. I told you to talk nice to 'em."

"I did."

"Wish I coulda seen 'em give you those," he said, in a wistful tone, grabbing him by the arm and yanking him upright. "I do love to watch a good flogging. Most of the sport we get, it's soon begun and sooner over, you know? Don't take long to cut a man's head off, nor to hang him neither, leastways not if you know what you're doing. Floggings, on the other hand, go on and on. But I expect you found that out, didn't you?"

He didn't answer.

"That looks like Torgill's work. Head torturer, he is. Man's got an arm. One lash is worth twenty, when he's holding the whip."

He was hustled out of the cell. The air outside was dry and hot and had the acrid smell of old smoke. His knees almost buckled from the combination of fear and pain, but willed himself not to faint.

He had to see this through, that's what that man had told him last night. And he had to keep his wits about him, or he'd miss his chance.

"Before we bring you to the Judge, one thing I'd like to show you," the fat soldier said. "Just by way of giving you an idea of what you're in for. So you can prepare yourself, you know." They crossed the courtyard, but instead of going up the broad steps into the Judge's chamber, they turned left and went through a narrow gate, and then up a winding staircase that smelled of mildew, through a wooden door, and into what appeared to be a stone guard tower. There was a bench and a couple of rickety wooden chairs, and leaning against the wall was a bundle of spears. Otherwise the room was empty.

He was pushed up to a window that was nothing much more than a rectangular hole in the wall, and found himself looking out over the town square.

"Look at that," the soldier said, gesturing with one hand. "All for your benefit, you know? Look at all the trouble they're going to. Hope you're properly impressed."

In the middle of the square was a scaffold. Stairs led up to a wide platform, in the center of which was a heavy wooden block. A broad axe stood next to it, and beside the block was a wicker basket. Dirty straw lay strewn about. Below there were booths being set up, and there were already people milling about, looking up at the scaffold and talking quietly among themselves, and men and women hawking food and trinkets.

"Sight to behold, ain't it?" the soldier said. "Already a crowd and the festivities ain't even scheduled to begin for another hour at least." He poked Duncan's bare chest. "You want to make a good show this morning. Otherwise, what's the point? Confess to the Judge quick, and get it over with like a good man. Nothing to be gained by prolonging your ordeal, and after a while, it spoils the whole thing for everyone. Them whip marks on your back are all right. Those'll get the crowd on your side, a little, make 'em sit up and pay attention. Mark of courage, you might say, shows you can take it like a man.

Also it'll put the fear of the Judge in 'em right enough, and that's all to the good for keeping law and order. But much more than that, and it's not fun for the spectators any more. You start protesting your innocence in front of Judge Bevans, and next thing you know you're missing so many body parts there ain't much of you left, specially if it's Torgill handling the equipment. One guy I remember never would confess, and by the time he went to the block he had to be carried up the stairs to it. Doubt he even knew what was happening at that point. Disappointing for everyone. My advice is, make a grand show of it. Confess what you done to the Judge, then go up there to the block with your head held high. Think up some defiant last words if it makes you happy. Better for all concerned, and a fine spectacle for them as come to see you off."

He looked at the scaffold and block, then at the fat soldier's grinning face, and the world started to go silver. His knees buckled, and the two guards caught him by the upper arms to keep him from falling.

"Oh, now, look what I done." The soldier's mocking voice came from what seemed a long way away. "Poor fellow, he's gone all wobbly. And me just trying to give him some sage advice."

He barely registered going back down the staircase, out into the courtyard, and then up toward the Judge's chambers.

Focus. Stay with it. There had to be a way out of this, other than up the steps to the scaffold. But he wouldn't get there by passing out. It was time to man up or give up. There weren't any other options.

Down the hall and into the broad, vaulted chamber where he had been flogged. Judge Bevans, still in his scarlet robes, stood behind the lectern as if he had never left the evening before, his face in its perpetual frown. The light was a little better, coming in through high slit windows in the stone wall, showing about a dozen men standing in the shadows watching.

"And what counsel has last night's punishment brought?" the Judge said.

"That I cannot confess to something I know I haven't done." He hoped his words sounded braver than he felt.

A murmur went around the room.

The Judge gave a gesture with one hand. Two men came forward, carrying a wooden rack filled with metal tools—pliers, pincers, knives, rasps—and set it in front of Duncan.

"Consider your words well," the Judge said. "And look at the tools that lie before your eyes. The evil will come out whatever you choose to do, but it can be with great pain or with less. That decision is yours."

"What if I'm innocent?"

Judge Bevans gave a dismissive wave of the hand. "Yet we know you are not."

"No," he said, his voice stronger. "Listen to me. What if you're wrong? Anyone can be wrong sometimes. What if you're wrong about me, and I'm telling the truth?"

"Useless sophistry. Trying to delay the inevitable."

"You didn't answer my question."

The Judge's hands clenched into fists. "You are guilty. There is no question to answer, other than whether you will admit to it before being tortured or after it."

"No!" he thundered. Even the Judge's impassive face showed some surprise. "Answer my question, dammit! Suppose I am innocent. You know it's possible. No man is infallible. Suppose when you go home, tonight, and are trying to sleep, the thought crosses your mind, 'Maybe I sent an innocent man to the executioner this morning.' What will you feel then, Judge Bevans? Are you as certain as you seem?"

For a moment, he thought that his words had struck home. The Judge's scowl deepened, and he didn't answer. Then he brought both hands, palm downward, onto the lectern.

"Lies from the pit of hell. You think to cloud my mind. You were seen talking to a demon. You ran from innocent, honest people, and compound your sins by lying to the High Judge of Gevurah. You wish this fate, even now that you see the tools that will be used on your body? You choose a difficult death rather than an easy one? You cried out pitifully under the whip, but you have not experienced pain yet." His mouth curled in a sneer. "Very well. So be it." He turned his head a little to the left. "The head torturer come forward. Bring me Duncan Kyle's right ear."

A massive figure stepped from the shadows. It was Torgill, the head torturer, the man who had whipped him the night before. He still wore a black hood, and was stripped to the waist, his massive arms folded across his chest. He went to the rack of tools and selected a long, thin knife with a blade that glowed crimson in the reddish light. Then he advanced toward him, mouth twisted in a cruel smile.

This was to be no slow, ceremonial act. The man was upon him in seconds. The knife came up. And with no conscious thought, he leaned back into the two soldiers who were still holding his upper arms, brought both feet up, and kicked Torgill solidly in his ample gut.

The breath went out of the man in a great *whoosh*. The blade went sideways, slicing a long gash in Duncan's cheek, and then fell clattering to the floor. The Judge gave a shout of, "You dare to strike out..." but was drowned out by a roar of rage from the head torturer, who retrieved the knife with one motion and bore down on Duncan like a charging bull.

"Stop!" the Judge shouted.

It was doubtful that Torgill even heard him. Bellowing with fury, he lunged at Duncan with the knife.

He twisted out of the way, but not far enough, and the point drove deep into his side.

Snarling, Torgill jerked the knife out. For a moment the two men were nose to nose, Duncan's eyes wide and terrified, Torgill's narrowed to slits, glowing with an anger that was barely human. Then the knife swept upward in a glittering, crimson-edged arc, as Torgill's thickly-muscled arm prepared to bring it down toward Duncan's naked chest and pierce him to the heart.

But before the knife could descend, two guards ran at the head torturer, who in short order found himself a prisoner, pinioned between them, struggling and still making inarticulate noises of anger. His arm was twisted back until he dropped the knife clattering to the floor. The other spectators erupted in a chaotic noise of shocked conversation. This was probably not the spectacle they had expected to see, but it was sport enough. There was even some harsh laughter and shouts of encouragement.

"Let 'em go at each other," said a rough voice. "This is better than letting Torgill butcher that fellow like a sheep. He's got some spunk. Give 'em both knives, and let 'em fight!"

The Judge shouted for silence, but no one listened.

"Fight!" someone else cried out, and then others took up the chant. "Fight! Let 'em fight to the death!"

His knees folded again, and this time he couldn't stop it. His guards let him collapse to the floor, perhaps because they thought he was mortally wounded or already dead.

Blood flowed from the wound in his side, and he clasped his right hand to it. He was on the floor, trying desperately to remain conscious, chest heaving. Blood fell in crimson drops from the gash in the side of his face, and as they hit the floor, the stone sizzled as if it were burning.

At first, staring down at the rough, stained rock of the torture chamber floor, he thought he was hallucinating, having visions borne of terror and pain and the nearness of death. The drops of blood looked like rubies, shining with their own light, and they left deep melted trails behind them as they moved, as if they were lava, burning away and purifying the filth of Gevurah, the tears and sweat and old blood of countless men and women who had suffered and died there.

And he understood. He looked at the glowing red droplets dancing on the rough gray rock beneath him, and he smiled.

Then laughed.

He crawled toward the lectern, and reached out with the index finger of his right hand to paint a vertical line on it with his own blood. The wood fumed and sizzled and blackened beneath it. He drew another upright line, and then connected the two. Smoke rose from it, but this wasn't the acrid fume of burning garbage that he had had in his nostrils ever since arriving in Gevurah. This was incense, this was every sacred and holy scent of burned sacrificial offering ever given and ever accepted with delight by the gods.

He reached out his left hand, and pushed in the center of the square of charred wood. The piece snapped like tinder, and fell forward. And in front of him was a wind-blown hillside covered with grass, and a blue sky.

But the Judge reached down and grabbed him by the hair, and dragged him to his feet. "Stop. You won't escape that easily. You have called up the infernal powers to assist you, but you will see that we are stronger."

"No," he said, and his voice was weak but clear. "That's the problem with you and your kind. You will never admit it when you're beaten." He reached out his blood-covered right hand and grabbed the man's face.

Judge Bevans recoiled and screamed, pawing at his face as tendrils of smoke curled upwards from the bloody handprint that covered it like a scarlet star. Duncan fell back to his knees, and crawled toward the doorway.

He was halfway through, the front part of his body already out in the sun and warmth and soft grass, when a hand caught him around the right ankle. He cried out and turned to see the face of the fat soldier peering through what looked like a square window into hell. Duncan twisted, his fingers digging into the soil.

"Oh, come now," the soldier said, and his piggy eyes regarded him with a crazy glee. "You mustn't cheat us of our morning's spectacle. The crowd wants blood. What shall we give them?"

"Your own," Duncan said, and with his last bit of strength he kicked his left heel into the man's face. There was a crunch and a scream, and the soldier let go of his ankle.

The portal winked out of existence. He half jumped, half collapsed into a blue-green expanse of deep grass, and there was a warmth that was like being enveloped by a tropical sea. He sank into it, and for a long while, knew nothing more.

CHAPTER 7

CHESED

Duncan opened his eyes to dim light filtering into a little room through slatted shades. A warm, humid breeze made the thin bamboo strips sway gently, and from outside there was a sound of wind chimes. He lay on his belly, and his bloodstained jeans had been removed, although he still wore the boxers Liam had given him in the hospital/prison in Tiferet. A soft blanket covered him to the waist.

His entire body was a mass of misery. His back felt like it had been sliced to ribbons. A deep throbbing ache came from his side and from the gash on his right cheek. He moved one hand, and even that small motion made the scabbed-over welts on his back cry out. But he probed his side, then moved his fingers up to his face, and found his wounds had been dressed, and were covered with a clean, dry cloth binding.

He turned his head, groaning as he did so. He was on a thin mattress, with a cylindrical pillow under his head. Trying to ignore the pain, he raised himself up onto his elbows and looked around.

The room he was in had a polished wooden floor, and walls that were painted a neutral cream color. Hanging from a peg by the door was a long, narrow painted scroll, with a sparse stylized image of a tree on a rocky hillside. A wicker chair sat near the window. There was a simple table next to the bed, on which sat a porcelain cup, a graceful blue ceramic pitcher, and a bowl of rice, next to which was a set of bamboo chopsticks.

"You're awake," came a soft voice.

He had to exert all of his self-control not to twist around in bed. He caught himself in time, with the realization that it would cost him in pain and possible re-injury to move that quickly.

I know that voice. Weak tears came to his eyes. *But she won't be any more real than any of the others have been—Gabe, Liam, my parents, Tania, Antonia, Maria. Don't get your hopes up...*

He slowly turned around, and found himself looking up into the eyes of his girlfriend, Libby Chen.

Her long black hair was pulled up into a complex knot at the base of her neck, and she wore a sky blue wrap with a broad indigo belt, knotted at the waist. She was barefoot. Around her neck was a slender silver chain, but that was the only jewelry she wore.

She never was much for adornments, he recalled, with a painful twist in his heart. *She is beautiful enough without them.*

But he knew immediately that he had been right not to accept what he saw. In her brown eyes there was nothing more than a gentle compassion. No recognition, no excitement of seeing a lover who had been lost. With an ache that for a moment outstripped the pain of his injuries, he knew that this was a strange woman in Libby's guise, just as the others had been strangers posing as people he knew.

She came to him and poured water from the pitcher into the cup and handed it to him, her eyes modestly lowered. He took it, and drank it gratefully.

"I'm glad to see that you've awakened," she said, and went to the chair. Her expression was one of deep sympathy. "Are you in much pain?"

"I'm hurting, yes. But it's tolerable. Thank you for caring for me."

"My father cleaned and dressed your wounds. He tried to wash the cuts on your back, but they were so many... he did what he could. He was afraid to hurt you too badly, and thought it better to let you sleep once the bleeding was stanched."

"Give him my thanks."

She nodded. "There is food. Nothing but cold rice at first, my father said. He did not know what your belly would tolerate after your injuries and loss of blood. But if you feel that you can, perhaps a little food would help." Her forehead creased, and her eyebrows drew together. "Who did these things to you? We found you on the hillside near my father's kiln, with the blood staining the ground underneath you. But there were no footprints in the grass, nothing to show where you'd come from, or how you had been hurt." She shook her head. "I thought at first you were dead."

"I was whipped. And then a man stabbed me. I got away in time to escape further torture and certain death. I don't know if I can explain how I got here."

She put one trembling hand to her mouth. "What had you done to deserve such treatment? Even the worst criminals are shown more mercy than this."

"As far as I know, I hadn't done anything. I was followed by someone who looked to their eyes like a demon, so they thought I had brought him there to harm them. Even though I told them the truth, they sentenced me to be flogged and then executed."

"To be able to treat someone so inhumanely. I cannot comprehend it."

"Me either." He laid his head back down on the pillow.

"If you wish to rest, you should," she said. "If the pain becomes too much, my father has a syrup made from poppies that will ease you into sleep. He will come in later to check on you, when his chores are finished."

"Thank you. It is wonderful to be treated with kindness, after being under the threat of death. For now, I don't need anything more."

Duncan slept uneasily. He awoke to the sound of rain, and a gray-blue twilight was all that was visible through the slatted window covering. He was hungry, and with many winces and groans he maneuvered himself into a sitting position on the edge of the bed and ate all of the rice in the bowl. It had been lightly seasoned, but he couldn't at first identify the flavors. Perhaps vinegar, and something a little garlicky. It was subtle, but his belly accepted it gratefully. The last time he'd eaten was the dry bread in the prison cell in Gevurah, before he was whipped, and that was a day ago, perhaps more.

He stood, moving carefully, and went to the window and pushed aside the shade. Silver sheets of rain fell over rolling hills covered with silky, rippling grass. A few cedar trees stood nearby, their frond-like branches dripping and glossy.

The door opened, and a small man came in. He had a narrow, shrewd face, with dark eyes set in a nearsighted squint. He moved with a brisk efficiency, hands clasped behind his back. Rainwater plastered his thinning black hair to his scalp and darkened the shoulders of his shirt, which was a plain-cut wrap a little like a short robe made of tan linen and tied closed with a cloth belt.

He looked at Duncan with a frown.

"Up, are you? You must be careful at this stage. All too easy to reopen a wound, and then where will you be?"

"I'm being careful."

"You have taken terrible injury. You are lucky to be alive. But with more luck, you will recover, although your skin will carry many scars." He looked at Duncan's back, and probed one of the cuts with his finger.

"Ow!" Duncan jerked.

"Yes. It will be a long recovery. I should clean those again. It will keep them from festering." He looked up at Duncan and raised a dark eyebrow. "It will hurt."

"I can take it."

"It seems that you can, to have survived such treatment at all. But you are not done with pain yet, I fear." He patted Duncan's bare shoulder. "I am called Shao Bolin. I think you have met my daughter, Shao Daiyu."

"Yes." Duncan opened his mouth to speak further, and then closed it again.

Shao Bolin laughed. "You wonder, I think, that a homely man like me has a daughter so beautiful. And I have no wife in another room whose appearance might explain it." He flashed a smile at him.

Well, that's not what he was wondering. But he couldn't ask the questions yet, not the ones he most wanted answered.

"Daiyu was a child of war. When our armies swept through a village in a neighboring country, the inhabitants fled or were killed. One of the soldiers found a baby girl, recently born, crying on a blanket in one of the huts. He took pity on her and brought her back, but could not care for her, so he looked for someone who was willing to raise her. I was married then, but childless, and took her in. And we gave her a name and raised her as our daughter, until my wife died three years ago. At that point Daiyu was old enough to marry, but she chose to stay on and help me. She is dearer to me than many a daughter to a father, however she is not of my blood."

He looked at Shao Bolin closely. Libby, too, had been an orphan, adopted by an older couple who raised her as family. So what other characteristics would Shao Daiyu bring from the Libby Chen he knew? Her gentleness?

Her sense of humor? The crooked little smile she wore when she was up to something?

But he couldn't let himself slip into thinking she was Libby. It was easier with the others, even with Maria, and his mother and father. But this struck near to the heart. And he knew that if he got sucked in, he'd never leave. What had Liam called it?

Falling for the lure and not seeing the lesson.

But Shao Bolin was speaking again.

"Lie back down. I will get warm water and see to washing your wounds. Then we will bring you food, if you feel that you are strong enough to eat."

"I am."

Bolin smiled. "Perhaps you should wait until after I am done with your back to decide that. Afterwards, you may not be thinking about eating."

Washing the blackened scabs on Duncan's back took nearly an hour. Shao Bolin painstakingly cleaned each of the hundreds of lacerations that the leather cords had cut in his skin, using a soft cloth and a bowl of warm water. Bolin's hand was extraordinarily gentle, but several times Duncan cried out with the pain of it, burying his face in the pillow to keep from screaming. But finally it was done, and Bolin gently dried his damaged skin. He peeled back the bandage on Duncan's side. That far deeper and more serious wound had already closed, and there was only a little blood staining the bandage.

"It will heal," Bolin pronounced. "Luck being with you. And luck you have already had, however you may not feel that way at the moment. A wound there, in your side, could have pierced your vitals, and you would very likely now be dying from it, and beyond my skill to save. Scars you will bear to your grave, but no worse than that." He replaced the bandages on Duncan's side and face with fresh ones, treated with a bit of ointment that reminded him of the salve that Fatima had used on the arrow graze on his thigh in the deserts of Hod.

"Why were the men who held you trying to kill you?" Bolin said, once he was lying comfortably on the bed once more.

"Because they thought I was conspiring with a demon. Which I wasn't. But when I said I wouldn't confess, they tortured me, and were going to send me to the executioner to be beheaded."

"Did it not occur to them that a man will say anything, true or false, to escape torture?"

He sighed. "I pointed that out to them."

"Fools, then," Bolin pronounced. "And a fool wielding a whip is still a fool."

"Didn't make it hurt any less."

"No. And such weapons are perhaps more dangerous in the hands of foolish men. Intelligent men you can reason with."

"There was no reasoning with these people. I was less than an hour from losing my head when I escaped."

"I would like to hear about your escape, but that must wait for another time. For an injured man, even conversation is tiring."

"I've done little but sleep, but I'm still exhausted."

Bolin nodded. "But before you rest, are you still hungry? Or has the ordeal of my doctoring you driven all thought of food from your mind?"

"I can still eat. It'll take more than that to put me off my feed."

Bolin laughed. "I left Daiyu preparing our meal. I will bring you some, and with it, a vial of a syrup I learned how to brew from my grandfather. It will assuage your pain and give you a night's comfortable sleep."

Bolin left, taking the bowl with the blood-fouled water and cloth with him, leaving him alone with his thoughts.

What would the catch be here? So far, it looked good, but so had Yesod at first. And trusting what he saw there nearly cost him his life.

But he'd grown since then. He wasn't the shallow guy he'd been back home. He wouldn't be fooled by Diana now. It would take more than an offer of sex, or friendship, or comfort, or even knowledge to trap him. In Gevurah he was able to fight back against pain and torture and the threat of execution with more courage than he knew he had. So whatever the twist was here, it would have to be pretty subtle to hook him.

Daiyu came in a few minutes afterwards, carrying a tray. He resisted the urge to ask her if she knew who Libby Chen was, if she knew that in another world, a woman exactly like her had been his lover. He knew what the answer would be.

Keeping his voice steady with an effort, he said, "Thank you."

"It is simple enough fare," Daiyu said. "Fish in broth, and rice, and wild vegetables."

"It sounds wonderful."

"Is it the sort of thing you eat, in the place where you are from?"

"Close enough." He smiled, and with some effort he sat up. She set the tray down on the bedside table, and he looked at the little china bowl with a serving of fragrant and steaming fish stew. "I'm sure it will be delicious."

She pointed to a blue ceramic cup, filled with a thick brown liquid. "The little cup has a measure of the poppy syrup I mentioned when we spoke earlier. When you are done with your meal, drink all of it. It takes perhaps fifteen minutes to work. You should do whatever is necessary for your comfort before then—afterwards, you will not be steady on your feet."

She blushed a little, and turned away from him.

"Daiyu?"

"Yes?" She looked back in his direction, but did not meet his eyes.

"Thank you. You and your father saved me. If it hadn't been for you, I would have bled my life away out there on the hillside. I don't know how I could ever repay you."

She lifted her eyes, and for a moment, they met his. She gave him a smile, and for a fleeting moment her expression was so like Libby's that the tears started to his eyes.

"There is no repayment," she said, in a quiet, low voice. "We could not do otherwise."

Then she turned and left.

The poppy syrup knocked Duncan out for a solid ten hours. When he woke the next morning, a warm breeze brushed his face, carrying with it the scent of the previous evening's rain. He carefully maneuvered himself into a sitting position and looked around. The whole place exuded peace, as if the house sat in a little oasis, saturated with calm, where the quiet and tranquility were nearly real, tangible substances, flowing down from the blue-green hills in a silent river.

He stood. Some time during the night, a pair of lightweight cream-colored pants had been laid across the chair. There would be no wearing a shirt for many days. Fortunately the weather was warm and comfortable. With many winces and groans, he got the pants on, knotted the tie around his waist, and went to the door and opened it.

The house was small, but long windows and a high ceiling made it look more spacious. There was a small table, and a kitchen area with a pot-bellied stove. Along one wall was a long set of wooden shelves, bearing the weight of stacks and rows of ceramic bowls, plates, jugs, cups, and pitchers. He went to the shelf and picked up a bowl. It had a graceful, sleek contour, simple in design, with a pale blue satiny glaze on it. On the inside, done with just a few brush strokes, was a stylized tree branch, in deep blue underglaze, with a white flower that looked a little like a single rose. The bowl was feather-light, and thin as an eggshell.

"My father's work," came a voice from behind him.

He turned, still holding the piece in his hand. Shao Daiyu stood in the doorway to the outside, carrying a bucket of water.

"It's beautiful."

"He is a master of his craft. He is at the wheel now. I will help him to fire his kiln later, if the rainy weather passes."

"I would like to see how he does such work. I've never seen anything like it."

"Does no one in your home place make such ware?"

"Not with this skill." He set the bowl gently on the shelf. "And I've never been artistic at all. It's beyond me how anyone could make something so wonderful."

She set the bucket down. "Then come into his workshop."

He followed her through the open door, and then along a curved gravel path toward a small building whose stone foundations had a strangely organic look, as if they had grown from the subsoil, not been erected by human hands. The rock from which the low foundation walls were constructed was deep, sea-green, with sinuous bands of lighter colors, and had a natural sheen. A little mossy plant with pink flowers grew in the seams between the stones, trailing long stems down onto the ground. Affixed to the foundation by some means he couldn't discern was a structure made from wood and bamboo, walls and doors and windows with their shutters standing wide open. Atop was a thatched roof from which rainwater still dripped.

Shao Daiyu motioned for him to enter.

The interior was dimly lit. The furnishings were utilitarian—a long table, rows of wooden buckets, and a stack of what looked like cannonballs wrapped in cloth. There were pitchers of liquids, the consistency of cream, in chalky pastel colors across the spectrum. On a shelf was a neat row of wide-mouthed glass bottles with powders, white, tan, gray, red, black. Tools of various sorts, some of odd shape and uncertain purpose, hung from the wall.

It struck him suddenly that this place was like the opposite of Gevurah. In Gevurah they used tools to destroy and cause pain. Here they used tools to create beauty.

But simultaneously, the cautious voice reasserted itself. *Take care.* Even if it seemed pleasant, even if they weren't jumping at the chance to torture him, this place still wasn't what it seemed. None of the worlds of the Sephirot had been what it seemed. He still had to stay on his guard.

He stepped forward, and in a corner saw Shao Bolin seated on a raised platform, behind a wide wheel that he turned with his feet. Bolin looked up as he approached, and said, "You are out of bed."

"Yes."

"Good. But take care not to stretch too far. This is the dangerous time, when you feel well enough to move around but are still not healed enough to do so safely. This is when you can tear open your injuries, make things worse."

"I'm being careful. Daiyu said I could watch you working, if that is all right?"

Bolin shrugged. "I don't mind." He picked up from a little shelf one of the cloth-wrapped cannonballs he had seen earlier, and removed the wrapping. Underneath was a spherical ball of white clay. Bolin threw it with some force into the center of the wheel, then with a quick motion of his feet set it spinning.

The wheel shaft was connected to a heavy disk of stone suspended underneath the platform on which Bolin sat. Once the stone disk was put in motion, its momentum kept the much lighter wheel spinning at a constant rate. Bolin dunked his hands in a bucket of water at his side, then placed them on the whirling ball of clay.

The process was mesmerizing. Within seconds, Bolin had the ball centered and flattened into a broad cylinder. He stuck his thumbs into the middle, and with a deft motion pulled outward and up, stretching the clay into a symmetrical bowl shape.

"He makes it look effortless," Duncan said to Daiyu. He was whispering. Any distraction might break the spell, send the piece collapsing in ruin to the wheelhead.

Daiyu just smiled.

Bolin once more drew his fingers upwards to pull the sides of the bowl, stretching the clay into a thin, even curve. Every few turns of the wheel, he would bend at the waist, looking at the piece from the side, utter a grunt of approval, and then give a kick to the stone disk to keep it spinning. He curled his fingers over the top of the little bowl, smoothing the rim, and took a wooden tool and cut a groove in the piece right at the wheelhead. Then he let the momentum spin down, slowing it by dragging his heel on the stone disk's surface, until it stopped. He picked up a long wire with two wooden pegs as handles, in one quick movement cut the newly-made bowl from the wheel, and transferred it to a shelf.

"That's amazing," Duncan said. "You work so quickly."

Bolin gave him a wry look. "Time is an odd thing. How long would you say it took me to make that bowl?"

"Maybe ten minutes."

"I see it differently," Bolin said. "For me, it took me forty years to make the bowl."

Duncan nodded. "I understand. It's not the time it took you to make that specific piece, but the forty years you put into becoming a master of your craft."

"Closer," Bolin said. "But still not quite correct. There is no mastery. There is no point when someone says, 'Now I am a master. I am done.' If you reach that conclusion, that the work is finished, that you have nowhere further to go, you can be sure that you have left the path. Your work, whatever it is, will stagnate."

"So you never are satisfied?"

"I didn't say that. If I couldn't look at what I created, and think, 'Yes. This is beautiful,' there would be no point. But there is a difference between 'beautiful' and 'perfect.' Perfection isn't even a good idea, because it gives an artist the impression that there is a destination. My hope is that when I die, I will still have my feet on the road, even if I know that the road doesn't lead anywhere."

By the time Duncan left the workshop, another shower had blown up from the hills to the west, and warm drops of rain stung the cuts on his shoulders and back as he returned to the house at a jog. He was amazed at how much better he felt. The pain was still there, but bearable. The whip welts only hurt when he moved suddenly. The stab wound in his side had subsided to a dull, low ache. Surprisingly, the gash across his right cheek was the most painful, sending electric jolts every time he spoke or smiled.

Bolin had been right. He sat down at the table, listening to the drumming of the rain on the roof. He would heal. He'd have scars, but he'd survive.

He considered the indolent man he'd been, back home in Colville, New York, complacent as an overfed cat. He looked down at his own body now. He was changed, inside and out, by the time he'd spent wandering from world to world. He'd lost weight, and converted much of what fat he'd had to lean muscle. Living by his wits had sharpened him. He was ready for whatever this world had in store for him, that the ease and healing he was experiencing here was storing up power in his legs, readying him to spring when he needed to act.

What would it be here? A sudden and unexpected attack, like in Hod? A discovery that Daiyu and Bolin were lulling him into relaxing, so they could get information from me, like in Netzach? What would it be this time?

Daiyu came in a few moments later, her wrap darkened with rainwater, and gave him a shy smile. "My father sent me to attend to you. Are you in need of anything?"

"I'm hungry." He returned her smile, trying not to let the pain of his bandaged cheek show in his face.

"I thought you might be. I can prepare something for you. Father and I have already eaten."

She busied herself in the kitchen, pulling out a small iron cookpot, filled it with water, and set it on the pot-bellied stove.

"What do you know about the Sephirot?" he asked her.

She looked up and shrugged. "It is where we are."

"But what *is* it?"

She frowned. "Look around you. That is what it is."

He shook his head. "That's not what I mean. The people in my world... they don't know about all of this. At least, I don't think most of them do. I certainly didn't."

"Do they truly believe that they are the only beings on the only world there is?"

"I don't know. I mean, we know about other stars and planets in space, and that sort of thing. But I don't think that's what the Sephirot is. Is it?"

Daiyu didn't answer.

"This is like a whole bunch of different realities, all connected to each other if you know how to get from one to the other. And no, I had no idea any of this even existed." He raised one hand, palm upward. "Until I fell into it. Which was not through anything I did deliberately. And I've been wandering from place to place ever since." He paused. "What is your world called?"

"Father once told me the old name for this place was Chesed. I don't know what it means. We don't call it anything, usually. It is here. The place where we live."

"Can I ask you a question?"

She picked up a cloth sack with grain in it, and poured a handful into the pot. "Of course."

"Everywhere I've been, there's been something that hasn't been what it seemed, and that in time has turned against me, tried to harm or kill me. What is this place hiding?"

She gave the contents of the pot a stir.

"I don't know what you mean."

"Each place, it's been something different. In one world, they tried to convince me I had a brain injury, and had dreamed everything I'd experienced. In another, that I was being cared for by my family, and it turned out to be a bunch of ghosts. In another, I was befriended, but then a wandering band of marauders attacked and threatened to kill my friends if I didn't reveal to them how I was getting from world to world."

He stopped for a moment, the color coming to his face. He had been about to mention his experiences with Diana in Yesod, but he couldn't bring himself to describe them to this shy, innocent young woman.

Odd. He'd made love to someone who looked exactly like her more times than he could recall, and now he couldn't even say the word "sex" in front of her.

"And you know what they did to me in the last world I visited."

"Yes." She looked down into the little pot. There was silence for a few moments.

He finally said, "I'm sorry if I've upset you."

"I'm not upset." Still she did not look up. "But I do not know how to answer your questions. This place..." She raised one long, slender hand, and gestured around her. "Nothing happens here but my father's work. There was war here, long ago. My father, I think, told you I was a child of that war. But I do not remember it. Peace came shortly afterwards, when I was still an infant. Since then, there has only been the craft—digging and refining clay, grinding glazes, making pottery, firing the finished pieces, and once a month bringing them into the town to sell them." She shrugged. "Nothing ever changes. Each day follows the one before, and that is that."

"After what I've been through, it sounds nice."

"Then why do you suspect us?"

"I don't suspect *you*," he said. "I'm sorry if I gave that impression. It's more that I can't quite believe what I'm seeing. Everywhere I've been, there's been something underneath that has been other than it seemed."

"Even the last world?"

He recalled his terror, and the excruciating pain of the flogging, and the hatred and condemnation in Judge Bevans's eyes.

"No. That place was exactly as it appeared. It was evil, but it wasn't hiding anything."

"Then perhaps," she said, lifting the pot and pouring its contents into a wide ceramic bowl, "this place is the opposite of that one. We only desire calm, and peace, and healing, and creating beauty. Why does that mean that what you are seeing is false?" She sprinkled a little something from each of three clay bottles into the bowl, then carried it to Duncan. It looked like oatmeal, but thicker, and his nostrils caught the aromatic scents of cinnamon and nutmeg. His stomach growled.

"I guess it doesn't."

"Doubting everything is as lazy as believing everything." She blushed, and once more cast her eyes downwards. "My apologies. That was discourteous."

He laughed. "Honesty isn't the same thing as discourtesy." She glanced up at him, a fleeting smile touching her lips.

"I will make us both some tea," she said.

Bolin came in later, face and arms flecked with drying bits of white clay. "Weather is clearing. I think the wind is shifting around to the north. It will bring sunshine and dry air. Good for firing the kiln."

"What is involved in firing the kiln?" Duncan asked.

"A lot of work," Bolin said dryly.

"What sort of work? I would like to help if I can."

"With your injuries, there is little you could do. We will load the kiln, and that will take most of the afternoon. Daiyu and I will do that part. It is an exacting process, and one that must be learned. Then, we will start the fire burning and close the door. It will be three days of stoking the firebox before the pieces inside are sufficiently tempered by the flame to be durable. Less, and they will shatter easily."

"I could help with tending the fire."

Bolin looked at him with a frown. "You must not lift anything heavier than a teacup." His voice was stern. "Not if you wish to heal. You lift firewood all night and all day, you will be helping no one, because you will open your wounds again, and all my daughter and I did for you will go for nothing."

"Can I watch, then?" he said meekly.

"Yes," Bolin said, mollified. "You can watch. But you must go into the house to rest when I tell you to. While you recover, you must let yourself be a child again. And a child takes his father's commands without question."

As Bolin predicted, the clouds were swept away by a cool, dry wind that rippled the blue-green grass on the hillside, and shortly after midday the three of them left the house and went down a well-trodden path that sloped away from the workshop and around the edge of a bank that was held back with an ancient stone wall. From there, Duncan could see another hill in the distance that had a tunnel projecting from its side, ending in a low, rounded doorway.

A Hobbit hole. But not for living in, not unless you like it hot.

The kiln was dug straight back into the hillside, and Bolin opened the door to reveal shelves built of some fire-blackened material that looked like rough brick. It was about ten feet deep, and perhaps five wide. Bolin walked through the doorway, barely ducking, and proceeded to poke and prod remnants of ash, dust, and broken ceramic still on the shelf.

"Huh," he said, his voice a little muffled. "I must clean up better after this firing. Such untidiness, it makes the work doubly hard."

Daiyu smiled. "He says that every time," she whispered.

Bolin had brought along a small broom and a wooden bucket, and he swept ash and dirt out of the doorway, but the broken shards he collected in the bucket. "These pieces I dump into the creek behind our house, where they will be ground down and washed away by the current. I give them back to the earth, and one day the earth will return them to me in the form of clay for making other things."

When the kiln was cleaned to his satisfaction, he returned to his workshop for a tray of glazed ware. The pieces were not much to look at—the unfired glazes that coated their surfaces were powdery, beige or white or pale green. One by one each piece was inspected and placed on one of the shelves, propped up on little balls of a special clay that Daiyu fashioned.

"How did you learn to make glazes that give you the colors you want?" Duncan asked.

"My father and grandfather taught me." Bolin held up a pitcher with a graceful, swooping handle and a narrow spout. It was a chalky gray color, like old ash. "This one will be a deep blue when it comes out, if all goes well. There is an earth you find some places—black, black like charcoal. A little of it in a white glaze makes a rich blue." He shrugged. "I do not know why. All I know is that it is so."

Duncan suddenly wished he'd paid more attention in high school chemistry. Maybe he could have explained it to him.

But then he realized that Shao Bolin wouldn't care about the reasons, about what chemicals made his pottery shine with a rainbow of colors, made them strong and functional and water-tight.

Likely he cared more about beauty than about details.

As Bolin had predicted, loading the kiln took several hours. Trays of ware were brought up from the workshop, and each one slowly emptied into the kiln, a piece at a time. The sun was sinking to the horizon, the cooler air raising goosebumps on Duncan's bare shoulders and arms, when finally, with a grunt of approbation, Bolin pronounced the task done.

"You may watch us begin the fire," Bolin said. "Then you must take some food and rest. Daiyu will give you another draught of the poppy syrup. However brave a face you are putting on, when you are in bed and trying to sleep, with nothing to distract you, the pain will once again claim your full attention."

"I won't argue."

"Good." Bolin pulled some pieces of firewood and kindling from a stack along the hillside that had been covered by a piece of waxed canvas, and using flint and tinder from a small metal box, he got a little fire started.

"A small fire that soon will be much bigger." He laughed, feeding it with more wood until he had a nice blaze going. "Now, the door closes. And will not open until it is done, for good or ill. Good fortune to you," he said to his work, sitting on shelves, barely visible in the deepening gloom. "May you come out more beautiful than you went in."

Duncan went back to the house, shivering a little as the cool night wind brushed his skin. He stoked the fire in the potbellied stove, heated water in the pot, and made himself another bowl of the oatmeal-like hot cereal he'd had earlier that day. Sated for the time being, he was just cleaning the bowl in a bucket of water when Daiyu came in.

"Father has the kiln fire roaring," she said. "He will tend it for half the night, then I will go out and mind it until morning. But before I sleep, I wanted to get you another draught of the poppy syrup, so that you will sleep as well." She went to a small cabinet with an ornate handle and extracted a blue glass bottle with a little cork, and poured out some of the thick brown syrup into a cup.

"Cheers," he said, holding up the cup, and then draining the sticky sweet liquid in a single swallow. Daiyu smiled and looked away, a gesture that was charming, but so unlike Libby Chen's quick forthrightness that he was once again struck to the heart by the fact that this woman was not his girlfriend, however much every feature was identical to hers.

And as he went towards his bedroom, just as the world started to spin, he thought, *Peace and tranquility. Not what I had back on Earth. But after what I've been through, I'll take it. No more questions.*

Duncan woke slowly the next morning, like a bubble rising to the surface of a still lake. The air coming in through the window was cool but not uncomfortable. He still could not tolerate a blanket covering his back, so he was thankful for the mild weather. He moved carefully. The pain was less, although it was uncertain whether from the aftereffects of the poppy syrup or because he was finally healing. He lay for a while, resting comfortably, listening to the wind chimes and the distant calling of birds, as his consciousness returned sufficiently that he felt like getting up.

The house was quiet. Daiyu, he knew, would be out tending the kiln, and Bolin was likely to be asleep after his long shift stoking the fire. He fixed himself breakfast, and put water on for tea. Once fed, he felt well enough that he decided to explore the house a little before going out to meet Daiyu.

Thus far, he'd only been in two rooms—his own bedroom, and the kitchen/eating area that also served as a living room. There was no bathroom indoors, but an outbuilding contained a bathing room and a toilet. He had not bathed since his arrival here, and was feeling terribly grimy, but immersing his wounds at this point was still off limits.

There were three other rooms off the short hallway where his room was. One was Daiyu's bedroom, and another Bolin's. The third, however, was a large room he'd only had a glimpse of once when Bolin was exiting. Bolin had not stopped him from looking in, not exactly, but Duncan still got the impression that he shut the door quickly when he saw Duncan peering around him.

He padded down the hall, still barefoot, looked both ways to make sure that he was not being observed, and quietly turned the handle of the door. It swung inward without a creak. He stepped inside.

He could see immediately that the room was some sort of shrine, but what kind was unclear. There was the smell of incense, and the walls were hung with tapestries woven in bright geometric patterns. Vases of flowers lined a set of steps up to an altar of sorts, a raised platform that held a table with votive candles and a bowl filled with dried rose petals. He raised his eyes, to see what sort of deity was being worshiped here.

Above the table was a huge mirror.

It was oval in shape, edged in a narrow band of silver filigree. Otherwise it was unadorned. He stepped up onto the platform, and looked at his own rather sorry reflection. The right side of his face and body were both swathed in bandages, and in several places, there were long scabbed cuts where a whip cord had curled around his ribcage or over his shoulder. Still, there was a certain glint in his eye that was different from the last time he'd looked in a mirror. When was that? Probably in the hospital/prison in Tiferet. He smiled, and the image in the mirror gave him a rakish smile back.

He'd been right, earlier. He *had* changed. He wasn't sure how, or why, or where it was leading, but it was as if he had grown up. He knew he might still die before all of this was over, before he finally got back home. But still and all, and even if he never got home, he'd rather be here than sleepwalking through a job at Carthen, Douglas, and Prescott, Financial Consultants.

Then his smile dimmed a little. Why a mirror on the altar? These people weren't narcissists. They didn't worship their own reflections. What did this mean?

He decided that when the time was right, he'd ask Bolin. Surely the man wouldn't be angry with him for exploring his surroundings a little.

With that thought, he left the room, closing the door silently behind him, and went out to join Daiyu at the kiln.

He walked up the gravel path, past the stone wall, and across to the hill with the kiln, but he heard it long before he got there. There was a roar like a jet engine, a continuous, low-frequency rumble that shook the ground and vibrated Duncan's innards. In the distance was Daiyu's lithe figure, clad in a simple wrap but wearing heavy gloves, as she picked up a large chunk of wood and shoved through a port in the door of the kiln.

The front end of the log blazed with fire before the back end made it all the way through.

Flames leapt up the chimney at the back, creating a heat shimmer against the blue of the clear sky. No smoke—this was burning so hot that there was nothing but a plume of blazing air, rising and dissipating into the cool morning.

Daiyu sat in one of two wooden chairs near the kiln door and passed a hand over her face in a clear gesture of fatigue.

"You look tired," he said.

She turned toward him and smiled in greeting, only making eye contact for the briefest of moments before dropping her gaze. "Firing the kiln is a great deal of labor. But it is all part of the work we do."

"I had no idea it was so loud."

"Father says that rage and heat and sound are the best for tempering the finest porcelain."

"Hard to imagine the pieces aren't blown to bits in there."

"Some are. It is part of the craft. Not all pottery can withstand firing. It is never predictable. Sometimes the soundest-looking pieces shatter, and ones with weaknesses and flaws come out the most beautiful. One never knows until the kiln cools and the door is opened."

"I like the things I do to be a little more certain."

"Nothing is certain." She picked up another piece of firewood to dump into the kiln's firebox.

They sat, silently, for some time, immersed in the thrumming vibrations of air pouring through the kiln vents and up the chimney.

He looked over at her. "Do you know what I'm supposed to be doing here?"

"Doing?" she said, raising an eyebrow. "Father said you were still not allowed to assist with the firing."

"That's not what I mean. I'm talking about here. Here, in Chesed. Why I came to this place."

"How would I know that?"

"I spoke with you yesterday about my experiences in other places. Each place, I've come upon danger, and had to get away or I'd have been injured or killed."

"Yes."

"But here... it's hard to see how I would ever have reason to leave."

"Why do you need to?"

"I..." He shook his head. "I don't know."

She did not answer for a moment, and he thought that perhaps she wouldn't speak again, that he might have breached some law of courtesy, or made her feel uncomfortable. But then she said, "Perhaps your travels have served to lead you here. And this..." She gestured around her, at the roaring kiln with its load of ceramics being tempered into beauty and utility, at the rolling blue-green hills dotted with the deeper, shadowed green of cedar trees. "Perhaps this was your destination all along. Perhaps all you have been through was a means to bring you here."

"I would like it if that were true," he said, but a misgiving rose in his heart.

That, he realized, was a lie. It wasn't like in Netzach, where he knew something was wrong, pretty much from the outset. There was nothing wrong here—or if there was, it was with Duncan himself. He was the disturbance, the ripples in the pond, the stick in the river around which the water had to flow.

And maybe that was the lure. Peace and contemplation and healing and calm. It wasn't a trick, like in Netzach. Daiyu was right. This place was the opposite of Gevurah. But what Gevurah could not do to him by force, Chesed was doing to him without any effort at all.

Stopping him in his tracks.

But he didn't know what, if anything, he could do to prevent that from happening.

There was something about the mirror room, as Duncan referred to it in his mind, that was magnetic. Over the next few days, he visited it as often as he had a chance. For some reason he could not quite put his finger on, he was still wary of being seen by Bolin or Daiyu, so he would only go there when they were both occupied. This was easy during the first few days, which were taken up with first completing the firing of the kiln, checking it repeatedly as it cooled, and then unloading the finished ware back onto shelves in the workshop. During it all Bolin was in motion constantly, either working himself—and he appeared to have nearly inexhaustible energy—or supervising Daiyu. He only came back to the house to sleep, taking his meals in the workshop, and in spare moments sitting at the wheel making pieces that would be in the next round of glazing and firing.

Duncan was drawn to the mirror room by its serenity, but also because he was fascinated with watching his own reflection as his healing progressed. The first bandage to come off was the one on his face. The knife gash was long but superficial, and it was already closed and dry, although still tender to the touch. The stab wound in his side was painful, but it, too, was mending, albeit more slowly. The whip-welts across his back had scabbed over, and some of the shallower cuts were already peeling, showing pink lines of healing skin beneath. He found that his back itched terribly, but he resisted scratching it after a careless pass of his fingernails across his shoulder opened up a cut that oozed blood for an hour afterwards.

He stood in front of the mirror, sometimes for a half-hour at a time, staring at himself. He was still uncomfortable wearing a shirt, so he was always clad only from the waist down in the cream-colored pants that Bolin had provided on his first day in Chesed. He realized he had never really looked at his own body, except in a completely utilitarian way. To shave, to brush his hair, to wash his face—those took a glance in the mirror, no more, and attention to one specific thing. Anything further always involved some sort of evaluation, usually negative. Frustration when his hair wouldn't lie flat as he got ready for a date. Irritation with discovering he had a pimple on his chin. Wishing, in some vague way, that his face or body was other than it was.

Now he found himself looking at every contour in his face and torso, considering himself without judgment. And he noticed things he had never seen before—the way the muscles in his forearm moved when he clenched his hand, the fact that his eyebrows were asymmetrical, the little white scar above his left nipple he'd gotten in a bicycle accident when he was seven years old. He watched as his beard grew in, at first dark stubble, then thick and prickly, changing the contours of his face, making him look older, wiser. His hair had needed cutting when he'd first started on this journey, and now it was a shaggy mane, not quite black, unkempt and at the moment unwashed. He raised both arms, lacing his hands behind his head, and stretched, arching his back like a cat. He had not been able to stretch, really stretch, since the flogging, and even now it stung, but the feeling was so pleasant he gave a little sigh of contentment as he dropped his arms to his sides.

Day followed day. A week after his arrival, he was able to don a shirt for the first time, but he was so comfortable without—and Daiyu and Bolin appeared not to care—that he often didn't bother as long as the weather was warm. That same day, he took a long, luxurious bath in the bathing house, glad to feel the grime of Gevurah, and the week's accumulation of sweat, wash away. Afterwards, he felt cleansed within and without, and when he dressed, he returned to the house refreshed.

But when he found that Daiyu and Bolin were both in the workshop, he went to the mirror room and spent another hour contemplating his own reflection.

Three weeks, and the last of the scabs from the flogging fell away. That day on his visit to the mirror room he twisted, peering over his own shoulder, looking at the lacework of livid lines on the tanned skin of his back. He remembered the unseen man who had spoken to him through his cell door in Gevurah, the night before he was to be executed—*You'll be carrying the scars of that whipping for the rest of your life.*

He would never have thought he could have survived this. If someone had told him when he fell, buck naked, into the catacombs of Malkuth, what was going to happen to him, he would have curled up and died of terror. Since then, he'd been nearly killed more than once, had to fight for his life, hunted for his own food, defended people who befriended him, seen through the lies of phantoms, and found his way out of a labyrinth meant to trap him. He'd been tortured, but he lived through it. He made love to Diana, and might be the first man ever who didn't pay for that pleasure with his life. He'd jumped now into seven worlds, and each time met whatever challenge it presented. He'd lived by his wits. And he was still alive.

When he turned back, his reflection smiled at him.

He fell into a routine, and gradually Bolin trusted Duncan enough to allow him to help out with chores in the workshop. At first, it was light work, grinding glazes using a mortar and pestle, then adding water to the powder until it was the consistency of heavy cream. Once his side had healed enough to pass Bolin's inspection, he was given heavier chores—hauling buckets of water from a nearby stream, running glazes through a sieve to mix them and remove impurities that would spoil the finish, kneading balls of clay until his arms and shoulder muscles ached. He assisted in firing the kiln, sitting up with it at night, feeding it wood like it was some sort of ravenous animal, watching the flames spout from the chimney and dissipate into the star-filled blackness overhead.

It was one morning, as Bolin relieved him at the kiln on the last day of a firing, that Bolin said, "What do you hope to learn, day after day, looking at yourself in the mirror?"

He froze, staring at Shao Bolin wide-eyed.

"You know..." he began, and then his face burned with embarrassment.

Bolin shrugged. "I have known for a long time. You are not so sneaky as you think you are." He laughed.

The heat of his shame spread. It was the helpless, self-conscious humiliation he hadn't known since he was a teenager, when his mother had walked in on him while he was masturbating. Neither of them had said a thing about it afterwards, but he hadn't been able to look his mother in the eye for days. He had felt no particular shame in the act itself, but to have been seen, to have his mother know what he was doing, was a height of embarrassment that even now, ten years later, could bring color to his cheeks when he thought about it.

But Bolin was not going to let him go that easily. He leaned back in the chair, smiling, watching Duncan squirm.

"What is that room for?" Duncan finally said, trying to think of something to distract Bolin from his question.

But the potter was not to be misdirected. "What do you think it is for? You must have learned some wisdom there."

Duncan thought of some things he might say in answer to that—that he was keeping tabs on how he was healing, that he was worried about how much his injuries had disfigured him. All sounded in his mind like the false-hoods they were.

Finally he spoke, saying the simple truth. "I couldn't look away."

Bolin nodded. "You see why it is there, then?"

He shook his head.

"Everything you learn, everything you do, becomes a part of you. It *becomes* you. You are not some static thing that never changes. Each act takes a little piece of you and turns it, this way, that way, makes you more beautiful, makes you more ugly, makes you stronger, makes you weaker. Some you cannot help, like those scars on your back. Others you choose. It is essential to know what we are, down to the smallest flaw, what we are at our core. Our best and worst. The mirror shows that." He looked up at the sky, where the red light of sunrise spread across the horizon. "Of course, it is easy to let self-study become a snare. To let it become a substitute for action."

"What if there is no action to be done?"

"There always is. Deciding who we are is less important than deciding what we must do."

He sat, watching the potter as he got up, shoved a log through the port in the kiln door, and shut it again. For a while, there was nothing but the roaring of the flames.

"And who are you? What do you see when you look in the mirror?" Duncan finally asked in a quiet voice.

"I am Shao Bolin. That is all."

"And you don't need more than that?"

"That is all there is." He plunked back down in the chair. "Perhaps that is why I don't go in there much, any more. I used to, when I was younger."

"And what did you learn?"

The older man laughed. "Not to ask questions for which there are no answers."

Duncan blushed again, looked away.

"Do not be ashamed. Better men than you have been trapped by such things. And bigger fools than you have recognized them as the traps they are, and escaped. Such is the way of the world."

"So how does the mirror do what it does? Is it magical?"

Now Bolin leaned back, and laughed loud and long. "Magical? No. It is only a simple piece of silvered glass. A pretty one, and the frame is beautifully made, but any mirror would have shown you the same thing."

"I've looked in mirrors before, though."

"No," Bolin gave him a frowning look, but still with a ghost of a smile playing about his lips. "No, I really don't think you have. Not until now."

Weeks passed into months. The weather became cool, then cold, the blue-green grass bleaching into a desiccated yellow. Duncan's hair grew long, and he tied it back with a twist of cloth when he worked. His strength grew, and with it his confidence, and Bolin's confidence in him. He carried heavy buckets of water to the workshop, two at a time, hanging from a yoke across his shoulders. Blocks of clay were pried from the creekside, sieved to remove dirt and rocks and other debris, and then were loaded into canvas bags and hauled up to the shop as well. Finally, he was allowed to load the kiln, and praised when his careful work was looked over with a critical eye.

"You've learned a lot," Bolin said. Coming from him, this was high praise.

"Thank you."

"Always more to learn, though. Don't get lazy."

"I won't."

It was that thought of *laziness* that haunted him, pushing at his mind like a pebble inside a shoe. It wasn't a physical laziness. He had done more hard work in the past months than he had ever done in his life. When he went into the mirror room, by now an infrequent occurrence as his memory still stung at Bolin's discovery of his visits, he saw a body grown lean and hard and powerful. His scars were still there, fading to white, but they seldom pained him. The one on his face had healed unevenly, and made his smile a little lopsided. But all said, he was pleased with the body he had, for perhaps the first time in his life.

What jabbed at him, though, was the knowledge that he had succumbed to the lure of Chesed, a lure he had recognized when he had only been there a week. The lure of peace, calm, contentment, the acceptance of tranquility as a destination, when in his heart he knew the journey wasn't over yet.

"Shao Bolin," he said, one day as they ate their evening meal.

He looked up, one eyebrow quizzical.

"I have to go."

"I know," was his simple reply.

Duncan frowned, feeling the frustration rising in him. "I have felt that way for a long time. As soon as I was well enough to consider the question. I have to go, but I don't know how."

Bolin took a slurping sip of the soup he was eating. "Certainly you do."

"I don't!" His voice rose. Daiyu looked at him, eyes wide with alarm, then she dropped her gaze. "My apologies," he went on, in a quieter tone. "I meant no discourtesy. You have shown me nothing but kindness, taking me in and healing me when I was gravely wounded. I would have died without your care, and Daiyu's. And I value everything I have learned here. But I can't stay. Chesed is beautiful, and I would have thought any man would be a fool to leave it, but..."

"It's not the end of your road."

"Yes."

"Then leave, and my blessing goes with you."

"It's not that easy. I have called up portals before, in Netzach, and Tiferet, by simply... I don't know, it was like I told them to appear, and they did. In Gevurah, I created a portal from my own blood. But here, I don't think that would work. This isn't a place you can push around in that way."

"No," Bolin said. "It isn't."

"Then?"

Bolin shrugged. "Then figure it out."

His forehead creased with frustration. "I've tried. Don't you think I've tried? All the doorways in this house lead to other rooms, or to the outside. None of them take me out, set my feet back on my path."

"Then you haven't tried the right door."

"You're being deliberately cryptic."

Bolin smiled. "No. Not that. Never that." He frowned, looked up at the ceiling, considering his words. "You have done mind puzzles, perhaps? The sort of riddles we give children, that require you to see things from a different angle?"

"Sure."

"When you have the flash of insight, the understanding that allows you to solve the riddle, it is an exhilarating feeling, yes?"

"Yes."

"Suppose instead of allowing you to think about it, I gave you a riddle and told you the answer immediately. What then?"

"There'd be no point to it."

"So." Bolin's shrewd gaze locked on his.

"So what?"

Bolin gave a harsh sigh of exasperation. "If I am not allowed to be deliberately cryptic, you are not allowed to be deliberately stupid."

He shook his head. "Okay, fine. I get your point. But it doesn't bring me any closer to the solution."

"That is because you have not had the flash of insight yet."

Duncan's frustration continued to ramp up through the evening, and after a few more fruitless attempts to get Bolin to give him an answer, *any* answer, he decided to go to bed early. He walked down the shadowed hallway toward his bedroom, and as he opened the door, he saw Daiyu standing in her own doorway, still, her hands clasped in front of her.

"Duncan," she said, her voice almost a whisper.

He turned, frowning. She rarely ever spoke to him without his speaking first, but now, she was looking directly into his eyes, with a resolve that he had not seen in her.

"What is it, Daiyu?" he said, dropping his own voice to a hush.

"When you were talking to my father tonight... It was in my mind to ask you, why are you so determined to leave us?"

"I thought I explained that."

She shook her head. "All of that vague speech about your not being done with your journey. It is foolishness, do you not see that?"

He looked at her in surprise. "I have never heard you speak so boldly. But I was only speaking from my heart. I'm sorry if it seems foolish to you."

"What if you are wrong? What if you leave now, only to go to another world like the one from which you escaped, one where you will be beaten and tortured and killed? You were fortunate enough to flee from them, and find healing, once. You might not be so fortunate a second time."

"I can't just stay here—"

"But why?" Her voice rose. "You still cannot answer that. Here there is work for you to do, good work, and the solace of a quiet home to return to." She looked down, and the fire died out of her speech. "And I had hoped... I hoped that one day, you would speak to me... about... that perhaps you and I could be together." The flush that spread across her cheeks was visible even in the gloom.

His heart gave an unsteady gallop. Why had he not anticipated this?

"Daiyu," he said, his voice stumbling, "I had no idea you felt this way. I would never want you to think I would spurn you."

"Then why? Why would you leave? Is there another, somewhere, in one of the worlds, who holds your heart?"

How could he answer that? *Yes, there is... and she looks exactly like you?*

But even Libby Chen now was a distant dream, like someone he had been involved with in another lifetime. He shook his head, and said, "Not anyone, not any more. It isn't that there's another woman. Or at least there hasn't been, not for a long time." How long ago, now? He wasn't even sure.

"Then why?"

He shook his head. "I feel like it's necessary, that if I stop here, that everything I went through in Gevurah will have been for nothing. That they will have won."

"I do not understand. We have nothing to do with the evil men who did those things to you." She was near tears, but held tight reins on her emotions. Her body was immobile, her lips barely moving as she spoke. But for her voice, she could have been a marble statue.

"I know." He passed a hand over his face. "I'm explaining myself badly. But the point of all I've been through—the fighting, and the running, and suffering under the whip and the threat of execution—is not to spend the rest of my life in idleness."

"Our work is not idleness—"

"No, but this *place* is. Chesed... it's like a wheel slowly turning, never a hitch, but never going anywhere. If I stayed here, I would get swallowed up. I would become part of the wheel."

A pair of tears coursed their way down Daiyu's carven marble cheeks. "I would have given myself to you."

"I know," he said, trying to think of a way to assuage her pain, and finding none. He reached out and touched her arm, but she pulled away, looked down, and took a step back into her room.

"Then there is nothing more to be said," she said, in a voice that was barely a breath.

She closed the door, leaving him standing alone in the shadowy hallway, feeling an ache worse than the physical pain he had endured, coupled with shame and helplessness and frustration that would have brought a shout of rage to his lips had such an outburst been possible in this tranquil place.

In the end, he simply turned, and went into his own bedroom and closed the door.

And it remains to be seen, he thought, as he undressed in the dark, *whether I will be able to leave in any case. So all of this anguish may, finally, accomplish nothing at all.*

Daiyu said nothing more about their encounter. When Duncan got up the next morning, and met her as she was preparing breakfast for herself and her father, she was as courteous as ever.

And as distant. She was dressed in a warm wrap of a deep ultramarine, hair up in a loose knot at the base of her neck. Beautiful as ever, but unreachable. She would not meet his eyes, and asked him only if he needed anything before she went out to join her father in the workshop.

"No," he said, his voice hollow. "No, I'm fine."

She gave a little bow, picked up the two bowls of hot cereal, and carried them outside, where the cold air made curls of steam rise from them, twist into the air, and vanish.

"Except for the fact that I feel like shit," he said, watching her retreating figure through the window. Then he put more water on to boil.

He sat by himself at the little table, eating his breakfast and drinking a cup of strong tea. There had to be a way out of here. The compulsion to leave was becoming overwhelming, even though he had every reason to stay. A promise of peace and quiet, doing work that was at least more meaningful than pushing around numbers on accounting sheets. A home to live in, with a man who was wise and kind, and who took him in to heal him of his wounds, and then allowed him to stay when he had no real necessity to do so. And a woman who, with no encouragement whatsoever, would be his lover, and who looked exactly like the lover he had left behind.

What man would say no to this?

"I would," he whispered into the still tranquility of the little house.

It was a beautiful life, but it was not for him.

After cleaning up, he went into the mirror room, and walked up onto the altar. He once more saw his reflection, wavy dark hair tied back into a thick pony tail, jaw edged with a neatly-trimmed beard, jagged white scar on the right cheek. A deep, anguished knowledge in the brown eyes.

"I understand, now," he said, to himself. "But what good does it do me if understanding sucks?"

He reached out, for the first time, to touch the cold glass surface of the mirror. And where his fingertips touched it, it rippled, as if he had been looking at his reflection in a still lake.

He jerked his fingers back as if stung, and frowned. "What the hell?" he said, under his breath.

He reached out again, and tapped the surface. The surface beneath his fingertips had the cool smoothness of glass, only a little less solid. Once more, waves radiated out from where he'd touched it, making his reflection shimmer. He pushed harder, and the tips of his fingers sunk into the mirror. When he retracted them, they were coated with silver, as if he'd dipped them in mercury. He flicked his hand at the mirror, and silvery drops scattered from his fingertips, flying glittering through the air. They skittered across the mirror's face and were absorbed, making little circular marks on the surface that were gone in an instant.

"It was easy enough once you saw it, wasn't it?" said an amused voice, and he turned to see Shao Bolin standing in the doorway. "But you had to discover it yourself. I don't even know if it would have worked if I had simply told you about it."

"So this is the portal."

"Apparently so."

"Where will it take me?"

Bolin shrugged. "I don't know. Does that matter?"

He shook his head. "No. No, I don't think it does."

Bolin nodded. "So." He gestured toward the mirror.

He hesitated. "Where is Shao Daiyu?"

"She is in the workshop. She could not bear to watch."

He looked down, feeling the anguish rising in his heart again, harder to endure than whips or knives. "I'm sorry. If I could stay, I could have loved her."

"She knows that. It doesn't make it less painful. But know you go with *her* love, however you were unable to reciprocate it."

"I never meant to hurt her."

"Most of the hurt in the world is accidental. Such is the way of things."

"Thank you for everything you have done for me. I will never forget it."

Bolin shrugged. "Much of the good is accidental, too. You came our way, we helped you. One day you may happen on someone, all by accident, and you will help him. It all balances, if you take a large enough view."

"Goodbye." He wondered whether this wry little man was expecting a hug, or a handshake, but Bolin only smiled and raised both hands in farewell.

"Feet back on the path, then," he said.

"Yes." Duncan swallowed. "Tell Daiyu I'm sorry. And tell her goodbye for me."

He turned, and stepped into the mirror. Like a stone falling into a pond, the glass swallowed him up, shuddering for a moment, and then once more becoming still, silver, inert, giving back only what was put into it.

CHAPTER 8

DA'AT

Duncan stepped forward, turned around, and found himself facing a mirror.

It wasn't an oval mirror with a silver filigree edge, as it had been in Shao Bolin's house. It was a long, rectangular mirror, from floor to ceiling. He half expected that from this side it would be a transparent window, and that he would see into the mirror room, perhaps catching a glimpse of Bolin watching him—but all he saw was his own reflection.

He reached out and touched the glass. It was solid, unyielding. He looked at his fingertips. There was no mercury silvering, nothing but his own skin.

He turned away, and about three feet in front of him was another pair of mirrors, angled toward each other. He looked into them, and saw two reflections of himself, one looking over his left shoulder, one over his right.

He took a tentative step forward, into the angle between the mirrors, until he could see multiple reflections of himself, front to back and back to front, vanishing into infinity. Once again, he reached out a hand, and found himself touching a cold polished surface, as hundreds, thousands of Duncan Kyles did the same thing.

A turn to the right brought him face first into another mirror, set at angles to the one through which he had arrived. But there was a gap between those two, a narrow passageway, also edged with mirrors that bounced his reflection back and forth as he squeezed through it. It led first straight, then down some shallow steps and onto a platform made of transparent glass.

Above him was yet another mirror, and he looked up to see his own face staring back down at him. Beneath his feet was room after room, as if he was on the top floor of a glass castle. In some of the rooms below were various mirrors and windows and tall columns that looked like giant prisms. Far down, perhaps three or four floors below, there was a rectangular white space that might have been a doorway made of something opaque, but there was no way to tell how it might be reached, nor where it would lead if he could reach it.

He had come here knowing he would be following his nose. He accepted that he was trading the safe, placid world of Chesed for whatever came his way. This mysterious world was no more and no less than what he had asked for.

He crossed the floor of the room, trying to ignore the disorientation caused by the hundreds of images his motion sent walking to and fro. He stopped... they stopped. In the nearest mirror, he could see himself from the back, a reflection of a reflection from some other surface in the room. This was a novel enough experience, but he quickly lost interest. Any obsession with looking at his own form was spent and over, now that it had apparently served its purpose in getting him here.

But where was here? He had yet to see anyone else. The place was totally silent except for his muffled foot-falls when he walked. He went across the room, hands held out in front of him in case some of the walls were closer than they appeared, then up a short set of steps and down another passageway.

It was in the next room, an octagonal space enclosed by alternating panes of mirror and transparent glass, that he found the first thing that was different. In the center was a sheet of what appeared also to be glass, but it was a different sort—milky and opaque, with an oily luster. As he looked, he saw it wasn't uniform. It was marbled with white and cream bands that swirled slowly, with a motion like the drifting of clouds. He reached out once more and touched it. Underneath his fingertips was a waxy sheet, rigid as plastic, slightly warm to the touch.

And as soon as he contacted it, it started to change.

The surface turned a murky scarlet, like the embers in a dying fire. Then the swirls coalesced into buildings and cobblestone streets underneath a cloudy sky at sunset. In the distance loomed the outlines of larger buildings against the dimly-lit horizon. The nearer ones were tumbledown and soot-covered. There were no people, but near at hand was the skeletal outline of a gallows, with the silhouette of a hanging body, its broken neck askew.

He was looking into the hellish landscape of Gevurah. His back and side ached with the memory of it.

As he watched, the glass went as yielding as clay, and his fingers sank into it. There was a pull on his arm, as if he were being drawn through the glass.

He yanked his hand back.

"Goddammit, no," he said in a yelp. "I sure as hell don't want to go back there."

And the glass instantly returned to its previous milky white opacity.

So that's how the portals would be in this world. At least it was more straightforward than having to draw one in his own blood.

He walked past the portal and down a long hallway that sloped gradually upwards. Mirrors at odd angles caught pieces of his reflection, some from the side, some from the back. He walked with one hand brushing the glassy walls. Without using a tactile sense to supplement his vision, the place was too disorienting, and he was afraid of falling.

This did not stop him from walking headlong into a transparent sheet of glass that blocked his way. He cracked his forehead and shoulder against it, swore profusely, and then turned away from it, proceeding more slowly now with his right hand on the wall and his left hand stretched out in front of him, as he had in the lightless caverns of Malkuth.

Vision was no good if all it did was confuse. Almost as bad as being in total darkness.

Another portal appeared in the distance. Getting to it took maneuvering around another clear glass wall, but he came up to it, and touched it. This time, the alabaster surface turned a sunny yellow, and when it cleared, he saw the labyrinth that lay in front of the hospital/prison of Tiferet, with its statuary and clumps of nodding sunflowers. His view was from above, perhaps from the balcony where Liam had said the people who ran the place watched the sport, when they fed the monster who lived in the middle. But there was no sign of movement, no guards, no lion-headed giant, nothing but a strangely innocent world of green and gold lanes, cloudless blue skies, and the gleam of bronze statuary.

He removed his hand, and the vision winked out.

A twisting corridor, lined with mirrors alternating with glass panels, led Duncan up to a platform with a third portal. A touch brought a wash of green to the surface, and at this point he wasn't surprised to see the broad lawn and well-appointed manor house that had been his home for a few days in Netzach. The immaculate gardens were in full bloom, with roses and hawthorns and the little white flowers of straight-sided holly hedges. He turned away. The false comfort he'd received there, floating on a matrix of lies, held as little appeal for him as the torture chambers of Gevurah.

A fourth portal was at the top of some stairs, and towered over him as he approached, like a marble wall from an ancient temple. This one briefly turned orange beneath his touch, then he was looking over the sandy expanses and azure skies of Hod. A tent, its flag snapping in the wind, was in the distance, and down a hill he could see palm trees and the glitter of water. He recalled the unexpected kindness he'd found there, amongst people who had no reason to befriend him. The memory brought with it a pang that one, perhaps more, of them had paid for that compassion with their lives.

He set out deliberately to find the next portal, and he came upon it around a bend made up of small glittering mirror fragments, like the facets of a fly's eye. He knew by now where this one would lead, and as he stepped toward it he felt a pull that was purely physical. How long had it been since he had made love to Diana? A warmth radiated from his belly down through his groin at the thought. At his touch the portal turned a deep violet, and then in front of him were the glades of Yesod, lying warm under the stars, and the little lake beside which he had been pleasured morning and night, sometimes more often than that. Diana was not there, but he remembered how good it was, and felt that old need rising in him.

Then he remembered how quickly she had turned on him. Her use of him was in no way a bond. She remained a virgin afterwards, and would never be otherwise, because she gave nothing of herself, only took from him, however fine it was at the time. With some reluctance, he pulled his hand away, and the portal returned to its original swirling white.

Another portal stood only a little farther on. At his touch it darkened, turned a brownish gray, and with the suddenness of a flipped switch, he found himself looking at the dead world of Malkuth. In the distance was the huge, blocky edifice of the Sphinx's temple. A dry wind vibrated the desiccated plants that had struggled their way up through the rocks millennia ago.

"Nope. Not really excited about going back there. But that's the first world I visited. Where now?"

"You should be able to answer that," came a deep voice, resonant, a little hoarse, from somewhere ahead. The passageway toward the voice was edged by a wide curved mirror that twisted his body's image like taffy, and he walked down an ever-widening path that opened outward like a giant glass funnel. At the end he found himself in the largest room he'd seen yet in this strange, glittering world of reflections. And in the middle was an elderly man seated in a chair, who gave Duncan a gap-toothed grin as he approached. The man wore a red plaid flannel shirt and worn blue jeans, legs stretched out in front of him, feet clad in ancient brown loafers with sprung soles.

"Grandpa?" Duncan said in a breathless whisper as he walked up to the man, his steps slowing. Finally, he stood, staring, heart pounding against his ribcage.

"Still falling for it, are you?" the man said. "I thought you'd figured it out."

He gave a convulsive swallow. "I... I did. It's just that it's... kind of a shock to see you."

"Why?"

"You... died."

"I did? Fancy that." The man looked down at himself, patted his sides and thighs, and then said, "I'm in pretty fine shape for a dead guy."

"What is your name?" His mouth was dry, and his tongue didn't want to work.

"Doesn't matter. You wouldn't believe it, no matter what I told you. What do you think my name is?"

"My mom's father was named Arthur Salazar," he said. "But you'll tell me you're not him."

"Will I?" The man shrugged. "All right, then."

"But what is your real name?"

"Whatever you choose to name me. You don't get to decide whether something's real. You discovered that the hard way in Gevurah. But you do get to decide what your posture toward it is going to be. If you want me to be your grandfather, well, you can do that."

"My deciding to go along with the illusion doesn't make it any more real, though."

"Doesn't make it any less, either."

He shook his head. "My grandfather was one of the smartest, kindest men I've ever known. And each place I've been, there's been someone there who has looked like a person I know. And they've all kept an essential part of the original person's character."

"It's a mystery," the man said, his eyes sparkling.

"Sure. You're trying to tell me I should know what all of this is about by now. But maybe because you look like my grandfather, who always helped me and supported me, you'll tell me what the hell is going on, here."

"Uh-huh. Support. Give you all the answers."

He frowned. "That's not what I meant."

"Sure sounded like it." The man cleared his throat. "Lookit, kid, it's not like this is supposed to be easy.

Why'd it be worth going through what you've been through, if the answer was some simple bullshit that anyone could have told you without you ever leaving your easy chair?"

"That's exactly what my grandpa would have told me."

"There you go, then."

"Okay. Where do I go from here?"

"Wherever you want to, seems to me. There's doorways to most anywhere in this place."

He looked around him. Everywhere he looked, reflections of himself and the man in the chair, and then reflections of those reflections, angled off into infinity. "What is this world?"

"Well, it's not really a world. Not a world on its own, y'understand. It's more of a way station. In the old days it was called Da'at. But I don't know that it's called much of anything, now, because it isn't much of anywhere. On the other hand, it's useful. You can jump from here to wherever you like."

"Wherever?" A hope rose in him, a hope that he at first tried not to pay attention to.

"Well, *most* anywhere."

"What about back home?"

He shrugged. "Could be. I don't know where all the portals lead. It's not like I go through 'em myself, or anything."

"Why not?"

"I'm not like most of the folks you meet. I don't need to go anywhere. People come to me."

"Like a spider in a web."

He smiled. "Just like. Except I'm not gonna eat you."

"That's a relief." He gestured around him. "I've wandered around here for a little while, and so far seen portals to all the worlds I've visited, but I don't have much desire to visit any of them again. You said that there are other portals?"

"Sure there are. Hundreds. There's one right up there." The man aimed one gnarled finger up a set of steps made of slabs of silvered glass.

"Where does that one lead?"

"Dunno. Nothing stopping you from taking a look, though."

He swiveled his head toward the staircase, then looked back at the man who looked like his grandfather. The man shrugged, in a gesture that was so like the Arthur Salazar that Duncan remembered and still missed that his eyes teared up. But he turned away again, then walked to the staircase and ascended it. At the top was a massive white block, solid, immovable. He reached out both hands, and pressed on its warm, greasy surface with his fingertips.

It immediately turned onyx black.

He squinted at it, waiting for something more to happen, and then the block became transparent, like a window without a speck of dust. And he peered through it into the interior of his own apartment.

It was night. The window was open, the curtains rippling in the breeze. Moonlight played on the surfaces, turning them a silvery gray, showing up every fiber in the carpet, the furniture casting angular, misshapen shadows against the wall. There was no hole in the floor, nothing amiss.

It looked exactly the way it had the moment before his plunge into the catacombs of Malkuth.

"Dear god," he said under his breath. And then with no conscious volition he stepped through the portal, and found himself once again standing, naked, in the living room of his apartment, the sounds of traffic coming in through the window, the warm, humid breeze of a July night brushing his bare skin.

CHAPTER 9

BINAH

Duncan looked around him, his expression dazed.

No. No, it can't be. It can't. Not after what I've been through.

He reached up, pulled fingers through his hair, and found that it was once again the short cut he'd had when he started, not the long, thick ponytail he'd worn when he stepped through the mirror in Chesed. His bare feet felt glued to the floor. All he could do was stand and stare in mute astonishment.

From where he was he could see into the kitchen. Piled in the sink were the dishes left from the evening's meal, still left unwashed because he and Libby had been too amorous to spend their time together cleaning dishes, and had retired to the bedroom shortly after the meal was over. A *Sports Illustrated* was face down on the coffee table, pages open to the last article he'd read, how long ago was it? Months? Years? A few hours?

There was no way to tell. And even if he'd decided, the answer wouldn't have meant anything.

Finally, he got his feet to move, and went across the room, avoiding the spot where the cave-in had occurred. Better safe than sorry. The last thing he wanted was to start over.

He opened the door to his bedroom. In the dim light from a distant street lamp, shining in through a gap in the curtains, he could see the rumpled blankets and twisted bedsheets, a pillow that was askew, and even the empty plastic water bottle he'd knocked off the night stand.

But Libby wasn't there.

He stepped out into the hall again, to see if maybe she was in the bathroom. The door was open, and the light was off, but he crossed the hall and peered in.

Empty.

"Libby?"

No answer.

He returned to the bedroom, put his hand on the mattress. On the right side, where he always slept when they were together, there was still warmth, as if he'd just arisen. The left side, though, was cool to the touch. Gone also was her pile of clothes, tossed one by one to the floor as they'd undressed each other.

His, of course, were still there, lying where they were thrown.

It was too much to wrap his brain around. Feeling a sudden uprush of emotion that left him near tears, he went to the bed and dropped into it, curled up on his side, pulled the blankets up around him, and fell into a deep sleep.

Duncan woke up when his alarm went off at seven o'clock. He blinked, yawned, and stretched, and looked over to the other side of the bed, half expecting Libby to be there, her long black hair fanning out over the pillow.

She wasn't.

He got up, grabbed his bathrobe from its hook on the door, and walked into the kitchen to put on coffee. Coffee... how long had it been since he'd had any coffee? Once again, the thought of *How much time has actually passed?* crossed his mind, floating past unanswered, likely unanswerable.

When the coffee pot was making comforting gurgling sounds, he decided to hit the shower. But as he was walking out of the kitchen, he glanced over at the telephone.

He picked it up, dialed Libby's number.. If he woke her up, that was too bad. He had to know where she was.

He picked up the receiver, and dialed Libby's number. On the sixth ring, there was a click, and her familiar voice saying, "Hi, this is Libby. I'm not here right now, or maybe I'm deliberately ignoring you. Either way, you can leave a message, and if I don't call you back you'll know which it was."

He smiled a little at hearing her voice, but the smile evaporated. If at seven in the morning she wasn't here, and wasn't in her own apartment, where was she?

He went into the bathroom, turned on the light and the tap, and then shucked his robe. He stuck a finger under the stream of water, and when he found it was just warming up he stood and stretched, arching his back like a cat.

And that's when he caught a glimpse of himself in the mirror.

There was a long, uneven white scar on his right cheek. He stared for a moment, as if he could not quite believe what he was seeing. He looked down at his belly, and smaller, fainter, was the scar of a knife-wound in his side.

His breathing accelerated. He leaned toward the mirror over the sink, twisting at the waist, looking at his back and shoulders. And crisscrossing his skin like a spider's web were dozens of long white scars, the remnants of the blows of a many-thonged leather whip that had been used on him in another world.

"What the *fuck*? Where am I?"

The water ran, steam rising from the bathtub, warming the air. Moving like a sleepwalker, he pulled the knob that turned on the shower, and stepped under the spray. He went through the motions of cleaning himself on auto-pilot, shampooing his hair, soaping and rinsing the rest of him, then shutting the shower off and reaching for his towel. He dried off, and while he was doing so, glanced in the direction of the mirror. It was now too fogged to see his own image.

That had to have been a hallucination. Post-traumatic stress disorder.

But post-traumatic stress after... what? A dream? What the fuck was all of that? All of the worlds and portals and so on, and then he ends up back in his apartment, apparently on the same night he left it?

And then a more sinister voice added, *But if it was only a dream, where is Libby?*

He rehung his towel, opened the bathroom door, and went into his bedroom. He stood, naked, in front of the full-length mirror affixed to the inside of his closet door.

The scars were still there. He stared at them, trying to make sense of it, and finally gave up. He walked to his dresser, pulled boxers, shorts, and a t-shirt out, and tossed them on the bed. Was it a work day? Should he be getting ready for another exciting day of paper pushing at Carthen, Douglas, and Prescott? He decided he didn't give a damn if it was.

No way was he going in. He'd call in sick. He had to have some time to get this all figured out.

He dressed, walking out into the living room as he was tugging his t-shirt into place, and gave Libby another call. He got her voicemail again.

Okay, call work. Maybe Tania was already there. At least she'd be able to tell him if he'd gone batshit insane or not.

But a call to Carthen, Douglas, and Prescott Financial Consultants also connected to voicemail. He glanced at the clock. It was 7:42, and the office didn't open until nine. So that wasn't that odd.

Yes, it is, the sinister voice in his head said. *It's all odd. There's something seriously wrong here.*

He poured himself a cup of coffee, and returned to the phone and dialed his parents' number. His dad was an early riser, and would already be off to work at the electrical repair company he owned and managed. His mom, on the other hand, was a nurse at Colville General Hospital, and she usually worked the afternoon-into-evening shift. Chances are, she should be home...

... but six rings in, it went to voicemail. "You have reached the home of Thalia and Dennis Kyle," came his mother's voice. "We're not able to come to the phone right now, but leave your name and number—"

He hung up.

Who else? Who else could he call?

No one, said the sinister voice. *They're all gone. Everyone you know is gone, like in those creepy movies where people vanish one by one, and eventually only the main character is left, slowly going crazy...*

"Oh, shut up." He picked up his cup of coffee and went to the window. It still stood open, the curtains fluttering a little. He pulled them back, and looked out from his vantage point on the second floor of the building.

He saw just what he expected to see. Cars moving down Lee Street, slowing as they approached the stop sign a little further on. A tweedy elderly man walking a little white shih-tzu down the sidewalk. Trees, bright green in the July sunshine. A corner of the apartment parking lot, where an overweight woman was trying to maneuver a car seat into the back of a little Toyota

Corolla while clutching a screaming infant in the other hand.

All ordinary, nothing that was inexplicable or mysterious or ominous.

He took a sip of coffee.

So he was home. He was home and it looked like no time at all elapsed, through all of those weeks and months he'd spent in other worlds, trying to find his way back. Whatever the meaning of it all, at least he was back where he belonged.

But the scars, came the sinister voice, the one he thought he had successfully silenced. *What about the scars? You don't get scars in a dream or a hallucination.*

There was no good answer to that. He drained the rest of his coffee, and walked back to the telephone, and dialed work again. This time when he got voicemail, he said, "Hi. This is Duncan Kyle. I'm feeling sick today, and won't be in. If anything urgent comes up, give me a call. I'll be in tomorrow. Thanks."

He hung up, then grabbed his sandals and slipped them on, took his keys from a hook next to the door, and left his apartment.

Duncan spent the morning driving around Colville. He passed his workplace, but the windows were still dark, the parking lot empty. He went to the Colville Bakery, got a scone and another cup of coffee, and then got the idea of going to see if his dad was at work. Dennis

Kyle would undoubtedly wonder why Duncan wasn't at work himself, but he decided he'd make up some excuse on the fly. There had to be something, someone to tie him down, bring him back into the familiar world he'd left, and in which everyone who had appeared in both worlds seemed to have blown away in the night like leaves in a storm.

K & G Electrical Repair was on North Pine Street, across town from his apartment. Dennis Kyle had started the company over twenty years ago with a friend, Adrian Gartner, who had wanted out of the business five years in. Dennis Kyle had bought out Adrian's share, but the company stayed K & G, mostly because the name mattered less to him than the quality of the work and the loyalty of the customers. The business was housed in a long, narrow two-room space in a large, low brick building that also was home to an appliance rental store and a place that sold pet supplies. The front room had bins and cabinets filled with parts, tools, and equipment, the back room was a small office containing Dennis's desk, a computer, and a file cabinet with twenty years' worth of receipts and records. It was a spare, practical place, no frills, orderly and pragmatic.

Just as Dennis himself was.

He turned from Gates Avenue onto North Pine, drove a block, and stopped at the stoplight where North Pine intersected Warren Road. He peered around the car ahead of him, trying to see the shop.

Shouldn't he be able to see the sign from here?

The light turned green. He pressed the accelerator, looking over to the right as he passed Northside Pet Supply. K & G should be next door.

But there was no K & G. Next to Northside Pet Supply was Frederick's Appliance Rentals, Inc. It was as if someone had excised the electrical repair company, and sewed the rent up without leaving a seam.

"What...?"

A horn blew behind him, and he realized that he'd slowed to a stop in the middle of the road without even being aware of it. He gave a distracted wave of the hand to the driver behind him, and then pulled up to the curb, and got out.

The appliance rental store windows were still dark, but there were fluorescent lights on in the pet store. He got out of his car and walked over to the door, feeling almost like he was watching someone else do these things. An actor in a play, perhaps, or simply acting as a spectator to the behavior of a total stranger, doing things for reasons only apparent to himself. He felt disembodied, lost, dazed.

He slipped his hand under his t-shirt, letting his fingertips trail across the scar on his side. Then he reached up and touched the one on his cheek. Only then did he grasp and turn the doorknob.

The door opened with a jingling of a bell, and he stepped up onto a wooden floor and past a cash register. Stacks of bags of dog and cat food lined shelves, along with trays of canned foods of various sorts, brushes, collars, leashes, toys. A little farther on were small animal supplies, hamster bedding, guinea pig food, little wheels and plastic balls and water bottles.

"Hello?" he said.

There was a noise of footsteps, and an elderly woman came out from the back of the shop. She was tall, a little stoop-shouldered, and had steel gray curls held back by a flowered scarf.

"Oh, hello," she said. "Sorry, I must have not heard the bell. Can I help you?"

"I'm... I'm wondering about a place, a place that used to be here. Or near here. It was an electrical repair company called K & G. I was told that it was next to the pet supply store, but I can't find it."

The woman frowned, and pushed wire-rim glasses up the bridge of her nose. "An electrician's place?" she said. "Now, I don't recall any electricians around here. I think there's one up towards Foxcroft. Dey Street, I think. Right near the Farmer's Market."

"No, it's not that I need an electrician. I was trying to find this particular one."

"Oh. Well, I've been here for about fifteen years, and it's always just been us and Mr. Frederick's place. Are you sure you're on the right block?"

"I'm sure."

The woman shrugged and smiled. "I'm sorry..." she said, a little tentatively.

"Me too." He turned and walked past the rows of brightly-colored pet supplies and out of the store, setting the little bell over the door jingling again.

He got back into his car and started the engine. His dad's business was gone. But their voicemail still said "Thalia and Dennis Kyle." They didn't answer the phone, even though his mom should have been home when he called.

It was as if they were here, but at the same time not here.

He drove back to his apartment, his thoughts spinning, evading his grasp as easily as fluttering butterflies. He pulled into his parking space in the lot, got out, and went through the door and up the stairs to the second floor. He unlocked his apartment door, went inside, and looked around, his eyes distant, unfocused.

Everything looked the same as always. Stereo, television, sofa, little table near the window with a framed photograph of him and Libby at the beach the previous year, magazine on the coffee table, dirty dishes in the sink. It was all exactly right, and at the same time all completely wrong.

He went into the kitchen, and saw that on his telephone there was the message "New Voicemail" on the digital display. He picked up the receiver, punched a few numbers to enter his access code, and heard a halting, mechanical voice say, "You have... one... new voicemail. Please press one to hear your messages." He did so.

There was a beep, and then a deep male voice said, "Duncan. This is Drew Consentino. I know I'm the last person you expected to hear from, but you need to give me a call right away. It's important. 287-3482." There was a pause. "Oh, yeah, and one other thing... you shouldn't talk to anyone else until I've had a chance to speak to you, okay, buddy?"

Duncan hung up the phone, his face a study in perplexity. "Mr. Consentino? Why the fuck would Mr. Consentino call me?"

Drew Consentino had been his track coach in high school. He was a smart, funny man, a taskmaster as a coach, but someone he had looked up to during a period when he'd been an aimless, unfocused teenager, much more interested in girls and parties than in discipline and academics. And the track team wasn't only about athletics. Mr. Consentino had been clear on that. Your grades drop, you're off the team, I don't give a rat's ass about how well you run.

"And," the coach had said, "you can quote me on that."

Okay. Mr. C. represented clear thinking, honesty, straightforwardness. He could use a good dose of that.

He punched the number in, half expecting that it'd go to voicemail like all the others had, but on the third ring he picked up. A familiar voice said, "Consentino residence."

"Mr. C.?" He felt strangely like the high schooler he'd been the last time they'd spoken. "It's Duncan Kyle."

"Duncan," Mr. Consentino said. "I'm glad you called back. Can we talk?"

"Sure."

"I'd rather do it face to face. But it has to be soon."

"Why?"

"Because you're in danger, here. Not that you haven't been before, but it's different. And you need to get this one figured out quickly. Before nightfall."

"Why?" It was hard to imagine being in deeper trouble than he'd been in Gevurah, or while being hunted by Diana in Yesod. He looked around at the familiar surroundings, and tried to imagine what could be as dangerous as what he'd already faced, and failed. Bizarre? Yes. An actual risk? Hard to believe.

But Mr. Consentino said, "I'll tell you more when we meet. But let me say that the other places you've been, they've been after your knowledge, or your loyalty, or your body, or your mind. Here they want your soul."

A shudder twanged its way up his backbone. "Where do you want to meet?"

"You know where Worlds Apart Café is?"

"It's near downtown, right?"

"Yup. Second Street, just across from the big travel agency."

"I can be there in twenty minutes."

"Me too." Mr. Consentino paused. "Oh, and Duncan? If you see anyone who looks like me, anywhere else but in the café, don't talk to him."

Duncan left his apartment again, so shaken up by the conversation with his old track coach that he went from the door of the apartment building to his car at a jog. He slid in behind the steering wheel, closed the door, and punched the auto-lock button, a shiver of relief going through him at the *clunk* noise of the locks shooting into place. He started the car, backed up, and then pulled out onto Lee Street, this time turning right toward downtown Colville.

And as soon as he pulled into traffic, he saw the smiling figure of Drew Consentino walking down the sidewalk. He met Duncan's eyes, waved in a friendly fashion, and motioned for him to pull over.

Instead, he hit the accelerator. He looked in the rearview mirror as Mr. Consentino turned, frowning, holding both hands palm upwards in a "what the hell?" gesture.

He turned the corner, and the man followed him with his eyes until he was lost to view.

A trickle of sweat ran down his chest.

Calm down. He had to calm down. He didn't even know what he was up against, yet. And whatever Mr. C. told him, it was hard to believe this place could do anything worse than whips, axes, and arrows.

But he couldn't shake the feeling of terror that the combination of the phone call, and seeing a second Mr. Consentino outside his apartment building, had left in him. He drove downtown in a shivering panic, checking his mirrors often, but seeing nothing more out of the ordinary. And when he saw first the sophisticated glass front of Exotic Destinations Travel Agency, and across the street the smaller, quaint front of Worlds Apart Café, he felt like he had navigated a minefield and somehow reached a safe haven.

He pulled over in an open spot, right in front of the café.

When had he ever been able to find parking this quickly downtown?

The feeling escalated when he saw that there was still thirty-two minutes left on the parking meter. He got out, locking his car behind him, and went in. It was the usual bustle of near-noon, with a wide assortment of patrons, from businesspeople to students to young mothers with toddlers in tow. He looked around through the crowds of people, and spotted Drew Consentino's face from the back, already seated at a table.

"I got you coffee," he said, sliding a cup toward Duncan as he sat down.

"Thanks."

Mr. C. looked much the same as he remembered—a little grayer around the temples, perhaps, and one or two more smile lines than he'd had eight years earlier. But the smile was authentic, as was the firm handshake.

"So, we could spend time in pleasantries, but I'm guessing you don't want that," Mr. Consentino said. "We can catch up afterwards. If you still want to."

"I saw you. As I was leaving. Right outside my apartment building."

Mr. Consentino nodded. "I warned you. You didn't talk to him, then?"

"No."

"I figured. You wouldn't be here if you had."

He frowned, shook his head. "What the hell is going on? I don't understand any of this."

"Well, you know you're not home, right?"

"I had sort of figured that out, yeah."

"And you've already figured out that some key players in your life are missing."

"My girlfriend, my parents. I tried calling them, and there's no answer. And my dad's business is gone."

The older man nodded. "You see what is happening, right?"

"No. I have no idea."

"The people you know best—your folks, your girlfriend, a few others—they can't replicate closely enough to fool you. You'd notice the difference. So it's easier for them to play the game of pretend-they're-out-of-the-office. Other folks, acquaintances and so on, if they don't get every mannerism just right, you wouldn't see it."

"And you...?" he started, and then realized that he didn't even know how to formulate the question that was in his mind.

Mr. Consentino grinned. "Me? Well, I'm not Drew Consentino. But I think you know that."

"You said you were."

"I had to get you out of the apartment, before you got in more trouble than you already are."

"But if..."

"Yes?"

"If you're one of them... I mean, if you're not who you say you are... then why should I trust you, either? You might be leading me into a trap." Maybe even meeting here was the trap. He resisted the urge to jump up and run.

"Good question. Best one you've asked yet." Mr. Consentino leaned back, stretching his long legs out in front of him. "You've been told this before, but I guess you need a reminder. You can't do this by logic. You have to feel your way forward. It's intuition or nothing, here."

"If this place isn't my home, where am I?"

"It's called Binah. But it can be anywhere you want it to be. Or, more accurately, anywhere *it* wants to be. But at night... it shows its true color."

"And what are its true colors?"

"Only one color. Black."

He shook his head. "Why are you helping me?"

Mr. Consentino shrugged. "In every world, there are powers. For want of a better name. There are good ones, bad ones, and ones that don't care a damn one way or the other, at least not with respect to humans. You must have noticed that you've had help."

"Yes."

"So think of it as being the powers that would like to see you keep going, and the powers that would like to see you fail. And, of course, the ones who have no interest in the outcome, but some of which might trip you up just for the fun of it." He took a sip of his coffee. "I'm one of the ones that would like to see you make it."

"Thanks."

"But here, the deck is stacked against you. There are a lot *more* of the ones who'd like you to fall. So they aren't only going to try to stop you, they're going to try to stop anyone who helps you."

"That's why they impersonated you."

"Yes. And you'll have to stay on your toes, because they haven't shot nearly all of their arrows yet. As you get closer to making it through, they're going to be more desperate to slow you down."

"How?"

"I don't know."

"And what am I looking for? Is it another portal?"

"I don't know that, either. Intuition, remember? I think the expression is 'you'll know it when you see it.'"

"So what happens if I'm still here at night?"

He looked down, and sloshed his coffee cup back and forth gently. "Well, the masks will fall away. That's good and bad, of course. You'll see this place, and its inhabitants, as they truly are, not as they want you to see them." He gestured around him at the crowd, at the smiling faces of patrons in animated conversation with friends, the serious faces of businesspeople picking up lunch and anxious to get back to work in time, the eager, fresh faces of college students, with their backpacks and laptops. "None of what you see now will look like this once the sun goes down." His voice fell to a near whisper, but it was still clearly audible through the background babel of talk and espresso machines and microwaves and cash registers. "All of these people? None of them are human." He smiled. "Of course, neither am I."

He stared at the familiar face of his old track coach, silent.

"I know," Mr. Consentino said. "You're still wondering, 'Why should I believe this guy?'"

"No. I believe you. I'm wondering what the hell I should do now."

"My guess is they won't get too blatant about it until nightfall. It'll be subtle stuff, like your meeting another me on the way here. All to slow you down, distract you."

"From what, though? That's what you haven't told me yet. What am I supposed to be doing?"

Mr. Consentino considered. "Some of the places you've been, it's been about revealing what you know, about trusting too easily. Other places you had to be careful not to be led by your heart or"—here he grinned— "your balls. You know what I'm talking about. You almost got caught that way."

"Yes."

"Easy enough to let that happen. I'm a guy, I understand, you know? And in other places you've been, it was about keeping your head on your shoulders and your skin in one piece. Here, though..." He looked up toward the ceiling, as if choosing his words. "They want *all* of you. They want to convince you to eat the illusion, so that you become part of it. They want you to become one of us, body and soul."

"Then these people..." He once again gestured around him.

"Some came in from outside. It's tempting not to leave. You'll see. They'll pull out all the stops." He considered the café patrons, drinking their cappuccinos and eating their sandwiches. "Some of the people here were probably in Binah from the beginning. But most of them,

I'd guess, are ones who came in from outside, and then fell for the illusion."

"What about you?"

Mr. Consentino shrugged and gave him a little smile. "I don't know. There's probably no way to know. Because, you fall for it, it wipes your memory of what you were. You want the illusion, it *becomes* you, and what you were sort of... ceases to be." He paused, finished his coffee. "So I have no idea. I don't remember any previous life, before I was here. But then, you see, I wouldn't, would I?"

"That's worse than being killed."

"I told you it was. I think some of us have kept a little of what we were before, though, which is why there are ones who want to help you, and others who want to stop you."

"So what do I do?"

"Keep focused on what you *know*. You know who you are, and you also know you're not where you seem to be. Keep putting one foot in front of the other, and when the time comes to act, you'll do it. But waver for an instant, and you'll never leave." He looked around. "You should go now. We've spent long enough talking. If you stay in one spot, they'll find you, and it'll be too late to get away. You'll be done for."

He stood, and the older man reached out to shake his hand.

"Thanks," he said. "I hope you haven't put yourself at risk by warning me."

"Me? Nah. I'm trapped already. What more can they do?"

Duncan turned away from the table, and wove his way through the crowded café. He paused before he left, and looked back at his old track coach. Mr. Consentino had stood, and was in quiet conversation with one of the baristas, a dark-haired young woman who looked like she might be a student at Colville College. Both of them laughed, then Mr. Consentino picked up his empty coffee cup, walked it to the trash, and headed for the exit.

Was he really on Duncan's side? Immediately the answer came. Intuition. Whatever else he'd said, he was right about that. Rely on his gut. And his gut was telling him he was speaking the truth.

He left Worlds Apart Café and walked toward his car, pulling out his keys. He clicked the unlock button on his keyring, and the car lights flashed as the locks unbolted.

A voice behind him said, "Duncan? Is that you?"

He turned, heart beating a little faster, to find himself facing a red-haired woman in an alluringly V-necked blouse and tight jeans, with a little silver cross on a necklace and dangly earrings that swayed as she moved. She smiled, revealing a row of perfect teeth.

"Oh, my god, it really *is*," she said, and the next thing he knew, he was in her arms. He hugged her back, reflexively. She smelled spicy and a little sweet, just a hint of perfume. He knew most of it was her body's own scent, *like when I was with her last...*

"Allison," he said.

"You remember me?" She gave a delighted laugh.

"How could I not?"

Like a guy could forget the woman he lost his virginity to, on a rug in front of a roaring fire in her father's hunting cabin...

Danger. Don't get taken in. And get away as soon as possible.

"How have you been?" she was saying. "It's been, what, five years?"

"More like six or seven. And I'm fine."

"Married yet?"

"Nope. You?"

She held up a left hand that was bare of adornments. "Not yet. I won't be easy to trap, I don't think."

Trap. Yup. Good choice of words, Allison, or whoever you are.

"I would have thought you'd have wanted to marry and settle down, honestly."

"Really? Well, I thought some lucky woman would have had you tied up, too. But maybe I'm the lucky one. You want to... do lunch?"

Something about the way she said "do lunch" almost made him laugh.

Mr. Consentino had been right. They were good with the mimicry, but not spot on. Allison loved having sex, but she wasn't this... sultry. They got the surface right and the details wrong.

"I'd love to," he said. "But I've got an appointment I have to get to. Maybe another time?"

Allison put out her lower lip a little. "Oh, that's too bad. I work as a paralegal, and I have a long lunch break today, I thought running into you was fortuitous, you know?" Again, there was more than a hint of come-on, and one that would have worked fine under most circumstances.

Such as if they were really in Colville, New York. Not in some strange world of masks.

"Don't you think lunch would be fun?" she said, still pouting.

"It would have been. But I gotta go." He shrugged. "Sorry. Give me a call, though. I'm in the phone book."

There was the sound of shrieking tires and blowing horns, and then a dull, hideous thump, followed by an outcry of many voices. Allison gave a little shriek.

"Oh, my god," she said, putting one finely-manicured hand to her mouth. "Someone's been hit!"

He turned, and looked over at where a group of bystanders were crowded. A silver Mazda was angled across both lanes, both doors open. Even from where he was standing, he could see a dent and a crimson stain on the hood.

"C'mon!" Allison walked toward the scene as fast as her high-heeled shoes would allow.

A man lay on his back, one leg twisted at a grotesque angle. Blood covered the side of his face, and more was seeping through his t-shirt. His eyes were half-closed, and he moaned, moving his head from side to side.

It was Drew Consentino.

"Lay still, buddy," someone said. "We've already called for an ambulance."

"I didn't mean to hit him," came a tearful female voice. "He walked right out in front of my car."

He walked up to his fallen coach, moving like a somnambulist. People parted as he came through, and he knelt by the stricken man. "This is because of me," he said. "They did this because of me."

Mr. Consentino opened his mouth, and licked his lips, and groaned. "I guess I was wrong when I asked what more they could do."

"I'll stay with you until the ambulance comes."

"No!" Mr. Consentino tried to sit up, and failed. "You can't stay here. That's why they did this to me. It's to keep you here, to keep you entangled. Get out of here. I'm done for anyway, no matter what." He coughed, and blood sprayed from his mouth and spattered Duncan's clothing. "Go. Now."

Duncan half turned. The accident had happened right in front of his car. There'd be no driving away, not for some time. "My car—"

"Doesn't matter how," Mr. Consentino said. "As long as you don't stay here. They'll be converging on this place, now they think you're trapped here."

He looked over at Allison, standing a little behind him, her beautiful face radiating sympathy and a desire to comfort. He knew what she'd say. *Now you can't go off alone, you need to be with someone when you've had a shock like this, I'll make you feel all better...*

And she would. He'd feel all kinds of better. And then he wouldn't need to remember anything, ever again.

He stood, knees straightening in a sudden, jerky movement, and backed away. Allison reached for his arm, touched him, but he pulled away from her as well, and turned and ran. He heard, as he fled, voices saying, "Why is that man running?" and "He said this was his fault!" and "He said the accident happened because of him."

The voices faded into silence as he ducked around a corner at a full run, sprinting down the familiar streets of Colville that, if Drew Consentino was right, wasn't Colville at all.

He ran past the columned façade of the Colville Public Library, then took off at a diagonal to cut through Clifford Park. People eating takeout food and chatting occupied long park benches. Solitary sorts reading books or texting occupied shady spots under trees. A pair of shirtless teenage boys laughed and tossed a frisbee around. The whole scene was idyllic, and could have had the caption "A Summer Day In The Park." No one looked up as he ran past. His shorts and t-shirt gave him the look of a jogger, and the drying blood spatters on his t-shirt looked like a smudge of dirt unless looked at closely.

Which no one did. No one tried to stop him. He exited the park at the other corner, and only then turned to see if he'd been pursued.

It appeared he had not.

But where to now? It was possible to get back to his apartment on foot, although a good hour's walk at least. And there was no certainty he'd be any safer in his apartment than anywhere else. He crossed a bridge over the swirling current of the Catanic River, tumbling over its shaly bed, and halted for a while in the middle, looking down into the water.

He didn't even know what he was looking for. It could be a portal, or it could be almost anything else. Even Mr. Consentino couldn't tell him exactly what he was trying to find. He said if he kept putting one foot in front of the other, he'd be okay.

And that he'd know it when he saw it. Whatever it was.

But spending hours aimlessly wandering through Colville wasn't all that appealing. And there was also the warning he'd received about this place being more dangerous after dark. "The masks fall away," Mr. Consentino had said, which sounded terrifying. The idea that all of these people, and all of the places as well, were mere appearances hiding something inhuman was far scarier than the up-front horror of Gevurah.

And he was hungry. All he'd consumed so far that day was a scone and three cups of coffee. He found a little deli just on the other side of the bridge and got a roast beef sandwich to go, which he ate sitting on a bench watching people go into and out of a little bookstore whose sign said "Flying Centaur Books."

Wasting time. He finished the last of the sandwich and wiped his mouth with a paper napkin. This was getting him nowhere. Although he did need to eat.

He got up, deposited the napkin and the sandwich bag into a trash can, then walked down the sidewalk under the shade from some ancient sugar maple trees. The street ended in a t-intersection, and he faced the soaring steeple of a church, with wide marble steps leading up to heavy double doors. Set in the center of the front wall was a circular stained glass window, and above that was a gap where a huge brass bell hung. A sign, its modernness a little jarring next to the classic architecture of the church, said, "Colville Methodist Church. Rev. Katherine Courtwright, Minister. All who are seeking answers, come inside, for what you seek is here."

"Well, that sounds hopeful." He stepped forward to cross the street toward the church.

He still had one foot on the sidewalk when the barking started. Tearing down the middle of the road, its eyes fixed on Duncan, was a huge dog. Its feet were a blur, but the savagery in its eyes was unmistakable. Teeth were bared, and a streamer of drool trailed it, splattering on the road. Its barks were deep-throated, guttural, primal. The black fur had an oily look, but along the back of its neck the hair stood up like spikes.

He froze. He'd never been afraid of dogs, but this one looked easily capable of tearing his throat out. He yelled, "Hey! Stop!" The dog slowed, perhaps ten feet from him, its breath coming out in one continuous grinding snarl.

"Back off," he said, in as stern a voice as he could manage while trembling. The dog didn't come closer, but it wasn't cowed, either. It stood between him and the church, bristling and growling.

"Well, they're trying to stop me, and that tells me I'm on the right track," he said under his breath, and then to the dog he said, "What now? Wait for you to attack? Or try to run past you? That'd end with me getting mauled. And I've been patched up enough times on this merry adventure."

The dog walked a pace or two, then turned back, as if it were drawing a line on the pavement beyond which Duncan could not cross.

"Yeah, I get it, you ugly sonofabitch. No going into the church. But why?"

A distressed voice came down the road, causing both Duncan and the dog to turn. "Moddy! Moddy, where are you?"

Around the corner of the next block came a middle-aged woman in a checkered blouse and tan slacks, wearing an apron. She took in the scene in front of her, and gave a horrified yelp. "Oh, Moddy, Moddy!" And then to Duncan she said, "He hasn't hurt you, has he?"

"No," he yelled back, still keeping his eye on the dog. "But he's damn determined not to let me move from this spot."

The woman trotted up to them, her face a study in agitation. "Oh, young man, I'm so sorry." Without a moment's hesitation reached down and grabbed the dog's collar. Duncan frowned. The dog seemed to shrink when she touched it, diminishing into a quite ordinary-looking black lab, looking up at her sheepishly and wagging his tail.

"He's not dangerous, but he's got a loud bark. He wouldn't have hurt you, I promise."

"He acted like he was ready to rip my guts out." He looked at the woman and dog through narrowed eyes.

"Oh, but he wouldn't have, really. Although I can see why you were scared. Are you sure you're okay?"

"I'm fine."

"Perhaps you should sit for a while, after your fright? I could get you some tea, and I've just taken cookies out of the oven. My house is right around the corner. It's the least I can do, after what naughty, naughty Moddy did." She looked down, and scolded, "You are such a bad boy. Pushing open the screen door like that. You could have been hit by a car, and you scared this poor man half to death."

Moddy whined, and his tail went down. A more ab-ject-looking dog Duncan had never seen. Not a trace of the slavering savagery he'd shown only minutes earlier.

"No, it's quite all right," he said. "I'll be fine. None the worse for having been a little frightened."

"Are you sure?" she said, a wheedling tone entering her voice.

"I'm sure."

And Moddy looked up at him, and for a fraction of a second, his lip curled back, exposing one white canine tooth.

"Well, if you're sure, then. Come along, you bad dog." She turned, and still holding Moddy's collar, she walked back down the street. Duncan followed them with his eyes until they turned the corner.

"Okay, then," he said. "And note how I'm looking both ways before I cross, so I don't get mowed down by a speeding cyclist, or something." He crossed the street, then went up the marble stairs to the front door of the Colville Methodist Church, opened the door, and stepped into a warm, dim space that smelled of old books and candle wax.

The door shut behind him, and a voice in his mind said, *Safe. At least this far.*

The entryway was utilitarian, a cork board had notices headed "Ladies' Altar Society" and "Ministry and Oversight Committee" and "Signups for Community Food Pantry." A pile of last Sunday's church bulletins sat on a little wooden table near the inner doors. On the left, a staircase downward was labeled with an arrow and the words "Sunday School," and to the right, a staircase upward had a similar sign that said, "Choir."

He went to up to the inside door, put his hand out, and paused.

He had not seen the inside of a church for perhaps fifteen years, since visiting his maternal grandparents in their native New Mexico as an eleven-year-old, and being dragged, protesting, to Saint Anne's Catholic Church in Albuquerque. The whole thing seemed to his young mind a mix between silly ritual, bad singing, mumbo-jumbo, and extreme boredom. His grandfather's surreptitious wisecracking, and a promise of a hike with him up into the Sangre de Cristo Mountains that afternoon, had made the experience bearable. But churches still had those bad associations—adults doing weird and pointless things, having to sit still and be quiet, and then life going on exactly as before after the whole thing was over.

He pushed the door open a little, and the sensations became overpowering. The way the light filtered through angled panes of colored glass. The dark wood pews. The marble baptismal font. The brass plaques honoring parishioners who had passed away and who, probably, had also been generous donors. And in the front, like some grotesque icon of torture, a crucifix, with the beaten and bleeding body of Jesus hanging by its hands and feet.

"Feel your pain, dude," Duncan said, and went in.

The interior contained an immense silence, a cavernous emptiness waiting to be filled. The pews, row on row, stood in orderly lines to the left and right, and he walked soundlessly between them toward the altar. There was only one other person in the church—a small, birdlike woman, dressed casually in jeans and a sweatshirt, standing behind the lectern straightening out a stack of handwritten notes.

She looked up as he approached, and gave him a tentative smile. She was perhaps forty years old, with straight brown hair in a neat, simple cut, and small round glasses that reflected the light as she moved.

"Hello?" she said, setting down the handful of papers. "Can I help you?"

"I'm looking for Reverend Courtwright," he said, without exactly knowing why.

Intuition. Mr. Consentino said he'd know what to do.

"You've found her." There was some relief in her tone. Understandable. A woman, alone in a church, and a strange man walks in, it's bound to raise some fears, even if you trust that God is watching over you.

She walked out from behind the lectern, and stepped down from the altar. "People call me Reverend Kate. Or just Kate. I don't stand on much ceremony." She put out one hand, and gripped his in a brisk handshake.

"I'm Duncan Kyle."

"Nice to meet you. What can I do for you?"

Good question. How could he find out what he needed to know, without betraying his knowledge to her? Then he did a mental shrug. No, never mind that. Screw being subtle. Just because everyone here was behind a mask of lies, didn't mean that he had to be.

"I'm trying to find a way out of Binah." He looked directly into her eyes.

Her forehead creased. "Out of where?"

"Binah."

"Is that some sort of word for *trouble*?"

"No. It's a place. In fact, it's where we are. But I'm guessing you knew that." He gave a grim chuckle. "But you're right, in a way. *Trouble* is exactly what this place is going to turn out to be, I think."

"I'm..." she started, and then stopped, frowning and smiling at the same time. "This is the Colville United Methodist Church, Colville, New York." Her voice was kind, patronizing. "I've never heard of a place called *Binah*. So I really don't have any idea what you're talking about."

"I think you do."

"Perhaps we could contact someone, someone who might be able to help you. Colville Social Services—"

"Oh, come on, Reverend, cut the crap," he snapped. "I don't need Social Services, I need help. I know where I am. I know, or at least I have an idea, of what's going to happen when the sun sets. And I want to get my ass well clear of this place by then."

Reverend Kate's eyes met his, only for a moment, and then she looked across the empty pews toward the door. When her gaze moved back to his face, she wore a different expression, a mixture of wariness, curiosity, and fear.

"Now, let's start over," he said. "I want to find a way out of here before nightfall. I think you know why."

"Yes." All of the condescension was gone from her voice. "I know why."

"So you get why I need to act quickly."

"Yes." She turned her hands toward him palm upwards. "But I don't know how I can help you."

"You can tell me how to find a way out of Binah."

"A way out of the world." She paused, rubbed a hand across her forehead. "It's a peculiar request."

"But you understand what I'm asking. So stop stalling."

Again, there was a pause, as if she were considering how to answer. Then she said, "Oh, yes. Yes, I understand."

"So...?"

She gave a fluttery little motion with one hand. "So, it's not really that easy. Which I'm guessing you know. If you can even make the request, you know that."

"Yes. But I was told I needed to find a way out before dark."

She frowned. "I suppose that's right. But that doesn't mean that things couldn't be dangerous before then. The fact that you know all of this—well, they'll try to stop you from leaving, and taking that knowledge with you. Or, better yet, they'll try to convince you to forget."

"Make me swallow the illusion."

"Yes. That's the right way to put it."

"A man I met said it that way. And the others tried to kill him. May have succeeded, I don't know. I didn't stick around long enough to find out."

She looked out into the shadowy space of the empty church. "They did that, did they? You must be awfully important."

"I'm not sure why that would be. But yes, they've tried more than once to stop me, and I don't think they're done trying yet."

"No," she said, shaking her head. "I expect not. But what is it you want from me?"

"Some direction. If you'll stop dancing around long enough to give it to me. Your sign outside said that if I wanted answers, I'd find them in here."

She smiled in a distracted way, and said, "Oh, that? The assistant pastor put that up. He gets a little categorical, sometimes. But I suppose... yes, it could be interpreted that way."

"So I've come to the right place?"

"One of many, but yes."

"So where now?"

She pressed her hands against her blouse as if to straighten it, and seemed to come to a decision. "There's no way out from here. The others—they know my sympathies well enough that they'd never allow a portal near here. I feel sorry, you know? If someone's made it this far, it's pitiful to see them fail." She gave him a searching look. "Most do, you know. If they can't stop you outright, they'll try to slow you down, and eventually most people give up."

"Then I'd better get going quickly. Where do I find a portal?"

Her expression became dubious. "I only know one that's close enough for you to walk to and have a hope of getting there before nightfall. And even then, it'll be a near run thing. It's in the old cemetery up near the college. Sandown Hill Cemetery, I think it's called. Do you know where the Arts Quad is?"

"Yes."

"If you walk lengthwise through the Arts Quad, on the north end you'll see an alley that passes between two of the buildings. It leads up a hill, behind some old storage buildings, and then around a little grove of trees. Once you get past the trees you'll see a metal arch through a stone wall. That's how you get in."

"And where in the cemetery is the portal?"

"Look for another arch. That's it."

"Where does it lead?"

"How would I know that?" Her voice had a hint of exasperation. "What more do you want from me? I've taken more of a chance than I should have just by telling you what I did." Then she stopped, cleared her throat, and shook her head. "I'm sorry. That was unkind of me. I've grown a little timid, I suppose. But even so, it *is* the best I can do. I don't know anything more. I certainly haven't tried going through the portal myself."

"Why not?"

She opened her mouth, closed it again.

He gestured around him. "This is a horrible place. You can't tell me you like living here. If you know of a portal, why don't you use it?"

She gave a nervous little laugh. "The devil you know versus the devil you don't, I suppose."

That was the common thread. The realization came upon him like a flash of lightning. They were all trapped because they'd trapped themselves. Not only here, but everywhere else. In Hod, they were willing to kill him to find out how he jumped from world to world—but they missed the truth, which was that he could do it mainly because he hadn't convinced myself that he couldn't.

Or wouldn't. Reverend Kate was a little like Fatima. Both of them stayed with what they knew rather than taking a chance and jumping to somewhere else. And it cost Fatima her life.

"I'd still take the chance, if I were you."

"If you were me?" The corner of her mouth curled a little, and the light caught on the lenses of her glasses, turning her eyes to flat circles of white. "But that's it. You don't know what I am. And if I went through the portal, what would I be then?" Again there was the shuddery little smile. "You haven't seen me at night, you know. If

I went through the portal, maybe I'd be that... all of the time. Day and night. Better at least to have half of my life to be human."

"I hadn't thought about that."

"No. You wouldn't, of course. No reason for you to. But none of that concerns you, not really. Because you're right, you need to get going, if you're to have any chance at all."

"Thanks," he said, looking at her and feeling a strange sense of pity. "You've been very helpful."

"I hope you make it."

"Me too. What happens if I don't, though?"

She laughed again, but her face showed fear, and perhaps something more than fear. Envy? Sorrow? Longing?

"Well, then, I might see you back here some Sunday morning." Her smile faded. "You won't remember that we ever met, though."

He shivered. "I'd really rather that didn't happen. No offense."

"None taken. Good luck."

"Thanks." He turned, and made his way back down the aisle toward the door.

"Duncan?" she said, and he turned. She looked tiny, fragile, standing there alone in front of the altar, like a china-painted statue.

"Whoever told you to be gone by nightfall was right. This place... once the sun sets, it's much easier to see where the evil is. But most people... when they see it, they collapse, give up. It appears to be invincible."

"Is it?"

"No." Both hands came out, either in a gesture of helplessness or in a benediction, it was impossible to tell which. "But it's much easier to *believe* that it is. And once you believe it, you've already been defeated."

He pushed open the door into the entryway, and then, more cautiously, opened the heavy door to the outside, and peered out. He half expected to see Moddy the dog, snarling and slobbering on the doorstep, waiting to devour him, or any of a hundred other less well-formed fears of what this world might have in store. But the wide stone landing was empty, as was the street in front of him. The warm July sun shone down, and a humid breeze ruffled his hair. Somewhere nearby, a bird sang.

All completely innocent, welcoming, like a honey trap for flies. *Come on out,* it said. *It's perfectly safe out here. Come on, little fly, a little farther now, there's nothing to be afraid of.*

He stepped out onto the landing. The church door closed behind him with a thud. He looked up the street, in the direction the woman in the checkered blouse had taken Moddy, but there was nothing that way but some parked cars, and in the distance, a little kid riding a tricycle on a driveway.

Okay. It was either give his best shot at getting to Sandown Hill Cemetery, or give up and stay here and wait for the sun to set.

And both Mr. Consentino and Reverend Kate were in agreement that that would be a bad idea.

So it was off toward Colville College, which meant cutting directly across downtown again. Maybe he could get to his car, though. That'd make it a lot faster, and a lot safer.

Which meant that they'd be looking for a way to stop him. But he still had to give it a shot before he set out on foot.

He retraced his steps, down the street and past the bench where he'd eaten lunch. At the corner was a shabbily-dressed man of perhaps Duncan's age, although his posture and demeanor were of someone much older. He held a sign up in front of him that said, "Homeless and jobless. Looking for work, will do anything. If you don't have a job for me, can you spare some change? If not even that, God bless anyway."

He considered crossing to the other side of the street, but by the time he got a good look at the man, such a move would have been blatant. The man turned his tired, blank eyes upon him, kept them fixed on his face. The eyes had no hope, no spark of life, only an exhausted resignation. Despite himself, Duncan felt pity for him.

Even though he knew the man was not really who he appeared to be, he couldn't stop himself from feeling sorry for him.

"Spare a dollar, dude?" the man said, in a hoarse voice.

"If I've got it." He pulled out his wallet.

Hell, he could afford five. The money wasn't real anyway.

He dropped a five-dollar bill into the man's outstretched hand.

"Gee, thank you, mister," the man said, in a dreary monotone. "You know where I can find work?"

"Not really. And I need to go."

"No, but I'll do anything." A grimy hand reached out and clutched his sleeve. "Anything. I'm starving."

"Well, now you have five bucks. Go get yourself some food. There's a deli across the street."

"But that'll only get me through this evening." The man's voice took on a wheedling tone. "You've got to help me."

Shit. He shouldn't have stopped. Don't get slowed down. Don't argue. Get away.

"I'm leaving now." He walked off, but the man held on to his sleeve.

"No!" the man said, becoming agitated, panicky. "You don't know what it's like!"

"I know what you're trying to do." He pried the clutching fingers loose. "And it's not going to work."

The man reached out again, his fingers grasping, but he pushed away his arm. The man spun around and almost fell.

"Fuck!" the man said. "You don't have to hit me!"

Duncan didn't respond.

It was another ruse, meant to delay him.

He turned and strode away, but still the man followed, shouting abuse. "You think it's easy, being homeless and penniless? You act like it's fun to push around poor people! Asshole! I hope one day you find out how it feels!"

Don't respond. He wasn't real. None of it was real.

But that was easier to tell himself than to believe. A lifetime of lessons in Being Nice To Others wasn't so easy to shuck, even if he was certain that the Others weren't actually human.

Certain. Was he certain?

He had to stop himself from turning to look at the beggar, who had finally stopped following him. Then he thought about Reverend Kate's words. *Once you believe it, you've already been defeated.*

He kept walking.

He passed the public library, its granite steps glinting in the sun. A fresh-faced young man in front of it was handing out pamphlets and asked him if he'd mind taking a quick survey. He didn't answer. He took a left on Second Street, meeting no further impediments, and noted with some relief that the accident in front of Worlds Apart Café had been cleared.

Was Mr. Consentino all right? He knew it wasn't Mr. Consentino. But whoever, or whatever, it was that helped him. Without his advice, he'd have been screwed. Hopefully he was okay. But in either case, at least he could drive up to the college, and not have to avoid more homeless guys and rabid dogs.

His cheer, though, diminished as he came up to his car, and saw that the front tire had a huge yellow plastic clamp on it. The meter was blinking "0:00." Tucked under the windshield was a parking citation.

It took him a moment for the realization to sink in. Then he shouted, "What the fuck? They booted my car for letting the meter expire?"

A man and a woman, walking hand in hand down the sidewalk, turned and gave him a sympathetic look. He met their eyes, his mouth hanging open with frustrated anger.

"Those traffic cops can be bastards," the man said in a commiserating tone.

"No shit."

"Sorry," the woman said, and the couple strolled on.

"Me too," he mumbled. He leaned over and tugged ineffectually at the boot, but it didn't budge. "Shit. Clever of them. On foot it is, then."

He left the car behind. The digital clock in front of the Colville Savings and Loan said it was five minutes till four. Still plenty of time to make it up to the college by sunset, especially given that it was July. Just past the bank, Second Street curved sharply to the left and angled upwards, the beginning of the rise leading to the hill on which Colville College sat, looking down on the town and Carlisle Lake from its high eminence. Soon he was toiling up a steep slope, the first of three long, sweeping switchbacks that in three miles as the crow flies, and six to follow the road, would finally flatten out onto the top of Eastham Rise, where a hundred and fifty years ago Abraham Vanderzee had donated the land that would one day house the most prestigious research institution in the area.

But now he cursed Vanderzee's memory for not siting it closer to the town. After only a half-hour's walk, his t-shirt was plastered to his back with sweat. The afternoon sun beat down on his shoulders, and he had a stitch in his side, undoubtedly a remnant of his still-tender knife wound. He only pushed himself another twenty minutes before he sat, panting, on a low stone wall by a stately Queen Anne mansion that was set back from the road in the shade of an ash grove.

He had gotten his wind back, and was about to keep going, when he heard a small voice saying, "Mr.?"

He looked up. A little boy, perhaps six or seven, approached him with timid, halting steps. The boy was dressed in a ragged t-shirt and grass-stained shorts, and wore scuffed tennis shoes that had holes the sides. His face, though, was cherubic, topped by a shock of light blond, almost white, hair.

"Yes?" he said, but inward, a voice said, *Oh, fuck it. Here we go again. What now?*

"I'm lost." His voice trembled, and his lips quivered, but he was trying to put a brave face on it.

"Oh, yeah?" He immediately winced. God, that sounded callous. "Where are your parents?"

"I don't know," he said. "My mom is back home. I don't think she knows I'm gone. My cat got loose, and I was trying to find him, but he ran. And I ended up here, and I don't know how to find my way back to my house. Can you help me?"

"What's your address?"

The lower lip came out a little, and a single tear escaped and trailed down his cheek. "I don't know."

Man, they were pulling out all of the stops this time. What would the little boy would do if he started laughing? This was classic. Help the little lost boy to find his home. Couldn't they think of anything more original than that? What was next, Lassie running up to tell him that Timmy was in the well again?

"I'm sorry," he said. "If you don't know where you live, there's not much I can do."

"Can't you try?" the little boy pleaded. "There's no one else to help me. You're the only person around." He gestured with both hands, a frantic, terrified movement that looked utterly authentic. And sure enough, when he looked up and down the street, there was no one else driving past, not a pedestrian, not a retiree out for a brisk walk, not a homeowner mowing his lawn.

"Sorry, kid. I have to go."

"*Please.*" Now a hand came out, reaching toward him, just as the homeless man's had.

He stood, and backed away.

"Can't you walk around with me for a while? I know I'll recognize my house if I see it. And maybe we'll find my kitty. My kitty is lost, too, he'll die if you don't help me find him—"

He turned and ran. The little boy's whining sobs died away behind him.

Jesus. I wish they'd find a way to stop me that didn't make me feel like a dick.

But he kept walking, as the road twisted its way up the side of Eastham Rise, up toward the college and the cemetery where Reverend Kate had said there was a portal.

An arch. She'd said that there was an arch at the entrance, and the portal was the only other arch in the cemetery. Should be easy. Get there, walk through, find himself somewhere else. Anywhere but here.

Of course, he still didn't really know what happened at dark. On the other hand, all of the warnings had been vague. Could it really be any worse than what he'd already been through? The whole thing sounded pretty nebulous. Probably not worth getting himself all worked up.

With that comforting thought, he walked up around the bend and onto the second long stretch, skirting the edge of Mill Creek Gorge. His watch said it was a little past six o'clock. He encountered two more people who tried to stop him, ignoring one who asked for help jump-starting a car, and then being forced to a stop by a broad-shouldered teenager with a swagger who blocked his way, grinning, and said, "Bro, you're on *my* sidewalk."

Duncan barely paused. He cocked one fist back, and punched the kid directly in the jaw. The teenager reeled backwards, caught his heel on a crack in the pavement, and sat down with a thud, a stunned look on his face.

He stepped over the kid's sprawled legs, massaging his hand. "Nice story, bro," he said, without turning.

But time was running out. By the time he made the next turn, this one up and to the right, across the Mill

Creek Bridge and into the last straight sweep to the edge of the rise, his legs burned with the exertion and the sun was dropping rapidly toward the west, turning the clouds orange and scarlet and molten gold. But there was a sign that said, "Colville College, est. 1868" on it, and then a series of more prosaic signs that gave directions to the various libraries, the medical and veterinary schools, the law school, the biological research building, labs, and greenhouses. The twisting maze of Colville College opened out before him.

There weren't many students out. It was summer session, but even so, the campus looked more quiet than usual.

Maybe they'd decided not to mess with him, since he knocked the last guy on his ass. He chuckled. Then his laughter died on his lips. No, not likely. Nowhere he'd been was that easy. They weren't ready to let him go yet.

Another fifteen minutes brought him to the rectangle of buildings surrounding the arts quad. He walked past the Law Library and into the grassy, tree-dotted expanse of the quad. The shadows were long, but the middle of the quad still had streaks of red-gold sunlight illuminating the tops of some towering pine trees. He crossed it diagonally, and spotted the entrance to a narrow alley on the north side, exactly where Reverend Kate said it would be. The entry to the alley lay between two venerable ivy-covered buildings, whose brickwork glowed red in the light from the setting sun.

"Excuse me, but can you show me some ID?" came a harsh male voice from behind him.

"Oh, for fuck's sake," he said, turning. Of course. Here we go, then.

A campus cop marched up to him, a suspicious look on his face. "Are you a student at the college?"

"No."

"Then I'll repeat my request. Can you show me some ID?"

"Why should I?"

The cop's scowl deepened. "Because a man answering your description was seen assaulting a student a half hour ago, only a quarter-mile from here. And you need to comply with my request, or I'm going to haul you in for questioning."

He stared. The cop stared back. And then Duncan laughed. The whole thing, all of the human obstacles set in his way, suddenly struck him as ludicrous.

"Really? In for questioning? Because the sun's about to set, and if I'm not mistaken, the whole place is really going to go to hell at that point. And that means I don't have much time left. So unless you want to fight me, or shoot me or something, you can back right the fuck off. And then I'm going to walk down that alley, and up to a little cemetery past a grove of trees, and with luck, I'll never visit this ridiculous place again."

The cop's lips tightened, and he took one threatening step toward him.

And he heard, as if it were coming from outside him, the words, *Run. Don't fight him, don't argue, run!*

The voice sounded a little like Mr. Consentino's.

With a lightning movement, he turned and fled, darting between the two buildings, his shoes slamming on the gravel of the alley.

Behind him, the cop shouted, "Hey! Stop!"

A rutted dirt road ran behind the buildings, curving gently around a small grove of trees. To the right were tin-sided pole barns, one with its doors open, revealing a dark interior and the front end of a piece of earthmoving equipment. He sprinted up the road with the cop panting behind him.

To his left, the trees thinned, then ended, to be replaced by a neat, well-maintained stone wall with a hedge behind it. In the middle of the wall was a gate with an arch, a sign curving around the top with the words "Sandown Hill Cemetery" cut into the metal. He gave it barely a glance as he sprinted toward the entrance.

That was when the last of the sun's rays were cut off by the advancing horizon of the rotating planet, and the spot of gold in the western sky faded into gray.

The color winked out of the world with a suddenness that brought him to a skidding halt. The familiar shapes around him melted, ran like wax in a fire, fusing into forms that were alien and unfamiliar. Everything became a sharp-edged nightmare of gray and black and silver and white. He was still right in front of the arch, but the arch was no longer a simple wrought-iron structure. It was heavy, of carven stone, with twisting figures of monsters incised in the side. The stone wall was made of rotted shale, and was partially collapsed. The neatly-trimmed hedge was now a tangle of weedy briars, their hook-thorned branches reaching out toward him like tentacles.

There was a gagging, snarling sound from behind him, and he slowly turned to face the campus cop.

Where the cop had been was an emaciated figure, dressed in grimy rags. Its bony arms ended in paw-like hands with long, heavy nails. The face was skeletal, its cheeks sunken, the mouth gaping open to show a row of broken teeth, eyes burning in deep, hollow sockets.

The policeman's hat still sat crookedly on the top of its head.

They were motionless only for a moment, and when the moment broke, both sprang simultaneously. Duncan ran through the arch as the cop's clasping hands snapped closed on the empty space his body had occupied only a fraction of a second earlier. The cop gave chase, his bony frame creaking as it moved.

But as he entered the cemetery, he saw that his problem was much bigger than a single adversary.

With a grating noise of stone on stone, graves slid open. Atop the graves were statues of angels and cherubs, but their faces were not kind and comforting. They were leering, looking out at the world with sly, wicked, knowing expressions. There was the groaning of coffin lids being pushed back, and the slithering sound of dirt being forced aside. And the dead clambered up, crawling from the earth, all moving toward where he stood, his eyes wide with terror.

A nearby headstone said, "Here lies Bethena Gray, beloved wife of Elijah Gray. 1811-1888. Rest in peace in the arms of the Lord." From this was coming a mere skeleton, missing some finger bones, its jaw slack and hanging to one side. It moved in a jerky, halting fashion, its white arms flailing and clattering. Another grave, that of one David Caldwell, was of more recent vintage, and the estimable Mr. Caldwell was arguably in better shape. He still had tatters of flesh clinging to his bones, and one eye was intact, glowering unblinking as he approached. Others, in various stages of decomposition, tottered or crawled along, moving however they could given the decrepitude of their joints.

All were converging toward the spot where Duncan stood.

About a hundred yards away was a stone building, its sides as stark-edged as a marble crypt. The windows were black, and the ivy that crept up the side had leaves that looked sculpted from black ice. But right in front of it was an arch, made not of stone or iron, but of the boughs of trees woven together by time, a pair of ancient maples that leaned toward each other, and over the centuries had become so tangled they had fused into one, twisted mass of branches.

This was the portal.

But between him and his goal were dozens, perhaps by now hundreds, of the dead denizens of Binah, as determined to block his way as its living inhabitants had been.

Once you believe, you're already defeated.

He looked at the horrific sea of animated corpses that were reaching, moaning, clutching at him.

Do not believe it. If what they looked like in the day time was an appearance, then so was this. And it could hurt him only if he gave it that power.

Slowly, taking a deep breath, he walked toward the arch.

And the dead fell back before him. One pathetic, mostly skeletal woman, still clad in what had once been a nice flower-print dress, tried to grab at his shirt, and he slapped her arm away with the ease of someone brushing away a mosquito. The woman gave a gurgling whine and cowered back.

He kept walking. No running now. The time for running was over. The race was already won.

Smiling to himself, he pushed over the last two of the dead that blocked his way, and strode through the arch, calmly and triumphantly leaving behind the macabre night world of Binah.

CHAPTER 10

CHOKHMAH

The world changed again, but color did not return. Duncan stood on a flat, featureless expanse of gray. The horrors in black and silver from the graveyard in Binah were gone, but what had replaced them appeared to be nothing at all.

His feet stirred up tendrils of fog that curled around his legs as he walked. He was still clad in his t-shirt, shorts, and sandals, but he once again had the long hair he'd worn in Chesed, tied back with a twist of cloth he'd gotten in the house of Shao Bolin. He brushed his fingers on his cheek, and felt the jagged line of the scar, and the prickliness of a neatly-trimmed beard.

So some things changed, some things remained. The illusion-world of Binah was able to hide some parts of him, but not others. The scars were visible through-out—maybe they were so integral to his memory of what had happened that whatever created the illusion couldn't override them. Binah was a sham world, a thin veil covering a terrible reality. But the veil was so at-tractive that it even worked for the creatures who lived there, and knew that it was all false.

Until darkness fell. Then they showed what they really were.

A troubling thought struck him. Were the people in Binah who had helped him, Mr. Consentino and Reverend Kate, also fleshless, bony horrors after dark? What did they see when they looked at themselves after night fell?

Maybe that was why Reverend Kate told him not to believe the illusion. She knew what it could do, because she'd let it happen to herself.

He kept walking. Nothing happened. The topography had no relief. It was perfectly flat, a gently swirling misty emptiness that stretched to the horizon. The sky was gray, but it didn't look like clouds hiding the sun—it looked as if there really was nothing there, just a pearly dome of diffuse light. The air held no smells, no sounds. Even the temperature was neither hot nor cold.

"It's an improvement over zombies," he said aloud. "But I don't think this place'll ever make it as a tourist attraction."

There wasn't much obvious purpose to walking, but on the whole, walking was more pleasant than standing still. So he kept going, his long legs kicking up streamers of fog, for perhaps another half hour before he saw something that broke the monotony of the landscape.

It was a dark shape, unmistakably solid and real in this nebulous void, like a little block of reality that had somehow dropped in from outside. And as he got closer, he saw that it was Drew Consentino, seated in a metal-framed chair like the ones in the café where they'd met. He was leaning back, the front two legs of the chair off the ground, and looked completely relaxed despite the odd setting. He wore a black t-shirt, sweat pants, and a pair of running shoes, much as he had been clad at track practices in Duncan's bygone high school days.

Mr. Consentino grinned as he saw him approaching.

"Made it out, I see," he said.

"Yeah. So did you, then?"

"In a way. I mean, I'm still back there, in Binah. Or would be, if you went back."

"So this isn't real."

"No. But you found out that what you were seeing in Binah wasn't real, either."

"Okay." He frowned.

"And you see what the problem is, right?"

"Well, I see a lot of problems, but I'm not sure if I know which one you're talking about."

"If something has two appearances, one pleasant and one horrible, then there are three possibilities. The horrible one could be the reality, and the pleasant one a mask. Or the pleasant one could be the reality, and the horrible one the mask." He fell silent, and raised his eyebrows a little. Duncan knew that look. It was the expression Mr. Consentino always had when he wanted Duncan to come up with an answer on his own.

"That's only two possibilities," he finally said, trying to keep an edge of annoyance out of his voice.

"Yup," Mr. Consentino said. "Glad you can count."

"So...?"

"Don't you see it?"

"No."

The older man's grin widened. "*Both* the horrible appearance and the pleasant one could be masks, hiding something else."

He frowned. "Okay, I guess I can see that. But which one is it?"

Mr. Consentino shrugged. "No idea."

"You live there. You must know."

"I'm not only talking about Binah. It's true everywhere. Once you start down that road of deciding that some things are real and others aren't, you have to be certain that you're using a valid criterion for determining which are which." He chuckled. "And look, Duncan. You started out by telling me I wasn't real, so why do you think any answer I would give you is relevant?"

"Shit," he said. "I'm not a philosopher. I'm just a guy. I don't have the brainpower to figure this stuff out."

"You don't have much choice. Unless you happen to come across a philosopher to help you out. And even then, I don't know if I'd trust them or not."

"So there's no guarantee that anything I'm seeing is real."

"No guarantees of anything, I'd say."

"On the whole, I'd rather be fighting zombies."

Mr. Consentino gave a belly laugh. "I relate, Duncan, I really do. Straightforward is nice. But most of life isn't straightforward, and you have to make a truce with that."

"How? Like I said, I'm not a deep thinker."

He reached into his shirt pocket, and pulled out a package of spearmint gum, and popped a slice into his mouth. "That's a tough one."

"Another thing I have to figure out for myself, I guess?"

"It all is, buddy. It *all* is." Mr. Consentino thwacked him on the arm. "And that is absolutely all I'm going to tell you." He held out the package of gum. "Want a piece?"

"No thanks," he said. "But I appreciate the advice. I guess." He stepped around Mr. Consentino.

And beyond the chair where he sat, the land was no longer mist-shrouded. It was still a slab of gray, but less amorphous, more solid, more *there*. The surface on which he walked had lines, like the seams between huge tiles, splitting up the featureless ground into squares.

He walked for perhaps a half-hour, as the figure of Mr. Consentino, still sitting in his café chair, diminished and finally disappeared behind him. Finally, he was completely alone, with nothing but a Cartesian grid of perfect squares extending in all directions as far as he could see.

He kept walking. The ground was smooth, solid, unyielding. He fell into a rhythm, measuring out paces. Three strides to a square. Fifty squares took him about five minutes, according to the watch he'd put on when he was in what he thought was his apartment in Binah. He'd counted out almost six hundred squares, which he estimated at a little more than a mile, when he came upon another interruption in the monotonous landscape.

Ahead of him, the rows of squares converged into the vanishing point. Then with a suddenness that made him stop in his tracks, there was a man in front of him. A moment before there was nothing, and then he was standing before his grandfather, Arthur Salazar, sitting in a rocking chair, looking up at him with a wry smile.

"Long time, no see," Arthur said.

"Where did you come from?"

"My Papa used to say he'd found me under a rotten log, but I think he may have been lying."

"That's not what I meant. You weren't here a moment ago."

Arthur gave a noncommittal little gesture with one hand. "These things happen." He looked around. "This isn't much better than living in a place made out of mirrors. You couldn't have conjured up something better for your grandfather?"

"Did you know where the black portal led?" he asked. "You said you didn't, but I wonder if you were telling the truth."

"Well, they all lead *somewhere*, and I've found that all the *somewheres* are dangerous, so it really doesn't matter much which one you choose. You can also choose to sit still and stay home, but that's dangerous too, you know? You never know what might happen to you in your own apartment."

"Tell me about it."

"I believe I am."

He frowned. "Is this all a dream?"

"Nope. I can tell you that for sure. You're not dreaming. You're wide awake, maybe the widest awakest you've ever been in your life. That's a gift. Not one to throw away."

"It's been a long journey to get there."

"Yes. And you're not done yet, you know."

"No. I wouldn't want to stop here."

Arthur laughed. "Give this place some time. It might grow on you."

The air quickened around him, as a breeze brushed his face.

"Now, get along. You don't have all the time in the world."

"No, I suppose not." He leaned over and gave his grandfather a hug. "I miss you, Grandpa."

"I know." The old man hugged him back, in an embrace that was strong and warm and comforting. "You'll do okay, Duncan."

He moved past, trying to suppress the tears that were rising in his eyes and tightening his throat, and he walked on without looking back.

A little less than an hour, walking in the tiled plain, with the warm breeze on his right cheek and his feet pacing out the miles, and he saw another of the denizens of this strange world. This one stood, still and blue, lissome and fragile as an iris flower. He knew even before he was close enough to see features that it was Shao Daiyu, wrapped in an indigo garment with a wide belt, watching him approach with a sorrowful expression, standing perfectly still, just as she had when she had revealed to him that she wanted him to stay with her in Chesed.

"I'm glad you have come this far," she said, as he walked up to her.

"Me, too." He gestured at the expanse of flat gridlines, as unremarkable as a sheet of graph paper. "Where is this?"

"It's called Chokhmah. Not that the name matters."

"I'm sorry I couldn't stay in Chesed," he said, feeling impelled to apologize even though he guessed that like Mr. Consentino, this was not the same Shao Daiyu as he had met in another world. Just as Daiyu was not the same as Libby Chen. Just as appearances aren't reality, ever, and the masks may simply cover up other masks, like the layers of an onion, so that when you're finally finished peeling each one away, you're left empty-handed.

"Are you truly sorry, Duncan Kyle?" she said. "Do you wish you had stayed with us in Chesed?"

He gave her a sheepish look, and didn't answer for a moment. Finally he said, "No. I guess not. But I didn't want to hurt you."

"Not wanting to hurt me is not the same as wishing that you could meet my desires. You can be honest about that. I understand that you had to leave."

"I know. But I am still not entirely certain why. All I know is that I felt compelled, even though your world was a pleasant place to be."

"Sometimes even a pleasure becomes a burden if it never changes."

"Yes. And I felt that..." He looked down. The patient gaze of her brown eyes was becoming impossible to meet, and he was ashamed of himself, although he couldn't see why. "It seemed to me that the path was not at an end, yet."

"Did it occur to you that perhaps there is no path?"

A fleeting smiled passed across his lips. "It is what I would have thought, before I started on this journey. I never thought there was a purpose for anything. Everything was random. Not that it bothered me. Honestly, I never even thought to ask the question."

"And now? Do you think there is a reason for everything that has happened to you?"

"It'd be nice."

"Nice, yes. But is it so?"

"I don't know."

"Then perhaps I should ask a different question. Would it make a difference to you, if you knew that there was no ultimate purpose?"

He considered. "It wouldn't change what I do, no."

"Then you are no different from my father and I. We mine clay and glazes, and make pottery. There is no purpose for it other than the fact that creating beauty is what we do. It is our nature. And you jump from world to world for the same reason."

Behind where Daiyu stood, he saw that the silver-gray grid had been replaced by a long, sweeping expanse of deep green grass, stretching off to the horizon, and the flatness had given way to gentle curves and swales.

"It's enough to know that you're doing what you were made for," Daiyu said, and a shy smile touched her mouth.

He leaned forward and kissed her on the cheek. "Thank you."

He stepped around her, and his feet touched the springy softness of grass. As he walked, the smell of vegetation rose to his nostrils, the scent of green and growing things. He only then recognized how sterile the air had been, no smells, no humid warmth of life. Moved by some impulse, he took off his sandals and continued barefoot, feeling the edges of the blades of grass bend under the soles of his feet. He carried the sandals swinging from his hand for a time, but finally tossed them aside.

He'd started out this adventure naked. Which is how all humans start out their adventure. It would be ridiculous to be afraid of being barefoot now.

He walked on for perhaps an hour, enjoying the feeling of the soft grass between his toes. The sky was still a uniform gray, and there was nothing else to look at, but on the whole it was still more pleasant than fog or a flat gray expanse of grid lines. When he saw the next interruption in the monotony, he thought at first that it was some kind of optical illusion, an afterimage from staring at the sheet of saturated greenness. But it refused to disappear, a reddish blotch on the horizon that stayed the same size however much he walked toward it.

But finally it resolved, becoming clearer and larger, and revealed itself to be Darick Bevans, High Judge of Gevurah, still wearing his scarlet robes, seated in an ornate chair that looked like a throne, trimmed in gold. There was a twinge of pain from his back, and a defiant anger rose in his chest.

Good. He actually wanted to have a word with that bastard, when he didn't have his goons around. Find out how he felt about the fact that Duncan had beat him fair and square.

"I told you that your kind never admits defeat," Duncan said, as he came up to the scowling man, who looked down at him with an expression of arrogance and certainty and judgment. "How does it feel, having lost?"

"You slipped from our clutches by trickery," Judge Bevans said. "This does not mean you are right."

"And the fact that you can command men with whips and knives and axes does not mean that *you* are right."

"You would tear down order and the rule of law. This must be stopped, by whatever means necessary."

"I have no quarrel with the rule of law. But fairness and decency are more important."

Judge Bevans gave a dismissive snort. "It is more moral to be over-harsh than over-kind. Purity and sanctity are the twin pillars holding up righteous society. The soft and weak will only hasten its destruction by inducing men not to undertake the drastic steps needed to protect what we have."

He laughed. "You're calling me soft and weak? You saw me take the whip, and even gravely injured, defy you and your lackeys. Is that weakness?"

"You show weakness of spirit," Judge Bevans said. "Those who intend evil always start that way. Pity is the opening of the door. You showed pity to that demon, who was rightly dying in our streets, and who would have been burned alive had he survived. Pitying leads to empathy, and empathy leads to acceptance. The Evil One uses your pity as a path to destruction."

"Yet I escaped, and your world remains undestroyed. Odd thing, that."

"You think to throw my failure back in my face..." Judge Bevans spat.

"No. Only to point out that your assumptions are wrong." His voice rose, and he wondered at his own sternness and authority in the face of the man who had put him to torture. "You mistake steadfastness and spirit for rebellion and anarchy, and throw away half of the world because it doesn't bow its head to your cruelty. But what you haven't been able to tell me is why you do it. If you are torturing and killing people on the off chance of saving your world, you must think it's awfully important to save. I've been in a lot of places since I started my travels, and I can say that without exception, Gevurah is the ugliest, bleakest, most humorless world I've ever seen. Why hurt others to defend that? If you can show me that by your desperation to eradicate evil, your world has more sweetness or compassion or pleasure in it, one more friendship forged or love brought to fruition or kindness performed, I will willingly go back to Gevurah with you and place my head on the block without complaint."

Judge Bevans stared at him for a moment, his expression frozen, eyes dark with fury. Then he bowed his head.

"You would live in a petty life of self-gratification rather than sanctity," he said, "seeking self-indulgence rather than what is right and holy. But here, I cannot stop you from doing so." His mouth curled as if he had tasted something bitter. "You may proceed."

And behind him, the grassy fields erupted in tens of thousands of crimson flowers, each one shaped like a tiny star.

Duncan stepped around the throne where Judge Bevans was seated, and mumbled, "Damn straight I may," under his breath.

He walked for another hour before he saw the next denizen of this land, a place that opened up before him like a flower. He was unsurprised to find it was his Uncle Liam, back in human form, lying on his back in the meadow with his eyes closed, a blissful expression on his face. He had his shirt off and balled up behind his head as a pillow, and both hands laced across his belly.

"Took you long enough," Liam said, without opening his eyes.

"Sunbathing?" Duncan said.

"Actually, yes," Liam said, and Duncan realized with a shock that he was casting a shadow. He looked up. The gray sky had turned a deep azure blue, and the yellow-white brilliance of the sun shone unobstructed on his shoulders.

"I suppose you have some sage advice for me, too," he said. "That's apparently what this place is about."

"Me? I don't believe in giving advice."

"Well, you did when we landed in Gevurah. You had a lot of advice then, as I recall."

Liam laughed, and opened his eyes. He stretched, cupping his hands behind his head. "First of all, I was dying. Figured that if there was a time to tell you some parting wisdom, it was then."

"Death doesn't seem to have slowed you down much."

"Let's say it was just a phase. But second, was I wrong? Not that you listened, of course."

"All you told me was to get out of there quickly. You didn't tell me how."

He sat up and shrugged. "No matter, I suppose. You made it through, which is the important thing, even if you lost a little skin in the process."

He sat down next to Liam on the flower-spangled grass. "So now what? Do I keep walking and see what happens?"

"That's what you've been doing all along, isn't it?"

"I suppose."

"Then no harm in continuing. It's worked okay so far."

He looked off toward the horizon, with its gentle curves of green and blue and red. "This place is, I don't know... evolving as I walk through it. What's that about?"

Liam picked a flower, and smelled it, then twirled it gently between his fingers. "I guess you could say that Chokhmah is a place that becomes what you need it to be. Or"—he frowned, and tossed the flower away— "it grabs on to what you bring into it, and shapes it into the next step you take."

"Where does it lead?"

Liam laughed, and shook his head. "You always want the answers to be laid out in front of you, don't you? Be willing to risk not knowing everything. Take what this place gives you, and be confident that you can meet its challenges standing on your feet. After what you've been through, you won't find them very hard."

"If I didn't know better, I'd think that was advice."

"That," Liam observed, "was a dirty trick."

"Can I ask you one more question?"

"I suppose. Even if you got more out of me already than I should have told you."

"Will I meet everyone that I came across in my travels? All the ones who I knew from my old life?"

"Don't know. You'll have to keep going to find out. But that's always true, of course. You keep going in order to find out how the story ends." He lay back down in the grass, folded his hands across his belly again, and closed his eyes.

Duncan stood, and walked off through the sunlit meadow.

He crested the top of a hill, where the breeze rippled through the little scarlet flowers and whispered through the grass, and before him saw the first trees he'd encountered. They were massive oaks, spreading their branches out over a little creek that wound its way through the hills, bubbling over a stony bed. And seated on a flat slab of rock next to the stream were his mother and father, still in the antiquated garb they'd worn in Netzach. Thalia Kyle had her knees tucked under her, and leaned against his father Dennis, who had one arm protectively around her shoulders. Thalia looked worried, Dennis stern, and both followed their son with their gazes as he approached, but did not smile.

"I'm disappointed in you, Duncan," his father said.

"Why? Because I saw through your lies?"

Dennis's lips tightened, and Thalia said, "We only wanted to help you, Duncan. We've only ever wanted to help you."

"And you wanted me to swallow your reality. It was like Binah, a watered-down version of what Binah is. You couldn't even be as authentically kind as Mr. Consentino and Reverend Kate, and the worst of you weren't as evil as the horrors that Binah conjured up. You wanted me to keep quiet and join in, and Binah wanted to eat me alive. But it was the same lie, really, on two different levels."

"And you never considered how your rejection affected others," Dennis said. "It was all about you. A selfish little boy, that's what you are."

He laughed, the first real belly laugh he'd had since his journey had begun. Thalia wilted a little beneath the power of that laugh, a sound that blew away all artifice, made the air around them a little clearer.

"And to be unselfish is to let you mold me into what you wanted me to be," he said. "That's always been your way, hasn't it, Dad? If I don't fit your mold, bend me till I do fit. Here, Duncan, look at the world through my lenses, because yours don't show you the truth. And Mom... you always let him, didn't you? Too hard to fight it, especially after Maria died. Too hard to stand up and say, 'Hey, Dennis? Maybe you're wrong.'"

"You always were a stubborn child," Thalia said.

"And you're right to put it in the past tense," he said. "I'm not a child. I have the scars to prove it. You can't shame me or bully me into seeing things your way any more, and if that bothers you… I'm sorry. I still love you, because you're my parents and I know the sacrifices you made for me and Maria. I know how hard it was when she died. But I won't pay myself in tribute on that debt for the rest of my life."

Neither of them spoke. They looked at him, Dennis still disapproving, Thalia still nervous, the fingers of one hand twisting at a bit of her sleeve.

"Goodbye, Mom, Dad," he said. "I don't know if I'll see you again. Maybe if I get home, we can discuss this again. If you… if the *real* you knows anything about it."

He walked past them, a little upstream, and saw an arched bridge spanning the creek, and on the other side, a neat little stone wall edging a road paved with cobblestones.

The road curved through a grove of oaks and maples, hoary with age. There were signs of inhabitants here. Besides the road and the wall were little clearings with neat rows of vegetables, a vineyard, and once, the gnarled gray-green of a cluster of olive trees. A little farther on were some small cottages, and standing in front of the last cottage was Fatima, wearing a kind smile. She leaned on the wall, and next to her was a tray piled high with figs, and cheese, and a fat loaf of freshly-baked bread.

"I thought by now you might be hungry and thirsty," she said.

"Famished."

"Then eat."

He helped himself to a fig, and Fatima picked up a pitcher of straw-colored wine and poured out two cups, then handed him one.

"There is much that could be said." She held up her cup. "But for now, food and drink and companionship are all I have to give."

"It is enough."

The next hour was spent sitting on the stone wall in the sunshine, and by the time it was passed the platter and pitcher were both empty.

"Did the jackal-man win?" he asked, as the sun climbed steadily into the clear sky, sending its dappled light through the moving leaves.

"Does it matter?"

"It does to me."

"Then no," she said. "No, he didn't win. He died, just as I did."

"Good."

"But so did Anir, and so did my cousins, and so did their families. All go to dust eventually. No one wins, not in the final tally. The most we can hope for is to have what we have." She gestured at the platter, now holding only crumbs and the stems of figs. "An empty plate and a full belly, and a good companion by your side, at least for a little while. And no regrets."

"Thank you." He took her hand and kissed it, and left her sitting on the wall in the sunshine, a bemused smile on her face.

The road wound up a hill, and the wall grew to a massive barrier over Duncan's head. It swept around and crossed the road, but was pierced by a gate, at this hour standing wide open, and on the other side of it were buildings and houses and hear the noise and bustle of a town. He passed through the gate, and inside was a tavern. Leaning against the door, watching him with an appreciative eye, was Diana, dressed in a diaphanous lavender garment that revealed as much as it hid.

"Never thought you'd see me again, did you, Duncan Kyle?" she said, giving him an alluring smile.

"Well, at this point, it was kind of inevitable. You're not going to try to kill me again, are you?"

"That'd hardly be sporting, given that you escaped me fairly, and considering how far you've come. And I don't have my bow handy in any case. But I wouldn't say no to a tumble, if you have the time. I wasn't lying when I said that I enjoyed your body."

"Flattered, but I think I'll pass," he said. "There's one more person I've got to see, and tempting as you are, it led to nothing but trouble last time."

Diana looked at him in silence for a moment, and then shook her head, still smiling. "You have grown, Duncan Kyle. You were as easy to trap last time as a randy teenager."

"Don't forget that I was half-dead from drowning when you hooked me."

She laughed. "Oh, come now. You're not going to stand there, look me in the eye, and tell me that you would have responded any differently had you been hale and hearty and sound when I found you."

He returned her laugh. "All right. You got me there."

"Thank you." She gave a mocking little bow. "Having conceded to me that far, you may go on. I'm not so proud that I don't realize it when I'm defeated."

She blew him a kiss in farewell, and he proceeded up into the streets of the city, now populated by throngs of people, buying and selling at the market, women hawking baked goods, butchers stacking cuts of meat for purchase, fruit-grocers setting out bins of oranges, hanging up heavy bunches of bananas, arranging baskets of figs and grapes and dates. A warm wind brushed his face, carrying with it the salt smell of the sea.

One more person to find. If she was a person at all. But he really wanted to see what she had to say. The Sphinx could have told him a lot had she chosen to. But perhaps it wouldn't have meant anything to him back then.

Maybe some things had to be lived, not told.

He found her sitting like a guardian by a gate that opened onto a broad and busy seaport. The blue-green waves beat incessantly on a pebbly shore, and moored out in the harbor were dozens of sailing ships. Nearer at hand was a long stone jetty where men, shoulders burnished to a deep bronze by the sun, unloaded baskets of fish from rowboats. She sat, her face impassive as always, but her glossy golden eyes were wide open.

"Welcome back," she said as he approached, her voice resonant and deep as a cello.

"Back?" he said, looking up into her huge stone face, shielding his eyes from the sun. "I've never been here before."

"That's true."

Duncan gave her a wry scowl. "Still speaking in riddles, I see."

"Call it a habit. You found some clothes."

"Yup. And I made it through the ten worlds. Where now?"

"Ten?" she said, and with a creak, a stone eyebrow lifted a little. "This is the ninth."

"I count ten."

"No," she said. "The mirror-realm of Da'at is not itself a world. It is only a passageway. I believe you were told that."

"Oh," he said, his face falling a little.

"Your expression is as if you were facing a prison sentence."

"No, it's more that I was looking forward to sleeping in my own bed again." He frowned. "I *will* get to go home, won't I?"

"You will have that option, yes."

"Well, that's good. Can I ask you a question?"

"Such opportunities are what I live for. Proceed."

"How much of what I experienced was real?"

"This point really bothers you, doesn't it?"

"Of course. It's kind of critical, you know?"

"Why?" Her *basso profundo* voice dropped even lower, making his innards vibrate. "Everyone else goes about their lives without worrying much about it."

"Even so, I'd like to know."

She considered for a moment. "I could answer you, but I think you're asking the wrong question."

"What question should I be asking?"

"Well, if you're wondering whether what you're seeing is real or not, the first thing to establish is whether or not *you* are real. Because if you're not real, then it rather makes everyone else's reality status a moot point, don't you think?"

He opened his mouth, stared at her for a moment, and then closed it again.

"Surely you have some kind of clever response meant to dismiss what I have said entirely," she said. "You can't come this far, meeting me again after such a long journey, only to find out you've run out of words."

"I'm not sure what to say."

The Sphinx gave a snort, and a shower of rock dust floated down onto his head and shoulders. "Well, say something. I mean, I'm not going anywhere, but at some point you'll undoubtedly want to."

"Okay, let's start with this. How can I not be real? That question doesn't even make sense. If I'm not real, then who is asking the question?"

"And you say you're not a philosopher," the Sphinx said, her voice shuddering a little with a deep laugh.

"No, but really. Answer my question."

"I cannot answer it, because you don't really know what you're asking. You looked into the mirrors of Da'at, and saw reflections of yourself, over and over, finally vanishing into the glass, yes? Millions of Duncan Kyles, all looking this way and that, each one complete and whole and wearing the charming befuddled expression you excel at."

"Yes."

"Had you asked one of those reflections, 'Which is the real Duncan Kyle, and which the copies?' what do you think he would have said?"

"I see what you're saying. But still... all of the reflections, even if they'd insisted that they were the real one, they'd have been wrong. I'm the original, they're the copies."

"You're so sure?"

"I feel real." He slapped his belly with his open palm. "See? Solid."

"Oh, my, you've convinced me," the Sphinx said. "There's no arguing that logic."

"You're impossible."

"You're improbable, and that's far worse."

"Fine," he said. "I may or may not be real. Everything around me may or may not be real. Where does that get me?"

"First, allow me to remind you that *you* were the one who insisted on discussing the point. But leaving that aside, you might consider the advantages. If you are certain you know where the boundaries are, you can't step beyond them, even if you were the one who built the walls with your own hands. You are only constrained in your choices if you're convinced you know what is possible."

"So if I wanted to fly, I could sprout wings from my shoulders, and fly away?"

"See?" the Sphinx said. "You ask that question because you are already so sure you know the answer."

"It's a matter of practicality."

"No. It is a matter of Duncan Kyle deciding that he knows what is possible and what is impossible. Who appointed you the Arbiter of Truth?"

"Isn't that what all humans do?"

"It's what they stop doing," the Sphinx said, "if they want to know what the Truth actually is. You really think your puny, nearsighted eyes, your weak ears, your dull and calloused skin, can sense everything there is to sense? That your feeble brain can know everything there is to know? How arrogant of you."

"I never thought of it that way."

"So a man who cannot prove that he isn't a reflection of a reflection, who doesn't know whether he is flesh and blood or a character in someone else's tale, sets himself up to determine what is possible." She chuckled. "That's rich."

"I don't know how to stop."

"You only have gotten as far as you have because you've muted that voice a little. You'd have been squashed like a bug in the first world you visited if it hadn't been for the fact that the door was already open a crack. In your travels, you've shoved the door open wide. But you've yet to take the final step."

"Which is?"

"To see that there never was a door in the first place."

"Every time I talk to you, it makes my brain hurt."

The Sphinx lowered her enormous head in a sardonic little bow. "I live to serve."

"Anyway, where do I go from here? Now that I've failed Philosophy 101, it's time to be moving on. I've got one more world to get through, and I'd like to get at it. So I need to find a portal."

"Why?"

"Oh, for fuck's sake. You know why."

"Do I?"

"Yes," he said, his voice rising in exasperation. "I need to find a portal, so I can get out of here and into wherever the tenth world is."

"Doors again. Maybe you could use a different path, this time."

"Such as?"

"Anything you choose. If you were only a little further along, you could grow those wings you spoke of earlier, and fly there. Perhaps another time for that. But you're in a seaport, maybe you can find a ship to carry you where you wish to go."

"What do I do? Go up to the captain, and say, 'Hey, dude, how'd you like to give me a ride out of the world?'"

The Sphinx inclined her head. "Just so."

"This is ridiculous."

"If you think that the 'real world' you are so fond of is any less ridiculous, you haven't been paying attention."

"Touché," he said. "Well, I guess I'll be going, now. Thanks for the thought-provoking conversation."

"It has been my pleasure. Come back to visit as often as you like."

"I'll see what I can do."

He walked past the Sphinx's great stone paws, and went down a shallow slope toward the beach. The waves lapped the shore, and near at hand, a little rowboat bobbed in the waves. A man stood in the gently rocking boat, hauling in a net. He had a muscular tanned back, and curling black hair that hung in a shaggy lion's mane to his shoulders. Duncan called out to him, and he turned, flashing a white smile in a darkly handsome face.

I should have known. His heart hammered against his ribs. *There wasn't anyone else left.*

The man in the boat was Duncan himself.

CHAPTER 11

KETER

"Fine day," said the man in the boat.

"It is," Duncan agreed.

The man gave him another joyful smile, and continued pulling in the net, powerful arms flexing in the sunshine, reveling in the pleasure of being young and strong and human.

"Where are you going, when you are done with your net?"

"Back out to my ship," the man said, not breaking his rhythm.

"Can I come along?"

Now the man slowed a little, and laughed. "It is only a simple fishing boat. It is no great sailing vessel, with luxuries. And the work there is hard. Are you fond of such labor?"

"I've never done it."

The man pulled the last of the net in, and dropped it, dark and dripping, into the hull. He shook his hands, sending droplets of water glittering through the air. "I could use extra help. My cousin worked for me for three years, but last month he started courting a girl from

Troianata, and now he's more interested in slipping away with her to make love in the olive groves than he is in helping me on a boat. Not that I can blame him," he added, laughing.

"I'd be glad to help you."

"You can swim, yes?"

"Yes. Don't want to take that for granted, I'd guess."

"No. You'd be surprised the grown men who have never learned." The man sat, and rowed the little boat over to the jetty where Duncan stood.

"I'm a good swimmer. And I can work hard." He reached out and grabbed the outstretched hand of the man, and with a long stride, stepped into the boat. It rocked a little, but he kept his feet long enough to sit down near the stern.

"I am called Lukas," the man said, turning the rowboat expertly, and sending it gliding out toward a sleek sailboat that lay at anchor in the harbor.

"I'm Duncan. But my middle name is Lukas."

The man laughed again. "Then you will never have cause to forget my name."

They crossed the glittering blue-green water to the sailboat in short order, and after climbing in, he helped Lukas to pull up the rowboat and lash it to the side. Lukas unfurled a long, triangular sail, untied the ropes holding the tiller in place, and then they worked together to pull up the anchor. The breeze filled the sail, and Lukas, hand on the tiller, guided the sailboat out to sea.

"Doesn't it strike you as odd that we look alike?" Duncan said, as the noise of the seaport was left behind. At this distance the jetty and the other boats in the harbor looked like little toys bobbing in the sea. The buildings of the town, rising in rank upon rank on the hill behind it, were no more than a green and blue and tan blur in the warm, humid air.

"Are we so much the same as all that?" Lukas said, his voice light.

"Exactly, I think."

"I wonder. A man is more than his appearance, you know."

"I know. But we could be twins." Duncan leaned back, letting the sun fall full on his face. "I have a few more scars, I'll admit."

"A fighting man, then? I noticed the one on your cheek. That came from a knife, I'd say."

"I got two wounds from that knife. The second would have killed me had the blade gone in at a different angle. And I have other scars besides, from arrows and whips. But no, I'm not a fighting man unless I have to be. I'd much rather live in peace."

"So, I think, would many warriors."

He smiled to hear that word applied to him, but he didn't correct Lukas.

He may not have been through war, but he'd been through a lot.

"Where are we going?" he asked, after they'd sailed for about a half hour.

"I am nearly done for the day. My net was torn badly two days ago, after it was caught on a floating log that had been washed out to sea in a storm. There is a man in

Chokhmah who is clever at repairing nets, and he owed me a favor, so I brought it to him to mend. He did a fine job of it, and I am glad, because it is my livelihood." By this time, the shore behind them was a faint line of darker green along the flat turquoise expanse of water. Ahead of them was nothing but more ocean.

"So you're going home?"

Lukas pointed ahead. "I live in Keter. It is yonder."

So the Sphinx had been right. All he had to do to leave Chokhmah was to ask someone to hitch a ride. It would have been nice to know it was that easy months ago.

"What is Keter like?"

Lukas shrugged. "It is beautiful. It has trees and rivers and pasturage for sheep. Everything one might need."

He grinned. "Where I come from, I don't think anyone would think that 'trees, rivers, and sheep' are everything you need."

"Oh?" His dark eyebrows went up. "What more do you need?"

"I don't know. I'm not saying I agree with them. It seems to me now that the people where I come from are a remarkably needy bunch."

"They must not be very happy."

"No," he said. "A lot of the time, they're not."

"It is well that you came here, then."

For some time, there was no sound but the waves and the wind, and the gentle motion of the sailboat rocked him to sleep. He only awoke when Lukas said, "There. You can see my home from here."

He sat up, blinking, and gazed into the distance, where Lukas's arm was pointing. Along the horizon, he could see a white line, no other features. Had Lukas not spoken with such assurance, he would not have thought it was land, but a low line of clouds, or the tops of whitecaps. As they approached, it gradually resolved into a low, sloping beach of pure white sand, and a grassy slope behind it. In the distance was the deep green of a forest, and directly ahead a long wooden pier jutted out from the beach, supported by heavy posts made of whole tree trunks.

Lukas deftly steered the boat in toward the pier, and minutes later, they pulled up alongside. With a grace borne of long practice, he leapt out of the boat onto the pier, and with ropes secured it to rings set in the posts, fore and aft. He then gave a hand to Duncan, who stepped onto the pier a little less steadily. As he walked down toward the beach, it felt as if he were still rocking gently, making his gait sway a little, but he made it to solid ground without losing his balance, or worse, taking a tumble into the ocean.

The warm white sand stuck to his bare feet as he walked up the beach, following Lukas toward a little cottage nestled amongst the trees. Its single window faced out toward the sea. Along the side of the house was a profusion of small trees in abundant pink flower.

"Welcome to my home," Lukas said.

"You live alone?"

"I have no woman to share my bed, if that is what you mean."

"Doesn't it get lonely?"

He shrugged. "When I am lonely, I go to the town farther up the shore, or across the water to Chokhmah. I have no particular need for companionship, although it is welcome when it comes." He held the door open for Duncan, and they went inside.

The interior of the cottage was spare and clean, with a single bed, a chair, a table with a candle in a bowl sitting in the center, and a small wooden cabinet.

"I usually take my meals outside," Lukas said, as Duncan looked around. "And sleep outside, as well, when the weather allows. There is a hammock in the trees yonder that makes for a sound night's rest. While you are with me, you may take either the bed or the hammock, whichever you prefer."

"I don't think I care. I'll be comfortable wherever I am."

Lukas flashed a grin at him. "Perhaps you and I are alike after all." He went to the cabinet, and took out a ceramic jug, which he uncorked. He poured out two measures of a clear liquid into two small cups, and handed one to him.

"It is a liquor I brew. It is flavored with the almonds you saw flowering outside my house. There is much cheer in it, if you do not drink it too liberally." He held up the cup. "May we learn much from each other." He drained the cup at one swallow.

"Hear, hear." He downed his as well. The drink was sweet and strong, and warmed his throat, stinging a little as it went down. "That's delicious."

"The bottle is still nearly full," Lukas said, his white smile gleaming in the dim light.

Food was brought out, fruit and bread and salted fish, and in an hour's time the plates were empty and the bottle of almond liquor was considerably lighter. Stars twinkled in a black velvet sky, odd constellations he had never seen before. He and Lukas ended up out on the beach, lying on their backs in the sand. He was mostly drunk, but instead of the usual spinning disorientation he knew from benders he'd had back home, here he was clear-headed, giddy, euphoric. He held up one hand in front of his face, half expecting that he'd be able to see starlight through his own skin, but all he saw was the dim outline of his five fingers against the star-spangled expanse of sky.

"Perhaps soon," came Lukas's voice. "You're still too solid for that. Maybe when you've moved on, you will be as transparent as a glass goblet, filled only with light."

"Moved on? I thought I was going home."

"Is that what you want?"

"Yes," he said, but his voice was tentative.

Lukas laughed. "That is the reply of a man who is answering what he thinks others expect him to."

"No, that's not it. It *is* what I wanted. I've been through hell on this journey, and I've always dreamed about eventually finding my way home."

"But...?"

"But when I think of the life I had, it was bland. Boring. It's hard to consider returning to that after all of..." He gestured up into the sky. "This."

"Why do you have to?"

"I'm not sure I want to spend the rest of my life working on a fishing boat, either," he said. "Not that I don't appreciate your hospitality."

"Those aren't the only two options."

"No? I don't see any others." He paused. "Now that I come to think of it, I don't even see the possibility of going home. There's no portal anywhere I can see."

"You didn't need one to get here, why do you think you need one to get there?"

"I'm not sure it's that simple."

"Why is it not?"

"Because I don't know what I want any more."

"Then the portal is not the problem," Lukas said. "The problem is to decide what it is you want."

The next days and weeks were spent working side by side with Lukas, casting and reeling in the net, handling the anchor, setting out and pulling up crab traps. The work was exhausting. He had thought that hauling and processing clay in Shao Bolin's workshop had been backbreaking, but Lukas's work was more strenuous still. Lukas threw himself into it with a joyous exuberance, often singing with a lilting voice in some strange and mellifluous language, and simply laughing when Duncan asked for a translation. For him, his work was an expression of life, and life an opportunity to experience his work. The two formed a seamless whole.

One evening, Duncan lay on his back in the hammock, a hand hanging loosely over the edge. There were stars overhead, but on the horizon, over the ocean, was the slate gray of clouds, and a white flash of lightning. Softly, almost beyond the range of hearing, there was the growl of thunder.

He was nearly asleep, lulled by the voices in the air, when he heard some soft footsteps in the sand. He opened his eyes, and saw Lukas silhouetted against the sky.

"There is likely to be rain tonight," he said. "You'll get soaked if you stay outside."

Duncan laughed. "And if I do? I, and my shorts, will both dry out."

Lukas leaned against one of the trees that supported the hammock, his wiry frame like a bowstring, all taut energy even when at rest. He did not speak for several minutes, his eyes turned out toward the sea, the intermittent lightning flashes showing every angle of a face that was Duncan's own.

Finally, he said, "How many days will it be before you know what path your feet need to follow? For all that I have valued your help, you said yourself that life on a fisherman's boat is not for you." He paused. "It is not that I do not value your help, but I know your heart lies elsewhere."

"I don't know where else to go."

"There is a place," Lukas said, and his voice for the first time sounded tentative, "where you might find some answers. Or at least, guidance."

"Where is this place?"

"Southward along the shore, the beach folds up into rocky prominences, and finally onto a great cliff. The top of it can be reached only if you venture inland a little. But it was said that my ancestors went up there, when they wished counsel from the gods. From the edge, they said that you can see all of the worlds."

"All ten, from one place?" The smile was clear in his voice.

"Ten?" Lukas said, his voice perplexed.

"The ten worlds of the Sephirot."

"Who told you that there were ten?"

"A Sphinx. In the first world I visited. And it was said again, when I spoke to a wise man who had read many books, in a desert world where I was befriended and taken in by kind people, some of whom paid with their lives for their compassion. He said that there was a great library in his world, and he had read much on the subject."

"I have no wish to diminish your friend's knowledge, or his people's sacrifice on your behalf, but they are wrong about the Sephirot."

A panic rose up in him, coupled with a deep sense of fatigue. Every time he thought he might be done with this journey, something more got in the way. How many worlds were there? Eleven? Twelve? Twenty?

"I already thought I'd visited eleven, but I was told that one didn't count," he said, trying to keep the peevishness out of his voice. "Is there yet another, beyond Keter, that I have to pass through before I will be allowed to go home?"

"I do not know about your going home," Lukas said. "But I do know that there are not ten worlds in the Sephirot."

"How many are there?"

"Countless. My mother's father, who was wise in such matters and who knew about the gateways and the passages, said there were so many different worlds that a man could visit one a day and not be done in a lifetime."

He didn't answer for a moment. He finally said, "Well, shit."

Lukas laughed softly in the dark. "But this doesn't mean you're compelled to visit any more than you wish. Let me take you up onto the cliff top tomorrow. It will do me no harm to spend a day away from the boat. Then, we will see what we will see. You may find your way home from there."

The first big drops of warm rain splattered against his bare chest. There was a zigzag flash of lightning, somewhere out to sea, and thunder rolled, closer than before.

"You should come indoors with me," Lukas said.

"No, I think I'd like to stay here."

Lukas chuckled again, and it was lost in another rumble of thunder. "As you wish, my friend. I will keep a dry corner for you if you change your mind."

He went off at a jog as the skies opened up. Water poured from the heavens, a drenching baptism that washed away all expectations, all hopes, all fears, and left him a vessel waiting to be filled, a bell ringing in the empty sky.

Countless. World without end, amen. Hadn't that been the end of the prayer in his grandmother's church? Were the ten worlds of the Sephirot only the first steps on the path?

Finally the rain slackened, and he slept. The storm passed, and the stars turned in their courses. And when he woke, his skin and hair were dry, and the sun was shining. Gentle waves lapped the shore, and a light breeze brought him the smell of salt and the keening of gulls.

Duncan took a quick swim in the shallows while waiting for Lukas to wake. The water was warm, and his body slipped through the waves as easily as a fish. Afterwards, he sat on a rock to dry off in the sunshine, and had just dressed when the door of the cottage opened.

Lukas came out, stretching and yawning, and said, "You passed the night without being washed away?"

"I like the rain. It leaves you alone with your thoughts."

"And what counsel has the rain brought?"

"That I should try your suggestion. Go up onto the cliff, and see what I can see."

"It may be that you will learn nothing," Lukas admitted. "Perhaps the powers attributed to the place are only superstition."

"Have you ever been up there yourself?"

"Once. My grandfather went up with me." Lukas gave him a crooked smile. "All I saw was the sea and the sun and the horizon. But honestly, that was all I was looking for. If you go up there with a different question in your heart, maybe you will see something else."

"There's only one way to find out." He stood. "I'm ready to leave when you are."

They packed satchels with some dried fruit and two water skins and set off up the beach. White sand gave way to rock, its surface smoothed by millennia of polishing by the ocean waves, and for a time they made better progress than they had on the soft sand. After they had hiked for a little more than an hour, Lukas raised his arm and pointed inland. There was a stone statue of a man, robed and hooded, standing under the eaves of the trees. One hand was out, palm upward, and the other held a lantern. The stone was eroded with the passage of time, and cracks showed in the carven folds of the sleeves and hood. A vining plant had twisted its way up the statue, the thin stems ending in a drapery of little white flowers.

"That marks the beginning of the path inland," Lukas said.

They walked into the deep shade of the woods. A carpet of leaves crunched under their bare feet, and for a while, they went forward in the green silence, around hoary tree trunks furred with moss. The terrain rose, and the forest climbed upwards amongst jagged rock outcroppings and boulders that had tumbled down in ruin from the mountain face ahead of them. An hour after that the trees grew more sparse, the broadleaved oaks replaced by wind-writhen pines and firs as they ascended. They stopped, sitting on a fallen log to eat the meager meal they had brought along, and to drink some of the water in the skins.

"How much farther?" Duncan asked.

"If we were birds, we'd reckon the distance short. But the climb gets steeper from here."

"And you and your grandfather did this journey when you were a child?"

"I was a youth, but strong and willful and cocky. And my grandfather thought it important. We took it slowly, with many rests."

They recommenced walking, as the rocky path twisted around jutting arms of the mountain, always heading upward, finding a way even when the nearly vertical face of the cliff seemed impassable. Each time they were brought to a place where it appeared that there was no way through, the path would snake its way into a barely-seen cleft that opened out into a narrow valley, and they would ascend farther, upwards toward the sky.

Late in the day, the path made one last steep scramble up onto a flat, treeless tableland, where the wind rippled through grass up to their knees. Duncan and Lukas stood for a moment at the top of the path, chests heaving with exertion, and then Lukas struck out across the broad expanse of the cliff top.

The sky looked closer, the warm, humid azure of sea level replaced by a deep ultramarine. The sun shone full on his face as they went forward, and the wind had a dry chill to it, but the grass was kind under his sore feet. Soon they approached a place where the cliff hung out over the ocean, where the rock was broken into torn edges that protruded into empty space, seeming held up by nothing at all. Lukas motioned him forward, and together, they went out onto one of the piers of stone, and lay down on their bellies, their eyes cast downward at the sea, a dizzying distance below them. They looked downward at white specks that seemed like floating bits of debris on the water, but he realized that those were gulls, kiting over the waves, thousands of feet below.

"What do you see?" Lukas said.

As Duncan watched, the incessant motion of the sea stopped, as if it had crystallized. The surface was covered with millions of glittering shards, reflecting back up to his gaze a myriad colors. When he moved his eyes, ordinary motion returned, but whenever he focused on one spot, the ocean froze, shattering into facets like a fly's eye.

"I see..." He swallowed. "I do not know how to describe it. It's like the surface of the sea is covered with windows."

"Each of those windows is a gateway," Lukas said.

He turned toward his twin, and frowned. "And is that what you see?"

Lukas smiled, and shook his head. "All I see is the ocean's waves, and the birds and the clouds. Those are the end of my path. I have no desire to tread a step outside of this land."

"Then how do you know about it?"

"My grandfather told me about such things. If it is your fate to travel between the worlds, you'll see the gates, and that is how you will know it is your path. Others do not see them."

He looked back down toward the sea, and fixed his gaze. Beneath him, the surface cracked into countless bright fragments. "Would one of those gateways bring me back home?"

"Certainly."

"How do I find it?"

"Are you asking," Lukas said, and Duncan could hear the smile in his voice, "because you wish to go through it, or because you wish to avoid doing so?"

"I don't know. I always wanted to go home. But so many worlds..." He looked over at Lukas again, and there were tears in his eyes. "When I was in Tiferet, a man there told me that the Sephirot was a journey toward enlightenment. I know I'm different now than when I started, but I don't feel enlightened, I feel overwhelmed."

"Perhaps enlightenment isn't a place you arrive. Maybe it's finding the path you need to be on, and taking that as far as you can."

"But why me?" His voice cracked. "It is something I have wondered, throughout all of this. I'm an ordinary man, with ordinary thoughts, ordinary fears, ordinary desires. There is nothing about me that makes me better than anyone else, that makes me worth... all of this."

"That is your error, then. There is no better path, no worse one. I am a fisherman, the man in Chokhmah I met is a net-maker. You are a traveler. All paths are equal, because in the end, they all lead to the same place."

"Where?"

"Nowhere."

A sense of bleakness rose up in him. "If that is true, then I have no choice."

Lukas put one hand on his shoulder. "You always have choice. Even if at the end, you look back and say, 'I could not have done differently,' the truth is that you always can stray from the path you should be on. If you know an answer, you can still turn your face away from it."

"So I could stand up, and walk back down the mountain, and live here in Keter for the rest of my life."

"Yes."

He felt a surge of wild hope. Keter was as close as a paradise he'd found on his journey. But like the static world of Chesed, it was not for him.

"You would not stop me, then? Even if you knew I was making the wrong choice?"

"If I did, it would no longer be a choice," Lukas said. "But from your voice, I would guess that you are no longer in any real doubt about which path to take."

"Yes. I know what to do, but I'm scared to do it."

"We all are."

Glowing prismatic colors shimmered from the crystalline faces of the waves, as if the ocean were a basin filled with jewels. Each one was a portal, within which were other portals to other places, a fractal snowflake of a universe where every piece contained the entire whole.

Worlds without end, amen.

Duncan stood, and walked a little way back from the cliff edge. He unsnapped and unzipped his shorts, and pulled them and his boxers off, tossed them aside. Standing, naked to the sky, he looked out toward the horizon.

"I started this journey wearing nothing but my skin. I shouldn't be afraid to end it the same way."

Lukas rolled over, and in a single graceful motion, moved into a crosslegged position. "I probably won't see you again," he said, in a conversational tone.

"It doesn't matter. It isn't as if you don't know who I am."

"Good luck. I hope you see wonders."

"I already have."

Lukas gave him a crooked grin. "I wouldn't be surprised if you sprout wings from your shoulders on the way down."

Duncan returned his smile, then facing outward toward the empty air, he took a deep breath, feeling the cool mountain air fill his chest. He sprinted forward, his bare feet pushing against the roughness of the rock face, and flung himself off.

He fell headfirst, hands out in front of him, his body flashing like a meteor as it cleaved the air. The glittering windows into a thousand different realities swirled upwards to meet him, caught him up, and in the blink of an eye, he was gone.

ABOUT GORDON BONNET

Gordon Bonnet has been writing fiction for decades. Encouraged when his story "Crazy Bird Bends His Beak" won critical acclaim in Mrs. Moore's 1st grade class at Central Elementary School in St. Albans, West Virginia, he embarked on a long love affair with the written word.

His interest in the paranormal goes back almost that far. Introduced to speculative, fantasy, and science fiction by such giants in the tradition as Madeleine L'Engle, Lloyd Alexander, Isaac Asimov, C. S. Lewis, and J. R. R. Tolkien, he was captivated by those writers' abilities to take the reader to a fictional world and make it seem tangible, to breathe life and passion and personality into characters who were (sometimes) not even human. He made journeys into darker realms upon meeting the works of Edgar Allen Poe and H. P. Lovecraft during his teenage years, and those authors still influence his imagination and his writing to this day.

This fascination with the paranormal, however, has always been tempered by Gordon's scientific training. This has led to a strange duality: his work as a teacher, skeptic and debunker on the popular blog *Skeptophilia*, while simultaneously writing paranormal and speculative novels, novellas, and short stories. Gordon explains this, with a smile: "Well, I do know it's fiction, after all."

He blogs daily, and is never without a piece of fiction in progress—driven to continue (as he puts it) "because I want to find out how the story ends." From historical fiction (*Kári the Lucky*), to murder mysteries (the Parsifal Snowe Mysteries, beginning with *Poison the Well*), to paranormal fiction with a humorous twist (*Periphery* and *Lock & Key*) to the truly terrifying (*Gears* and *Descent into Ulthoa*), Gordon's fiction has something for all tastes!

Find him conversing with his dogs (and perhaps his wife) in Trumansburg, NY, or the following platforms:

- YouTube *https://youtube.com/@skeptophilia1509*

- Skeptophilia blog *http://www.skeptophilia.com/*

- Books and stuff *http://www.gordonbonnet.com*

- Twitter *@TalesOfWhoa*

- TikTok *@GordonBonnetAuthor*

- Instagram *@skygazer227*

Or, ya know, the Google.

ALSO BY GORDON BONNET

The Communion of Shadows

Kári the Lucky

Descent into Ulthoa

Kill Switch

The Fifth Day

The Shambles

Snowe Mysteries (Series)

Black-eyed Children (Series)

Sign up for Gordon's Little Bustard Books Newsletter and Obscure Weird Tidbits at his website:
http://www.gordonbonnet.com

from The Communion of Shadows

August 1850

A desolate moan, and the wooden shutters rattled like there was something unholy trying to enter, but it was only the wind.

Leandre Naquin jumped at the sound, then turned back toward his friends, the heat of embarrassment rising in his cheeks. Thunder rolled in the distance and the air coming in through the cracks smelled like rain.

"Scared of some noise?" J. P. Ayo's characteristic grin flashed out in the dim lantern light. "*Loup garou* come out of the swamp to get you?"

Leandre gave a genial laugh, and the three other men joined in. "No, it just startled me. But it's coming faster than we thought. Good thing we got the cane cut. Wind like this could blow it flat. Lose the whole field."

J. P. gave a dismissive wave. "It's not a hurricane, it's just a summer thunderstorm. But you know what that means, T-Joe. You better stay the night here."

Joseph Lirette, the youngest of the four, put on an expression so comically distraught that J. P. snorted laughter and slapped his knee.

"Won't hurt you none to miss a night with your pretty wife, T-Joe. You can just make sure and do it twice tomorrow night."

T-Joe's face turned scarlet. "That's not it. I'm just... I hope she'll be all right by herself. A storm, you know, she could get scared."

Clovis Dantin snorted. "Better scared for a night than alone forever because you walked home in a storm and got struck by lightning." He took a swig of the liquor J. P. had poured into tin cups from a heavy ceramic bottle, then leaned back in his chair and crossed his arms.

"I guess you're right." T-Joe didn't look convinced. He took a sip from his own cup, and grimaced. "Damn, J. P., what did you make this from? Lye and horse piss?"

"You get used to it."

"Not sure I want to."

Another roll of thunder shook the house. Leandre dropped into a wicker-backed chair, stretching out his long legs and propping his feet on the table. "Refill my cup with some of that lye and horse piss, J. P."

J. P. obliged with a smile.

"Must be nice, living alone." Clovis's habitual scowl deepened, and he took another sip." My wife'd never let me put my feet on the table like that. You got nobody telling you what to do day in, day out."

"Nobody to welcome you to bed, either," T-Joe said earnestly.

"Huh." Clovis shook his head. "Happens seldom enough in my house, I'd be better off able to put my feet on the table." He glanced over at J. P., and his expression softened. "Say, sorry, J. P. I didn't mean..."

J. P. gave him a dismissive wave of the hand. "Don't worry about it. Marie-Elise died almost two years ago. I'm not over missing her—doubt I ever will be, honestly—but I'm over feeling like every mention of wives or being alone is a knife in my heart. *Tiens*, you can't mourn forever."

"You think you'll remarry?" T-Joe asked.

J. P. shrugged. "I don't have a pretty lady ready to take me off to the church, if that's what you mean. Right now I'm content to go to the *fais-do-do* and dance with all of them, then come back to my own little house when it's over."

"That's my thought," Leandre said.

"How about you, though?" T-Joe turned his gaze toward Leandre. "You're what, twenty-eight?"

"Thirty."

"And never married?"

"Never."

"Why not?"

Leandre smiled and shrugged. "Too much else to do."

T-Joe shook his head, his expression baffled. "I don't understand y'all."

Lightning flashed, its blue-white radiance shining for an instant through the cracks in the shutters. The thunder followed almost immediately, a deep-throated rumble that made the liquor in Leandre's cup vibrate. "Sometimes there are good reasons for not having a woman, you know."

The corners of J. P.'s mouth quirked upward. "Such as?"

Leandre's eyes met his friend's, and he didn't answer for a moment. Then he grinned. "So I can put my feet on the table." Rain began to slash against the roof, and another gust of wind made the shutters vibrate. Enough of it made its way through gaps that the flame in the oil lamp guttered and almost went out. "Hell of a night. The kind of nights when the ghosts walk."

Clovis gave him a raised eyebrow. "Ghosts? What ghosts?"

Leandre shrugged. "Whatever ghosts are out there. There've got to be millions. How many people are alive now, and how many people have died since Adam and Eve left the Garden? The dead outnumber the living, no question about it."

"That doesn't mean they're ghosts."

"Not *all* of them, no. But tell me, Clovis, you've never seen a ghost? Or known someone who has?"

Clovis opened his mouth to answer, then closed it without saying anything.

"Thought so." Leandre laughed. "I bet we all have."

"I don't know why they'd be out in the rain, though." J. P.'s smile flashed out in the semi-darkness. "Night like this, I would stay in my nice dry coffin. If I was a ghost, only time you'd see me is on a sunny afternoon. And to hell with appearing in a graveyard, you know? I'd show up in the middle of Sunday Mass. I'd love to see the look on Father Rousseau's face." His smile faded. "But you're right, Leandre. I have seen a ghost. It was a long time ago, but I remember it like it was yesterday."

"Whose ghost was it?" T-Joe leaned forward in his chair. His eyes were wide, but whether with fear or interest was impossible to tell.

"Her name was Thérèse. Thérèse Clerot. A woman who I knew when I was a child. She lived nearby, by herself, but it wasn't so she could put her feet on the table." He flashed a quick grin at Leandre. "My mama said about her that she was no better than she had to be, you know? A lot of the young men in the parish showed up to her house in the evening, only stayed a half-hour or so. But she never wanted for money or food. Even at my age then—couldn't'a been more than eleven or twelve at the time—I knew what was going on. And now, looking back, I realize why the young men sought her company. She was beautiful, no doubt about that. Long black hair, flashing blue eyes, skin like rich cream. No wonder she was never lonely."

"Then she died?" T-Joe said.

"Well, yes. But I'm getting ahead of myself. Because Thérèse Clerot finally gave up entertaining every young man who crossed her palm with a coin, and actually fell in love. The different men every night changed to one man who came to her cabin over and over again. His name was Michel Dominique." He frowned, remembering. "Nobody much would have thought about this, because after all, everyone approved of Thérèse settling down, maybe even getting married herself, rather than carrying on all evening with any men who happened along. There was only one problem.

"Michel Dominique was already married, to the daughter of one of the richest men in the parish, Clément Lagrange."

T-Joe gaped at him. "So his wife was Jacques Lagrange's sister?"

J. P. nodded.

"I've talked to Jacques a dozen times. He never mentioned he has a sister."

"No, he wouldn't. She's dead and gone, too, along with her husband Michel and his lover Thérèse. And the Lagrange family—well, let's say they were just as happy to forget Julienne Lagrange ever existed." He looked from one face to the other, and a flicker of his earlier smile returned to his face. "But like I said, that's getting things out of order. If I'm going to tell the story, I should tell it proper. So if you want to hear it...?"

T-Joe and Leandre both nodded, and Clovis gave a noncommittal shrug, which was about all the enthusiasm he usually expressed.

Leandre refilled his three friends' cups with liquor. "Then let's hear it, J. P."

"All right. Then I have to begin with the day Thérèse Clerot died. And I can tell you about that because I was the one who found her body."

T-Joe gave a little gasp. "*R'gardez-donc*," he said, in a near whisper. "So you're not joking, or telling us a tall tale because it's a stormy night."

This time the thunderclap was so close that they heard a noise like a whipcrack, almost at the same moment the bolt of lightning struck, followed by an earsplitting roll. "Oh, no. It's no tall tale." He took a swallow from his cup, and wiped his mouth with the back of his hand. "Now that I come to think of it, I wish it was. But I can't leave it there. Since I've started, I might as well tell you the whole story."

Please, do folks a favor and write a few words to review my books! It really helps other readers find writers they enjoy, and it helps me reach potential fans. If you have a minute, please go to Amazon or Apple (https://mybook.to/saNT) and tell the world how much you loved Sephirot :) Thanks! – Gordon